AN INSCRUTABLE GENTLEMAN

As she gazed defiantly into those smouldering grey eyes, Mary Challoner's heart melted. Against her will, against all her plans, the Marquis of Vidal had won her love forever. But she had tricked Vidal once, she had tried to make a fool of him—and he was not a man who forgot or who forgave easily.

Was his offer of marriage part of a devilish design of revenge?

DEVIL'S CUB

A thrilling romantic novel of deception and danger in 18th-century London and Paris.

GEORGETTE HEYER
DEVIL'S CUB

BANTAM BOOKS
TORONTO · NEW YORK · LONDON · SYDNEY

DEVIL'S CUB

A Bantam Book / published by arrangement with
E. P. Dutton Inc.

PRINTING HISTORY

E. P. Dutton edition published September 1966
2nd printing . . . . January 1967

Bantam edition published August 1967

2nd printing . . September 1967	7th printing . September 1971
3rd printing . . . . March 1968	8th printing . September 1972
4th printing . . September 1968	9th printing . . . October 1974
5th printing . . . . July 1969	10th printing . November 1975
6th printing . . . . January 1971	11th printing . . . . . April 1983

ISBN 0-553-23121-9

Published simultaneously in the United States and Canada

Bantam Books are published by Bantam Books, Inc. Its trade-
mark, consisting of the words "Bantam Books" and the por-
trayal of a rooster, is Registered in U.S. Patent and Trademark
Office and in other countries. Marca Registrada. Bantam
Books, Inc., 666 Fifth Avenue, New York, New York 10103.

PRINTED IN THE UNITED STATES OF AMERICA

H   20 19 18 17 16 15 14 13 12 11

∙§ Chapter I §∙

THERE was only one occupant of the coach, a gentleman who sprawled very much at his ease, with his legs stretched out before him, and his hands dug deep in the capacious pockets of his greatcoat. While the coach rattled over the cobbled streets of the town, the light from an occasional lantern or flambeau momentarily lit the interior of the vehicle and made a diamond pin or a pair of very large shoe-buckles flash, but since the gentleman lounging in the coach wore his gold-edged hat tilted low over his eyes, his face remained in shadow.

The coach was travelling fast, too fast for safety in a London street, and it soon drew out of the town, past the turnpike, on to Hounslow Heath. A faint moonlight showed the road to the coachman on the box, but so dimly that the groom beside him, who had been restive since the carriage drew out of St. James's, gasped presently, as though he could no longer keep back the words: "Lord! you'll overturn us! It's a wicked pace!"

The only answer vouchsafed was a shrug, and a somewhat derisive laugh. The coach swayed precariously over a rough stretch of ground, and the groom, clutching the seat with both hands, said angrily: "You're mad! D'you think the devil's on your heels, man? Doesn't he care? Or is he drunk?" The backward jerk of his head seemed to indicate that he was speaking of the man inside the coach.

"When you've been in his service a week you won't call this a wicked pace," replied the coachman. "When Vidal travels, he travels swift, d'ye see?"

1

"He's drunk—three parts asleep!" the groom said.

"Not he."

Yet the man inside the coach might well have been asleep for all the sign of life he gave. His long body swayed easily with the lurch of the coach, his chin was sunk in the folds of his cravat, and not even the worst bumps in the road had the effect of making him so much as grasp the strap that swung beside him. His hands remained buried in his pockets, remained so even when a shot rang out and the vehicle came to a plunging standstill. But apparently he was awake, for he raised his head, yawning, and leaning it back against the cushions turned it slightly towards the off-window.

There was a good deal of commotion outside; a rough voice was raised; the coachman was cursing the groom for his tardiness in firing the heavy blunderbuss in his charge; and the horses were kicking and rearing.

Someone rode up to the door of the coach and thrust in the muzzle of a big pistol. The moonlight cast a head in silhouette, and a voice said: "Hand over the pretties, my hearty!"

It did not seem as though the man inside the coach moved, but a gun spoke sharply, and a stabbing point of flame flashed in the darkness. The head and shoulders at the window vanished; there was the sound of a fall, of trampling hooves, of a startled shout, and the belated explosion of the blunderbuss.

The man in the coach drew his right hand out of his pocket at last. There was an elegant silver-mounted pistol in it, still smoking. The gentleman threw it on to the seat beside him, and crushed the charred and smouldering portion of his greatcoat between very long white fingers.

The door of the coach was pulled open, and the coachman jumped up on to the hastily let-down step. The lantern he held lit up the interior, and shone full into the face of the lounging man. It was a surprisingly young face, dark and extremely handsome, the curious vividness overlaid by an expression of restless boredom.

"Well?" said the gentleman coldly.

"Highwaymen, my lord. The new man being unused, so to say, to such doings, was late with the blunderbuss. There was three of them. They've made off—two of them, that is."

"Well?" said the gentleman again.

The coachman seemed rather discomposed. "You've killed the other, my lord."

"Certainly," said the gentleman. "But I presume you have not opened the door to inform me of that."

"Well, my lord—shan't we—do I—his brains are lying in the road, my lord. Do we leave him—like that?"

"My good fellow, are you suggesting that I should carry a footpad's corpse to my Lady Montacute's drum?"

"No, my lord," the coachman said hesitatingly. "Then—then—shall I drive on?"

"Of course drive on," said the gentleman, faintly surprised.

"Very good, my lord," the coachman said, and shut the door.

The groom on the box was still clasping the blunderbuss, and staring fascinated at the tumbled figure in the road. When the coachman climbed up on to the box again, and gathered the reins in his hands, he said: "Gawd, ain't you going to do anything?"

"There isn't anything you can do for him," replied the other grimly.

"His head's almost shot off!" shuddered the groom.

The equipage began to move forward. "Hold your tongue, can't you? He's dead, and that's all there is to it."

The groom licked his dry lips. "But don't his lordship know?"

"Of course he knows. He don't make mistakes, not with the pistols."

The groom drew a deep breath, thinking still of the dead man left to wallow in his blood. "How old is he?" he blurted out presently.

"Twenty-four all but a month or two."

"Twenty-four! and shoots his man and leaves the corpse as cool as you please! My Gawd!"

He did not speak again until the coach had arrived at its destination, and then he seemed to be so lost in meditation that the coachman had to nudge him sharply. He roused himself then and jumped off the box to open the coach door. As his master stepped languidly down, he looked covertly at him, trying to see some sign of agitation in his face. There was none. His lordship sauntered up the steps to the stone porch, and passed into the lighted hall.

"My Gawd!" said the groom again.

Inside the house two lackeys hovered about the late-comer to take his hat and coat.

There was another gentleman in the hall, just about to go up the wide stairway to the saloon. He was good-looking in a rather florid style, with very heavily-arched brows and a roving eye. His dress proclaimed the Macaroni, for he wore a short coat decorated with frog-buttons, fine striped breeches with bunches of strings at the knee, and a waistcoat hardly reaching below the waist. The frills of his shirt front stuck out at the top, and instead of the cravat, he displayed a very full handkerchief tied in a bow under his chin. On his head he wore an amazingly tall ladder-toupet, dusted with blue hair powder, and he carried in his hand a long tasselled cane.

He turned as my lord entered, and when he saw who it was, came across the hall. "I hoped I was the last," he complained. He raised his quizzing-glass, and through it peered at the hole in his lordship's coat. "My dear Vidal!" he said, shocked. "My dear fellow! Ecod, my lord, your coat!"

One of the lackeys had it over his arm. My lord shook out his Dresden ruffles, but carelessly as though it mattered very little to him to be *point-de-vice*. "Well, Charles, what of my coat?" he asked.

Mr. Fox achieved a shudder. "There's a damned hole in it, Vidal," he protested. He moved forward and very gingerly lifted a fold of the garment. "And a damned smell of powder, Vidal," he said. "You've been shooting someone."

His lordship leaned against the bannister, and opened his snuff-box. "Some scum of a footpad only," he said.

Mr. Fox abandoned his affectations for the moment. "Kill him, Dominic?"

"Of course," said my lord.

Mr. Fox grinned. "What have you done with the corpse, my boy?"

"Done with it?" said his lordship with a touch of impatience. "Nothing. What should I do with a corpse?"

Mr. Fox rubbed his chin. "Devil take me if I know," he said after some thought. "But you can't leave a corpse on the road, Dominic. People might see it on the way back to town. Ladies won't like it."

His lordship had raised a pinch of snuff to one classic nostril, but he paused before he sniffed. "I hadn't thought of that," he admitted. A gleam, possibly of amusement, stole into his eyes. He glanced at the lackey who still held his damaged greatcoat. "There is a corpse somewhere on the road to town. Mr. Fox does not wish it there. Remove it."

The lackey was far too well trained to display emotion, but he was a little shaken. "Yes, my lord," he said. "What does your lordship want done with it, if you please?"

"I have no idea," said his lordship. "Charles, what do you want done with it?"

"Egad, what is to be done with a corpse in the middle of Hounslow Heath?" demanded Mr. Fox. "I've a notion it should be delivered to a constable."

"You hear," said his lordship. "The corpse must be conveyed to town."

"Bow Street," interjected Mr. Fox.

"To Bow Street—with the compliments of Mr. Fox."

"No, damme, I don't take the credit for it, Dominic. Compliments of the Marquis of Vidal, my man."

The lackey swallowed something in his throat, and said with a palpable effort: "It shall be attended to, sir."

Mr. Fox looked at the Marquis. "I don't see what else we can do, Dominic, do you?"

"We seem to have been put to a vast deal of inconvenience already," replied the Marquis, dusting his sleeve with a very fine handkerchief. "I do not propose to bother my head further in the matter."

"Then we may as well go upstairs," said Mr. Fox.

"I await your pleasure, my dear Charles," returned his lordship, and began leisurely to mount the shallow stairs.

Mr. Fox fell in beside him, drawing an elegant brisé fan from his pocket. He opened it carefully, and held it for his friend to see. "Vernis Martin," he said.

His lordship glanced casually down at it. "Very pretty," he replied. "Chassereau, I suppose."

"Quite right," Mr. Fox said, waving it gently to and fro. "Subject, Télémaque, on ivory."

They passed round the bend in the stairway. Down in the hall the two lackeys looked at one another. "Corpses one moment, fans the next," said the man who held Vidal's coat. "There's the Quality for you!"

The episode of the corpse had by this time apparently faded from Lord Vidal's mind, but Mr. Fox, thinking it a very good tale, spoke of it to at least three people, who repeated it to others. It came in due course to the ears of

Lady Fanny Marling, who, in company with her son John, and her daughter Juliana, was present at the drum.

Lady Fanny had been a widow for a number of years, and the polite world had ceased to predict a second marriage for her. Flighty she had always been, but her affection for the late Mr. Edward Marling had been a very real thing. Her period of mourning had lasted a full year, and when she reappeared in society it was quite a long time before she had spirits to amuse herself with even the mildest flirtation. Now, with a daughter of marriageable age, she was becoming quite matronly, and had taken to arraying herself in purples and greys, and to wearing on her exceedingly elaborate coiffure turbans that spoke the dowager.

She was talking to an old friend, one Hugh Davenant, when she overheard the story of her nephew's latest exploit, and she at once broke off her own conversation to exclaim: "That abominable boy! I vow and declare I never go anywhere but what I hear of him. And never any good, Hugh. Never!"

Hugh Davenant's grey eyes travelled across the room to where the Marquis was standing, and dwelled rather thoughtfully on that arrogant figure. He did not say anything for a moment, and Lady Fanny rattled on.

"I am sure I have not the least objection to him shooting a highwayman—my dear Hugh, do but look at that odd gown! What a figure of fun—oh, it is Lady Mary Coke! Well, small wonder. She never could dress, and really she is become so strange of late, people say she is growing absolutely *English*. Yes, Hugh, I heard it from Mr. Walpole, and he vowed she was mad—what was I saying? Vidal! Oh, yes, well, if he must shoot highwaymen, it's very well, but to leave the poor man dead on the road—though I make no doubt he would have done the same to Vidal, for I believe they are horridly callous, these fellows—but that's neither here nor there. Vidal had no right to leave him. Now people will say that he is wickedly blood-thirsty, or something disagreeable, and it is quite true, only one does not want the whole world to say so." She drew a long breath. "And Léonie," she said—"and you know, Hugh, I am very fond of dear Léonie—Léonie will laugh, and say that her *méchant Dominique* is dreadfully thoughtless. Thoughtless!"

Davenant smiled. "I make no doubt she will," he agreed. "I sometimes think that the Duchess of Avon will always remain, at heart—Léon, a page."

"Hugh, do I beseech you, have a care! You do not know who may overhear you. As for Avon, I truly think he does not care at all what happens to Dominic."

"After all," Hugh said slowly, "Dominic is so very like him."

Lady Fanny shut her fan with a snap. "If you are minded to be unkind about my poor Avon, Hugh, I warn you I shall not listen. Lud, I'm sure he has been a perfect paragon ever since he married Léonie. I know he is monstrous disagreeable, and no one was ever more provoking, unless it be Rupert, who, by the way, encourages Dominic in every sort of excess, just as one would expect—but I'll stake my reputation Avon was never such a—yes, Hugh, such a *devil* as Vidal. Why, they call him Devil's Cub! And if you are going to tell me that is because he is Avon's son, all I can say is that you are in a very teasing mood, and it's no such thing."

"He is very young, Fanny," Hugh said, still watching the Marquis across the room.

"That makes it worse," declared her ladyship. "Oh, my dear Lady Dawlish, I wondered whether I should see you to-night! I protest, it's an age since I had a talk with you. . . . Odious woman, and as for her daughter, you may say what you choose, Hugh, but the girl *squints!* Where was I? Oh, Vidal, of course! Young? Yes, Hugh, I marvel that you should find that an excuse for him. The poor Hollands had trouble enough with their son, not but what I consider Holland was entirely to blame—but I never heard that Charles Fox ever did anything worse than lose a fortune at gaming, which is a thing no one could blame in him. It is very different with Vidal. From the day he left Eton he has been outrageous, and I make no doubt he was so in the nursery. It is not only his duels, Hugh—my dear, do you know he is considered positively deadly with the pistols? John tells me they say in the clubs that it makes no odds to the Devil's Cub whether he is drunk or sober, he can still pick out a playing card on the wall. He did that at White's once, and there was the most horrid scandal, for of course he was in his cups, and only fancy, Hugh, how angry all the people like old Queensberry and Mr. Walpole must have been! I wish I had seen it!"

"I did see it," said Hugh. "A silly boy's trick, no more."

"I dare say, but it was no boy's trick to kill young Ffolliot. A pretty to-do there was over that. But as I say, it is not only his duels. He plays high—well, so do we all, and he is a true

Alastair—and he drinks too much. No one ever saw Avon in his cups that I ever heard of, Hugh. And worse—worse than all——" she stopped and made a gesture with her fan. "Opera dancers," she said darkly.

Davenant smiled. "Well, Fanny, I deplore it as much as you do, but I believe you cannot say that no one ever saw Avon——"

He was interrupted. "I am very fond of Justin," said Lady Fanny tartly, "but I never pretended to approve of his conduct. And with all his faults Justin was ever *bon ton*. It is no such thing with Vidal. If he were my son, I should never have consented to let him live anywhere but under my roof. My own dear John scarce leaves my side."

Hugh bowed. "I know you are very fortunate in your son, Fanny," he said.

She sighed. "Indeed, he is prodigiously like his poor papa."

Hugh made no reply to this but merely bowed again. Knowing her ladyship as he did, he was perfectly well aware that her son's staid disposition was something of a disappointment to her.

"I am sure," said Lady Fanny, with a touch of defiance, "that if I heard of my John holding—holding orgies with all the wildest young rakes in town I should die of mortification."

He frowned. "Orgies, Fanny?"

"Orgies, Hugh. Pray do not ask more."

Davenant had heard a good many stories concerning the doings of Vidal's particular set, and bearing in mind what these stories were, he was somewhat surprised that they should have come to Lady Fanny's ears. From her expression of outraged virtue he inferred that she really had heard some of the worst tales. He wondered whether John Marling had been her informant, and reflected that in spite of his excesses one could not but like the Marquis better than his impeccable cousin.

At that moment Mr. John Marling came across the room towards his mother. He was a good-looking young man of rather stocky build, dressed very neatly in Spanish-brown velvet. He was in his thirtieth year, but the staidness of his demeanour made him appear older. He greeted Davenant with a bow and a grave smile, and had begun to inquire politely after the older man's health, when his mother interrupted him.

"Pray, John, where is your sister? I was put out to see that young Comyn was present here to-night. I do trust you have not let her slip off with him?"

"No," John said. "She is with Vidal."

"Oh!" A curiously thoughtful expression came into her ladyship's face. "Well, I make no doubt they were glad to see each other."

"I don't know," John said painstakingly. "Juliana cried out: 'Why, my dear Dominic, you here?' or some such thing, and Vidal said: 'Good God! Have I stumbled on a family gathering?'"

"That is just his way," Lady Fanny assured him. She turned her limpid gaze upon Davenant. "Vidal has a great kindness for his cousin, you know, Hugh."

Davenant did not know it, but he was perfectly well aware of Lady Fanny's ambition. Whatever might be the imperfections of Vidal's character, he was one of the biggest prizes on the matrimonial market, and for years her ladyship had cherished hopes which she fondly believed to be secret.

John seemed disposed to argue the matter. "For my part I do not believe that Vidal cares a fig for Juliana," he said. "And as for her, I very much fear this Frederick Comyn has taken her fancy to an alarming degree."

"How can you be so teasing, John?" Fanny demanded petulantly. "You know very well she is nothing but a child, and I am sure no thought of—of marriage, or love, or any such folly has entered her head. And if it had, it is no great matter, and when she has been in Paris a week, she will have forgotten the young man's very existence."

"Paris?" said Hugh, foreseeing that John was going to try and convince his mother for her own good. "Is Juliana going to Paris?"

"Why yes, Hugh. Have you forgotten that my dear mamma was a Frenchwoman? I am sure it is no matter for wonder that the child should visit her French relatives. They are quite wild to know her, so John is to take her next week. I don't doubt they will make so much rout with her she will hardly wish to come home again."

"But I do not feel at all hopeful that it will answer the purpose," said John heavily.

"Pray, John, do not be so provoking!" implored Lady Fanny, somewhat tartly. "You make it sound as though I were one of those odious scheming females whom I detest."

Hugh thought it time to withdraw, and tactfully did so, leaving mother and son to argue in comfort.

Meanwhile, Miss Juliana Marling, a charming blonde dressed in blue lustring with spangled shoes, and her curls arranged *à la Gorgonne,* had dragged her cousin into one of the adjoining saloons. "You are the very person I wished to see!" she informed him.

The Marquis said with conspicuous lack of gallantry: "If you want me to do something for you, Juliana, I warn you I never do anything for anybody."

Miss Marling opened her blue eyes very wide. "Not even for me, Dominic?" she said soulfully.

His lordship remained unmoved. "No," he replied.

Miss Marling sighed and shook her head. "You are horridly disobliging, you know. It quite decides me not to marry you."

"I hoped it might," said his lordship calmly.

Miss Marling made an effort to look affronted, but only succeeded in giggling. "You needn't be afraid. I am going to marry someone quite different," she said.

His lordship evinced signs of faint interest at that. "Are you?" he inquired. "Does my aunt know?"

"You may be very wicked, and quite hatefully rude," said Miss Marling, "but I will say one thing for you, Dominic: you do not need to have things explained to you like John. Mamma does not mean me to marry him, and that is why I am to be packed off to France next week."

"Who is 'he?' Ought I to know?" inquired the Marquis.

"I don't suppose you know him. He is not at all the sort of person who would know your set," said Miss Marling severely.

"Ah, then I was right," retorted my lord. "You are contemplating a *mésalliance.*"

Miss Marling stiffened in every line of her small figure. "It's no such thing! He may not be a brilliant match, or have a title, but all the men I have met who are brilliant matches are just like you, and would make the most horrid husbands."

"You may as well let me know the worst," said my lord. "If you think it would annoy Aunt Fanny, I'll do what I can for you."

She clasped both hands on his arm. "Dear, dear Dominic! I knew you would! It is Frederick Comyn."

"And who," said the Marquis, "might he be?"

"He comes from Gloucestershire—or is it Somerset? Well, it doesn't signify—and his papa is Sir Malcolm Comyn, and it is all perfectly respectable, as dear Aunt Léonie would say, for they have always lived there, and there is an estate, though not very large, I believe, and Frederick is the eldest son, and he was at Cambridge, and this is his first stay in town, and Lord Carlisle is his sponsor, so you see it is not a *mésalliance* at all."

"I don't," said his lordship. "You may as well give up the notion, my dear. They'll never let you throw yourself away on this nobody."

"Dominic," said Miss Marling with dangerous quiet.

My lord looked lazily down at her.

"I just want you to know that my mind is made up," she said, giving him back look for look. "So that it is no use to talk to me like that."

"Very well," said my lord.

"And you will make a push to help us, won't you, dearest Dominic?"

"Oh certainly, child. I will tell Aunt Fanny that the alliance has my full approval."

"You are quite abominable," said his cousin. "I know you dislike of all things to bestir yourself, but recollect, my lord, if once I am wed you need not be afraid any more that mamma will make you marry me."

"I am not in the least afraid of that," replied his lordship.

"I declare it would serve you right if I did marry you!" cried Miss Marling indignantly. "You are being quite atrocious and all I want you to do is to write a letter to Tante Elisabeth in Paris!"

His lordship's attention seemed to have wandered, but at this he brought his gaze back from the contemplation of a ripe blonde who was trying to appear unconscious of his scrutiny, and looked down into Miss Marling's face.

"Why?" he asked.

"It's perfectly plain, Dominic, I should have thought. Tante Elisabeth so dotes on you she will do whatever you wish, and if you were to solicit her kindness for a friend of yours about to make his début in Paris——"

"Oh, that's it, is it?" said the Marquis. "Much good will a letter from me avail you if my respected Aunt Fanny has already warned Tante against your nobody."

"She won't do that," Miss Marling replied confidently. "And

he is not a nobody. She has no notion, you see, that Frederick means to follow me to Paris. So you will write, will you not, Dominic?"

"No, certainly not," said my lord. "I've never set eyes on the fellow."

"I knew you would say something disagreeable like that," said Miss Marling, unperturbed. "So I told Frederick to be ready." She turned her head and made a gesture with her fan, rather in the manner of a sorceress about to conjure up visions. In response to the signal a young man who had been watching her anxiously disengaged himself from a knot of persons near the door, and came towards her.

He was not so tall as Vidal, and of a very different *ton*. From his moderate-sized pigeon's-wing wig to his low-heeled black shoes, there did not seem to be a hair or a pin out of place. His dress was in the mode, but not designed to attract attention. He wore Lunardi lace at his throat and wrists, and a black solitaire adorned his cravat. Such usual adjuncts to a gentleman's costume as quizzing-glass, fobs, and watches, he had altogether dispensed with, but he had a snuff-box in one hand, and wore a cameo-ring on one finger.

The Marquis watched his approach through his quizzing-glass. "Lord!" he said. "What's the matter with you Ju?"

Miss Marling chose to ignore this. She sprang up as Mr. Comyn reached them, and laid her hand on his arm. "Frederick, I have told my cousin all!" she said dramatically. "This is my cousin, by the way. I dare say you know of him. He is very wicked and kills people in duels. Vidal, this is Frederick."

His lordship had risen. "You talk too much, Juliana," he drawled. His dark eyes held a distinct menace, but his cousin remained unabashed. He exchanged bows with Mr. Comyn. "Sir, your most obedient."

Mr. Comyn, who had blushed at his Juliana's introduction, said that he was honoured.

"Vidal is going going to write to my French aunt about you," stated Miss Marling blithely. "She is really the only person in the family who is not shocked by him. Except me, of course."

The Marquis caught her eye once more. Knowing that dangerous look of old, Miss Marling capitulated. "I won't say another word," she promised. "And you will write, will you not, dear Dominic?"

Mr. Comyn said in his grave young voice: "I think my

Lord Vidal must require to know my credentials. My lord, though I am aware that I must sound like a mere adventurer, I can assure you it is no such thing. My family is well known in the West of England, and my Lord Carlisle will speak for me at need."

"Good God, sir! I'm not the girl's guardian!" said his lordship. "You had better address all this to her brother."

Mr. Comyn and Miss Marling exchanged rueful glances.

"Mr. Marling and Lady Fanny can hardly be unaware of my estate, sir, but—but in short I cannot flatter myself that they look upon my suit with any favour."

"Of course they don't," agreed the Marquis. "You'll have to elope with her."

Mr. Comyn looked extremely taken aback. "Elope, my lord!" he said.

"Or give the chit up," replied his lordship.

"My lord," said Mr. Comyn earnestly, "I ask you to believe that in journeying to Paris, I have no such impropriety in mind. It was always my father's intention that I should visit France. Miss Marling's going there but puts my own journey forward."

"Yes," said Juliana thoughtfully, "but for all that I'm not sure it wouldn't be a very good thing to do, Frederick. I must say, Vidal, you do take some prodigious clever notions into your head! I wonder I did not think of it myself."

Mr. Comyn regarded her with a hint of sternness in his frank gaze. "Juliana—madam! You could not suppose that I would steal you away clandestinely? His lordship was jesting."

"Oh no, indeed he wasn't. It is just the kind of thing he would do himself. It is no good being proper and respectable, Frederick; we may be forced to elope in the end. Unless ——" She paused, and looked doubtfully up at Vidal. "You don't suppose, do you, Dominic, that my Uncle Justin could be induced to speak for us to mamma?"

My lord answered this without hesitation. "Don't be a fool, Ju."

She sighed. "No, I was afraid he would not. It is a vast pity, for mamma always does what Uncle Justin says." She caught sight of a stocky figure at the far end of the room. "There's John! You had best go away, Frederick, for it will not do at all for John to see you talking to my cousin."

She watched him bow, and retreat, and turned enthusiastically to the Marquis. "Is he not a delightful creature, Vidal?" she demanded.

My lord looked at her frowningly. "Juliana," he said, "do I understand that you prefer him as a husband to myself?"

"Infinitely," Miss Marling assured him.

"You have very bad taste, my girl," said my lord calmly.

"Indeed, cousin! And may I ask whether you prefer that yellow-haired chit I saw you with at Vauxhall as a wife to me?" retorted Juliana.

"Ill-judged, my dear. I do not contemplate marriage either with her or you. Nor am I at all certain which yellow-haired chit you mean."

Miss Marling prepared to depart. She swept a dignified curtsey, and said: "I do not mix with the company you keep, dear cousin, so I cannot tell you her name."

The Marquis bowed gracefully. "I still live, dear Juliana."

"You are shameless and provoking," Miss Marling said crossly and left him.

ᴇᵍ *Chapter II* ᴊᴥ

IN the sunny withdrawing-room which overlooked the street
sat the Duchess of Avon, listening to her sister-in-law, Lady
Fanny Marling, who had called to pay her a morning visit, and
to talk over the week's doings over a cup of chocolate and
little sweet biscuits.

Lady Fanny no longer looked her best in the crude light
of day, but her grace, though turned forty now, still retained
a youthful bloom in her cheeks, and had no need at all to
shrink from the sunlight. Lady Fanny, who had taken care
to seat herself with her back to the window, could not help
feeling slightly resentful. There really seemed to be so little
difference between her grace, and the boy-girl whom Avon
had brought to England twenty-four years ago. Léonie's
figure was as slim as ever, her Titian hair, worn just now
en négligé, was untouched by grey, and her eyes, those great
dark-blue eyes which had first attracted the Duke, held all
their old sparkle. Twenty-four years of marriage had given
her dignity—when she chose to assume it, and much feminine
wisdom, which she had lacked in the old days, but no wifely
or motherly responsibility, no weight of honours, of social
eminence had succeeded in subduing the *gamin* spirit in her.
Lady Fanny considered her far too impulsive, but since she
was, at the bottom of her somewhat shallow heart, very
fond of her sister-in-law, she admitted that Léonie's impetu-
osity only added to her charm.

To-day, however, she was in no mood to admire the Duchess. Life was proving itself a tiresome business, full of unpaid
bills, and undutiful daughters. Vaguely it annoyed her that

15

Léonie (who had a thoroughly unsatisfactory son if only she could be brought to realize it) should look so carefree.

"I vow," she said rather sharply, "I do not know why we poor creatures slave and fret our lives out for our children, for they are all ungrateful and provoking and only want to disgrace one."

Léonie wrinkled her brow at that. "I do not think," she said seriously, "that John would ever want to disgrace you, Fanny."

"Oh, I was not talking of John!" said her ladyship. "Sons are another matter, though to be sure I should not say so to you, for you have trouble enough with poor dear Dominic, and indeed I wonder how it is he has not turned your hair white with worry already, and young as he is."

"I do not have trouble with Dominique," said Léonie flatly. "I find him *fort amusant.*"

"Then I trust you will find his latest exploit *fort amusant,*" said Lady Fanny tartly. "I make no doubt he will break his neck over it, for what must he do at the drum last night but wager young Crossly—as mad a rake as ever I set eyes on, and I should be prodigious sorry to see my son in his company—that he would drive his curricle from London to Newmarket in four hours. Five hundred guineas on it, so I heard—play or pay!"

"He drives very well," Léonie said hopefully. "I do not think that he will break his neck, but you are quite right, *tout même,* Fanny: it makes one very anxious."

"And not content with making absurd wagers, which of course he must lose——"

"He will not lose," cried her grace indignantly. "And if you like I will lay you a wager that he will win!"

"Lord, my dear, I don't know what you would have me stake," said Lady Fanny, forgetting the main issue for the moment. "It's very well for you with all the pin money and the jewels Avon gives you, but I give you my word I expect to find myself at any moment in that horrid place Rupert used to be clapped up in. If you can believe it I've not won once at loo this past month or at silver-pharaoh, and as for whist, I vow and declare to you I wish the game had never been thought of. But that's neither here nor there, and at least I have not to stand by and watch my only son make himself the talk of the town with his bets and his highwaymen, and I don't know what more beside."

Léonie looked interested at this. "But tell!" she commanded. "What highwayman?"

"Oh, it was nothing but just to match the rest of his conduct. He shot one last night on Hounslow Heath, and must needs leave the body upon the road."

"He is a very good shot," Léonie said. "For me, I like best to fight with swords, and so does Monseigneur, but Dominique chooses pistols."

Lady Fanny almost stamped her foot. "I declare you are as incorrigible as that worthless boy himself!" she cried. "It's very well for the world to call Dominic Devil's Cub, and place all his wildness at poor Avon's door, but for my part I find him very like his mamma."

Léonie was delighted. "*Voyons,* that pleases me very much!" she said. "Do you really think so?"

What Fanny might have been goaded to reply to this was checked by the quiet opening of the door behind her. She had no need to turn her head to see who had come in, for Léonie's face told her.

A soft voice spoke. "Ah, my dear Fanny," it said, "lamenting my son's wickedness as usual, I perceive."

"Monseigneur, Dominique has shot a highwayman!" Léonie said, before Fanny had time to speak.

His Grace of Avon came slowly to the fire, and stretched one thin white hand to the blaze. He carried an ebony stick, but it was noticeable that he leaned on it but slightly. He was still very upright, and only his lined face showed his age. He wore a suit of black velvet with silver lacing, and his wig, which was curled in the latest French fashion, was thickly powdered. His eyes held all their old mockery, and mockery sounded in his voice as he answered: "Very proper."

"And left the body to rot on the road!" snapped Lady Fanny.

His grace's delicate brows rose. "I appreciate your indignation, my dear. An untidy ending."

"But not at all, Monseigneur!" Léonie said practically. "I do not see that a corpse is of any use at all."

"La, child, will you never lose those callous notions of yours?" demanded Fanny. "It might be Vidal himself speaking! All he would say was that he could not bring a corpse to the drum. Yes, Avon; that is positively the only excuse he gave for his inhuman conduct."

"I did not know that Vidal had so much proper feeling,"

remarked his grace. He moved towards a chair and sat down. "Doubtless you had some other reason for visiting us to-day—other than to mourn Vidal's exploits."

"Of course, I might have known you would uphold him, just to be disagreeable," said Lady Fanny crossly.

"I never uphold Vidal—even to be disagreeable," replied his grace.

"Indeed, and I cannot conceive how you should. I was only saying to Léonie when you came in that I have never seen my son in such scrapes as he is always in. I do not believe John has ever caused me one moment's anxiety in all his life."

The Duke opened his snuff-box—a plain gold case delicately painted *en grisaille* by Degault and protected by *cristal de roche.* "I can do nothing about it, my dear Fanny," he said. "Recollect that you wanted to marry Edward."

Under her rouge additional and quite natural colour rose in Fanny's cheeks. "I won't hear one word against my sainted Edward!" she said, her voice quivering a little. "And if you mean that John is like his dear father, I am sure I am thankful for it."

Léonie interposed hurriedly. "Monseigneur did not mean anything like that, did you, Monseigneur? And me, I was always very fond of Edward. And certainly John is like him, which is a good thing, just as Juliana is very like you, only not, I think, as pretty as you were."

"Oh my dear, do you say so indeed?" Lady Fanny's angry flush died down. "You flatter me, but I believe I was accounted something of a beauty in my young days, was I not, Justin? Only I hope I was never so headstrong as Juliana, who is likely to ruin everything by her stupid behaviour." She turned to Avon. "Justin, it is too provoking! The foolish chit has taken a fancy to the veriest nobody, and I am forced—yes, forced to pack her off to France till she has got over it."

Léonie at once pricked up her ears. "Oh, is Juliana in love? But who is he?"

"Pray do not put such an idea into her head!" besought Lady Fanny. "It's no such matter, I'll be bound. Lord, if I had married the first man whom I fancied I loved——! It's nothing but a silly girl's first affair, but she is such a headstrong child I vow I do not know what she will be at next. So off she goes to France. John is to take her."

"Who," inquired his grace languidly, "is the nobody?"

"Oh, no one of account, my dear Justin. Some country squire's son whom young Carlisle is sponsoring."

"Is he nice?" Léonie asked.

"I dare say, my love, but that's nothing to the point. I have other plans for Juliana." She gave her laces a little shake, and went on airily: "I am sure we have spoken of it often enough, you and I, and I cannot help feeling that it would be a charming match, besides fulfilling my dearest wish. And I have always thought them remarkably well suited, and I make no doubt at all that everything would have been on the road to being settled by now had Juliana not taken it into her head to flout me in this way, though to be sure, I do not in the least blame her for appearing cold to him, for it is no more than he deserves."

She paused for breath, and shot a look at Avon out of the corners of her eyes. He was quite unperturbed; a faint smile hovered over his thin lips, and he regarded his sister with an air of cynical amusement. "I find your conversation somewhat difficult to follow, my dear Fanny," he said. "Pray enlighten me."

Lady Fanny said shrewdly: "Indeed, and I think you follow me very well, Justin."

"But I don't," Léonie said. "Who deserves that Juliana should be cold? It is not the poor nobody?"

"Of course not!" replied her ladyship impatiently. She seemed strangely loth to explain herself. Léonie glanced inquiringly at the Duke.

He had opened his snuff-box again, and held a pinch to one nostril before he spoke. "I apprehend, my love, that Fanny is referring to your son."

A blank look came into Léonie's face. "Dominique? But ——" She stopped and looked at Fanny. "No," she said flatly.

Lady Fanny was hardly prepared for anything so downright. "Lord, my dear, what can you mean?"

"I do not at all want Dominique to marry Juliana," Léonie explained.

"Perhaps," said Lady Fanny, sitting very erect in her chair, "you will be good enough to explain what that signifies."

"I am sorry if I seemed rude," Léonie apologized. "Did I, Monseigneur?"

"Very," he answered, shutting his snuff-box with an expert flick of the finger. "But, unlike Fanny, beautifully frank."

"Well, I am sorry," she repeated. "It is not that I do not like Juliana, but I do not think it would amuse Dominic to marry her."

"Amuse him!" Fanny turned with pardonable exasperation to her brother. "If that is all——! Have you also forgotten the plans we made, Avon, years back?"

"Acquit me, Fanny. I never make plans."

Léonie interrupted a heated rejoinder to say: "It is true, Fanny: we did say Dominique should marry Juliana. Not Monseigneur, but you and I. But they were babies, and me, I think it is all quite different now."

"What is different, pray?" demanded her ladyship.

Léonie reflected. "Well, Dominique is," she replied naïvely. "He is not enough respectable for Juliana."

"Lord, child, do you look to see him bring home one of his opera dancers on his arm?" Lady Fanny said with a shrill little laugh.

From a doorway a cool, faintly insolent voice spoke. "My good aunt interests herself in my affairs, I infer." The Marquis of Vidal came into the room, his chapeau-bras under his arm, the wings of his riding coat clipped back, French fashion, and top boots on his feet. There was a sparkle in his eyes, but he bowed with great politeness to his aunt, and went towards the Duchess.

She flew out of her chair. "Ah, my little one! *Voyons*, this makes me very happy!"

He put his arms round her. The red light went out of his eyes, and a softer look transformed his face. " 'My dear and only love,' I give you good morrow," he said. He shot a glance of mockery at his aunt, and took both Léonie's hands in his. " 'My dear—and—only—love,' " he repeated maliciously, and kissed her fingers.

The Duchess gave a little crow of laughter. "Truly?" she inquired.

Fanny saw him smile into her eyes, a smile he kept for her alone. "Oh, quite, my dear!" he said negligently. Upon which my lady arose with an angry flounce of her armazine skirts, and announced that it was time she took her leave of them.

Léonie pressed her son's hand coaxingly. "Dominique, you will escort your aunt to her carriage, will you not?"

"With the greatest pleasure on earth, madam," he replied

with promptitude, and offered his arm to the outraged lady.

She made her adieux stiffly, and went out with him. Half-way down the stairs her air of offended dignity deserted her. To be sure the boy was so very handsome, and she had ever a soft corner for a rake. She stole a glance at his profile, and suddenly laughed. "I declare you're as disdainful as Avon," she remarked. "But you need not be so cross, even if I do interest myself in your affairs." She tapped his arm with her gloved hand. "You know, Dominic, I have a great fond-ness for you."

The Marquis looked down at her rather enigmatically. "I shall strive to deserve your regard, ma'am," he said.

"Shall you, my dear?" Lady Fanny's tone was dry. "I wonder! Well, there's no use denying I had hoped you would have made me happy, you and Juliana."

"Console yourself, dear aunt, with the reflection that I shall cause neither you nor Juliana unhappiness."

"Why, what do you mean?" she asked.

He laughed. "I should make a devil of a husband, aunt."

"I believe you would," she said slowly. "But——well, never mind." They had come to the big door that gave on to the street. The porter swung it open and stood waiting. Lady Fanny gave her hand to the Marquis, who kissed it punctil-iously. "Yes," she said. "A devil of a husband. I am sorry for your wife—or I should be if I were a man." On which obscure utterance she departed.

His lordship went back to the sunny room upstairs.

"I hope you did not engage her, *mon petit?*" Léonie said anxiously.

"Far from it," replied the Marquis. "I think—but she became profound so that I cannot be sure—that she is now glad I am not going to marry my cousin."

"I told her you would not. I knew you would not like it at all," Léonie said.

His grace surveyed her blandly. "You put yourself to un-necessary trouble, my love. I cannot conceive that Juliana, who seems to me to have more sense than one would ex-pect to find in a child of Fanny's, would contemplate marriage with Vidal."

The Marquis grinned. "As usual, sir, you are right."

"But I do not think so at all," objected Léonie. "And if you are right, then I say that Juliana is a little fool, and without any sense at all."

"She is in love," answered the Marquis, "with a man called Frederick."

"Incroyable!" Léonie exclaimed. "Tell me all about him at once. He sounds very disagreeable."

The Duke looked across the room at his son. "One was led to suppose from Fanny's somewhat incoherent discourse that the young man is impossible!"

"Oh, quite, sir," agreed Vidal. "But she'll have him for all that."

"Well, if she loves him, I hope she will marry him," said Léonie, with a bewildering change of front. "You do not mind, do you, Monseigneur?"

"It is not, thank God, my affair," replied his grace. "I am not concerned with the Marlings' futures."

The Marquis met his glance squarely. "Very well, sir. The point is taken."

Avon held out one of his very white hands towards the fire, and regarded through half-closed eyes the big emerald ring he wore. "It is not my custom," he said smoothly, "to inquire into your affairs, but I have heard talk of a girl who is not an opera dancer."

The Marquis answered with perfect composure. "But not, I think, talk of my approaching nuptials."

"Hardly," said his grace, with a faint lift of the brows. "Nor will you, sir."

"You relieve me," said his grace politely. He got up, leaning lightly on his ebony cane. "Permit me to tell you, my son, that when you trifle with a girl of the *bourgeoisie,* you run the risk of creating the kind of scandal I deplore."

A smile flickered across Vidal's mouth. "Your pardon, sir, but do you speak from your wide experience?"

"Naturally," said his grace.

"I do not believe," said Léonie, who had been listening calmly to this interchange, "that you ever trifled with a *bourgeoise,* Justin."

"You flatter me, child." He looked again at his son. "I do not need your assurance that you amuse yourself only. I have no doubt that you will commit almost every indiscretion, but one you will not commit. You are, after all, my son. But I would advise you, Dominic, to amuse yourself with women of a certain class, or with your own kind, who understand how the game should be played."

The Marquis bowed. "You are a fount of wisdom, sir."

"Of worldly wisdom, yes," said his grace. In the doorway he paused and looked back. "Ah, there was another little matter, as I remember. What kind of cattle do you keep in your stables that it must needs take you four hours to reach Newmarket?"

The Marquis' eye gleamed appreciation, but Léonie was inclined to be indignant. "Monseigneur, I find you *fort exigeant* to-day. Four hours! *ma foi*, but of a surety he will break his neck."

"It has been done in less," his grace said tranquilly.

"That I do not at all believe," stated the Duchess. "Who did it in less?"

"I did," said Avon.

"Oh, then I do believe it," said Léonie as a matter of course.

"How long, sir?" the Marquis said swiftly.

"Three hours and forty-seven minutes."

"Still too generous, sir. Three hours and forty-five minutes should, I think, suffice. You would perhaps, like to lay me odds?"

"Not in the least," said his grace. "But three hours and forty-five minutes should certainly suffice."

He went out. Léonie said: "Of course I should like you to beat Monseigneur's record, my little one, but it is very dangerous. Do not kill yourself, Dominique, please."

"I won't," he answered. "That is a promise, my dear."

She tucked her hand in his. "Ah, but it is a promise you could break, *mon ange*."

"Devil a bit!" said his lordship cheerfully. "Ask my uncle. He will tell you I was born to be hanged."

"Rupert?" said Léonie scornfully. "*Voyons,* he would not tell me any such thing, because he would not dare." She retained her clasp on his hand. "Now you will talk to me a little, *mon enfant—tout bas.* Who is this *bourgeoise?*"

The laugh went out of Vidal's eyes at that, and his black brows drew close together. "Let be, madame. She is nothing. How did my father hear of her?"

She shook her head. "I don't know. But this I know, Dominique, you will never be able to hide anything from Monseigneur. And I think he is not quite pleased. It would be better, perhaps, if you did not amuse yourself there."

"Content you, maman. I can manage my affairs."

"Well, I hope so," Léonie said doubtfully. "You are quite

sure, I suppose, that this will not lead to a *mésalliance?*"

He looked at her rather sombrely. "You don't flatter my judgment, madame. Do you think I am so likely to forget what I owe to my name?"

"Yes," said her grace candidly, "I think, my dear, that when you have the devil in you—which I perfectly understand— you are likely to forget everything."

He disengaged himself, and stood up. "My devil don't prompt me to marriage, maman," he said.

❧ Chapter III ❧

MRS. CHALLONER occupied rooms in a genteel part of the town which might be said to touch the fringe of the more fashionable quarter. She was a widow with a jointure quite inadequate for a lady of her ambition, but she had an additional source of income in her brother, who was a city merchant of considerable affluence. From time to time he paid some of Mrs. Challoner's more pressing bills, and though he did it with a bad grace, and was consistently discouraged by his wife and daughters, he could always be relied upon to step into the breach before matters reached too serious a pass. He said, grumbling, that he did it for his little Sophy's sake, for he could not bear to see such a monstrous pretty girl go dressed in the rags Mrs. Challoner assured him she was reduced to. His elder niece awoke no such generous feeling in his breast, but since she never exerted herself to captivate him, and always stated in her calm way that she lacked nothing, this was perhaps not surprising. Though he would naturally never admit it, he stood a little in awe of Mary Challoner. She favoured her father, and Henry Simpkins had never been able to feel at ease with his handsome brother-in-law. Charles Challoner had been reckless and graceless, and his own noble family had declined having any intercourse with him after he had committed the crowning indescretion of marriage with Miss Clara Simpkins. He was indolent and spendthrift, and his morals shocked a decent-living merchant. But for all that he had an air, a faint hauteur of manner that set his wife's relations at a distance, and kept them there. They might assist materially in the upkeep of

25

his establishment, and he was not above permitting them to rescue him from the Spunging House, whenever he was unfortunate enough to fall a victim to his creditors, but a gentleman of his connections could not be expected to consort on equal terms with (as he neatly phrased it) a bundle of Cits. This easy air of assurance, and a patrician cast of countenance he bequeathed to his elder daughter. Her Uncle Henry found himself ill at ease in her presence, and wished that if his son Joshua must feel it incumbent on him to fall in love with one of his cousins, he would choose the easier and prettier Sophia.

Mrs. Challoner had only the two daughters, and since Mary's sixteenth birthday her main object in life had been to marry them both suitably as soon as possible. The signal success once achieved by a certain Irish widow put ideas into her head which her brother thought absurd, but though she admitted that Mary, in spite of her grand education, could scarcely hope to achieve more than a respectable alliance, she could not find that either Maria or Elizabeth Gunning in their prime had outshone her own Sophia. It was more than twenty years since the Gunning sisters had taken the town by storm, and Mrs. Challoner could not remember ever to have set eyes on either, but she knew several reliable persons who had, and they all assured her that Sophia far transcended the famous beauties. If Mrs. Gunning, who hadn't a penny, and was dreadfully Irish as well, could catch an earl and a duke in her matrimonial net, there seemed to be very little reason why Mrs. Challoner, with a respectable jointure, and no common Irish accent, should not do quite as well. Or if not quite, at least half—for she was not besotted about her daughters, and had made up her mind a long time ago that nothing great could be hoped for Mary.

It was not that the girl was ill-favoured. She had a fine pair of grey eyes, and her profile with its delightfully straight nose and short upper lip was quite lovely. But placed beside Sophia she was nothing beyond the common. What chance had chestnut curls when compared to a riot of bright gold ringlets? What chance had cool grey eyes when the most limpid blue ones peeped between preposterously long eyelashes?

She had, moreover, grave disadvantages. Those fine eyes of hers had a disconcertingly direct gaze, and very often twinkled in a manner disturbing to male egotism. She had common-sense too, and what man wanted the plainly matter-of-fact, when he could enjoy instead Sophia's delicious folly? Worst of all she had been educated at a very select seminary— Mrs. Challoner was sometimes afraid that she was almost a Bluestocking.

The education had been provided by the girl's paternal relatives, and at one time Mrs. Challoner had expected wonders to come of it. But Mary seemed to have acquired nothing from it but a quantity of useless knowledge, and a certain elegance of deportment. The select seminary had housed young ladies of the highest rank, but Mary's commonsense fell short of making fast-friends with any of them, so that Mrs. Challoner's visions of entering the Polite World through her daughter's friendships all vanished, and she was left to wish that she had never applied to the Challoners for help at all. Yet at the time of Charles Challoner's early demise, it had seemed to her to be an excellent thing to do. Her brother had said that she could hope for nothing from such high and mighty folk, and it certainly seemed now as though she had got worse than nothing. While evincing no desire to set eyes on his late son's spouse, General Sir Giles Challoner had expressed his willingness to provide for the education of his eldest granddaughter. Mrs. Challoner perforce had accepted this half-loaf, with the secret belief that it would lead to better things. It never had. On several occasions Mary had been bidden on a visit to Buckinghamshire, but no suggestion either of adopting her, or of inviting her mamma and sister to share the visit, had ever been made.

It was bitterly disappointing, but Mrs. Challoner was a just woman, and she had no doubt that the frustration of her ambitions was largely due to Mary herself. For all her wonderful learning, the girl had not the smallest notion of bettering her position. With every opportunity (if only she had known how to be ingratiating) of insinuating herself into the affections of her benefactors, she had apparently made no attempt to be indispensable to them, so that here she was, actually twenty years of age, still sharing the lodging of her mother and sister, and with no better prospect in view than marriage with her cousin Joshua.

Joshua, a stout and affluent young man, was not an earl, but then Mary was not Sophia, and Mrs. Challoner would have been quite satisfied with this match for her elder daughter. Inexplicably Joshua had no eyes for Sophia. He was obstinately and somewhat fiercely in love with Mary, and the mischief was that the stupid girl would have none of him.

"I don't know what you look for, I'm sure," Mrs. Challoner said, pardonably incensed. "If you think you will marry a titled gentlemen, let me tell you, Mary, that you have no notion how to go about the business."

Whereupon Mary had looked up from her stitchery, and said with a humorous inflexion in her calm voice: "Well, mamma, I have plenty of opportunity for learning, haven't I?"

"If all that fine education of yours taught you was to be odiously sarcastic about your sister, miss, you wasted your time!" said her mother sharply.

Mary bent her head over her work again. "Indeed I think so," she said.

There was nothing much to be made of this. Mrs. Challoner suspected her daughter of a hidden, and probably unpalatable meaning, but could not resist saying: "And though you may sneer at Sophia now, I wonder how you will look when she is my lady."

Mary re-threaded her needle. "I think I should look much surprised, mamma," she replied somewhat drily. Then as Mrs. Challoner began to bridle, she put her work aside, and said in her quiet way: "Madam, surely in your heart you know that Lord Vidal does not dream of marriage?"

"I will tell you what it is, miss!" said her mother with a heightened colour, "you are jealous of your sister's beauty, and all the suitors she has! Not dream of marriage? Why, what do you know of the matter, pray? Does he take you so deep into his confidence?"

"I do not think," said Mary, "that Lord Vidal is aware of my existence."

"I'm sure that's no wonder," declared Mrs. Challoner. "You've no notion how to make yourself agreeable to a gentleman. But that's no reason why you should be so prodigious unpleasant about poor Sophia's chances. If ever I saw a man fall head over ears in love, that one is Lord Vidal. Lord, he's for ever kicking his heels upon our doorstep, and as for the posies and the trinkets he brings——"

"They had better be given back to him," said her daughter prosaically. "I tell you that man means no good towards Sophia. Good God, mamma, don't you know his reputation?"

Mrs. Challoner failed to meet that straight gaze. "Fie, and pray what should you, a chit from the schoolroom, know of a gentleman's reputation?" she said virtuously. "If he has been something of a rake, that will all be changed when he weds my pretty Sophia."

"It seems fairly safe to say so," agreed Mary, picking up her work again. "You choose to be hoodwinked, ma'am, but if you will believe he means honestly by my sister, will you not at least consider how far apart are their fortunes?"

"As to that," replied Mrs. Challoner, preening herself, "I am sure the Challoners are good enough for anyone. Not that it signifies in the least, for we all know how the Gunnings, who were nobody, married into the nobility."

"They did us a great disservice thereby," sighed Mary.

More she would not say, deeming it useless, but it was with deep misgiving that she regarded her sister when that damsel danced in, fresh from an expedition with her bosom friends, the Matchams.

Sophia was just eighteen, and it would have been hard to have found a fault in her appearance. She had the biggest of cornflower-blue eyes, the daintiest of little noses, the softest, most adorable mouth in the world. Her curls, which her mamma nightly brushed for her, were of a gold that had nothing to do with flaxen, and her complexion was of that rose-leaf order that seems too perfect to be natural. She had a frippery brain, but she could dance very prettily, and knew just how to drive a man to desperation, so that it really did not matter in the least that she was amazingly ignorant, and found the mere writing of a letter the most arduous task.

Just now she was bubbling over with plans for the immediate future, and she broke in impatiently on her mother's lamentations over a torn muslin gown. "Oh, it doesn't signify, mamma, you will be able to mend it in a trice. But only fancy what a delightful scheme there is afoot! My Lord Vidal is to give a supper-party at Vauxhall, and we are all to go. There is to be dancing and fireworks, and Vidal promises we shall go by water, which makes Eliza Matcham so cross because I am to be in Vidal's boat, and he never asked her at all."

"Who is 'all,' Sophia?" inquired her sister.

"Oh, the Matchams, and their cousin Peggy Delaine, and I dare say some others," Sophia replied airily. "Can you conceive of anything more charming, mamma? But one thing is sure! I must have a new gown for it. I would die rather than wear the blue lustring again, if you can't contrive a new one, I vow I shan't go to the party at all, which would be a shame."

Mrs. Challoner quite saw the force of all this, and was at once prolific of plans for the acquiring of a suitable gown, and exclamatory over the pleasure in store for her daughter. Into their ecstasies Mary's matter-of-fact voice broke once again. "You'll hardly be seen at Vauxhall in Vidal's and Miss Delaine's company, Sophia, I should hope."

"And why not?" cried Sophia, beginning to pout. "Of course I knew you would try to spoil it for me, you cross thing! I dare say you would prefer I should stop at home."

"Infinitely," said Mary, unmoved by the hint of tears in her sister's eyes. She looked straightly across at her mother. "Will you think for a moment, ma'am? Do you see nothing amiss in allowing your daughter to go out in public with a play-actress and the most notorious rake in town?"

Mrs. Challoner said to be sure it was a pity Miss Delaine was to be of the party, but was immediately cheered by the reflection that Sophia would be accompanied by the two Misses Matcham.

Mary got up, and it was to be seen that she was of medium height and very neat figure. There was a sparkle in her eyes, and her voice took on a certain crispness. "Very well, ma'am, if that comforts you. But there's not a man alive would take my sister for the innocent girl she is who sees her in such company."

Sophia swept a curtsey. "La, and thank you, my dear! But perhaps I am not so innocent as you think. I know very well what I am about, let me tell you."

Mary looked at her for a moment. "Don't go, Sophy!"

Sophia tittered. "Lord, how serious you are! Have you any more advice, I wonder?"

Mary's hand dropped to her side again. "Certainly, child," she said. "Marry that nice boy who worships you."

Mrs. Challoner gave a small shriek of dismay. "Good God, you must be mad! Marry Dick Burnley? And she with her chances! I've a mind to box your ears, you stupid, provoking girl."

"Well, ma'am, and what are those fine chances? If you push her much further down the road she is travelling now, you'll have her Vidal's light o' love. A rare end, that, to your ambition."

"Oh, you wicked creature!" gasped Sophia. "As if I would!"

"Why, child, what hope would you have once Vidal got you in his clutches?" Mary said gently. "Oh, I allow he's hot for you! Who would not be? But it's not marriage he means by you, and it will be something quite otherwise if he sees you in such loose company as you keep." She stayed for a moment, awaiting any answer they might choose to give, but Mrs. Challoner for once had nothing to say, while Sophia sought refuge in a few sparkling easy tears. Having nothing further to say, Mary gathered up her embroidery and went out.

She might as well have held her peace. Uncle Henry having been coaxed into providing the necessary guineas to buy his pretty niece a new gown, Sophia went off to her party in high spirits, entirely, and quite rightly, satisfied with her appearance in pink tiffany, trimmed with rich blonde in scallops. Cousin Joshua, getting wind of it, came to condemn such behaviour, but got little satisfaction from Mary. She heard him out in a silence that seemed more abstracted than attentive and this so piqued him that he was unwise enough to ask her whether she were listening.

She brought her gaze back from the window, and surveyed him. "I beg your pardon, cousin?"

He was annoyed, and showed it. "I believe you've not heard one word!" he said.

"I was thinking," said Mary thoughtfully, "that puce does not become you, Joshua."

"Puce?" stammered Mr. Simpkins. "Become me? What —— Why——?"

"It is maybe your complexion that's too high for it," mused Miss Challoner.

Mr. Simpkins said with dignity: "I was speaking of Sophia, Mary."

"I'm sure she would agree with me," replied the lady maddeningly.

"She's too easy, cousin. She don't know the path she treads," Joshua said, trying to bring the conversation back to its original topic. "She's very different from you, you know."

A slow smile curled Miss Challoner's lips. "I do, of course, but it's hardly kind in you to tell me so," she said.

"In my eyes," declared Joshua, "you are the prettier."

Miss Challoner seemed to consider this. "Yes?" she said interestedly. "But then, you chose puce." She shook her head, and it was apparent she set no store by the compliment.

When Sophia returned from her party it was long past midnight. She shared a bedchamber with her sister, and found Mary awake, ready to hear an account of the night's doings. While she undressed she prattled on of this personage and that, of the toilettes she had seen, of the supper she had eaten, of the secret walk she had stolen, and the kiss she had received, of how Eliza had come upon them, and been near sick with jealousy, and much more to the same tune.

"And I'll tell you what, Mary," she ended jubilantly, "I shall be my Lady Vidal before the year's out, you mark my words." She curtsied to her own reflection in the mirror. " 'Your ladyship!' Don't you think I shall make a vastly pretty marchioness, sister? And everyone knows the Duke is getting very old, and I dare say he can't last very long now, and then I shall be your grace. If you don't wed my cousin, Mary, maybe I shall find you a husband."

"What, have I a place in all these schemes?" inquired Mary.

"To be sure, you need not fear I shall forget you," Sophia promised.

Mary regarded her curiously for a moment. "Sophia, what's in your mind?" she asked suddenly. "You're not fool enough to think Vidal means marriage."

Sophia began to plait her hair for the night. "He'll mean it before the end. Mamma will see to that."

"Oh?" Mary sat up in bed, and cupped her chin in her hands. "How?"

Sophia laughed. "You think no one has brain but yourself, don't you? But you'll see I shan't manage so ill. Of course Vidal don't mean marriage! Lord, I'm not so simple that I don't know the reputation he bears. What if I let him run off with me?" She looked over her shoulder. "What then, do you suppose?"

Mary blinked. "I'm too mealy-mouthed to hazard a guess, my love."

"Don't fear for my virtue!" Sophia laughed. "Vidal may think I'm easy, but he'll find he'll get nothing from me without marriage. What do you think of that?"

Mary shook her head. "We should quarrel if I told you."

"And if he won't wed me," Sophia continued, "then mamma will have something to say, I promise you."

"Nothing is more certain than that," agreed Miss Challoner.

"Oh, not to Vidal!" Sophia said. "To the Duke himself! And I think Vidal will be glad to marry me to prevent the scandal. For there is my uncle as well as mamma, you know, and he would create a rare to-do. Vidal will have to marry me."

Miss Challoner drew a deep breath, and lay back on her pillows. "My dear, I'd no notion you were so romantic," she drawled.

"I am, I think," nodded Sophia innocently. "I have always thought I should like to elope."

Miss Challoner continued to observe her. "Do you care for him?" she asked. "Do you care at all?"

"Oh, I like him very well, though to be sure, I think Mr. Fletcher dresses better, and Harry Marshall has prettier manners. But Vidal's a marquis, you see." She took a last complacent look at her own image, and jumped into bed. "I've given you something to think of now, haven't I?"

"I rather believe you have," concurred Miss Challoner.

It was certainly long before she fell asleep. Beside her Sophia lay dreaming of the honours in store for her, but Mary lay staring into the darkness, and seeing before her mind's eye, a black-browed face, with a haughty thin-lipped mouth, and eyes that seemed to her fancy to look indifferently through her.

"You're a fool, my girl," Mary told herself. "Why should he look at you?"

She could find no reason at all, being singularly free from conceit. She could find very little reason either why she should want the gentleman to look at her. She took herself to task over it. What, was she to turn into a languishing miss? A bread-and-butter schoolgirl, sighing for a handsome face? God help the woman Vidal's fancy lighted on! Ay, that was a better tune. Like father, like son. The old Duke's affairs had been the talk of the town. He had a pretty-sounding name once, though he might be as virtuous as you please to-day. Satan, was it? Some such thing. They called the son Devil's Cub, and not without reason, if the half of the tales told were true. Lord! Sophia was no match for the man. He would break her like a china doll. And how to prevent it?

Again there seemed to be no answer. The plan the chit had in mind would have been laughable had it not been nauseating. To be sure Vidal deserved to get paid in his own coin, but that—no, that was nasty work, even if it succeeded. And what a plan it was! Faith, it seemed mamma was so foolish as Sophia. What would the noble family of Alastair care for one more scandal added to their list? The plague was, mamma and Sophia would never be brought to realize that they would come off the worst from that encounter. Uncle Henry? Miss Challoner grimaced in the darkness. From Uncle Henry to Aunt Bella was no great step, and from Aunt Bella to the world a shorter one still. Miss Challoner had no desire to publish Sophia's indiscretions abroad. She began to nibble one finger-tip, pondering her problem, and so, at last, fell asleep.

The morrow brought his lordship before her again, this time no picture of the mind. Nothing would do but that Sophia must go walking in Kensington Gardens with her sister to meet Eliza Matcham. When Mary perceived the Marquis approaching them down one of the paths, she understood the reason for this unwonted desire for exercise.

As usual, he was richly, if somewhat negligently dressed. Miss Challoner, incurably neat, wondered that a carelessly tied cravat and unpowdered hair could so well become a man. Not a doubt but that the Marquis had an air.

Sophia was blushing and peeping through her eyelashes. His lordship possessed himself of her hand, kissed it, and placed it on his arm.

"Oh, my lord!" Sophia murmured, casting down her eyes.

His smile was indulgent. "Well, child, what?" he said.

"I did not think to meet you," Sophia explained, for her sister's benefit.

The Marquis pinched her chin. "You've a short memory, my love."

Miss Challoner with difficulty suppressed a chuckle. My lord disdained the art of dissimulation, did he? Faith, one could not help liking the creature.

"Indeed, I don't know what you mean," Sophia pouted. "We came expressly to meet Eliza Matcham and her brother. I wonder where they can be got to?"

"Confess you came to meet me!" the Marquis said. "What, was I really forgotten?"

There was a toss of the head for this. "La, do you suppose I think of you all day long, sir?"

"Egad, I hoped I had a place in your memory."

Miss Challoner broke in on them. "I think I have just seen Miss Matcham cross the end of this walk," she remarked.

His lordship glanced down at her impatiently, but Sophia said at once: "Oh, where? I would not miss her for the world!"

Miss Matcham, with her brother James, was soon overtaken, and Miss Challoner at once perceived that their mission was to engage her in talk while the Marquis and Sophia lost themselves. This friendly office was frustrated by the exasperating behaviour to their quarry, who refused to be separated from her sister.

Since neither the Marquis nor Sophia put themselves to the trouble of including her in their conversation, and Miss Matcham was wholly engaged in keeping the hem of her muslin gown from getting wet on the grass, she had ample opportunity to observe her sister's lover. A very little time was enough to convince her that love, as she understood it, was felt by neither. Her sister, she thought, would bore his lordship in a week, and as she listened to him, and watched him, she found herself wondering again how Sophia could imagine that he felt any more than a passing fancy for her. Certainly he wanted the chit; he was of the type that would go to any lengths to get what he wanted, and, unless she was much mistaken, Miss Challoner was sure that once the prize was won, he would cease to desire it. Then woe betide Sophia with her artless ideas of shaming him into marriage. Why, thought Mary, one could never shame my Lord Vidal, because he did not care what was said of him, and had already given the world to understand, beyond possibility of mistake, that he would do exactly as he pleased on every occasion. Scandal! Mary almost laughed aloud. Lord, he would carry off anything with that insolent high-bred manner of his, while as for being afraid of public opinion, he'd raise those black brows of his in faint surprise at such a notion.

These reflections occupied her mind till the expedition broke up. From something the Marquis said to Sophia in a low voice at parting she gathered that a future assignation had been made, but Sophia did not tell her where it was to be. Her smiles vanished with the Marquis, and on the way home she complained ceaselessly of her sister's lack of tact in remaining at her side all the morning.

As for the Marquis, finding himself with time on his hands,

he strolled round to Half Moon Street to visit the most congenial of his relatives.

Although it was past noon, he found this worthy still attired in a dressing-gown, and without his wig. The remains
of breakfast stood upon the table, but my Lord Rupert Alastair seemed to have finished this repast, and was smoking
a long pipe, and reading his letters. He looked up as the door
opened, and made a grab at his wig, which lay conveniently
on the sofa beside him, but when he saw his nephew he
relaxed again.

"Oh, it's you, is it?" he said. "Here, what the devil do you
make of this?" He tossed over the sheet of paper he had
been perusing, and tore open another of his letters.

Vidal laid down his hat and cane and came to the fire,
running his eye over the note he held. He grinned. "Ain't
it plain enough, O my uncle? Mr. Tremlowe would be gratified
by the payment of his bill. Who the devil's Mr. Tremlowe?"

"Damned barber," growled Lord Rupert. "What's he say
I owe him?"

The Marquis read out a startling total.

"Pack of lies," said Lord Rupert. "Never saw so much
money all at once in all my life. Damme, what have I had
from him? Nothing at all! A couple of wigs (a Crutch and a
She-dragon, and I never wore the Crutch) and maybe a bottle of Pomatum. Blister it, does the fellow think I'm going
to pay him?"

The question was purely rhetorical, but the Marquis said:
"How long has he known you, Rupert?"

"Lord, all my life, curse his impudence!"

"Then I don't suppose he does," said Vidal calmly.

Lord Rupert pointed the stem of his pipe at Mr. Tremlowe's missive. "I'll tell you what it is, my boy. The fellow's
dunning me. Put it in the fire."

The Marquis obeyed without the slightest hesitation. Lord
Rupert was scanning another sheet of paper. "Here's another,"
he exclaimed. It went the way of the first. "Never see anything but bills!" he said. "What's your post bring you, Vidal?"

"Love letters," promptly replied his lordship.

"Young dog," chuckled his uncle. He disposed of the rest
of his correspondence, and suddenly became solemn. "I'd
something to say to you. Now what the plague was it?" He
shook his head. "Gone clean out of my head. Which reminds
me, my boy, I've a piece of advice to give you. I was din-

ing with Ponsonby last night, and he said you was bound
to him for Friday next."

"Oh, God, am I?" said the Marquis wearily.

"Don't touch the brandy!" his uncle adjured him. "The
burgundy's well enough, and you can swallow the port, but
the brandy's devilish bad."

"Given you a head, Rupert?" inquired his lordship solici-
tously.

"Worst I've had in years," declared Lord Rupert. He
stretched his long legs out before him, and lay looking up
somewhat owlishly at his nephew. It seemed to dawn on him
that the hour was an unusually early one for the Marquis to
be abroad. "What brings you here?" he asked suspiciously. "If
you want to borrow money, Vidal, I tell you plainly, I'm
cleaned out. Lost a milleleva last night. Never seen anything
like the run of the luck. Bank's won for weeks. Burn it, I
believe I'll give up pharaoh and take to whist."

Vidal leaned his shoulders against the mantelpiece, and
thrust his hands deep into his pockets. "I never pursue for-
lorn hopes, uncle," he said sweetly. "I've come for the pleasure of seeing you. Can you doubt it?"

His lordship shot out a hand. "Now don't do that, my
boy!" he said. "Damme, when you start talking like Avon
I'm off! If you've not come to borrow money——"

"Boot's on the other leg," interrupted the Marquis.

Lord Rupert's jaw dropped. "Ecod, was it you lent me
five hundred pounds last month? When did I say I'd pay?"

"Judgment Day, belike," said his undutiful nephew.

Lord Rupert, shook his head. "Won't be before, if the
luck don't turn soon," he agreed gloomily. "If you stand
in need of it, my boy, I might ask Avon for a trifle."

"Lord, I could ask him myself, couldn't I?" the Marquis
said.

"Well, I don't mind telling you, Vidal, that's a thing I
don't do till the tipstaffs are after me," confessed Rupert.
"I'm not saying Avon's mean, but he's devilish unpleasant
over these little affairs."

The Marquis glanced down at him with a glint in his
eyes. "Sir, I am constrained to remind you that his grace
has the honour to be my sire."

"Don't do it," roared his uncle. "Look'ee, Vidal, if you're
going to look down your nose, and turn into the living
spit of Justin, you've one friend the less. I'm done with you."

"My God, could I survive?" mocked the Marquis.

Lord Rupert started to get up, but was thrust back again. "Easy now," said his nephew. "I've done."

Rupert relaxed again. "Y'know, you'll have to watch it, Dominic," he said severely. "One in the family's too much already. Avon's got a damned nasty way with him, and if you fall into it you'll find yourself with a whole pack of enemies." He stopped and scratched his head. "Not but what you've got them already, ha'n't you?"

Vidal shrugged. "I dare say," he replied indifferently. "I don't lose sleep over them."

"Cool fish, ain't you?" said Rupert, eyeing him. "Ever let anything trouble you?"

The Marquis yawned. "I've never found anything worth troubling over."

"H'm! Not even women?"

The thin lips curled. "Least of all women."

Lord Rupert looked solemn. "Won't do, y'know. Must care about something, Dominic."

"Sermon, uncle?"

"Advice, my boy. Damn it, there's something wrong with you, so there is! Never see you but what you're after some wench or other, and the devil's in it you don't care for one of 'em——" He broke off and clapped a hand to his brow. "That's got it!" he exclaimed. "Put me in mind of what I had to say to you!"

"Oh?" A faint interest sounded in Vidal's voice. "Have you found a charmer, Rupert? At your age, too!"

"Fiend seize it! D'you think I'm in my dotage!" said his lordship indignantly. "But that's not it. This is serious, Dominic. Where's the burgundy? Take a drop, my boy; it won't do you a mite of harm." He picked up the bottle, and poured out two glasses. "Ay, it's serious this time, I warn you —— What do you think of the wine? Not so bad, eh? Forget where I got it."

"It's good," said the Marquis positively, and poured out two more glasses. "You had it from my cellar."

"Did I so? I'll say this for you, Vidal, you've inherited your father's palate. It's the best thing I know of either of you."

The Marquis bowed. "We thank you. What's your serious warning?"

"I'm just about to tell you, aren't I? Don't keep breaking

in, my boy; it's a devilish bad habit." He drained his glass, and set it down. "That's cleared my head a trifle. It's that yellow-headed chit, Dominic. Filly you had on your arm at Vauxhall Gardens t'other night. Can't remember her name."

"Well?" said his lordship.

Rupert reached out a long arm for the bottle. "Avon's got wind of her."

"Well?"

Rupert turned his head to look at him. "Don't keep on saying 'Well,' burn you!" he said testily. "I'm telling you Avon's heard things, and he ain't pleased."

"Do you expect me to break out in a sweat?" asked Vidal. "Of course my father knows. It's a habit with him."

"And a damned bad habit, too," said Rupert feelingly. "You know your own business best, or, at any rate, you think you do, but if you take my advice, you'll go easy with—what in hell's the girl's name?"

"You can pass over her name."

"No, I can't," contradicted Rupert. "I can't go on calling her girl, filly, chit, yaller-head; it throws me out."

"Just as you please," yawned Vidal. "You'll forget it in five minutes. Sophia."

"That's it," nodded my lord. "Never could stand the name since I got entangled with a widow called Sophia. D'you know, boy, that woman well-nigh married me?"

"That wasn't Sophia," objected Vidal. "That was Maria Hiscock."

"No, no, that's a different one," said Rupert impatiently. "Sophia was years before your time. And she devilish nearly had me. You be warned, Dominic."

"You are kindness itself," answered Vidal politely. "I can only repeat what I seem to have said already several times; I do not at this present contemplate marriage."

"But ain't this Sophia a thought different from the others?" asked his lordship curiously. "Daughter of a cit? Lay you odds you stir up trouble there."

"Not I. If it were the sister now——!" Vidal gave a short laugh. "That's one of those enemies of mine you spoke of, or I'm much mistaken."

"Didn't see the sister, did I? The mother will do what she can to see you tied up in wedlock. 'Pon my soul, if I ever set eyes on a worse harpy!"

"And the sister would send me to the devil," Vidal said. "I don't please Miss Prunes and Prisms."

Lord Rupert cocked an eyebrow. "Don't you, begad? And does she please you?"

"Good God, no! We don't deal together. She'd spoil sport if she could." He showed his teeth in a rather saturnine smile. "Well, if she chooses to cross swords with me, she'll maybe learn something in the encounter." He picked up his hat and cane, and strolled to the door. "I'll leave you, beloved. You're becoming damned moral, you know." He went out and the door shut behind him before Lord Rupert, astonished and indignant at the charge, could think of a suitable retort.

❧ Chapter IV ❧

MY Lord Carlisle having discovered that his sedate protégé had an incongruous passion for gambling, thought he could do no better for him than to introduce him to the newest of the hells. The young man seemed to have plenty of money at his command, and if he chose to lose it over the dice, it was no business of my lord's. Of late Mr. Comyn's face had worn a very serious expression, and my lord had no hesitation in laying this at Miss Marlin's door, that sprightly damsel having been bundled off to Paris in charge of her brother.

"Hang all women!" Carlisle said blithely. "Why, man, there's not one worth the half of these glum looks of yours."

Mr. Comyn eyed him calmly. "You are merry, sir, but you mistake," he said politely. "I believe I have a natural gravity which perhaps misleads you."

"Devil a bit," said his lordship. "I know all about you, my friend. Gone to France, hasn't she? I see young Marlin's back again."

Mr. Comyn compressed his lips. My lord laughed. "Don't like him, do you? Well, it's a dull dog." He clapped Mr. Comyn on the shoulder. "You'll forget the fair Juliana over a bottle. Tell you what, I'll take you to Timothy's."

"I shall be happy to accompany your lordship," bowed Mr. Comyn.

"You're not in society until you've crossed that threshold," Carlisle went on. "It's the newest of the hells. Vidal and Fox made it the fashion. The play's high; you're not the man to mind that, I take it. All the same," he added thoughtfully,

"I'd not play at Vidal's table if I were you. The pace he sets is a trifle too hot for most of us. Don't know if you've run across the Devil's Cub yet?"

"I had the honour of meeting his lordship at the drum last week," said Mr. Comyn. "I shall be happy to renew my acquaintance with him."

Carlisle stared. "Will you, by gad?" he said.

Timothy's was a discreet-looking establishment in a street off St. James's. An unobtrusive individual, casually strolling up and down the road, was pointed out to Mr. Comyn as the orderly-man, engaged to give warning if any constables approached. The windows were thickly curtained, but when a funereally clad porter admitted my Lord Carlisle and his protégé, Mr. Comyn fairly blinked at the blaze of lights within the house. The porter, who was clothed in black, rather startled him, but on the way upstairs my lord explained that this sombre livery was a whim of Mr. Fox's, who was given to such conceits.

"Surely, sir, Mr. Fox is not the owner of a gaming-house?" said Mr. Comyn, greatly surprised.

"Oh no, but he's Vidal's crony, and Timothy, so I'm told, was in the Duke of Avon's employ until he discovered in himself a genius for this sort of thing. Thus, you see, what Vidal or his intimates want is all that signifies to Master Timothy."

They had reached the head of the stairway, and Lord Carlisle led the way into the first of the gaming-rooms. It was somewhat crowded, and was apparently given over to pharaoh and deep basset.

My lord passed through it, exchanging a greeting here and there, and led Mr. Comyn through an archway into a second and smaller apartment. The rattle of dice sounded here, and Mr. Comyn's eye brightened. There was only one table, and that occupied the centre of the room, and was surrounded by a fair number of onlookers.

"H'm! Vidal's bank," grunted Carlisle. "Shouldn't play if I were you."

Mr. Comyn perceived my Lord Vidal at the end of the table, a glass at his elbow. His cravat was loosened, and a strand of lightly-powdered hair had escaped the riband that tied it in his neck. He wore a coat of purple velvet, heavily laced, and a flowered waistcoat, one or two of the buttons of which had come undone. He looked pale in the candle-light, and rather more dissipated than usual. He glanced up as Mr. Comyn drew near the table, but his eyes, which seemed unusually brilliant, betrayed no recognition.

Carlisle tugged at Mr. Comyn's sleeve. "Better play pharaoh," he muttered under his breath. "Vidal's in a wild humour by the look of it. See who's at the table? Oh! you wouldn't know! Fellow beside Jack Bowling—red-faced fellow in a bag-wig. His name's Quarles. There's something of a bone lies between him and the Cub. There'll be trouble before the morning. Best out of it."

Mr. Comyn regarded the red-faced gentleman with interest. "But I hardly suppose, my lord, that I could be concerned in the trouble," he said precisely.

"Oh lord, no! Just some pother over a wench that Vidal snapped from under Quarles's nose."

"I apprehend," said Mr. Comyn, "that most of my Lord Vidal's quarrels owe their existence to a female."

He returned to the contemplation of the table. At Vidal's right hand, Mr. Fox lolled in his chair, busy with a gold toothpick. He raised a languid hand in greeting to Carlisle. "Coming in, my lord? Take the bank?"

A heap of gold and paper lay before Vidal. Carlisle shook his head. "Not I, Fox."

The Marquis tossed off what remained in his glass. "I'll throw you for it," he offered.

"I advise against it, my lard," one of the players said mincingly. "Vidal has had the devil's luck all this week."

"I'm not dicing to-night," Carlisle replied. "If you have a place at the table, Mr. Comyn here is of a mind to play."

My lord paused in the act of refilling his glass, and again looked up at Mr. Comyn. "Oh, it's you, is it?" he said carelessly. "I thought I knew you. Do you want to throw for the bank?"

"I thank your lordship, but I would prefer to throw against the bank," replied Mr. Comyn, and sat down beside Lord Rupert Alastair.

Lord Carlisle, having done what he could to prevent his protégé from joining the table, shrugged fatalistically, and withdrew.

"Raise you to a hundred, gentlemen," Vidal said, and lay back in his chair, feeling in his capacious coat-pocket for his snuff-box. He pulled it out, and opened it, and took a pinch, flashing a quick look round the table. A gentleman

Devil's Cub 44

in puce satin, and a very large stock buckle, protested that
fifty was deep enough.

Mr. Fox lifted weary eyebrows, and stretched out his
hand for Vidal's snuff-box. He regarded it closely, and remarked with a sigh: "Le Sueur. *Email en plain*. Very pretty.
A hundred, I think you said?" He put it down and picked up
the dice-box.

Someone at the other end of the table said that the game
went too deep, but was overruled.

"Standing out, Cholmondley?" asked the Marquis.

"By God, I'm not, then! You've too many of my notes
under your hand, Vidal. Keep it at fifty."

"Raising you to a hundred," the Marquis repeated.

Mr. Fox took the dice. "A hundred it is, and those afraid
of it stand out," he drawled. He called a main of eight
and threw fives. "Rot you, Vidal," he said good-humouredly,
and scribbled his name on a slip of paper, and pushed it across
the table.

The red-faced gentleman seated midway down the table
opposite Lord Rupert Alastair looked under his brows at
the Marquis, and said loud enough to be heard: "I'd say
it was time another man held the bank. This is a damned
one-sided game."

His neighbour, Mr. Bowling, saw the glitter in the Marquis's eye, and nudged him warningly. "Easy, now, easy,
Montague," he said quietly. "Ever known the luck to run
evenly?"

Someone standing amongst the spectators said beneath his
breath: "Vidal's three parts drunk. There'll be trouble soon."

Drunk the Marquis might be, but his speech and intellect
were unimpaired. He lay back in his chair, one hand in his
breeches pocket, the other with its long fingers curled round
the stem of his wineglass; and his hard stare challenged the
dissatisfied player. "Had enough, Quarles?"

The tone was an insult. Mr. Fox took snuff, and looked
sideways under the incredible arch of his brows. Lord Rupert
picked up the dice-box. "Ah, you're wasting time. I'll call
seven." He threw and lost. "Rabbit it, I've called 'em for
the last hour, and the cursed dice turn up aces and threes."

Montague Quarles said with bitter distinctness: "Enough?
No, by God, but let someone else hold the bank! What do
you say, gentlemen?" He looked round the table, but met
with no response till Lord Cholmondley said gruffly: "I'm sat-

isfied. Egad, I hope we know how to stand against a run
of bad luck. Too much talk, is what I say."

The Marquis was still looking at Montague Quarles. "There's
a matter of some four thousand pounds in the bank. Throw
you for it."

"Come, that's fair enough!" declared a bluff man on the
Marquis's left.

Mr. Quarles said angrily: "Damned if I will! Not against
you, my lord!"

"My God, do we sit all night arguing?" Bowling cried.
"Let's be done with this!" He took up the dice-box, called a
main and threw. Vidal pushed a little pile of guineas towards
him, and the game went on.

Money passed backwards and forwards, but the bank was
still an easy winner at the end of a couple of hours' play.
The Marquis was drinking steadily. So were several others,
notably Mr. Quarles, whose scowl deepened with each glass.
On the Marquis the wine seemed to have little or no effect.
His hand was steady enough, and there was only that glitter
in his eyes to betray to one who knew him how much he
had drunk.

My Lord Rupert, another heavy drinker, had reached the
rollicking stage, and was sitting with his wig askew. Mr. Fox
had broached his second bottle, and seemed somnolent. My
Lord Rupert won a little, lost again, and called up the table
to his nephew: "Rot you, Vidal, this is poor sport! Quicken
the game, my boy!"

"Take the bank, Rupert?"

My lord pulled his pocket linings out, and began to count
the guineas that lay before him. It was a difficult business.
"I make it eleven," he announced with a hiccough. "Can't
start a bank on 'leven guineas, Vidal. Can't start bank at
Timothy's on less than sixty guineas."

The Marquis said recklessly: "Raise you to two hundred,
gentlemen."

Mr. Fox nodded. Bowling pushed back his chair. "I'm out,"
he said. "That's too deep for me, Vidal."

"Bank can't win for ever," the Marquis replied. "Stay the
course, Jack, the night's young yet."

Mr. Bowling blinked at the clock on the far wall. "Young?
I make it past four."

"That's young, ain't it?" said Lord Rupert. "Four? Why,
that's devilish young!"

Mr. Bowling laughed. "Oh, I protest! I'm a man of sedate habits. Do you mean to take your breakfast here? I'm for my bed."

"Sit it out!" recommended Lord Cholmondley. "We'll break Vidal yet. Vidal! Is that bay mare by Sunshine out of Mad Molly still in your stables? I'll stake my Blue Lightning against the mare I break your bank before six."

The Marquis poured more wine. "Make it five, and I'll take you."

Mr. Fox opened his eyes. "What's amiss? You for bed too?"

"I don't sit after five," the Marquis said. "I'm for Newmarket and back again."

Lord Cholmondley gaped at him. "God save us all, it's not the day of your race? Man, you're crazy to think to drive to Newmarket! Damme, Vidal, you're drunk. You can't do it! And here's me with a cool five hundred backing you!"

"Be calm, my loved one," mocked Vidal. "I drive best when I'm drunk."

"But up all night—no, blister me, that's too much. Get to bed, you madman!"

"What, to save your stake for you? Be damned if I do! My coach calls for me at five. Does the bet stand? You'll break my bank before five—your colt to my mare."

"I'll do it!" Cholmondley said, slapping the table with his open hand. "Got an hour, ha'n't I? Time enough. Where's the betting-book?"

The bet was duly entered. The waiter was about to remove the book when the Marquis drawled: "I'll lay you a further five hundred I reach Newmarket under the given time, Cholmondley—play or pay."

"Done!" said Cholmondley promptly. "Now I'm for you, my boy. Playing two hundred!"

"Two hundred it is," the Marquis agreed, and put up his eyeglass to watch the throw of the dice.

Cholmondley called sixes. Lord Rupert looked solemnly at the dice as they fell on the table. "Deuce ace," he declared. "Bank can't win for ever, eh, Vidal?"

Mr. Quarles, who had been tapping an impatient foot, burst out: "I'd say my Lord Vidal can't lose!"

The eyeglass dangled on its black ribbon from between my lord's fingers. "Would you?" said the Marquis gently, and as though he waited for more.

"Oh, stand out, Quarles, if you can't stay the course!" said Cholmondley impatiently.

It was evident that Mr. Quarles had reached the quarrelsome stage. "I'll stay the course well enough, sir, but the luck's too damned uneven for my taste."

Mr. Fox took a mirror from his capacious pocket, and studied his reflection in it. With considerable care he straightened his toupet, and flicked a speck of snuff from the lapel of his coat. "Dominic," he said wearily.

The Marquis shot him a look.

"Dominic, how did this place grow to be so devilish vulgar?"

"Hush, Charles, hush!" said the Marquis. "You interrupt my dear friend. He is about to explain himself."

The bluff man, who had as yet taken no part in the swiftly brewing quarrel, leaned over Mr. Bowling's vacant chair, and plucked at Quarles's sleeve. "Hold your peace, man. You're out of tune. Don't play if you're shy of the luck, but for God's sake let's have an end to this bickering."

"I'll play," Mr. Quarles said obstinately. "But I say it's time another man took the bank!"

"Lord, man, there's a bet on! The bank stays with Vidal."

"Dominic," said Mr. Fox plaintively. "Dominic, my dear fellow, I shall have to give up this place, positively I shall have to give it up now the herd has discovered it."

My lord was still watching Quarles. "Patience, Charles, Mr. Quarles don't like to see the bank win. You should sympathize."

Quarles started up. "I don't like the way this game has gone, my lord," he said loudly, "and if you won't give up the bank, I say give us fresh dice!"

His words brought about a sudden uneasy silence. Cholmondley tried to fill the breach, saying quickly: "Lord, you're too drunk to know what you're saying, Quarles. Let's get on with the game."

"I think not." The voice came from the end of the table. The Marquis was leaning forward, his wineglass still in his hand. "So you don't like the dice, eh?"

"No, I don't like them, curse you!" Quarles shouted. "And I don't like your high-handed ways, my lord. They won't serve. I've sat three nights and seen you win——"

He got no further; the Marquis was up and had dashed the contents of his glass full in Quarles's face. He was smiling now and his eyes blazed. "And that's a waste of good wine," he said, and turned and said something to the waiter at his elbow. Mr. Quarles, with the burgundy dripping down his front, sprang up and made a clumsy lunge at him. Cholmondley and Captain Wraxall, the bluff gentleman, forced him back.

"Damn it, you asked for that!" Cholmondley swore. "Take it back, you fool! We all know you're drunk."

The Marquis had resumed his seat. The waiter looked frightened, and whispered to him. My lord turned on him with something like a snarl, and the man fled.

Lord Rupert got up rather unsteadily. "Fiend seize it, the champagne's got into my head!" he said. But the sudden interlude seemed to have jerked him back to sobriety. "There's been enough of this," he said authoritatively. "You be damned for a fool, Vidal. Can't you see the fellow's drunk?"

Lord Vidal laughed. "I'm drunk myself, Rupert, but I can tell when a man calls me cheat."

"Good God, my lord, you'll never care for what's said after the third bottle!" cried Captain Wraxall.

Lord Cholmondley gave Mr. Quarles's arm a shake. "Take it back, man; you're out of your senses."

Mr. Quarles wrenched himself free. "You'll meet me for this, my lord!" he roared.

"Be sure I will," said the Marquis. "We'll settle it now, my buck."

Rupert took up the dice. "Break 'em," he said briefly. "Where's that rogue Timothy? I want a hammer."

Sir Horace Tremlett, he of the mincing speech, protested. "I vow it's not necessary, my lard. We know my Lard Vidal, I believe. Break the dice? 'Pon my soul, sir, it's to insult his lardship."

"To hell with that!" said Rupert. "I'm breaking 'em, see? If they're true, Quarles apologizes. That's fair, ain't it?"

"Ay, that's the best," Captain Wraxall agreed.

Mr. Quarles was wiping his face. "I say my lord will meet me! By God, I'll not take a glass of wine in the face and say thank you for it!"

Cholmondley spoke in Lord Rupert's ear. "It's gone too far now. Rot that nephew of yours! What's to do?"

"Break the dice," Rupert said obstinately. "Can't have it said an Alastair plays crooked."

"Oh, you're as drunk as Vidal! Who's to say so? Quarles

will take it back when he's sober if you can stop Vidal forc-
ing it on now."

The waiter had come back into the room carrying a flat
case. With a scared look at the Marquis he laid this on the
table. Vidal opened it, and it was to be seen that a brace of
pistols lay within. "Take your choice," he said.

Rupert stared. "What's this? Can't fight here, Dominic. Arrange it for you out at Barn Elms, nine o'clock."

"By nine o'clock I shall be in Newmarket," said the Marquis.
"I'll settle my score before I leave."

Mr. Fox roused himself. He inspected the pistols through
his eyeglass, and looked inquiringly at Vidal. "Where did they
come from?" he said. "Don't carry pistols to gaming houses
myself."

"They come out of my coach," replied Vidal. He looked
at the clock. "It waits. Choose, you!"

"I'm for you!" Mr. Quarles declared. He rolled an eye at
Captain Wraxall. "Sir, will you act for me?"

"Act for you?" exploded the Captain. "I'll have nothing
to do with the business. My lord, you're in no fit case to
fight, and I recommend you to go home and let your seconds
arrange the matter more seemly."

Vidal laughed. "Not fit? By God, that's rich, Wraxall. You
don't know me very well, do you?"

"I am happy to say I do not, sir!" said the Captain stiffly.

"Watch then!" My lord drew a small gold-mounted pistol
from his pocket. He levelled it, still lounging in his chair,
and fired before any could stop him. There was a loud report,
and the smash of glass as the bullet shattered the big mirror
at the end of the room.

"What in hell's name——?" began Wraxall furiously, and
broke off, staring in the direction of my lord's pointing finger.
One of a cluster of three candles was no longer burning.
The voice of Mr. Comyn said calmly: "Quite remarkable
shooting—under the circumstances."

Lord Rupert, forgetting larger issues, called out: "Outed it,
begad, and not touched the wax! Good lad!"

The explosion brought those still remaining in the other
rooms hurrying to the scene. Vidal paid no heed. "Don't
know me very well, do you?" he repeated, and laughed again.

Cholmondley, casting a glance of rebuke at Rupert, ad-
monished Mr. Quarles once more. "Go home and sleep on it,

Quarles. If you want to fight, fight sober. You're no match for Vidal else."

A stout individual dressed in discreet black pushed his way through the knot of men in the doorway. "What's this, gentlemen?" he said. "Who fired that shot?"

Vidal raised his brows. "You interrupt, Timothy. I fired that shot."

The stout man looked aghast. "My lord, my lord, what wild work is this? You'll ruin me, my lord!" He saw the case containing the pistols and made a pounce for them. My lord's hand shot out and grasped his wrist. Timothy met his eyes for a moment, and said distressfully: "My lord, I beg of you—my lord, don't do it here!"

He was thrust back. "Damn you, stop whining!" Vidal sprang up, overturning his chair. "Am I to sit here till noon while Mr. Quarles makes up his mind? Name your friends!"

Quarles rolled a hot eye round the circle. No one came forward. "I'll act for myself since you're all so shy," he sneered.

Mr. Comyn, his sedateness quite unimpaired, rose from his seat. "Since it's my Lord Vidal's honour that is in question it will be wise to have a gentleman to act for you, sir," he said.

"To hell with the lot of you!" swore Quarles. "I'll act for myself."

"Your pardon, sir," returned Mr. Comyn smoothly, "but I think you must see that if you doubt his lordship's good faith, your seconds should carefully examine these pistols, which I apprehend are his lordship's own. In short, I offer myself at your disposal."

"Obliged to you," growled Quarles.

Vidal was leaning on a chair back. "That's a mighty long speech," he remarked, with just that faint suggestion of slurring his words together. "Is it to insult me, or not?"

"Such, my lord, is not at the moment my intention," replied Mr. Comyn.

The Marquis laughed. "Didn't know you had it in you. You're devilish correct, ain't you?"

"I trust I am conversant with the rules governing such affairs as these, my lord. Will you name your friends?"

The Marquis was still looking at him with an amused and not unkindly eye. "Charles, you might act for me," he said, without turning his head.

Mr. Fox arose, sighing. "Oh, very well, Dominic, if you

must behave so damned irregularly." He went apart with Mr.
Comyn, and they inspected the weapons with due solemnity,
and pronounced them identical.

Lord Rupert pushed his way unceremoniously to his neph-
ew's side. "Go put your head in a bucket of water, Vidal!"
he said. "Stap me if I ever heard the like of you to-night!
Mind you, I don't say the fellow don't deserve to have a hole
in him, but do the thing decently, my boy, that's all I ask!"
He broke off to hurl somewhat conflicting advice to Captain
Wraxall. "Move those candles a shade to the left, Wraxall.
Must have the light fair to both."

The table was pushed back. Mr. Fox and Mr. Comyn were
measuring the paces.

The pistols were presented. My lord took his in what looked
to be an alarmingly slack hold. Apparently his uncle did not
think so, for he said urgently: "Don't kill him, Dominic!"

The seconds stepped back, the word was given. My lord's
pistol hand jerked up swiftly; there was a flash and a report,
followed almost instantly by an answering shot. Mr. Quarles's
bullet buried itself in the wall beyond my lord, and Mr.
Quarles pitched forward on to his face.

The Marquis tossed his pistol to Mr. Fox. "Give 'em to
my man, Charles," he said, and turned away to pick up his
snuff-box, and handkerchief.

"Damn you, Vidal, I believe you have killed him!" Rupert
said angrily.

"I'm very nearly sure of it, dear uncle," said the Marquis.

Mr. Comyn, on his knees beside the fallen man, looked up.
"A surgeon should be fetched," he said. "I do not think that
life is extinct."

"I must be more drunk than I knew, then," remarked his
lordship. "I'm sorry, Charles; I meant to make the place
habitable for you."

Lord Cholmondley started towards him. "Devil take you,
Vidal, you'd best be gone. You've done enough for one night."

"I thought so, certainly," said the Marquis. "Mr. Comyn
apparently disagrees." He glanced at the clock. "Hell and
damnation, it's past five already!"

"You're surely not driving to Newmarket now?" cried Captain Wraxall, appalled by his callousness.

"Why not?" said Vidal coolly.

Captain Wraxall sought for words, and found none. The
Marquis turned on his heel and went out.

⊷§ Chapter V §⊷

IT was only a little past noon on the following day when her Grace of Avon, accompanied most unwillingly by Lord Rupert, first called at Vidal's home. The Marquis's major-domo responded to his lordship's anxious look with the smallest of bows. Lord Rupert heaved a sigh of relief. One never knew what might be found in Vidal's apartments.

"I want my son," her grace stated flatly.

But it appeared that the Marquis had not returned from Newmarket.

"There, what did I tell you?" said Rupert. "Leave a note for him, my dear. The devil alone knows when he'll be back, eh, Fletcher?"

"I have no precise knowledge myself, my lord."

"I shall come back again later," announced her grace.

"But, Léonie——"

"And again, and again, and again until he has returned," said her grace obstinately.

She kept her word, but on her last visit, in full ball dress at seven in the evening, she declared that she would enter the house and await her son there.

Lord Rupert followed her weakly into the hall. "Ay, but I'm on my way to Devereaux's card party," he expostulated. "I can't stay here all night!"

The Duchess flung out exasperated hands. "Well, go then!" she said. "I find you *fort ennuyant!* For me, I must see Dominique, and I do not need you at all."

"You always were an ungrateful chit," complained his lordship. "Here am I dancing attendance on you the whole day, and all you can say is that you don't need me."

Léonie's irrepressible dimple peeped out. "But it is quite true, Rupert; I do not need you. When I have seen Dominique I shall take a chair to my party. It is very simple."

"No, you won't," said Rupert. "Not with those diamonds on you." He followed her into the library, where a small fire burned, and struggled out of his greatcoat. "Where's that fellow gone off to? Fletcher! What's his lordship in the cellar that her grace would like?"

The suave Fletcher showed some small signs of perplexity at that. "I will endeavour, my lord . . ."

The Duchess had cast off her cloak, and seated herself by the fire. "Ah, bah, I do not want your ratafia, me. I will drink a glass of port with you, *mon vieux.*"

Lord Rupert scratched his head, tilting his wig slightly askew. "Oh, very well! But it's not what I'd call a lady's drink."

"Me, I am not a lady," announced her grace. "I have been very well educated, and I will drink port."

Fletcher withdrew, quite impassive. His lordship remonstrated once more. "Y'know you mustn't talk like that before servants, Léonie. 'Pon my soul——"

"If you like," interrupted Léonie, "I will play piquet with you till Dominique comes!"

Dominic came an hour later. A sulky dashed up the street and stopped outside the house. Léonie flung down her cards, and ran to the window, pulling aside the heavy curtains, but was too late to catch a glimpse of her son. A groom was already driving the sulky away, and inside the house a door slammed, and Fletcher's discreet voice sounded. A sharper one answered; a quick step trod in the hall, and Vidal came into the library.

He was pale, and his eyes were frowning and tired. Mud had generously splashed his breeches and plain buff coat, and his neckcloth was crumpled and limp. *"Ma mère!"* he said, surprise in his voice.

Léonie momentarily forgot her mission. She went to him, grasping the lapels of his coat. "Oh, you have not killed yourself! But tell me, Dominique, at once, did you get there in the time?"

His hands covered hers with a gesture rather mechanical.

"Yes, of course. But what are you doing here? Rupert, too? Is anything amiss?"

"Anything amiss," exploded Rupert. "That's rich! 'Pon my soul, that's rich! Oh, there's naught amiss, never fear! You've only killed that fellow Quarles and set the whole town in a roar."

"Dead, is he?" said his lordship. He put Léonie from him, and walked to the table. "Well, I thought as much."

"No, no, he is not dead!" Léonie said vehemently. "You shan't say so, Rupert!"

"It don't matter what I say," responded my lord. "If he ain't dead now he will be in a day's time. You fool, Vidal."

The Marquis had poured himself out a glass of wine, but was looking down at the red liquid instead of drinking it. "Runners after me?"

"They will be," his uncle said grimly.

A heavy frown was gathering. The Marquis's lips tightened. "Damnation!" His glance flickered to Léonie's troubled face. "Don't let it disturb you, madame, I beg."

"Dominique, did you—did you, in effect, mean to kill him?" she asked, her eyes on his face.

He shrugged. "Oh, since I fought at all, yes."

"I do not mind you killing people when you have reason, you know, but—but—was there a reason, *mon enfant?*" said her grace.

"The fellow was drunk, and you knew it, Vidal!" Rupert said.

"Perfectly." The Marquis sipped his wine. "But so was I drunk." Again he looked towards Léonie. What he saw in her face made him say with a kind of suppressed violence: "Why do you look at me like that? You know what I am, do you not? Do you not?"

"Here, Dominic!" his uncle said, in a voice of protest. "You're talking to your mother, boy."

Léonie raised an admonishing finger. "Enough, Rupert. Yes, I know, my little one, and I am very unhappy for you." She blinked away a tear. "You are too much my son."

"Fiddle!" said Vidal roughly. He put down his glass, the wine in it unfinished. The clock on the mantelpiece chimed the hour, and he looked quickly round at it. "I must go. Why did you come? To tell me Quarles is as good as dead? I knew it."

"No, not for that," Léonie replied. "I think—I think there is a billet for you from Monseigneur."

The Marquis's laugh held a note of recklessness. "Be sure. I have it in my pocket. Inform him, madame, that I shall wait upon him in the morning."

There was real trouble in Léonie's face. "Dominique, you do not seem to me to understand at all. Monseigneur is enraged. He says you must leave the country, and, oh, my dear one, I beg you not to anger him any more! You should wait on him at once."

"Who told him?" Vidal answered. "You, Rupert?"

"Fiend seize you, do you take me for a tale-bearer? You young fool, he saw it!"

The frowning eyes stared at him. "What the devil do you mean?"

"You'd no sooner got clear of the place—and a pretty turmoil you left behind you, I can tell you—than in walks Avon with Hugh Davenant." Lord Rupert, apparently overcome by the recollection, mopped his brow with his fine lace handkerchief.

"What, at five o'clock in the morning?" demanded the Marquis.

"It wasn't as much as that, not but what I thought myself 'twas the wine got into my head when I clapped eyes on him. He'd been at Old White's all night, d'ye see, playing pharaoh, and the devil put it into his head to call in at Timothy's, to see what sort of a hell it was that his precious son had honoured with his patronage. 'And I perceive,' said he, 'that it is indeed something beyond the common.' Now I put it to you, Vidal, isn't it Avon all over to walk in pat like that?"

The frown was lifting. A gleam shone in the Marquis's eyes. "Of course it was inevitable. Tell me it all."

"Lord, I was so rattled, I don't know what happened. There was young Comyn holding a napkin to the wound you'd blown through Quarles's chest, and someone splashing water about, and Wraxall shouting for the porter to run for a surgeon, and the rest of us in the devil of a fluster, and all at once I saw Avon standing in the doorway with his glass held up to his eye, and Davenant gaping beside him. Well, you know how it is when your father is about. There was an end to the noise; everyone was watching Avon, save Comyn—I'd say that lad is a cool hand—who went on staunching the blood as calm as you please. If you ask me, Avon saw the whole at a glance, but he chose to look all round, mighty bland, and then down at Quarles. Then he says to Davenant: 'I was informed, my dear Hugh, that Timothy's was unlike other hells. And I perceive,' says he—but I told you that bit. Of course, if I'd had my wits about me, I'd have left by the window, but I don't deny I had a deal of champagne in me. Well, your father turned his infernal quizzing-glass towards me. I was waiting for that. 'I suppose,' says he, 'I need not ask where is my son.'" Lord Rupert shook his head wisely. "Y'know, he's devilish acute, Vidal; you must grant him that."

"I do," said his lordship, with the ghost of a laugh. "Go on, what next? I wish I had seen all this."

"Do you, begad?" said his uncle. "You might have had my place for the asking. Well, I said you'd gone. Young Comyn took it up in that finicky voice of his. 'I apprehend, sir,' says he, 'that his lordship is by now upon the road to Newmarket.' Avon turns his glass on him at that. 'Indeed!' says he, devilish polite. 'I fear my son has untidy habits. This gentleman'—and he points his quizzing-glass at Quarles—'this gentleman—I think unknown to me—is no doubt his latest victim?' I can't give you his tone, but you know how he says things like that, Vidal."

"None better. Oh, but I make him my compliments. He comes off with the honours. Did he make my apologies?"

"Well, now you mention it, I believe he did," said Rupert. "But he divided the honours with that Comyn lad. We'd all lost our tongues. But Comyn says—which I thought handsome of him—'As to that, sir, the late affair was in a sort forced upon his lordship. I believe, sir, no man could swallow what was said, though I am bound to confess that neither of the principals was sober.' And I thought to myself, well, you must be damned sober, my lad, to get all that out without so much as a stammer."

The Marquis's face showed his interest. "Said that, did he? Mighty kind of him." He shrugged, half smiling. "Or mighty clever."

Léonie, who had been gazing into the fire, raised her head at that. "Why was it clever?"

"Madame, I spoke a thought aloud." He looked at the clock again. "I can't stay longer. Tell my father I will wait on him in the morning. To-night I have an engagement I can't break."

"Dominique, don't you understand that if that man dies, you must not be in England?" Léonie cried. "Monseigneur says that this time there will be trouble. It has happened too often."

"So I'm to make off like a scared mongrel, eh? I think not!" He bent over her hand for a moment. "Pray do not show that anxious face to the world, maman; it accords very ill with our dignity."

In another moment he was gone. Léonie looked dolefully at Lord Rupert. "Do you suppose it is that *bourgeoise,* Rupert?"

"Devil a doubt!" said his lordship glumly. "But I'll tell you what, Léonie; if we can pack him off to France there'll be an end to that affair."

It was as well for his peace of mind that he did not follow his nephew that evening. The Marquis stayed only to change his mud-stained garments, and was off again within twenty minutes, bound for the Theatre Royal. The play was more than half over, and in one of the boxes Sophia Challoner displayed a pouting countenance. Eliza Matcham had been twitting her the whole evening on the non-appearance of her fine beau, and she was in no very good humour. Her sister, with Cousin Joshua assiduously at her elbow, said tranquilly that the Marquis could hardly be expected to come after the happenings of the night before.

For the tale of the duel had spread like wildfire, so that the backwash of the sea of rumour had already reached Miss Challoner's ears. It had also reached those of Cousin Joshua, who was not slow to say what he thought of the profligate Marquis. Sophia told him sharply that it was presumption in him to judge one so far above him, and by the time he had thought out a suitable retort, she had turned her white shoulder, and was talking with great vivacity to Mr. Matcham. Cousin Joshua addressed the rest of his homily to Miss Challoner, who listened in silence. Her gaze was so abstracted that he was beginning to suspect her of inattention. Then he observed a change in her expression. She stiffened, and her eyes grew intent and widened a little. Even Joshua could not suppose that this sudden interest was caused by his discourse, and he turned his head to see what had caught her eye.

"Upon my soul!" he said, puffing out his cheeks. "Shameless! If he has the effrontery to approach Sophia I shall know how to act."

The Marquis of Vidal was standing in the pit, raking the boxes with his quizzing-glass.

A laugh trembled on Miss Challoner's lips. Shameless? Of course he was shameless, but he was sublimely unconscious of it, unconscious too of the notice he was attracting from all who recognized him.

Mary looked at her cousin at last. "That is just as well, Joshua," she said, "for I think he is going to approach her now."

Mr. Simpkins saw the Marquis elbowing his way through the crowd in the pit, and tugged at Sophia's sleeve. "Cousin!" said he, "I cannot but consider myself responsible for you, and I forbid you to speak with that profligate."

This had not quite the desired effect. Sophia's pout turned to an expression of sparkling eagerness. "Oh, is he here? Where? I do not see him. I knew he would never fail me. How I shall scold him for being so late!"

The Marquis had disappeared from the floor of the house by this time, and in a few minutes his knock fell on the door of the box, and he entered.

Sophia greeted him with a smile that reproached and yet beckoned. "Why, is it you indeed, my lord? I vow I had given you up. La, we have been hearing such tales of you! I declare I am half afraid of you."

"Are you? Why?" inquired his lordship, kissing her hand. "Do you think I would hurt anything half so pretty as you?"

"Oh, lord, I don't know what you might not do if I angered you," laughed Sophia.

"Then don't anger me," advised the Marquis. "Walk with me in the corridor instead. The curtain won't go up for a few minutes yet."

"No, but do you know this is the fifth act? Positively, you have only come in time to hear the end of the play, and the farce."

"Well, you had better instruct me in what it is all about," said his lordship coolly.

"You don't deserve that I should," Sophia said, getting up from her chair. "Well, if I do walk with you outside, it will only be for a moment."

Mr. Simpkins cleared his throat portentously, attracting the Marquis's somewhat bored notice. "You spoke, sir?" Vidal said with so much haughtiness that Mr. Simpkins became flustered, and stammered something quite inaudible.

The Marquis smiled a little, and was just about to leave the box, with Sophia on his arm, when he caught sight of Miss Challoner's flushed countenance. His brows lifted slightly. What the devil was the girl blushing for? She looked up as though she felt his gaze upon her, and her eyes met his steadily for a moment. He read disdain in them, and was amused, and asked Sophia as soon as they were out of the box what he had done to offend her sister.

She shrugged up her pretty shoulders. "Oh, sister doesn't approve of your dreadful wicked ways, my lord."

He suffered from a moment's surprise. Nothing in Sophia, or her mamma and cousins had led him to suspect that her sister was likely to be strait-laced. Mrs. Challoner he wrote down as an elderly harpy; the Matchams were frankly vulgar. He laid his right hand on Sophia's, lying on his arm. "Strait-laced, is she? Are you so, too?"

She raised her eyes to his, and saw them gleaming with some light that both frightened and excited her. Her colour fluctuated deliciously. The Marquis shot a quick look up and down the deserted corridor, and caught Sophia hard against his breast. "One kiss!" he said in a voice made suddenly husky with passion, and took it. She made a half-hearted struggle to break free. "Oh, my lord!" she protested. "Oh, no, you must not!" He had her fast round the waist, and with his free hand he cupped her chin, holding her head up so that he might look into her face. "You can't keep me at arm's length for ever, you little beauty. I want you. Will you come to me?"

The direct attack flustered her. She began to say: "I don't know what you mean," but he interrupted her: "Everything of the most dishonourable. Remember that, my pretty dear, for I don't cheat, at love or cards."

Her lips formed a soundless "oh" of astonishment. He kissed them, and partly from nervousness (for he had shaken her) and partly from coquetry, she giggled. He had no further doubts, but laughed back at her. She had an odd fancy, un-usual in one so matter-of-fact, that little devils danced in his eyes. "I see we understand each other," he said. "Listen to me now. I take it you've heard of last night's affair? I may have to leave the country for a spell in consequence."

She broke in with a little cry of dismay. "Leave the country? Oh, no, my lord!"

"I won't leave you, my pretty, I promise. I've a mind to take you to Paris with me. Will you come?"

The colour flooded her cheeks. "Paris!" she gasped. "Oh, Vidal! Oh, my lord! Paris!" To hear it spelled gaiety, fine dresses, trinkets, all that she craved of life. He had no difficulty in reading her thoughts. "I'm rich; you shall have all the pretty things your own prettiness deserves. I'll hire an hôtel for you; as its mistress you will play the hostess to my friends; in France these arrangements are understood. I know of a dozen such establishments. Do you choose to come with me, or not?"

Her native hardheadedness made her play for time, but her imagination was already running riot. The picture he drew lured her; she thought recklessly that she cared very little for the marriage-tie if she could live in Paris, where such arrangements, Vidal said, were understood. "How can I answer you, my lord? You—I protest you take me by surprise. I must have time!"

"There is no time. If Quarles dies, it's farewell to England for me. Give me your answer now, or kiss me and say goodbye."

She had only one steadfast thought, and that was that she would not let him slip through her fingers. "No, no, you cannot be so cruel!" she said with a tiny sob.

He was quite unmoved, but his hot gaze seemed to devour her. "I must. Come! Are you afraid of me that you hesitate?"

She drew away from him, a hand at her breast. "Yes, I am afraid," she said breathlessly. "You force me—you are cruel . . ."

"You need not be afraid: I adore you. Will you come?"

"If—if I say no?"

"Then let us kiss and part," he said.

"No, no, I cannot leave you like that! I—oh, if you say I must, I will come with you!"

Rather to her surprise he showed neither rapture nor relief. He said only: "It will be soon. I will send you word to your lodgings."

"Soon?" she faltered.

"To-morrow, Friday—I can't say. You need bring nothing but the clothes you stand in."

She gave an excited laugh. "An elopement! Oh, but how shall I contrive to slip off with you?"

"I'll spirit you away safe enough," he said, smiling.

"How? Where must I meet you?"

"I will let you know. But, remember, no word of this to a soul, and when you hear from me do exactly what I shall tell you."

"I will," she promised, larger and more mercenary issues for the moment forgotten.

When she returned to the box, alone, the curtain had already gone up on the fifth act. She was still flushed by excitement, and met her sister's look with a defiant toss of her head. Let Mary frown if she would: Mary had no brilliant future before her; Mary might consider herself fortunate if she caught Cousin Joshua for a husband. Sophia gave herself to ecstatic imaginings.

The Marquis, meanwhile, betook himself to Timothy's and created a sensation.

"Good God, it's Vidal!" ejaculated Lord Cholmondley.

Mr. Fox, who was playing piquet with him, tranquilly dealt a fresh hand. "Why not?" he inquired.

"Cold-blooded devil!" marvelled Cholmondley.

Mr. Fox looked bored, and waved a languid hand at the Marquis.

Vidal was standing just inside the card-room, apparently surveying the company. There was just a moment when all play was suspended, and heads turned in his direction. The sudden silence was broken by an inebriated gentleman seated by the window, who called out: "Hey, Vidal, what time did you make? Laid a monkey you'd not do it under the four hours."

"You have lost your stake, my lord," said the Marquis. He perceived Mr. Fox, and began to make his leisurely way across the room to his table.

A hum of talk broke out. Many disapproving glances were cast at Vidal's tall figure, but he seemed unaware of them and passed to Mr. Fox's side, a picture of cool unconcern.

Cholmondley had laid down his cards. "Is that true?" he demanded. "You made it in the four hours?"

The Marquis smiled. "I made it in three hours and forty-four minutes, my dear."

"Man, you were drunk!" Cholmondley cried. "I'd say it was impossible!"

"Ask the judges," shrugged the Marquis. "I warned you that I drive best when I am drunk." He was watching the next table as he spoke. Loo was being played, but someone was leaving, and the party was broken up. The Marquis raised his voice slightly, addressing one of the players. "A hand of piquet, Mr. Comyn?"

Mr. Comyn turned his head quickly. A flicker of surprise showed in his face. He bowed. "I shall count myself honoured, my lord."

Vidal strolled over to his table and waited while a waiter put fresh cards and placed chairs.

"Cut, Mr. Comyn," said the Marquis.

Mr. Comyn obeyed, and won the deal.

"The usual stakes?" drawled the Marquis.

Mr. Comyn met his eye firmly. "Whatever you will, my lord."

Vidal laughed suddenly, and abandoned his drawl. "We'll play for love, Mr. Comyn."

Mr. Comyn paused in the middle of his deal. "I can scarcely suppose, my lord, that that would amuse you."

"Not in the least," grinned the Marquis.

"Or me, my lord."

"I never gamble in the family," explained Vidal.

Mr. Comyn jumped. "Sir?"

"Well, sir?"

Mr. Comyn carefully laid down the pack. "Do I understand you to mean that you favour my suit, my lord?"

"Devilish precise, ain't you?" commented Vidal. "I suppose if Juliana wants you she'll have you. Get it out of your head that I have anything to do with it. It don't concern me."

Mr. Comyn leaned back in his chair. "I apprehend, my lord, that to play piquet with me was not your object in singling me out to-night."

"Oh, I'll play," said his lordship. "But I don't fleece my relatives, and I don't care to be fleeced by 'em. Call it ten shillings a hundred."

"Certainly—if that satisfies you," said Mr. Comyn.

The Marquis's eye twinkled. "Oh, I'm quite sober to-night."

Mr. Comyn completed the deal and said slowly: "Without wishing to be guilty of impoliteness, my lord, your temper is such that I should not wish to play with you were you not sober."

"Much wiser not," agreed Vidal, putting down his discard. "Four only. You think I might blow a hole through you?"

Mr. Comyn picked up the remaining four cards. "Oh, surely not—in the family, my lord?"

Vidal laughed. "Egad, I think you'd better make all speed to Paris and abduct Juliana. You will do very well in our family. If you want my advice, let me recommend you to better your acquaintance with my father. I've a strong notion he might approve your suit. A point of six, a quinte, and three aces. Six played."

Mr. Comyn drew six cards from his hand with some deliberation. "Taking into consideration, sir, the unfortunate circumstances under which I made his grace's acquaintance—if such I can call it—I cannot suppose that a further meeting with me could be anything but repugnant to him."

"It is evident," retorted his lordship, "that you don't know much of my father." He played the rest of the hand in silence, but as the cards were gathered up he said: "I have it from my uncle that you in some sort upheld me last night. I'm obliged to you. Why did you do it? Policy? You don't exactly love me, do you?"

A smile disturbed Mr. Comyn's gravity. "On the contrary, my lord, I was under the impression that I detested you, but I believe I have an innate passion for justice."

"I thought as much," said the Marquis. "But to-day you find that I can be quite agreeable, and you reserve judgment."

"True," said Mr. Comyn thoughtfully. "Yet I confess that from time to time I find your manner calculated to arouse feelings of animosity in my breast."

"Alas!" said his lordship. "Let us again endeavour. Sir, you were kind enough to speak in my defence yesterday. I am probably your debtor, since I dare say my respected father may have believed you. At any other season I might have put in a word for you to his grace, but I don't imagine my word will carry much weight with him at the moment. Failing that, I make you a present of my advice. Marry my cousin out of hand. You won't get her else."

Mr. Comyn's brow wrinkled. "So I have been given to understand. Yet I fail to see why Lady Fanny should consider my suit so ineligible. I do not desire to make a brag of my estate, but though not noble I believe it is not disgraceful, nor is my fortune contemptible. I am heir to a baronetcy of——"

"You may be heir to a dozen baronetcies," interrupted Vidal, "but you can't compete with the heir to a dukedom."

Mr. Comyn looked a question. "Myself," said the Marquis. "Failing me, some other—if I know my aunt. She's looking high, you see, and she's a damned obstinate woman."

"But, sir, to persuade Miss Marling into a runaway marriage is a course savouring strongly of the dishonourable."

"She won't need any persuading," said his lordship callously. "And she hasn't a fortune, so you needn't fear to be thought an adventurer. You'll do as you please about it, but that's my advice."

Mr. Comyn gathered up his hand and began to sort the cards. "I must thank you, I suppose, but anything in the nature of irregularity, or clandestine conduct, is distasteful to me—especially in this delicate affair."

"Then you shouldn't ally yourself with my family," replied his lordship.

⤜§ Chapter VI §⤛

THE Marquis of Vidal had not expected to enjoy his interview with Avon, but it turned out to be more unpleasant than he was prepared for. To begin with, his grace was writing at his desk when Vidal was ushered into the room, and although the lackey quite loudly announced his lordship, his fine hand continued to travel across the paper, and he neither looked up nor betrayed by even the smallest sign that he had heard the announcement.

The Marquis paused for a moment on the threshold, eyeing him; then he walked across to the fireplace and stretched one elegantly shod foot to the warmth. To all appearances he was thoughtfully observing the extremely high polish on his top boot, but once he put up his hand to the Mechlin lace round his throat, and gave it a tug as though it were too tight.

He was dressed with unusual care, possibly out of deference to his grace's known views, but, as was his habit in the forenoon, for riding. His buff breeches were of impeccable cut, his coat of blue cloth with silver buttons was somewhat severe, but admirably became his tall person. His fringed cravat was for once very neatly arranged, the ends thrust through a gold buttonhole, and his black locks strictly confined by a thin black riband. He wore no jewellery save a heavy gold signet ring, and his face was innocent of the patches and powder affected by the Macaronis.

The Duke had finished writing, and was now reading his letter through with maddening deliberation. Vidal felt his temper rising, and set his teeth.

Having made some slight alteration in his letter, the Duke folded it, and dipping his quill in the standish, began to write the direction. Without turning his head he said: "You may sit down, Vidal."

"Thank you, sir, I'll stand," replied his lordship curtly.

The Duke laid his letter aside, ready for sealing, and at last turned, shifting his chair so that he could survey his son. Vidal found himself wishing, for perhaps the hundredth time in his life, that it was possible to read his father's expression.

The eyes, faintly disdainful, travelled from Vidal's boots to his face, and there stayed. "I suppose I should count myself honoured that you have been able to visit me," said his grace gently.

There did not seem to be anything to say in answer to this. After a moment's uncomfortable silence the Duke continued: "Your presence in England is extremely—shall we say enlivening?—Vidal. But I believe I shall survive the loss of it."

At that the Marquis spoke. "Is he dead then?"

Avon's brows rose in polite surprise. "Is it possible that you don't know?"

"I don't, sir."

"I envy you your light-heartedness," said Avon. "So far as I am aware the gentleman still lives. Whether he continues to do so or not is a question that does not at the moment concern me. It will make very little difference to you. Three months ago I warned you that your next killing would prove serious. You will allow me to point out that it is never wise to disregard my warnings."

"Certainly, sir. I take it I may have to stand my trial?"

"Not at all," said his grace coldly. "I am still somebody. But you may take it that for some appreciable time to come your residence will be upon the Continent. An affair of honour, conducted honourably, might have been condoned. A pot-house brawl can only be—one trusts—eventually forgotten."

The Marquis flushed. "One moment, sir. My affairs, whether settled at Barn Elms or in a pot-house, are still honourably conducted."

"I make you my apologies," replied Avon, slightly inclining his head. "You must forgive my declining years, which make it difficult for me to appreciate the manners of your gen-

eration. In my day we did not fight in gaming-hells, or when
we were in our cups."

"A mistake, sir, I admit. I am sorry for it."

The Duke looked at him sardonically. "I am not in the
least interested in your emotions, Vidal. What I object to
is that you have had the impertinence to disturb your mother.
That I do not permit. You will leave England at once."

Vidal was very pale, and a muscle at the corner of his
mouth twitched. "I'll stand my trial, I believe."

The Duke put up his glass and surveyed Vidal through it.
"You do not appear to have much understanding of the
situation," he remarked. "You will leave England, not to save
your neck, nor because it is my will, but to spare your
mother any further anxiety concerning your safety. I trust I
make myself plain?"

Vidal looked at him with hard defiant eyes. Then he strode
restlessly to the window and back again. "Quite plain. Yet
if I say I'll not go, what then?"

"I should regret the necessity of course, but I should—er
—contrive your departure willy-nilly."

The Marquis gave a short laugh. "Egad, I believe you
would! I'll go."

"You had better bid your mother good-bye," recommended
his grace. "You will reach the coast quite easily by to-night."

"Just as you please, sir," Vidal said indifferently. He picked
up his hat and gloves from the table. "Is there anything more
you desire to say to me?"

"Very little," Avon answered. "Your restraint is quite admirable. I applaud it."

"I thought it was my lack of it that had offended your
sensibilities, sir," said Vidal grimly. "You go too fast for me."

Avon smiled. "You must not think me witless, my dear
boy. I am perfectly aware that you would like to throw
my extremely reprehensible past in my teeth."

"I confess, sir, I find your homily a little ironic."

"Quite amusing, is it not?" agreed his grace. "I am perfectly sensible of it. But the road I travelled is not the road
I should desire my son to take. And you will no doubt
agree that a liberal experience of vice gives me some right
to judge." He rose and came to the fire. "Concerning more
immediate matters, you may draw upon Foley's in Paris,
of course."

"Thank you, sir, I have enough for my needs," the Marquis said stiffly.

"I compliment you. You are certainly the first Alastair ever to say so. You will find your mother upstairs."

"Then I'll take my leave of you, sir," Vidal said. "Accept my apologies for the inconvenience I may have caused you." He bowed, unsmiling, and turned sharp on his heel. As he jerked open the door, Avon spoke again. "By the way, Vidal, does my record still stand?"

The Marquis looked back over his shoulder, frowning. "Your record, sir?"

"Three hours and forty-seven minutes was my time," said his grace pensively.

An unwilling laugh broke from Vidal. "No, sir, your record does not stand."

"I thought not," said Avon. "May I be permitted to know the new record?"

"Three hours and forty-four minutes. But the curricle was specially designed."

"So was mine," said Avon. "I am glad you bettered my time. If I were twenty years younger——"

"I beg you will not attempt it, sir!" said the Marquis quickly. He hesitated; the stormy look was still in his face, but his eyes had softened.

"Pray do not do violence to your feelings," Avon said. "You will find me remarkably hard to wound."

The Marquis let go the door handle, and came back to his father's side. "I beg your pardon, sir." He took Avon's thin hand in his, and bent to touch it with his lips. *"Adieu, mon père."*

"Let us say, rather, *au revoir,*" Avon answered. "I will spare you my blessing which I cannot conceive would benefit you in the least."

Upon which they parted, each one understanding the other tolerably well. Vidal's interview with his mother lasted much longer, and was to him even more unpleasant. Léonie had no reproaches for him, but she was plainly unhappy, and the Marquis hated to see his mother unhappy.

"It's my damnable temper, maman," he said ruefully.

She nodded. "I know. That is why I am feeling very miserable. It is no good people saying you are a devil like all the Alastairs, because me, I know that it is my temper that you have, *mon pauvre*. You see, there is very black

blood in my family." She shook her head sadly. "M. de
Saint-Vire—my father, you understand—was of a character
the most abominable. And hot-headed! He shot himself in
the end, which was a very good thing. He had red hair like
mine."

"I haven't that excuse," said her son, grinning.

"No, but you behave just as I should like to when I am
enraged," Léonie said candidly. "When I was young I was
very fond of shooting people dead. Of course, I never did
shoot anyone, but I wanted to—oh, often! I meant to shoot
my father once—which shocked Rupert—it was when M. de
Saint-Vire kidnapped me, and Rupert saved me—only Monseigneur arrived, and he would not at all permit it." She
paused, wrinkling her brow. "You see, Dominique, I am not
a respectable person, and you are not a respectable person
either. And I did want you to be."

"I'm sorry, maman. But I don't come of respectable stock,
either side."

"Ah, but the Alastairs are quite different," Léonie said
quickly. "No one minds if you have *affaires*. Of course, if you
are a very great rake people say you are a devil, but it
is quite in the mode and entirely respectable. Only when
you do things that other people do not do, like you, and
make scandals, then at once you are not respectable."

He looked down at her half-smiling. "What am I to do,
maman? If I made you a promise to become respectable I
am very sure I should break it."

She slipped her hand in his. "Well, I have been thinking,
Dominique, that perhaps the best thing would be for you to
be in love and marry somebody," she said confidentially. "I
do not like to say this, but it is true that before he married
me, Monseigneur was a very great rake. *A vrai dire,* his
reputation was what one does not talk about. When he made
me his page, and then his ward, it was not to be kind, but
because he wanted to be revenged upon M. de Saint-Vire.
Only then he found that he would like to marry me, and
do you know, ever since he has not been a rake at all,
or done anything particularly dreadful that I can remember."

"But I could never hope to find another woman like you,
maman. If I could I promise you I'd marry her."

"Then you would make a great mistake," said Léonie wisely.
"I am not at all the sort of wife for you."

He did not pursue the subject. He was with her for an

hour and more; it seemed as though she could not let him go. At last he wrenched himself away, knowing that for all her brave smiles she would weep her heart out once he was gone. He had given his word to her that he would leave London that night; he had much to do in the few hours left to him. His servants were sent flying on various errands, one to Newhaven to warn the captain of his yacht, the *Albatross*, that his lordship would sail for France next day, another to his bankers, a third to a quiet house in Bloomsbury with a billet, hastily scrawled.

This was delivered to an untidy abigail who received it in a hand hastily wiped upon her apron. She shut the door upon the messenger, and stood turning the heavily sealed letter over in her hand. Sealed with a crest it was; she wouldn't be surprised if it came from the handsome lord that was running after Miss Sophy, only that it was directed to Miss Challoner.

Miss Challoner was coming down the stairs with her marketing-basket on her arm, and her chip hat tied over her curls. Miss Challoner, for all she was better educated than her sister, was not too grand to do the shopping. She had constituted herself housekeeper to the establishment soon after her return from the seminary, and even Mrs. Challoner admitted that she had the knack of making the money last longer than ever it had done before.

"What is it, Betty?" Mary asked, pulling on her gloves.

"It's a letter, miss, brought by a footman. For you," added Betty, in congratulatory tones. Betty did not think it was fair that Miss Sophy should have all the beaux, for Miss Mary was a much nicer-spoken lady, if only the gentlemen had the sense to see it.

"Oh?" said Mary, rather surprised. She took the letter. "Thank you." Then she saw the direction, and recognized Vidal's bold handwriting. "But this is——" She stopped. It was adressed to Miss Challoner sure enough. "Ah yes! I remember," she said calmly, and slipped it into her reticule.

She went on out of the house, and down the street. It was Vidal's hand; not a doubt of that. Not a doubt either that it was intended for her sister. The scrawled direction indicated that the note had been written in haste; it would be very like the Marquis to forget the existence of an elder sister, thought Mary with a wry smile.

She was a little absent-minded over the marketing, and

came back with slow steps to the house. She ought to give the billet to Sophia, of course. Even as she admitted that, she realized that she would not give it to her, had never meant to from the moment it had been put into her hand. There had been an air of suppressed excitement about Sophia all the morning; she was full of mystery and importance, and had twice hinted at wonders in store for her, but when questioned she had only laughed, and said that it was a secret. Mary was anxious as she had not been before; this letter— and after all it was certainly directed to herself—might throw a little light on Sohpia's secret.

It threw a great deal of light. Safe upstairs in her bed-room, Mary broke open the seal, and spread out the single thick sheet of paper.

"*Love*——" the Marquis began—"*It is for to-night. My coach will be at the bottom of your street at eleven. Join me there and bring nothing that you cannot hide beneath your cloak. Vidal.*"

Miss Challoner's hand crept to her cheek in a little fright-ened gesture she had had from a child. She sat staring at the brief note till the words seemed to start at her from the page. Just that curt command to decide Sophia's future! Lord, but he must be sure of her! No word of love, though he called her by that sweet name; no word of coaxing; no entreaty to her not to fail him. Did he know then that she would go with him? Was this what they had arranged in that stolen interview last night?

Miss Challoner started up, crumpling the letter in her clenched hand. Something must be done and done quickly. She could burn the message, but if Sophia failed Vidal to-night, would there not be another to-morrow? She had no notion where Vidal meant to take her sister. A coach: that meant some distance. Doubtless he had a discreet house in the country. Or did he intend to cheat Sophia with a pre-tended flight to Gretna Green?

She sat down again, mechanically smoothing out the letter. It was of no use to show it to her mother; she knew from Sophia what absurd dreams Mrs. Challoner cherished, knew enough of that lady, too, to believe her capable of the crowning folly of winking at an elopement. Her uncle could do nothing, as far as she could see, and she had no wish to blazon Sophia's loose behaviour abroad.

When the idea first came to her she did not know; she

thought it must have been hidden away in her brain for a long while, slowly maturing. Again her hand stole to her cheek. It was so daring it frightened her. I can't! she thought. I can't!

The idea persisted. What could he do after all? What had she to fear from him? He was hot-tempered, but she could not suppose that he would actually harm her, however violent his rage.

She would need to act a part, a loathsome part, but if she could do it it would end the Marquis's passion for Sophia as nothing else could. She found that she was trembling. He will think me as light as Sophia! she reflected dismally, and at once scolded herself. It did not matter what he thought of her. And Sophia? What would she say? Into what transports of fury would she not fall? Well, that did not signify either. It would be better to bear Sophia's hatred than to see her ruined.

She consulted the letter. Eleven o'clock was the hour appointed. She remembered that she was to spend the evening with her mother and sister at Henry Simpkins' house, and began to lay her plans.

There was a table by the window with her writing-desk upon it. She drew up a chair to it, and began to write, slowly, with many pauses.

"*Mamma——*" she began, as abruptly as the Marquis— "*I have gone with Lord Vidal in Sophia's place. His letter came to my hand instead of hers; you will see how desperate is the case, for it is plain he has no thought of marriage. I have a plan to show him she is not to be had so easily. Do not be afraid for my safety or my honour, even tho' I may not reach home again till very late.*" She read this through, hesitated, and then signed her name. She dusted the sheet, folded it up with the Marquis's note to Sophia, and sealed it, directing it to her mother.

Neither Mrs. Challoner nor Sophia made much demur at leaving her behind that evening. Mrs. Challoner thought, to be sure, that it was a pity she must needs have a sick headache on this very evening when Uncle Henry had promised the young people a dance, but she made no attempt to persuade her into accompanying them.

Miss Challoner lay in bed with the hartshorn in her hand, and watched Sophia dress for the party.

"Oh, what do you think, Mary?" Sophia chattered. "My

uncle has contrived to get Dennis O'Halloran to come. I do think he is too dreadfully handsome, do you not?"

"Handsomer than Vidal?" said Mary, wondering how Sophia could prefer the florid good looks of Mr. O'Halloran to Vidal's dark stern beauty.

"Oh well, I never did admire black hair, you know," Sophia replied. "And Vidal is so careless. Only fancy, sister, nothing will induce him to wear a wig, and even when he does powder his hair the black shows through."

Mary raised herself on her elbow. "Sophy, you don't love him, do you?" she said anxiously.

Sophia shrugged and laughed. "La, sister, how stupid you are with all that talk of love. It is not at all necessary to love a husband, let me tell you. I like him very well. I do not mean to love anyone very much, for I am sure it is more comfortable if one doesn't. Do you like my hair dressed *à la Venus?*"

Mary relaxed again, satisfied. When Sophia and her mother had left the house she lay for a while, thinking. Betty came in with her supper on a tray. Her appetite seemed to have deserted her, and she sent the tray away again almost untouched. At ten o'clock Betty went up the steep stairs to her little chamber, and Mary got out of bed, and began to dress. Her fingers shook slightly as she struggled with laces and hooks, and she felt rather cold. A search through one of Sohpia's drawers, redolent of cedar-chips, brought to light a loo-mask, once worn at a carnival. She put it on, and thought, peering at herself in the mirror, how oddly her eyes glittered through the slits.

She had some of the housekeeping money in her reticule; not very much but enough for her needs, she hoped. She hung the bag on her arm, put on a cloak, and pulled the hood carefully over her head.

On the way down the stairs she stopped at her mother's room, and left the letter she had written on the dressing-table. Then she crept noiselessly down to the hall, and let herself out of the silent house.

The street was deserted, and a sharp wind whipped Mary's cloak out behind her. She dragged it together, and holding it close with one hand, set off down the road. The night was cold, and overhead hurrying storm-clouds from time to time hid the moon.

Mary came round the bend in the street, and saw ahead

of her the lights of a waiting chaise. She had an impulse to go back, but checked it, and walked resolutely on.

The light was very dim, but she was able as she drew closer to distinguish the outline of a travelling chaise drawn by four horses. She could see the postilions standing to the horses' heads and another figure, taller than theirs, pacing up and down in the light thrown by the flambeaux burning before the corner house.

She came up to this figure soft-footed. He swung round and grasped at her hand, held out timidly towards him. "You've come!" he said, and kissed her fingers. They shook in his strong hold. He drew her towards the chaise, his arm round her shoulders. "You're afraid? No need, my bird. I have you safe." He saw that she was masked, and laughed softly. "Oh, my little romantic love, was that needful?" he mocked, and his hand went up to find the string of the mask.

She contrived to hold him off. "Not yet! Not here!" she whispered. He did not persist, but he still seemed amused. "No one will see you," he remarked. "But keep it if you will." He handed her up into the chaise. "Try to sleep, my pretty; you've a long way to travel, I fear."

He sprang down from the step, and she realized with a shudder of relief that he was riding.

The chaise was very luxuriously upholstered, and there was a fur rug lying on the seat. Mary drew it over her, and leaned back in one corner. He had said she had a long way to travel. Could this mean the Scottish border after all? She suddenly thought that if Gretna was his goal, she had done her sister the greatest disservice imaginable.

She leaned forward, peering out of the window, but soon abandoned the attempt to mark their route. It was too dark, and she lacked the sense of direction that would have told her whether she was travelling northwards or not.

She had never ridden in a chaise so well sprung as this one. Even over the cobbled streets she was not conscious of any peculiar discomfort. She could catch no glimpse of her escort, and supposed that he must be riding behind. Presently a gleam of moonlight on water caught her eye, and she started forward to look out of the window once more. The chaise was crossing a bridge; she could see the Thames running beneath, and knew then that she must be travelling south. Gretna was not his goal. She felt a paradoxical relief.

Once clear of the town the horses seemed to leap for-

ward in their collars. For a little while Mary felt alarmed
at the wicked pace, expecting every moment some accident,
but after a time she grew accustomed to it, and even dozed
a little, lulled by the sway of the coach.

A sudden halt jerked her awake. She saw lights, and heard
voices and the trampling of hooves. She supposed the time
of reckoning had come, and waited, outwardly calm, to be
handed down from the coach. The moon was visible, but when
she tried to discover where she was she could see only a
signboard swinging in the wind, and knew that the equipage had merely stopped to change horses. The door of the
chaise was pulled open, and she drew back into the corner.
Vidal's voice spoke softly: "Awake, little Patience?"

She stayed still, not answering him. If she had the courage
she would disclose her identity now, she thought. She shrank
from it, visualizing the scene, at night on a windy road, with
sniggering ostlers to witness it.

She heard a low laugh, and the click of the door as it was
shut again. The Marquis had gone, and in a moment whips
cracked, and the chaise moved forward.

She slept no more, but sat bolt upright, clasping her
hands in her lap. Once she caught a glimpse of a rider
abreast of the coach window, but he drew ahead, and she
did not see him again.

They halted for the second time presently, but the change
of horses was accomplished in a twinkling, and no one came
to the chaise door. A cold grey light informed her that
the dawn was approaching. She had not anticipated that
her imposture would remain undetected for so long, and
wondered uneasily how far into the day it would be before
she reached home again.

As the light grew the interior of the chaise became dimly
visible. She observed a holster within easy reach of her
hand, and with calm forethought, possessed herself of the
pistol it contained. It was rather large for her small hand,
and having very little knowledge of firearms she had no idea
whether it was loaded or not. She managed to put it into
the big pocket of her cloak. It made the cloak very heavy,
but she felt safer. The quivering alarm that had possessed
her from the start of this queer journey began to leave
her. She discovered that her hands were now quite steady,
and felt that she could face whatever was to come with
tolerable composure. She began to chafe at the length of

the journey, and wondered with a kind of detached interest whether she had enough money in her reticule to pay for her return. She hoped she would be able to travel by the stage-coach to London. The hire of a chaise would be beyond her means, she was sure. That Vidal might convey her to her door again, never entered her head. Vidal was going to be far too angry to consider her plight.

At the next halt she caught sight of Vidal for a moment, as he mounted a fresh horse, but he did not come to the coach door. Apparently the lover was forgotten in his desire to press on. She had heard from Sophia that he travelled always at a break-neck pace, springing his horses; otherwise, she reflected, she might well have supposed that he was flying for his life.

Pale sunlight began at last to peep through the clouds. Mary tried to calculate how far they had journeyed, but could arrive at no satisfactory estimate. Houses came into sight, and presently the chaise swept into a cobbled street, and slackened speed.

A corner was turned. Mary saw a grey tumbling sea, and stared at it in bewilderment. That Vidal meant to carry Sophia out of England had never entered her head. She began to realize that such really was his intention, and remembering his late duel she felt that this possibility ought to have occurred to her before.

The chaise drew up with a lurch. She turned quickly from her contemplation of a yacht lying in the harbour and waited for the door to be opened.

Somebody let down the steps; it was Vidal who opened the door. "What, still masked?" he said. "I shall call you Prudence, love. Come!" He held out his hands to her, and before she could lay her fingers on his arm, caught her round the waist, and swung her lightly down. She had a momentary sensation of complete helplessness, and was annoyed to find that she liked it.

"In with you, sweetheart," he said gaily. "There is just time for you to drink some coffee before I must bundle you aboard ship."

A stout landlord was bowing her into the inn. Looking at him through the slits of her mask, she thought that she detected a sly expression on his discreet countenance, and concluded with a stab of anger, that she was not the first female Lord Vidal had brought to this inn.

He ushered her into a parlour overlooking the sea, and stood bowing and smirking while Vidal delivered his orders. Mary walked to the fireplace, and stood there with her back turned.

"Yes, my lord, yes!" the landlord said. "Some coffee for the lady, and a roll, and a tankard of small-beer for your lordship. Yes, my lord; on the instant!"

"Let it be on the instant," Vidal said, "or I miss the tide."

"My lord, it shall be!" the landlord assured him, and bustled out.

Mary heard the door shut, and turned. Vidal had thrown down his whip and gloves, and was watching her in some amusement. "Well, Mistress Discretion?" he said. "Do you take off that mask, or must I?"

She put up her hands to the strings, and untied it. "I think it has served its turn," she said composedly, and put back her hood.

The smile was wiped from his face; he stood staring at her. "What the devil——?" he began.

She took off her cloak and laid it carefully on a chair; she had quite forgotten her pistol, for she had a part to play. She tried to smile archly, as Sophia could, and hoped she did not boggle it.

"Oh, my lord, I vow you are too easy to trick!" she said, and tittered, quite in Sophia's manner.

He strode up to her, and caught her wrists in a painful grasp. "I am, am I? We shall see, my girl. Where's your sister?"

"La, where should she be but in her bed?" Mary answered. "Lord, how we laughed when she showed me your letter! She was all for playing some jest on you to punish you for your impudence. So we put our heads together, my lord, and hit on the very thing. Oh, she will die of laughing when I tell her how you never suspected 'twas I you had in the coach, and not her at all!" There was not a tremor in Miss Challoner's voice as she spoke her part; she was all flippant vulgarity upon the surface. But under the surface, good God, is he going to murder me? she thought.

Murder certainly looked out of his eyes, his grip on her wrists made her wince. "A jest, is it?" he said. "Her jest—or yours? Answer me!"

Her rôle was hard to maintain, but she continued airily enough: "Oh well, to be sure 'twas I carried it through, and I dare say I should have thought of it if she had not."

"She thought of it?" he interrupted.

She nodded. "Yes, but I did not at all like it at first, only when she threatened to get Eliza Matcham to go if I would not I consented." She glanced up at him fleetingly, but dared not keep her eyes on his. "You need not think, my lord, that you can seduce Sophia so easily. She led you on finely, did she not? But when she found you'd no thought of marriage, she determined to teach you a lesson!"

"Marriage!" he said, and threw back his head and laughed. "Marriage! By God, that's rich!"

Her cheeks were stained crimson. His laughter had a jeering, wicked ring; he looked like a devil, she thought.

He let her go all at once, and cast himself down in a chair by the table. The murderous look had left his face, but in his half-closed eyes was a gleam that alarmed her more. The man meant mischief. His glance stripped her naked. Her cheeks grew hotter, and she saw that an ugly smile had curled his thin lips. His very attitude, while she still stood, was an insult. He lounged at his ease, one leg stretched out before him, a hand driven deep into his breeches pocket.

"You'll forgive my amusement," he drawled. "I suppose the truth is that Miss Sophia has found some other fool who offered more than I did, eh?"

She shrugged carelessly. "Oh, I tell no secrets, sir!"

The door opened and the landlord came in, followed by a serving-man with a tray. Miss Challoner walked over to the window while the cloth was laid. When they were alone again my lord said: "Your coffee—have I ever heard your name? Mary, isn't it?"

She forgot her rôle, and said coldly: "I have not given you the right to use it, sir."

Again he laughed. "My good girl, you've given me whatever rights I choose to claim. Sit down."

She remained where she was, eyeing him.

"Obstinate, eh? I'll tame you," Vidal said, and got up.

She had an impulse to run from him, and curbed it. She was swept off her feet and dumped down, none too gently, on a chair by the table. A heavy hand on her shoulder kept her there. "You elected to come with me," the Marquis said, "and by God you'll obey me, if I have to lay my whip about your sides!"

He looked so grim that she could not but believe he would do as he threatened. She sat still and he removed his hand from her shoulder. "Drink your coffee," he said. "You've not much time."

Her hands were no longer quite steady, but she contrived to pour some coffee into the cup.

"Shaking, eh?" said that hateful voice. "I shan't beat you if you behave yourself. Let me have a look at you." He turned up her face with a careless hand under her chin. "You're not so bad-looking after all," he remarked. "I dare say we shall deal extremely together."

She drank a little of the hot coffee; it put heart into her; she replied calmly: "Unfortunately we shall have no opportunity of judging. I go back to London by the first coach."

"Oh no, my dear," said his lordship. "You'll go to Paris with me, in Sophia's stead."

She pushed her cup and saucer away from her. "You're talking wildly, my lord. You won't expect me to believe that it is me you want to run away with."

"Why not?" said his lordship, coolly. "One wench is much like another after all."

She sat very upright, her hands lightly folded in her lap. "You've been worsted, sir, but need you insult me?"

He laughed. "We'll see who's worsted when we reach the end of the jest, my girl. As to insults, egad! I wish you would tell me how I may insult so bold a piece as yourself. Don't put on that missish face, my dear. It won't serve after this night's escapade."

"You can't take me to France," she persisted. "You think because Sophia was indiscreet—that I—that we are loose women, but——"

"If you're trying to make me believe in your virtue, you're wasting your breath," interrupted his lordship. "I knew what your sister was from the start, and as for you, whatever doubts I may have had you've set at rest. Virtuous young ladies, my dear, don't lend themselves to these jests. I may not be very much to your taste, but if you contrive to please me, you won't find me less generous than any other man."

"You are unpardonable!" she said in a suffocated voice. She got up, and this time he made no effort to prevent her. "Have the goodness to tell me how far I am from London. What is this place?"

"Newhaven," he replied, draining his tankard.

"Can I travel by stage-coach from here?"

"I've no idea," said his lordship with a yawn. "It need not concern you. I meant what I said."

"To take me to Paris? You're absurd, my lord. Do you suppose I should make no outcry? In these days even a noble marquis could scarcely force a young female aboard his yacht."

"Scarcely," agreed his lordship. "But I can make you so damned drunk that you'll be in no fit case to struggle, my girl." He drew a flask from the pocket of his greatcoat and held it up. "Hollands," he said briefly.

She was scandalized. "I think you are mad," she said with conviction.

He got up and came towards her. "You can think what you like, Mary, but you'll drink my Hollands."

She moved back till the wall stayed her. "If you touch me, I'll scream," she warned him. "I don't desire to make a scene, but I will."

"Scream away," he said. "You'll find old Simon is very deaf—when he doesn't want to hear."

She was shrewd enough to know that the landlord would hesitate to interfere with his noble patron if he could avoid it, and felt suddenly very helpless. The Marquis towered over her, and it seemed likely that he really would force the contents of his flask down her throat. She said quietly: "Please do not make me drink that. I am not a shameless woman, my lord, though I must seem to be one. I can—I think I can make you understand, if you will listen to me."

"I'll listen to you later," he replied. "There's no time now."

As though to corroborate him, someone knocked loudly at the door, and called: "My lord, we'll miss the tide!"

"I'm coming," he answered, and turned back to Mary. "Quickly, you!"

She held him off, both her hands clasping his wrist. "You need not make me drunk," she said. "Since there's no help for it I'll come."

"I thought you would," said the Marquis with a grim little smile.

He turned away from her to the table, and picked up his tankard, and drained it. He never took his eyes off her, and she found herself unable to look boldly back at him as she would have liked to do. He set down the tankard as she came to pick up her cloak from the chair where she had laid it, and said with a drawling note in his voice: "You'll see no one but my own fellows on the quay, but if you should be tempted to make a scene, remember I shall be beside you, and can throttle you before you've time to make more than one screech."

He strolled over to her as she drew her cloak round her, and before she realized what he was about, he had grasped her arm, and taken her throat in one of his shapely hands. He let her feel what strength lay in his fingers, and though for dignity's sake she forced herself to be passive the blood drummed unpleasantly in her head, and she felt herself to be in danger of losing her senses. "Like that," the Marquis said, smiling mockingly down at her. He let her go, and she put up her hands to her bruised throat. "Unpleasant, eh?" he said. "If you force me to do it again you'll find yourself unable to speak for quite a little while. Having throttled you—and I can do it in a flash, my dear—I shall carry you aboard, informing anyone who might chance to be about that you have swooned. Do you quite understand, wench?"

The muscles of her throat felt stiff. She managed to say: "Perfectly, sir."

"I thought you would," he said softly. "Now come!"

He dragged her arm through his, and led her to the door. The pistol in the pocket of her cloak knocked against her knee, and she remembered its existence with a start.

She did not think that she could pull it out with one hand, with the Marquis holding her other in his. She was very much afraid that it might go off if carelessly handled, nor had she any intention of firing it, and creating thereby the very scandal she wished to avoid. When she took it from its holster she had been prompted by no more than a vague notion that it might be well to possess a pistol. No plan of using it had entered her head; she had not even foreseen the need of it. It was too late now, but at the first opportunity she would manage to extricate it from the coat pocket into which it fitted so tightly.

The Marquis led her out. He stopped in the coffee-room to pay his bill. The landlord was all obsequious attention. Miss Challoner made a mental resolve never again to set foot in Newhaven.

She accompanied the Marquis, willy-nilly, out on to the quay. White horses raised their crests in the troubled sea;

Miss Challoner eyed them with inward trepidation. Then she saw the graceful yacht she had observed from the coach; it was heaving on the water even in the shelter of the quay. Miss Challoner began to feel squeamish, and glanced imploringly up at the dark face above her.

My lord paid not the slightest attention, but compelled her to walk down the gangway on to the deck of the *Albatross*. She was aware of a few curious looks from some rough-looking men who were busy with a maze of ropes, but his lordship marched her past these to a steep companion-way. Evidently feeling that she was incapable of negotiating it, he tossed her up over his shoulder, and so took her down it. On the lower deck she was set down, and thrust into a fair-sized cabin.

"Go inside," he commanded. "You should be comfortable enough, I trust. Stay there till I come; I shall not be long."

When he had gone Miss Challoner made her precarious way to the bunk against the bulkhead and sank down upon it. Now was undoubtedly the time to possess herself of the pistol, but curiously enough she made no attempt to do this. The cloak slipped from her fingers unheeded she put her hand to her head.

Outside men were shouting and stamping about the deck. The yacht heaved more than ever, and Miss Challoner was almost flung from the bunk. She decided to lie down; she had, at the moment, no interest in what was going forward on deck.

A little while later the Marquis entered the cabin, without ceremony. "Well, my dear, we've weighed anchor," he said with that detestable smile of his.

Miss Challoner opened her eyes, marvelled to see his lordship so untroubled, and shut them again with a shudder.

"And now," said Vidal silkily, "and *now*, Miss Mary Challoner . . . !"

Miss Challoner made a heroic effort, and raised herself on her elbow. "Sir," she said, self-possessed to the last, "I do not care whether you go or stay, but I desire to warn you that I am about to be extremely unwell." She pressed her handkerchief to her mouth, and said through it in muffled accents: "Immediately!"

His laugh sounded heartless, she thought. "Egad, I never thought of that," he said. "Take this, my girl."

She opened her eyes once more, and found that his lordship was holding a basin towards her. She found nothing at all incongruous in the sight. "Thank you!" gasped Miss Challoner, with real gratitude.

◆§ Chapter VII §◆

MISS CHALLONER awoke with a long sigh, and lay for a moment with her eyes still closed. To open them would be to court disaster, and she had borne enough, she decided. Then she began to realize that the yacht was no longer pitching and tossing, but was, in fact, almost motionless. She opened her eyes and looked distrustfully at the furnishings of her cabin, but these no longer rose and fell before her indignant gaze.

"Thank God!" said Miss Challoner devoutly.

She felt extremely weak, and her head when she raised it from the pillow swam unpleasantly. She lay still, therefore, trying to recollect the happenings of the past interminable hours. She found that her memory was somewhat blurred, but she remembered that Lord Vidal, having presented her with a basin, had retired. He had certainly come back later— hours later, when she was too exhausted even to speak, and he had forced something exceedingly fiery down her throat. With a vague fear of his threat to make her drunk she had tried to struggle, whereupon he had said, still apparently amused: "It's only brandy, my dear. Drink it."

So she had drunk it, and it had sent her to sleep. She supposed his lordship must have tucked her up; she had not suspected him of so much consideration.

In the middle of these reflections the door opened, and the Marquis himself came in. He was bright-eyed and a little dishevelled. "You're awake, are you?" he said. "Up you get, then."

"I don't think I can," said Miss Challoner candidly. "My head swims."

"You must. We're at Dieppe. What you want is food," his lordship informed her callously.

Miss Challoner was impelled to sit up. "You can force your presence on me, I suppose," she said bitterly, "but if you have any feeling at all you will not talk to me of food."

"I haven't," said Vidal. "You don't know it but you will be perfectly well when you have dined. Get up and come ashore."

That last magic word brought Miss Challoner to her feet. His lordship offered his arm. "That's better," he encouraged her. "I've bespoken dinner and beds at the Coq d'Or."

They came up on to the deck. Miss Challoner, having requested my lord to precede her, climbed up the companion as quickly as a swimming head would allow. Once on deck she observed that the sea was miraculously calm and blue, and blinked at it in surprise. Then she saw the long shadows on the quay, and asked what time it was.

"Close on six," replied Vidal. "We met rough weather."

Her brain refused to work. She kept on repeating to herself: "I'm in France. I can't get home now. It's of no avail to ask the time. I'm in France."

The Marquis led her up the gangway and along the quayside until the Coq d'Or was reached. "Your gear has been taken up," he said.

She looked at him, puzzled. "But I have none," she said.

"You are forgetting," he replied ironically, "I told Sophia to bring nothing, but promised I would provide her with what she might need."

"Have you bought—*dresses* for Sophia?" she demanded incredulously.

He grinned. "Oh, not only dresses," he replied. "You can teach me nothing of what a lady requires. Shifts, négligées, lappets, beads, perfume from Warren's, Poudre à la Maréchale —you'll find 'em all there. I have endless experience, I can assure you."

"That I do not doubt," she said.

He bowed. "I trust you will approve my taste," he said, and handed her over to the waiting abigail.

Miss Challoner saw nothing for it but to go upstairs in the wake of this damsel. She had a very fair notion of what her appearance must be, and she felt quite unequal to the coming scene with the Marquis until she had tidied her person.

She spoke French prettily enough, and had no difficulty in making the maid-servant understand her wants. She washed her face and hands, did up her hair again, using the brush and comb of his lordship's providing, and very gingerly withdrew the pistol from the pocket of her cloak. She thought she would be able to hold it so that the panniers of her gown concealed it from view, and practised this in front of the mirror. Deciding that it was hardly successful, she held the pistol in her right hand and draped her cloak over her arm, so that its folds fell over the weapon. Satisfied, she left her chamber and went downstairs to the private parlour his lordship had engaged.

He was standing by the fire with a glass in his hand. Suddenly she knew why his eyes glittered so strangely; his lordship had been drinking, and was drinking still.

She took one quick look at him, and went to the table, and seated herself, holding the pistol under her skirts, and putting her cloak over the back of her chair.

"I find that you were right, sir," she remarked politely. "I shall be the better for some food."

He strolled over to his chair and sat down. "You look as though you need something to warm you," he said. "Will you drink burgundy with me, or ratafia by yourself?"

"Thank you, my lord, I will drink water," answered Miss Challoner firmly.

"As you please," he shrugged and leaned back in his chair, lazily watching her.

The entrance of a liveried man, followed by one of the inn-servants created a welcome diversion. The discreet-looking man began to serve them, and surprised Miss Challoner by addressing her in her own tongue.

"I always travel with my own servants," explained the Marquis, observing her surprise.

"An agreeable luxury, sir," commented Miss Challoner.

She made an excellent dinner, and maintained a flow of easy conversation for the benefit of his lordship's servant. The Marquis emptied his bottle of burgundy, and sent for a second. Miss Challoner's heart sank, but the wine only seemed to make his lordship readier of tongue. There was a certain air of recklessness about him, but he was far from being drunk.

Miss Challoner, dreading the inevitable *tête-à-tête,* lingered over the sweetmeats. When she at last ended her repast, the Marquis signed to his servant, who, in his turn, directed the French hireling to clear away the covers. Vidal got up and lounged over to the fire again. Miss Challoner stayed where she was, only pushing her chair back a little way from the table.

"Will your lordship require anything further tonight?" asked the servant.

"Nothing," Vidal answered.

The man bowed, and withdrew. Vidal spoke softly: "Come here."

"I have something to say to you first, my lord," returned Miss Challoner calmly.

"Good God, girl, do you suppose it was to hear you talk that I brought you to France?" Vidal said derisively. "I'll swear you know better than that!"

"Perhaps," admitted Miss Challoner. "Nevertheless, sir, I beg you will listen to me. You won't pretend, I hope, that you are fallen in love with me."

"Love?" he said scornfully. "No, madam. I feel no more love for you than I felt for your pretty sister. But you've thrown yourself at my head, and by God I'll take you!" His eyes ran over her. "You've a mighty trim figure, my dear, and from what I can discover, more brain than Sophia. You lack her beauty, but I'm not repining."

She looked gravely up at him. "My lord, if you take me, it will be for revenge, I think. Have I deserved so bitter a punishment?"

"You're not very complimentary, are you?" he mocked.

She rose, holding her pistol behind her. "Let me go now," she said. "You do not want me, and indeed I think you have punished me enough."

"Oh, that's it, is it?" he said. "Are you piqued that I liked Sophia better? Never heed it, my dear; I've forgotten the wench already."

"My lord," she said desperately, "indeed I am not what you think me!"

He burst into one of his wild laughs, and she realized that in this mood she could make no impression on him.

He was advancing towards her. She brought her right hand from behind her, and levelled the pistol. "Stand where you are!" she said. "If you come one step nearer I shall shoot you down."

He stopped short. "Where did you get that thing?" he demanded.

"Out of your coach," she answered.

"Is it loaded?"

"I don't know," said Miss Challoner, incurably truthful.

He began to laugh again, and walked forward. "Shoot then," he invited, "and we shall know. For I am coming several steps nearer, my lady."

Miss Challoner saw that he meant it, shut her eyes and resolutely pulled the trigger. There was a deafening report and the Marquis went staggering back. He recovered in a moment. "It was loaded," he said coolly.

Miss Challoner's eyes flew open. She saw that Vidal was feeling his left arm above the elbow, and to her dismay she watched a red stain grow upon his sleeve. She dropped the pistol, and her hand went up to her cheek. "Oh, what have I done?" she cried. "Have I hurt you very badly?"

He was laughing again, but quite differently now, as though he were really amused. "You've hurt old Plançon's wall more than you've hurt me," he answered.

M. Plançon himself burst into the room at this moment, his eyes fairly starting from his head. A flood of questions broke from him, accompanied by much excited gesticulation. My lord disposed of him summarily enough. "Calm yourself, my friend. Madame merely wished to assure herself that my pistol was in order."

"But milor', in my hôtel! My beautiful *salle* he is spoiled! Ah, *mon Dieu*, but regard me that hole in the wall!"

"Put it down on the shot, you old villain, and remove your fat carcase from my sight," said his lordship. He saw his steward behind the agitated landlord. "Fletcher, take the fool away."

"Certainly, my lord," said Fletcher impassively, and drew M. Plançon out of the room.

Miss Challoner said guiltily: "Oh dear, I am sorry! I did not know it would make such a stir."

Vidal's eyes began to twinkle. "You've spoiled his beautiful *salle*, and you've spoiled my no less beautiful coat."

"I know," said Miss Challoner, hanging her head. "But, after all, it was your fault," she said with spirit. "You told me to do it."

"I may have told you to do it, but I can't say I thought that you would," replied his lordship.

"You shouldn't have come any nearer," she said severely.

"Obviously," he agreed. He began to strip off his coat. "I make you my compliments. I know of only one other woman who would have had the courage to pull that trigger."

"Who is she?" inquired Miss Challoner.

"My mother. Come and bind up your handiwork. I'm spoiling old Plançon's carpet."

Miss Challoner came promptly and took the handkerchief he held out to her. "Are you sure it is not serious?" she asked anxiously. "It bleeds dreadfully."

"Quite sure. I observe that the sight of blood don't turn you queasy."

"I am not such a fool, sir." Miss Challoner began to roll up his sleeve. "I fear the lace is ruined, my lord. Am I hurting you?"

"Not at all," said Vidal politely.

Miss Challoner made a pad of her own handkerchief, and bound the wound up tightly with my lord's.

"Thank you," he said when this operation was over. "Now if you will help me to put on my coat again, we will talk."

"Do you think you had better put it on?" asked Miss Challoner doubtfully. "Perhaps it may start to bleed again."

"My good girl, it's the veriest scratch!" said Vidal.

"I was afraid I had killed you," confided Miss Challoner.

He grinned. "You're not a good enough shot, my dear." He struggled into his coat, and then pulled a chair to the fire. "Sit down," he said. She hesitated and he drew one of his own pistols from his pocket and gave it to her. "Shoot me with that next time," he recommended. "You'll find it easier."

She sat down, but though she smiled, her voice was serious when she answered. "If I shoot again, it had better be myself," she said.

He leaned forward and took the pistol away from her. "In that case, I'll keep it." He looked at her frowningly. "You had better explain," he said abruptly. "I've a notion I was right in my first reading of your character."

"What was that, sir?"

"I thought you were devilish strait-laced."

She nodded. "Yes, my lord," she said simply.

"Then in God's name, girl, what possessed you to play this hoyden's trick on me?"

She clasped her hands in her lap. "If I tell you, my lord, I fear it will make you very angry."

"You can't make me more angry than you've done already," he said. "I want the truth now. Let me have it, if you please!"

She was silent for a moment, looking into the fire. He sat still, watching her, and presently she said in her quiet way: "Sophia thought that she could make you wed her. She is very young and silly. My mother too——" she coloured painfully—"is not very wise. I did not think that you would marry Sophia. I thought that you would try to make her your mistress, and I was afraid for her because—because she behaved—foolishly, and because I knew that you would ruin her." She paused, but he said nothing. "That letter you sent," she went on, "was directed to Miss Challoner. I am the elder, you see, and it came to my hand. I knew it was writ by you, but I opened it. Sophia never saw it, my lord."

"Then all you told me at Newhaven was a lie?"

Miss Challoner flushed. "Yes, sir, it was a lie. I wanted to be sure that you would never want to see Sophia again and it seemed to me that if only I could make you believe that she had tricked you—like that—you would be done with her for ever."

"You were right," said Vidal grimly.

"Yes. Only I did not know that you would force me to go instead. I didn't know I should be obliged to tell you all this. I thought you would let me go at once, and I could travel back to London, and only my mother and Sophia be the wiser. Of course, I see now that I was very foolish. But that is the whole truth, my lord."

"Foolish?" he said. "You were mad! Good God, what a damnable muddle!" He sprang up, and began to pace to and fro. Over his shoulder he threw at her: "You little fool, Sophia was never worth the risk you took. You may have saved her from me, but there will be others soon enough."

"Oh no," she said distressfully. "Oh no, my lord!"

"I tell you, yes. Now what the devil's to be done to get you out of this coil?"

"If you would arrange a passage for me on the packet, my lord, I could manage very well," she said.

A swift smile lit his eyes. "What, dare you brave the sea again?"

"I must," she answered. "I dare say it will not be so rough this time."

The smile died; he shook his head impatiently. "No, you can't do that. There's no going home now."

She looked startled. "Where else can I go? I must go home."

"You can't," he repeated. "Do you realize you've been in my company since yesterday? My poor girl, it's you who are ruined, not Sophia."

She said placidly: "But I am not ruined. I can think of some tale to tell that will satisfy people."

He gave a short laugh. "Once it's known you were aboard my yacht, no one will believe you innocent, my dear," he said.

"But no one need——" She stopped, remembering the note she had left for her mother.

He read her thought. "Left a letter, did you? Of course you did! What woman ever did not?"

She felt abashed, and said nothing. He came back to the fireplace, and stood scowling down at her. "Let's finish this bout with buttons off," he said. "I don't care to make mistakes. The fault may be mine, but what business have you with a mother—with a sister such as Sophia?"

"Sir," said Miss Challoner, giving him a very straight look, "I don't design to be thought above mamma or Sophia."

"Design!" he said scornfully. "You are above them. They ——but I don't wish to offend you more than I have done."

Miss Challoner said with composure: "You have insulted me in every conceivable way, sir, so pray do not boggle at plain speaking now. I assure you I shall hear you with equanimity."

"Very well," said his lordship, cold as ice. "Then I shall take leave to inform you, ma'am, that the manners of your parent and sister are neither those of persons of Quality, nor those of virtuous females. You, upon the other hand, are apparently both virtuous and gently bred. And," continued his lordship with a flash of anger, "it is not my custom to abduct respectable young females."

"I did not want you to abduct me," Miss Challoner pointed out. "I am very sorry for your mistake, and I fear that my own conduct may have been partially to blame."

"Your conduct," said the Marquis crushingly, "was damnable! The manners you assumed at Newhaven were those of the veriest trollop; your whole escapade was rash, wanton, and ill-judged. If I had used my riding whip to school you as I promised you would have had no more than your just deserts."

Miss Challoner sat very straight in her chair, and looked steadfastly down into her lap. "I could not think of any other way to keep Sophia safe from you," she said in a small voice. "Of course, I see now that it was madness." She swallowed something in her throat. "I never thought that you would take me instead."

"You are a little fool," replied the Marquis irritably.

"I may be a little fool," retorted Miss Challoner, plucking up spirit, "but at least I meant it for the best. While as for you, my lord, you meant nothing but wicked mischief right from the start. You tried to ruin Sophia, and when I would not let you, you ruined me instead."

"Acquit me," said his lordship coldly. "I don't ruin persons of your quality."

"If you call me a respectable young female again, my lord, you will induce a fit of the vapours in me," interrupted Miss Challoner with asperity. "If you had discovered my respectability earlier, it would have been the better for both of us."

"It would indeed," he agreed.

Miss Challoner hunted for her handkerchief, and blew her little nose defiantly. It was a prosaic action. In her place Sophia would have made play with wet eyelashes. Further, Sophia would never have permitted herself to sniff. Miss Challoner undoubtedly sniffed. Lord Vidal, whom feminine tears would have left unmoved, was touched. He dropped his hand on her shoulder, and said in a softer voice: "You've no need to cry, my dear. I told you I don't ruin ladies of your quality."

She said, with a challenging gleam in her eye: "I am rather tired or I assure you I should not indulge in a weakness I despise."

"Egad, I believe you wouldn't," said his lordship.

Miss Challoner put the handkerchief away. "If you know what I must do next, I wish you would tell me, sir."

"There's only one thing you can do," said his lordship. "You must marry me."

The inn parlour spun round before Miss Challoner's eyes. She shut them, unable to bear a sight so reminiscent of all she had undergone aboard the *Albatross*. "What?" she said faintly.

Vidal raised his brows. "You seem amazed," he said.

"I am amazed," replied Miss Challoner, venturing to open her eyes again.

"You have a remarkably pretty notion of my character, ma'am," he said ironically.

Miss Challoner rose from her chair, and curtsied. "You are extremely obliging, my lord, but I must humbly decline the honour of becoming your wife."

"You will marry me," said his lordship, "if I have to force you to the altar."

She blinked at him. "Are you mad, sir? You cannot possibly wish to marry me."

"Of course I don't wish to marry you!" he said impatiently. "I scarcely know you. But I play my cards in accordance with the rules. I have a number of vices, but abducting innocent damsels and casting them adrift on the world is not one of them. Pray have a little sense, ma'am! You eloped with me, leaving word of it with your mother; if I let you go you could not reach your home again until tomorrow night at the earliest. By that time—if I know your mother and sister at all—the whole of your acquaintance will be apprised of your conduct. Your reputation will be so smirched not a soul will receive you. And this, ma'am, is to go down to my account! I tell you plainly, I've no mind to become an object of infamy."

Miss Challoner pressed a hand to her forehead. "Am I to marry you to save my face, or yours?" she demanded.

"Both," replied his lordship.

She looked doubtfully at him for a moment. "My lord, I fear I am too tired to think very clearly," she sighed.

"You'd best go to bed," he said. He put his hand on her shoulder, and held her away from him, looking down at her. She met his gaze frankly, wondering what he would say next. He surprised her yet again. "Don't look so worn, my dear; it's the devil of a coil, but I won't let it harm you. Good night."

Unaccountable tears stung her eyelids. She stepped back, and dropped a curtsy. "Thank you," she said shakily. "Good night, my lord."

✧§ Chapter VIII ‡∞

MISS CHALLONER had pleaded fatigue, but it was long before she slept. Her desperate problem leered at her half through the night, and it was not until she had reached some sort of a decision that she could achieve slumber.

She was shocked to realize that for a few breathless moments she had forgotten Sophia in a brief vision of herself wedded to his lordship. "So that's the truth, is it?" said Miss Challoner severely to herself. "You are in love with him, and you've known it for weeks."

But it was not a notorious Marquis with whom she had fallen in love; it was with the wild, sulky, unmanageable boy that she saw behind the rake.

"I could manage him," she sighed. "Oh, but I could!"

She did not permit herself to indulge in this dream for long. Marriage, on all counts, was out of the question. He did not give the snap of his fingers for her; he must marry, when the time came, some demure damsel of his own degree; and—the greatest bar of all—she could not steal a bridegroom from under Sophia's nose.

Having disposed thus of his lordship, Miss Challoner set herself resolutely to think of her own future. Vidal had shown her the impossibility of a return to Bloomsbury; it would be equally impossible to seek shelter with her grandfather. After pondering somewhat drearily upon this sudden isolation, she dried her eyes, and tried to think of an asylum. At the end of two hours, being a female of considerable strength of mind, she decided that her wisest course would be to remain in France, to assume a new name, and to try to obtain a post as governess in a respectable French household.

She began, eventually, to compose a letter to her mother, and in the middle of a phrase which had become strangely involved, she fell asleep.

She partook of chocolate and a roll in bed next morning, and when she at length came downstairs to the private parlour, she was met by the discreet Fletcher, who informed her, not without a note of severity in his voice, that his lordship's arm had broken out bleeding again in the night, and looked this morning uncommon nasty. His lordship was still abed, but meant to travel.

"Has a surgeon been sent for?" inquired Miss Challoner, feeling like a murderess.

"His lordship will not have a surgeon, madam," said Fletcher. "It is the opinion of Mr. Timms, his lordship's valet, and myself, that he should see one."

"Then pray go and fetch one," said Miss Challoner briskly.

Fletcher shook his head. "I daren't take it upon myself, ma'am."

"I don't ask you to," Miss Challoner replied. "Have the goodness to do as I bid you."

"I beg pardon, madam, but in the event of his lordship desiring to know who sent for the surgeon——?"

"You will tell the truth, of course," said Miss Challoner. "Where is his lordship's bedchamber?"

Fletcher eyed her with dawning respect. "If you will allow me to show you, madam," he said, and led the way upstairs.

He went ahead of her into the room. Miss Challoner heard Vidal say: "Oh, let her come in!" and awaited no further invitation. She went in, and when the door had shut behind Fletcher, walked up to the big four-poster bed and said contritely: "I did hurt you. Indeed, I am sorry, my lord."

Vidal was sitting up in bed, propped by pillows; his eyes looked a little feverish, and his cheeks were flushed.

"Don't apologize," he said. "You did very well for a beginner. I regret receiving you like this. I hoped you'd sleep later. Will you be ready to set forward at noon?"

"No, I fear I shall not," she answered. "We will stay where we are for to-day." She picked up a pillow from the floor, and arranged it carefully under Vidal's injured arm. "Is that more comfortable, sir?"

"Perfectly, I thank you. But whether you are ready, or not, we start for Paris today."

She smiled lovingly at him. "It's my turn to play the tyrant, sir. You will stay in bed."

"You are mistaken; I shall do no such thing."

He sounded cross; she wanted to take his face between her hands and kiss away his ill-humour. "No, sir, I am not mistaken."

"May I ask, ma'am, how you propose to keep me a-bed?"

"Why yes, I have only to remove your clothes," Miss Challoner pointed out.

"Very wifely," he commented.

She winced a little at that, but said without a tremor: "I have sent your man for a surgeon. Pray do not blame him."

"The devil you have!" said his lordship. "I'm not dying, you know."

"Certainly not," replied Miss Challoner. "But you drank a great deal too much wine yesterday, and I have little doubt it is that that has made you feverish, and maybe inflamed the wound. I think you should be blooded."

My lord regarded her speechlessly. She drew a chair up and sat down. "Do you feel well enough to talk with me for a few minutes, sir?"

"Of course I am well enough to talk with you. What do you want to talk about?"

"My future, if you please."

He looked frowningly at her. "That's my affair, ma'am."

She shook her head. "It is kind in you, my lord, but I do not aspire to be your wife. I have thought very deeply, and I believe I know what will be best for me to do. May I tell you what I have decided?"

He said with a flash of humour: "There seems to be a vast deal of decision about you this morning, my dear. Tell me, by all means."

She folded her hands in her lap; it occurred to him that she was a very restful woman. "What you said last night, my lord, was true; I cannot return to my home. You must not think that this will grieve me overmuch. I have never been very happy there. So I have formed a plan for my future which I believe to be tolerably sensible. If you will take me to Paris I shall be grateful for your escort. Once I am there it is my intention to seek a post in a genteel family as governess. I thought, perhaps you would be able to put me in the way of it, since I suppose you have a large acquaintance in Paris."

His lordship broke in at this point. "My good child, are you proposing that I should recommend you to some respectable matron?"

"Couldn't you?" asked Miss Challoner anxiously.

"I could, of course, but—— Lord, I'd give a monkey to see the matron's face!"

"Oh!" said Miss Challoner. "I see. It was stupid of me not to think of that." She relapsed into profound thought. "Well, if I cannot find anyone to recommend me as a governess, I think I shall become a milliner," she announced.

He stretched out his right hand, and clasped both of hers in it. He was no longer laughing. "I don't often suffer from remorse, Mary, but you are fast teaching me. Come, can't you stomach me as a husband?"

"Even if I could, my lord, do you think I would steal you from my sister? It was not for that I took her place."

"Steal me be damned!" said his lordship rudely. "I'd never the smallest notion of marrying Sophia."

"Nevertheless, sir, I could not do it. The very thought of marriage is absurd. You do not care for me nor I for you, and my estate is too far removed from yours."

"What is your estate?" he asked. "Who was your father?"

"Does it matter?" she said.

"Not a whit, but you puzzle me. You did not get your breeding on the distaff side."

"I was fortunate enough to be educated at a very select seminary, sir."

"You were, were you? Who placed you there?"

"My grandfather," answered Miss Challoner unexpansively.

"Your father's father? Is he alive? Who is he?"

"He is a general, sir."

Vidal's brows drew together. "What county?"

"He lives in Buckinghamshire, my lord."

"Good God, never tell me you are Sir Giles Challoner's grandchild?"

"I am," said Miss Challoner calmly.

"Then I am undone, and we must be married at once," said Vidal. "That stiff-necked old martinet is a friend of my father's."

Miss Challoner smiled. "You need not be alarmed, sir. My grandfather has been very kind to me in the past, but he disowned my father upon his marriage, and has washed his hands of me since I choose to live with my mother and sister. He will not concern himself with my fate."

"He'll concern himself fast enough if he gets wind of his granddaughter in a milliner's shop," said Vidal.

"Of course I shall not become a milliner under my own name," Miss Challoner explained.

"You won't become one under any name, my girl. Make the best of it: marriage with me is the only thing for you now. I am sorry for it, but as a husband I believe you won't find me exacting. You may go your own road—I shan't interfere with you so long as you remain discreet—I'll go mine. You need see very little of me."

The prospect chilled Miss Challoner to the soul, but observing my lord's heightened colour she judged it wiser not to argue with him any further at present. She got up, saying quietly: "We will talk of it again presently, my lord. You are tired now, and the surgeon will soon be here."

He caught her wrist and held it. "Give me your word you'll not slip off while I'm laid by the heels!"

She could not resist the temptation of touching his hand. "I promise I'll not do that," she said reassuringly. "I won't leave your protection till we reach Paris."

When the surgeon came he talked volubly and learnedly, with a great many exclamations and hand-wavings. His lordship suffered this for some time, but presently became annoyed and opened his eyes (which he had closed after the first five minutes) and disposed of the little surgeon's diagnosis and proposed remedies in one rude and extremely idiomatic sentence.

The doctor started back as from a stinging nettle unwarily grasped: "Monsieur, I was informed that you were an Englishman!" he said.

My lord said, amongst other things, that he did not propose to burden the doctor with the details of his genealogy. He consigned the doctor and all his works, severally and comprehensively described, to hell, and finished up his epic speech by a pungent and Rabelaisian criticism of the whole race of leeches.

Whereupon the doctor, who had listened rapt to the unfaltering diatribe, said with enthusiasm: "But it is wonderful! An Englishman to have so great a command of the French tongue! It is what compels the admiration! I shall now bleed you. Madame will have the goodness to hold the basin. The English have such phlegm!"

Vidal became aware of Miss Challoner standing demurely by the door. "What, are you here?" he said. "Do you understand French?"

"Tolerably well, sir," she replied placidly.

"How well?" demanded his lordship.

A glint of amusement shone in her grey eyes. "Well enough to understand the doctor, my lord. But I could not follow very much of what you said. Most of the words you used were strange to me."

"Thank God for that!" said Vidal. "Now go away, there's a good girl, and leave me to deal with this fellow."

"Having phlegm, sir, I am to hold the basin," replied Miss Challoner. "You did as much for me, after all."

He grinned. "I'd a notion you'd never forgive me for that, whatever else you forgave."

"Forgive you? I was exceedingly grateful," said Miss Challoner matter-of-factly.

"You're a remarkable woman," he said. "But I'll have none of this blood-letting for all that."

Miss Challoner had the bowl ready. She said kindly: "It will not hurt you, sir, I assure you."

For the second time that morning his lordship was bereft of speech.

Miss Challoner said, as one reasoning with a rebellious child: "If you desire to be well, and able to make the journey to Paris, you will do as the surgeon advises. But if you are minded to be stupid and obstinate, I shall find the means to go to Paris by myself."

His lordship sat up. "Thunder and turf, how old do you take me for?"

"Not very old," said Miss Challoner, "or you would have more sense." She smiled at him, a warm smile of understanding. "Please permit this poor man to blood you, my lord."

"Oh, very well!" snapped his lordship, relaxing again. "And for the future, ma'am, I'll thank you not to interfere in my concerns."

"I'll try and remember your expressed wish, sir," promised Miss Challoner.

My lord gave his wrist up to the surgeon, but continued to look at Mary. "If I don't end by wringing your neck, my girl, you will be in no way to blame," he informed her.

The cupping left his lordship too weak to attempt the journey to Paris. He slept most of the day, and when he lay awake seemed disinclined to talk. Miss Challoner, a capable female, took charge of the entire party, and issued a number of orders concerning my lord's well-being that made Mr. Fletcher exchange startled looks with Mr. Timms. Both these highly discreet gentlemen treated her from the first with proper respect (which surprised her), but by the end of the day their respect was no longer due to their fear of his lordship.

The Marquis had the first intimation of the change that was taking place in his household at four in the afternoon, when Fletcher, his face like a mask, presented him with a bowl of thin gruel. He had received it from Miss Challoner, and meeting Mr. Timms upon the stairs, had said with great presence of mind: "You may take this to his lordship, Horace."

Mr. Timms, after one glance at the tray, declined the office. "And if I was you, Mr. Fletcher, I would send it by one of these Frenchies," he recommended.

The suggestion offended Mr. Fletcher's dignity, and he said stiffly: "And why, my lad, can you not wait upon his lordship?"

"Because I don't want a basin of gruel thrown at my head," replied Mr. Timms with brutal frankness.

The Marquis looked at the contents of the bowl in the silence of amazement. Then he looked at his major-domo, who stared woodenly at the bed-post. "My good fool," said the Marquis, "what is this repulsive pap?"

"Gruel, my lord," replied Fletcher, expressionless.

The Marquis leaned his head back on the pillows, and continued to survey his henchman. "Have you taken leave of your senses?" he inquired softly.

"No, my lord."

"Then what the devil do you mean by bringing me a bowl of gruel? Where did you get it? Don't dare to tell me a Frenchman perpetrated such an abomination!"

"The lady prepared it, my lord."

There was a short but pregnant silence. "Take it away," said his lordship, with dangerous restraint.

"The lady told me, my lord, that I was on no account to do so," said Fletcher apologetically.

My lord's fingers crooked themselves round one of the handles of the bowl. "Are you going to take it away, Fletcher?" he inquired very gently.

Fletcher, with one eye warily on the movement of that white hand, said, abandoning the struggle: "Certainly, my lord."

Vidal removed his hand from the bowl. "I thought so. Bring me something fit to eat, and a bottle of claret."

Fletcher bowed and removed both himself and the tray. Three minutes later the door was opened again. Miss Challoner came in bearing the same tray. She set it down on the table by the bed, and handed his lordship a napkin. "I am sorry I cannot let you have your bottle of claret, sir," she said. "But I think you won't find my gruel so very bad. I am thought to make it tolerably well."

There was a spark of anger in Vidal's eyes. "You're outside your rôle, ma'am," he told her. "I don't require either your solicitude or your gruel. Have the goodness to refrain in future from meddling in my concerns."

Miss Challoner was not noticeably dashed. "Very well, sir, but will you not, to oblige me, at least taste my gruel?"

"No, ma'am, I will not."

Miss Challoner picked the tray up again, with a small unhappy sigh. "I did not mean to offend you, my lord," she said wistfully. "I thought, perhaps, that if I prepared it very carefully you would not be so unkind as to refuse even to partake of a spoonful."

"Then you are wrong, ma'am," replied his lordship icily.

"Yes," Miss Challoner said rather sadly "I see that I was. I suppose it was presumptuous of me. I am sorry, sir."

She went slowly to the door. My lord said, in the voice of one goaded beyond endurance: "Oh, bring it back, girl— bring it back! I'll swallow the brew if it will please you."

Miss Challoner seemed to hesitate. "Yes, indeed, it would please me, but I do not at all desire to plague you with it."

"For God's sake let's have no more words!" besought Vidal. "Give it to me, and have done!"

Miss Challoner obediently brought back the tray. She sat down by the bed, and watched his lordship drink the gruel. He looked suspiciously at her, but she preserved an innocent front. He finished what was left in the bowl, and put it down. "Mary," said he, "come a little closer and present your left cheek."

A dimple quivered. "Why, sir?"

"Don't you know?" said Vidal.

She laughed. "Why yes, sir. You would dearly love to box my ears."

"I should," he said. "Don't think I'm deceived by that meek face! Where are you going?"

"Down to the parlour, sir."

"Stay with me. I want to talk to you." This was decidedly a command. Miss Challoner raised her eyebrows in faint hauteur. Vidal grinned. "Dear Mary, pray do me the honour of remaining at my side."

She sat down again, slightly inclining her head. "Certainly, sir, but I do not think I gave you leave to call me Mary."

"Give me leave now, then," said Vidal. "Are we not betrothed?"

She shook her head. "No, my lord."

"Dominic," he corrected.

"No, my lord," repeated Miss Challoner steadily.

"Mary," said his lordship, "may I proffer a piece of good advice?" She looked inquiring. "Do not be for ever arguing with me," said the Marquis. "It will be very much better for you to refrain. My intentions are admirable, but I seldom act up to them, and I should not like to lose my temper with you again."

"But, indeed, my lord, I cannot——"

"Dear Mary," said his lordship, "hold your tongue!"

"Very well, sir," replied Miss Challoner obediently.

"First," Vidal said, "I must ask you to keep within doors while we remain in Dieppe. I don't want a chance traveller to see you here."

Miss Challoner wrinkled her brow thoughtfully. "I will do as you wish, of course, but I do not think I number among my acquaintance anyone likely to be visiting France at this season."

"Possibly not," answered the Marquis. "But I number many. Second, I much regret that it will not be possible for me to marry you immediately we arrive in Paris."

"Do you mean, sir, that you have, upon reflection, perceived the wisdom of my plans?"

"No, ma'am, I do not," Vidal said. "I mean that there are

certain difficulties attendant upon the marriage of English Protestants in France."

"Oh!" said Miss Challoner hopefully.

"The obvious course is to visit the Embassy," said my lord, "but since the Ambassador is related to me and I know personally at least three of the Secretaries, the Embassy is the last place I shall visit."

"If," said Miss Challoner, "you feel so much aversion from displaying me to your numerous friends, sir, I wonder that you still persist in this determination to wed me."

"And if," said the Marquis with some asperity, "you would put yourself to the trouble of employing the brain I imagine you must possess, you might possibly perceive that my reluctance to display you to my numerous friends arises from motives of the most disinterested chivalry."

"Indeed?" Miss Challoner said, unabashed. "Well, I could scarce be expected to think that, could I?"

"Oho!" said his lordship. "So you've claws, have you?" Miss Challoner said nothing. "To put it plainly, Miss Challoner, the Ambassador, my esteemed cousin, and his Secretaries, my unregenerate friends, have not infrequently visited my hôtel when a lady was there to act as hostess. They would not consider the presence of a lady under my roof worthy of comment. But were I to walk into the Embassy with a request to be married at once to a lady, living already under my protection, I should cause, not comment, but something in the nature of an uproar. Within a week, my dear, it would be all over town that you'd run off with me, and trapped me into wedding you."

"Oh!" said Miss Challoner, flushing.

"Precisely, my love," said his lordship sardonically. "So since the reason for our marriage is to stop any breath of scandal attaching to your fair name, we shall be wed as quietly as I can contrive. After which, I can easily make it appear that I met you, very properly, in Paris, where you were sojourning with friends, and married you, most romantically, out of hand."

"I see," said Miss Challoner. "And how do you propose to achieve all this, my lord?"

"There are still Protestants in France, my dear. All I have to do is to find a pastor. But it may not be easy, and until I have done it you will have to remain hidden in my house. I can't trust my aunt or I'd place you in her charge." He paused. "There is of course my obese great-uncle Armand de Saint-Vire. No. His tongue wags too much."

"You would appear to have many relatives in Paris, sir," remarked Miss Challoner. "I felicitate you."

"You need not," said Vidal. "I am more in the habit, myself, of consigning 'em all to the devil. Not only is my mother a Frenchwoman, but my paternal grandmother must needs have been one too. The result, ma'am, is that my damned French cousins litter Paris. There is the aunt in whose charge I'll not place you. She is more properly a cousin, but is known to my generation as Tante Elisabeth. You'll meet her. She has a fondness for me. The rest of the family need not concern you. I never permit 'em to disturb me."

"And your obese great-uncle?" inquired Miss Challoner.

"Ah, he don't belong to that side of the family. He's the head of my mother's family. He married upon coming into the title, very late in life. He is a friend of my father's, and like him, has one son, my cousin Bertrand. You'll meet him, too."

"Shall I?" said Miss Challoner. "When?"

"When I've married you."

"The prospect is naturally alluring, sir," said Miss Challoner, rising, "but even these treats in store don't tempt me to marriage." Upon which she curtsied gracefully and walked to the door.

"Vixen," said his lordship, as she opened it.

Miss Challoner curtsied again, and withdrew.

Upon the following morning she found his lordship partaking of a substantial breakfast, and since he seemed to be very much better, she made no demur. The surgeon visited the inn at noon, and although he exclaimed aloud against Vidal's intention to travel that day, he had no objection, he said, to his patient leaving his bed for a short time. When he had gone Miss Challoner prevailed upon the Marquis to postpone their departure one more day. She spent the afternoon in her own room, but came down to the private *salle* shortly before the dinner hour, and walked plump into an agitated conference at the foot of the stairs.

Several excited persons were gathered about a neat and unemotional gentleman in travelling dress of unmistakable English cut. M. Plançon, the landlord, was apparently trying to make himself intelligible to this gentleman, but in the intervals of volubility, he cast up despairing hands to heaven, while two serving-men and an ostler took up the tale with the maximum amount of gesticulation and noise.

Miss Challoner hesitated, mindful of his lordship's instructions, but at that moment the traveller said in a placid voice: "I regret, my good fellows, that I do not understand more than one word in ten of your extremely obliging advice, but I am English—*Anglais, vous savez,* and I do not speak French. *Ne comprenny pas.*"

Miss Challoner's motherly instincts were aroused. She moved forward. "If I could be of assistance, sir?"

The neat gentleman turned quickly, and executed a bow. "You are very kind, madam. I find myself unable to converse with these fellows. It is amazing to me that amongst them all there is not one with a knowledge of the English tongue."

Miss Challoner smiled. "It is most reprehensible, sir, I agree. But if you will explain your difficulties to me, I may be able to interpret them to the landlord."

"I shall be excessively indebted to you, ma'am. Permit me to make myself known to you. My name is Comyn, and I have but this moment landed from the packet. It is my intention to travel by the stage-coach to Paris, and I was endeavouring when you came upon me to ascertain from these fellows when and where I may find the *diligence.*"

"I will ask Plançon," said Miss Challoner, and turned to the landlord.

Perceiving that she had constituted herself interpreter, M. Plançon opened negotiations with an impassioned plea to be preserved from these mad Englishmen who expected honest Frenchmen to understand their own barbarous language— and this in France, *voyez-vous!*

At the end of an animated dialogue lasting for five minutes, Miss Challoner was able to inform Mr. Comyn that the *diligence* would start for Paris in an hour's time, and from this very inn.

Mr. Comyn thanked her, and begged that she would add to her kindness by informing the landlord that he required dinner immediately.

Cheered by this information, M. Plançon disappeared to execute the order, and his hirelings drifted away upon their respective businesses.

Mr. Comyn said that he had been prodigiously fortunate

to have found a countrywoman in Dieppe, and inquired politely whether Miss Challoner was also bound for Paris.

Miss Challoner replied tranquilly that her plans were uncertain, and was about to retreat to the shelter of the parlour when Timms came down the stairs, bowed to her and said with distressing clarity: "His lordship's compliments, madam, and he will do himself the honour of dining with you at five o'clock."

Miss Challoner blushed scarlet, felt herself quite unable to meet Mr. Comyn's look of mild surprise, and fled.

Ten minutes later, one of the inn-servants scratched at Vidal's door, and upon being bidden to come in, presented his lordship with a note.

Vidal was seated before the dressing-table. He took the note and read in Miss Challoner's handwriting: *"Pray, my lord, be careful. There is an Englishman here, of the name of Comyn. I fear I have been indiscreet, but I was obliged to speak with him, and while I was still in his company, your message was delivered to me, so that I was quite undone."*

My lord swore softly and appeared to meditate for a moment. Then he tore up the note and resumed his toilet. In a few minutes he was ready, and made his way downstairs to the coffee-room. Mr. Comyn was standing by the window, consulting his watch. He looked up as the Marquis came in, and exclaimed: "Lord Vidal! So it was——" He broke off, and coughed.

"It was," said his lordship. "But why in the fiend's name you must needs come to Dieppe is a matter passing my comprehension."

"I cannot conceive why it should pass your comprehension, sir," replied Mr. Comyn. "Considering that it was yourself who told me to journey to France."

"I seem to spend my time telling people to do things I have not the smallest desire they should do," said the Marquis bitterly. "Mr. Comyn, you have, I think, met a lady in this inn."

"I have, sir."

The Marquis said: "Contrive to forget it."

"Certainly," said Mr. Comyn, bowing.

Vidal smiled. "Egad, I'm beginning to like you, my prospective relative. That lady is shortly to become my wife."

"You surprise me," said Mr. Comyn truthfully.

"I am sure I do. Permit me to inform you that her presence

in this inn is due, not to her own choice, but to my forcible abduction of her. She is a lady of unimpeachable virtue, and I shall be obliged if you will forget that you have ever seen her in my company."

"Sir," said Mr. Comyn, a stickler for exactitude, "I never have seen her in your company, and I have therefore nothing to forget."

"You're a good fellow," said his lordship, with unusual kindness. "I'll trust you." He sat himself down in the window, and favoured Mr. Comyn with a brief, unvarnished account of the happenings of the past two days.

Mr. Comyn listened with grave attention, and remarked at the end that it was an edifying story. He added that he was honoured by his lordship's confidence, and begged to proffer his felicitations upon his approaching nuptials.

"Oh, go to the devil!" snapped the Marquis, exasperated.

Chapter IX

HIS lordship's remarks to Miss Challoner on the impropriety and folly of addressing strangers in French inns were caustic and denunciatory, but had no visible effect upon the lady. She continued to eat her dinner, lending no more than a polite ear to his homily, and appeared to consider Mr. Comyn's inability to speak French an adequate excuse. My lord speedily undeceived her. "You do not seem to me to comprehend the extreme delicacy of your situation," he said.

Miss Challoner subjected a dish of sweetmeats to close inspection, and finally selected the best of them. "I do," she replied. "I have had plenty of time for reflection, my lord, and I cannot but realize that I've not a shred of reputation left to me."

The Marquis laughed. "You're mighty cool over it, ma'am."

"You should be glad of that," Miss Challoner said serenely. "The task of conveying to Paris a female suffering from a series of strong hysterics would, I imagine, be vastly distasteful to you."

"It would," said the Marquis with conviction.

"Moreover," pursued Miss Challoner, once more inspecting the dish of sweetmeats, "I cannot discover that a display of agitation on my part would achieve much beyond my own exhaustion and your annoyance." She bit into a sugar plum. "Also," she said meditatively, "you have upon several occasions threatened me with extreme violence, so that I should be excessively fearful of the results of driving you to distraction."

The Marquis brought his open hand down upon the table,

and the glasses jumped. "Don't lie!" he said. "You are not in the least afraid of what I may do to you! Are you?"

"Not at the moment, sir," she admitted. "But when you have broached your second bottle, I own to some qualms."

"Let me inform you, ma'am, that I am not considered dangerous until the third bottle."

Miss Challoner looked at him with a faint smile. "My lord," she said frankly, "you become dangerous immediately your will is crossed. I find you spoiled, impetuous, and shockingly overbearing."

"Thank you," said his lordship. "Perhaps you prefer the sedate demeanour of your friend Mr. Comyn?"

"He seemed to be a gentleman of ordinary propriety, certainly," concurred Miss Challoner.

"I, on the other hand, am a gentleman of extraordinary impropriety, of course."

"Oh, not a gentleman, sir, a nobleman," said Miss Challoner with irony.

"You hit hard, ma'am. Pray, was there anything else in Mr. Comyn that you found worthy of remark?"

"To be sure, sir. His manners were of the most amiable."

"I've none at all," said his lordship blandly. "Being a nobleman, ma'am, I don't need 'em. Pray let me pass you this second dish of comfits which has apparently escaped your notice."

"Thank you," said Miss Challoner.

The Marquis sipped his wine, watching her over the rim of his glass. "I think it only fair to warn you, ma'am, that this paragon is secretly contracted to a cousin of mine. In fact, his business in Paris, and I mistake not, is to elope with her."

"Indeed?" Miss Challoner said innocently. "Your cousin is no doubt very like you?"

"Oh, just a family likeness, ma'am," retorted his lordship. "She should be pleased with you," he added thoughtfully.

"I cannot conceive why, sir."

"She'd be pleased with any female who married me."

Miss Challoner looked at him curiously. "She is so fond of you?"

"No, that ain't the reason. Her mamma, my ambitious Aunt Fanny, intends her to be my bride—a prospect Juliana dislikes as much as I do."

Miss Challoner said quickly: "Juliana?"

"My cousin."

"Yes, I understand that, my lord. But what is her sur-name?"

"Marling," said his lordship. "Now what's to do?"

Miss Challoner jumped in her chair. "Your cousin! Juliana Marling! But I know her!"

"Do you?" said Vidal, not visibly excited. "A mad piece, ain't she?"

"Oh, she was my very dearest friend!" Miss Challoner said. "But I never dreamed she was your cousin! We were at the same seminary, you see."

"I'll wager Juliana learned precious little there," remarked Vidal.

"Not very much," allowed Miss Challoner. "They nearly sent her away once, for—er—flirting with the drawing-master. She always said they only forgave her because her uncle was a duke."

"Kissed the drawing-master, did she? She would!"

"Is she really going to marry Mr. Comyn?" inquired Miss Challoner.

"She says so. But she can't run off with him now until our affair is settled. Egad, it's providential that you know her!" He pushed back his chair and got up. "She's staying with my cousin Elisabeth—bundled off too young to be out of Comyn's way. I'll go and pay my respects to her im-mediately we reach Paris, and tell her the whole story. She's a rattle-pate, but she's fond of me, and she'll do as I bid her. She shall have met you in Paris, just as you were on the point of returning to England with—oh, an aunt, or some such thing. She will tell Tante Elisabeth that she has pre-vailed upon you to visit her for a week or two and you will go to the Hôtel Charbonne surrounded by a positive fog of respectability. From whence, my dear, I shall presently elope with you—before, I trust, Tante has had time to dis-cover the truth."

Miss Challoner was thinking fast. If Juliana were in Paris, Juliana could help her to obtain a post in some genteel house-hold. Knowing that lively damsel, she had no fear that she might be shocked at her friend's extraordinary escapade. "Yes, my lord, that is a very good notion—some of it, but I believe you have not perceived the whole good of Juliana's presence in Paris. You have said yourself, sir, that I shall be surrounded by a positive fog of respectability. I have only to pretend to my mother that Juliana was with you from the start of our journey, and my reputation is saved."

He shook his head. "I fear not, Mary. It's a good lie, but too many people would know it for a lie. Moreover, my dear, if I know aught of your mamma, her first care will have been to apprise my parents of your abduction, and to create as much stir as possible. I am well aware that she meant to try and force me into marriage with Sophia by some such method. Didn't she?"

"Yes," said Miss Challoner, flushing and shamefaced.

The Marquis touched her cheek with a careless finger as he passed her chair. "No need to look like that, child; I know. Happily, these plans will be delayed a little by the absence of both my parents from town. My father was to have left for the races at Newmarket upon the day I took my leave of him; and my mother was to have gone with him as far as Bedford, where she will be at this moment, staying with the Vanes. We have, therefore, at least a fortnight's grace, I imagine, but certainly not longer. Write to your mother, apprising her of your bethrothal: that should silence her."

"And you?" she said, watching him as he wandered restlessly about the room. "Do you intend to write your father?"

An involuntary smile twisted his mouth. He refrained from telling her that it was not his libertine behaviour that would annoy his grace, but his honourable intention to marry. He said only: "No need: his grace is not likely to concern himself with my affairs."

"I do not desire to speak with any disrespect of your father, sir, but from the little I have heard of him I take it that though he might not concern himself with your more clandestine affairs, he would do all in his power to prevent your marriage with one so unsuitable as myself."

"I devoutly hope you are wrong, my dear," replied his lordship humourously. "For when my father uses every means to achieve an end, he invariably does achieve it."

Miss Challoner got up, smiling a little ironically. "Vastly pretty, my lord. I could almost suppose that you wanted to marry me."

She moved towards the door which his lordship held open for her. "I assure you, ma'am, I am becoming hourly more reconciled to the prospect," he said, and surprised her by taking her hand and kissing it, very much in the grand manner.

She reflected on her way upstairs that the sooner she left his lordship's protection the better it would be for her peace of mind.

Upon the following day they resumed their journey, travelling by easy stages, and, at Miss Challoner's request, at a moderately decorous pace.

She was somewhat amused at the Marquis's entourage. Besides the chaise that carried her, there was a light coach bearing a quantity of luggage, and Mr. Timms. His lordship rode, and seemed to be accompanied by half his household. Miss Challoner remarked on the size of the *cortège*, and learned that the Marquis had thought himself to be travelling light. He described his mother's frequent progresses, and made her feel sad to think that she would never meet the Duchess of Avon. Her grace, it appeared, had only two ways of travelling. Either she set forth carrying all her wardrobe, and most of her furnishings, with a small army of servants preceding her to make ready at every inn she stopped at, or she started out in an immense hurry, forgetting to provide herself with so much as a change of dress.

Miss Challoner soon discovered that the Marquis adored his mother, and by the end of the journey she had learned much concerning the engaging Duchess. She learned something, too, of the Duke, enough to make her feel thankful that the sea separated her from him. He seemed to be a somewhat sinister person, with uncanny powers of penetration.

They spent four days upon the road to Paris, and the Marquis only twice lost his temper. The first occasion was at Rouen, when Miss Challoner slipped off to see the cathedral, narrowly escaped being seen by a party of English persons, and was treated by her return to a furious tirade; and the second was induced by her refusal to wear the clothes of his lordship's providing. This quarrel began to assume alarming proportions, and when the Marquis announced his intention of dressing Miss Challoner with his own hands, she thought it prudent to capitulate. His eyes were still smouldering when she reappeared in a gown of blue dimity, and it took her some time to coax him out of his wrath.

Upon their arrival in Paris his lordship conducted Miss Challoner immediately to the Hôtel Avon and left her there while he went in search of his cousin. It was already late in the evening, and neither Miss Marling nor Mme. de Charbonne was to be found at home. The Marquis learned that

they had gone to a ball at the house of one Mme. de Château-
Morny, and promptly followed them there. He had taken the
precaution of changing his travelling clothes for a coat of
yellow velvet rather heavily laced with gold, and satin breeches.
Mr. Timms, on his mettle in this land of exquisites, managed
to powder his raven locks with fair thoroughness, and further
to fix a diamond buckle over the black riband that tied them
back. There were diamond buckles on the Marquis's shoes,
and a diamond pin in the foaming lace at his throat. Mr.
Timms would dearly have liked to slip a few rings on to my
lord's long white fingers, but the Marquis pushed them all
aside, and would wear nothing but his gold signet. He was
impatient of the hares-foot, and the patch-box, but when
Timms besought him almost in tears not to go to a ball in
Paris with his face entirely free from rouge, he laughed, and
submitted. Consequently when he took his leave of Miss
Challoner, cosily ensconced beside the fire in the big library,
she thought for a moment that a stranger had entered the
room. The sight of his lordship in full ball dress with diamonds
glinting, ruffles of the finest lace falling over his hands, his
hair adequately powdered and arranged in neat curls, and a
patch at the corner of his mouth, almost took her breath
away. She laughed at him, but thought privately that he
looked magnificent. He grimaced at his reflection in the mirror
over the mantelpiece. "I look like a damned Macaroni, don't
I?" he said. "If I know anything of Juliana, I shall find
her at some ball or rout. Don't go to bed till I get back."

He had no difficulty in entering Mme. de Château-Morny's
hôtel, and when he reached the head of the stairway Madame
herself greeted him with a cry of mingled surprise and delight,
and laughed to scorn his apology for coming uninvited to her
party. He escaped from her presently, and, entering the ballroom, stood looking round through his eye-glass. His very
height at once attracted attention; several persons hailed him,
demanding to know whence he had sprung, and more than
half the young ladies in the room determined to dance with
him before the night was done.

Miss Marling, at the moment of the Marquis's entry, was
going down the dance with a slim young gentleman dressed
in the very latest mode. She caught sight of her cousin, gave
an unmaidenly shriek, and seizing her partner by the hand,
left the dance without ceremony, and rushed to greet him.

"Vidal!" she exclaimed, and gave him both her hands.

Half the young ladies in the room regarded her enviously.

"Don't be a hoyden, Ju," said his lordship, raising first one hand and then the other to his lips. "God defend me, is it you, Bertrand?"

"It is her cousin, the wicked Marquis," whispered a brunette to a languishing blonde.

"How she is fortunate!" sighed the blonde, gazing soulfully at Vidal.

The modish young gentleman swept a deep bow, flourishing a handkerchief strongly scented with amber. He had a mobile and somewhat mischievous countenance, and was known to every anxious parent as a desperate flirt. "*Cher Dominique*, it is even I, thy so unworthy cousin. What villainy has brought you here?"

"Damn your impudence," said his lordship cheerfully. "And what's the meaning of all this, Bertrand?" He let fall his glass, and took the lively Vicomte's ear between finger and thumb.

"English, you understand," murmured a dowager to her *vis à-vis*. "They are all quite *sans gêne*, I have heard."

"My earrings? But it is *de règle*, my dear! Oh, but the very, very latest mode!" the Vicomte answered. "Let go, barbarian!"

Juliana tugged at his lordship's sleeve. "Vidal, it is amazingly pleasant to see you again, but what in the world are you doing here? Never will you tell me my uncle has sent you to—to be a dragon because of my dearest Frederick!"

"Lord, no!" replied Vidal. "Where is your dearest Frederick? Not here tonight?"

"No, but he is in Paris. Oh, Vidal, where can we talk? I have so much to tell you!"

The Vicomte broke in on this and said in English: "Vidal, I am with pistols quite incompetent, but you who are so much in the habit of it, will you not shoot me this abominable Frederick?"

Juliana gave a little crow of laughter, but told the Vicomte she would not permit him to talk in such a fashion.

"But he must be slain, my adored one! It is well seen that he must be slain. Anyone who aspires to steal you from me must be slain. Behold Vidal, the very man to do it!"

"Do it yourself, puppy," said his lordship. "Pink him with that pretty sword of yours. Juliana would love to have a duel fought in her honour."

"It is an idea," agreed the Vicomte. "Decidedly it is an

idea. But I must ask myself, can I do it? Is he perhaps a master of sword-play? That gives to think! I cannot fight for the hand of the peerless Juliana unless I am sure I win. You perceive how ridiculous that would make me to appear."

"It won't make you more ridiculous than those earrings," said his lordship. "I wish you would go away; I want to talk to Juliana."

"You inspire me with jealousy the most profound. Do I find you at the Hôtel Avon? I shall see you perhaps to-morrow, then."

"Come and dine with me," Vidal said, "but no earrings, mind!"

The Vicomte laughed, waved an airy good-bye, and went off in search of further amusement.

"Ju, I want your help," the Marquis said quickly. "Where can we be undisturbed?"

Her eyes sparkled. "My dearest Vidal, what can you have done now? Tell me at once, dreadful creature. Of course, I'll help you! I know of a little room where we shall be quite alone."

The Marquis followed her to where a curtain hung over an archway, and held it back for her to pass through.

"Juliana, you minx, were you ever at a ball without finding a little room where you could be quite alone?"

"No, never," answered Miss Marling with simple pride. She seated herself on a couch, and patted the place beside her invitingly. "Now tell me!"

He sat down, and began to play with her fan. "Do you recall the blonde piece you once saw me with at Vauxhall Gardens?"

She thought for a moment, then nodded. "Yes, she had blue eyes and looked stupid."

"She was stupid. I've run off with her sister instead of her, and the devil's in it, I must marry the girl."

"What?" shrieked Miss Marling.

"If you screech again, Ju, I'll strangle you," said his lordship. "This is serious. The girl's not like the one you saw. She's a lady. You know her."

"I don't," contradicted Miss Marling positively. "Mamma would never let me know the sort of female who would run off with you, Dominic."

"Don't keep interrupting!" commanded Vidal. "I meant

to bring the other sister to Paris, since I had to leave England——"

"Merciful heavens, what have you done that you had to leave England?" cried Miss Marling.

"Shot a man in a duel. But that's not important. The fair sister was to have come with me, but this one got wind of it and took her place to save her."

"I expect she wanted you herself," said the sceptical Miss Marling.

"She don't want me; she's too strait-laced. I didn't discover the cheat till Newhaven was reached. The girl thought to make me believe Sophia had planned the trick. I did believe it." He frowned down at the fan he still held. "You know what I'm like when I lose my cursed temper, Ju?" Miss Marling shuddered dramatically. "Well, I did lose it. I forced the girl to come aboard the *Albatross,* and brought her over to France. At Dieppe, I discovered the mistake I'd made. She was no Sophia, but a lady, and virtuous to boot."

"I'll be bound she enjoyed it prodigiously for all that," sighed Miss Marling. "I should."

"I dare say," said his lordship crushingly, "but this girl is not a minx. There's nothing for it but to marry her. I want to do that as quickly as may be, and until I can arrange it I want you to befriend her."

"Vidal, I never, never thought that you would turn romantic!" said Miss Marling. "Tell me her name at once!"

"Challoner—Mary Challoner," replied the Marquis.

She fairly leaped up from the couch. "Mary! What, my own dear Mary, who left school and was never more heard of? Dominic, you wicked, abominable creature! Where is she? If you've frightened her, I vow I'll never speak to you again!"

"Frightened her?" he said. "Frightened Miss Challoner? Don't you know her better than that? She's the coolest woman that ever I met."

"Oh, do take me to her at once!" begged his cousin. "I should like of all things to see her again. Where is she?"

"At the Hôtel Avon. Listen to what I want you to do."

He told her his plan; she nodded her approval, and straightway dragged him off to the card-room where Mme. de Charbonne was playing at euchre. "Tante, here is Vidal!" she announced.

Madame gave him her hand and a preoccupied smile. *"Cher*

Dominique!" she murmured. "One told me that you were here. Come and visit me tomorrow."

"Tante, only fancy!—Vidal tells me one of my dearest friends is in Paris. Tante, pray listen to me! I am going to see her at this very moment, for Vidal says she leaves to-morrow for England with her aunt."

"But how can you go this moment?" objected madame.

"Vidal says he will escort me. You know mamma will let me go anywhere with Vidal. And he will bring me safe home when I've seen Mary. So do not wait for me, will you, Tante Elisabeth? Not here, I mean."

"It's all very irregular," complained madame, "and you interrupt the game, my dear. Take her away, Dominique, and do not be late."

Half an hour later Miss Challoner, dozing before the fire, was roused by an opening door, and looked up to see her friend Juliana come quickly into the room. "Juliana!" she cried joyfully.

"Mary!" squeaked Juliana, and flung herself into Miss Challoner's arms.

⋅⊰ Chapter X ⊱⋅

MRS. CHALLONER'S emotions upon reading her elder daughter's letter found expression in a series of loud shrieks that brought Sophia running to her room. "Read that!" gasped the afflicted parent, and thrust the note into Sophia's hands.

When Sophia had mastered its contents she wasted no time, but went off into strong hysterics, drumming her feet on the carpet, and becoming alarmingly rigid. Mrs. Challoner, a practical woman, dashed the contents of a jug of water over her, and upon Sophia recovering sufficiently to break into a flood of tears mixed with sobbing complaints of her sister's wickedness, she sat down by her dressing-table, and thought very deeply. After some time, during which Sophia had worked herself into a white heat of fury, Mrs. Challoner said abruptly: "Hold your tongue, Sophy. It may do very well, after all."

Sophia stared at her. Mrs. Challoner threw her a look of unusual impatience, and said: "If Vidal has run off with Mary, I'll make him marry her."

Sophia gave a choked scream of rage. "She shan't have him! She shan't, she shan't! Oh, I shall die of mortification!"

"I never thought to marry Mary well," went on her mother, unheeding, "but I begin to see that nothing in the world could be better than this. Lord, the Gunnings will be nothing to it! To think I was intending Joshua for Mary, and all the time the sly minx was meaning to steal Vidal from under your nose, Sophy! I declare I could positively laugh at myself for being so simple."

Sophia sprang up, clenching her fists. "Mary to be a Marchioness? I tell you I'll kill myself if she gets him!"

"Oh, don't fret, Sophy," Mrs. Challoner reassured her. "With your looks you will never want for a husband. But Mary, whom I never dreamed would be wed, unless it were to Joshua——! La, it is the most amazingly fortunate thing that could ever be."

"She isn't going to marry Vidal!" Sophia said in a voice that shook with passion. "She's gone to save my honour, the interfering, hateful wretch! And now it's her honour will be ruined, and I'm glad of it! I'm glad of it!"

Mrs. Challoner folded up Mary's letter. "It's for me to see she's not ruined, and I promise you I shall see to it. My Lady Vidal—oh, it is famous! I don't know whether I'm on my head or my heels."

Sophia's fingers curled like a kitten's claws. "It's me Vidal wants, not Mary!"

"Lord, what has that to say to anything?" said Mrs. Challoner. "It's Mary he has run off with. Now don't pout at me, miss! You will do very well, I don't doubt. There's O'Halloran, mad for you, or Fraser."

Sophia gave a little scream. "O'Halloran! Fraser! I won't marry a plain mister! I won't! I'd sooner drown myself!"

"Oh well, I'm not saying you might not do better for yourself," replied Mrs. Challoner. "And if only I can get Mary safe wedded to Vidal there's no saying who she may not find you. For she has a good heart; I always said Mary had a good heart; and she'll not forget her mamma and sister, however grand she's to become."

The prospect of having a husband found for her by Mary proved too much for Sophia's self-control. She fell into renewed hysterics, but was startled into silence by a smart box on the ear from a mother who had suddenly discovered that her elder daughter was of more account than her pampered self.

She was bundled off to bed; Mrs. Challoner had no time to waste on tantrums. Her chief fear at that moment was that Mary might return uncompromised, and her night's repose was quite spoiled by her dread of hearing a knock on the front door. When morning came bringing no news of Mary, her maternal anxieties were allayed, and telling Sophia sharply to stop crying, she set about making herself smart for a visit to his grace of Avon. She chose a gown of stiff damson-hued armazine, with one of the new German collars, and a caravan bonnet with a blind of white sarsenet to be let down at will, and thus attired set forth shortly before noon for Avon House. The door was opened by a liveried porter, and she inquired haughtily for his grace of Avon.

The porter informed her that his grace was from home, and having formed his own opinion of Mrs. Challoner's estate, prepared to shut the door.

That redoubtable lady promptly put her foot in the way. "Then be so good as to take me to the Duchess," she said.

"Her grace is h'also h'out of town," replied the porter.

Mrs. Challoner's face fell. "When do you expect her back?" she demanded.

The porter looked down his nose. "H'it is not my place to h'expect her grace," he said loftily.

Feeling much inclined to hit him, Mrs. Challoner next inquired where the Duke and Duchess might be found. The porter said that he had no idea. "And h'if," he continued blandly, "you will have the goodness to remove your foot h'out of the way, I shall be h'able to close the door."

But it was not until the porter had been reinforced by the appearance of a very superior personage indeed that Mrs. Challoner could be induced to leave the doorstep. The superior personage required to know Mrs. Challoner's business, and when she replied that this concerned the Duke and Duchess only, he shrugged in a very insulting manner, and said that he was sorry for it, as neither the Duke nor the Duchess was in town.

"I want to know where I can find them!" said Mrs. Challoner belligerently.

The superior personage ran her over with a dispassionately appraising eye. He then said suavely: "Their graces' acquaintances, madam, are cognisant of their graces' whereabouts."

Mrs. Challoner went off with a flounce of her wide skirts at that, and reached home again in a very bad temper. She found Eliza Matcham sitting with Sophia, and it was plain from Eliza's demeanour that she had been the recipient of all Sophia's angry confidences. She greeted Mrs. Challoner with an excited laugh, saying: "Oh, dear ma'am, I never was more shocked in my life! Only conceive how we have been hoodwinked, for I could have sworn 'twas Sophia he wanted, could not you?"

"It was me! It is me!" choked poor Sophia "I hope he strangles Mary! And I dare say he has strangled her by now, for he has a horrid temper. And it will serve her right, the mean, designing thing!"

Finding Mrs. Challoner in an unresponsive mood, Miss Matcham soon took her leave of Sophia, and went away agog with her news. When she had gone Mrs. Challoner soundly rated Sophia for her indiscretion. "It will be all over town by to-night!" she said. "I would not have had you tell Eliza for the world."

"I don't care," Sophia answered viciously. "People shan't think that he preferred her to me, for it's not true! She's a shameless hussy, and so I shall tell everyone."

"You'll be a fool if you do," her mother informed her. "Pray who would believe such a tale? People will only laugh at you the more, and say you are jealous."

She did not tell Sophia of her fruitless mission to Avon House, but went off again directly after luncheon to visit her brother Henry.

She found only her sister-in-law at home, Henry Simpkins being in the city, but Mrs. Simpkins, perceiving her to be big with news, pressed her warmly to await his return, and dine with them. It did not take Mrs. Simpkins long to possess herself of her sister's news, and the two dames spent a very comfortable few hours, discussing and exclaiming, and forming plans for the runaways' marriage.

When Henry and Joshua came in, shortly before five, they were immediately apprised of the whole story. Mrs. Challoner told it with a wealth of detail and surmise, and Mrs. Simpkins added riders here and there.

"And only fancy, Henry," Mrs. Challoner ended triumphantly, "she is the slyest thing! For she pretended she was gone off to save Sophy's reputation, and all the time she must have meant to run away with the Marquis herself, for if she did not, why didn't she return as she said she would? Oh, she is the naughtiest piece imaginable!"

A deep groan brought her attention to bear upon her nephew. "Ay, Joshua, it is a sad thing for you," she said kindly. "But you know I never thought she would have you; for she's a monstrous pretty girl, and I always said she would make a brilliant marriage."

"Marriage?" Joshua said deeply. "I wish you don't live to see her something far other than a wife. Shameless, shameless!"

Mr. Simpkins supported his son. "Time enough to brag of

marriages when you have her safe tied to the Marquis," he said. "If the Duke is indeed from home you must find him. Good God, Clara, one would think you were glad the girl's gone off like this!"

Mrs. Challoner, knowing her brother's Puritanical views, hastily dissembled. She told him how she had found both the Duke and the Duchess of Avon absent from town, and he said that she must lose no time in running one or the other to earth. She had no notion how to set about this task, but her sister-in-law was able to assist her. Mrs. Simpkins had not read all the Court journals for years past in vain. Not only could she recite, unerringly, all his grace of Avon's names and titles, but she was able to inform her sister-in-law that he had a brother living in Half Moon Street, and a sister who had married a commoner, and was now a widow.

Mr. Simpkins, upon hearing the name of his grace's brother, brushed him aside. Lord Rupert Alastair was known to him by reputation, and he could assure his sister that this noble-man was depraved, licentious, and a spendthrift, and would be the last person in the world likely to aid her to force Vidal into marriage. He advised her to visit Lady Fanny Marling in the morning, and this she in the end decided to do.

Lady Fanny's servants were not so well trained as those at Avon House, and Mrs. Challoner, by dint of saying that Lady Fanny would regret it if she refused to see her, managed to gain an entrance.

Lady Fanny, dressed in a négligée of Irish polonaise, with a gauze apron, and a point-lace lappet-head, received her in a small morning-room at the back of the house, and having a vague notion that she must be a mantua-maker, or milliner come to demand payment of bills long overdue, she was in no very good humour. Mrs. Challoner had prepared an opening speech, but had no opportunity of delivering it, for her ladyship spoke first, and in a disconcerting fashion. "I vow and declare," she said stringently, "things are come to a pretty pass when a lady is dunned in her own house! My good woman, you should be glad to have the dressing of me, and as for the people I've recommended you to, although I can't say I've ever heard your name before—(I suppose you are Cerisette, or Mirabelle)—I am sure there must be dozens of them. And in any case I've not a penny in the world, so it is of no avail to force your way into my house. Pray do not stand there goggling at me!"

Mrs. Challoner felt very much as though she had walked by mistake into a madhouse. Instead of her fine speech, all she could think of to say was: "I do not want money, ma'am! You are quite mistaken!"

"Then if you don't want money, what in the world do you want?" demanded her ladyship, opening her blue eyes very wide.

She had not offered her unwelcome visitor a chair, and somehow Mrs. Challoner did not care to take one without permission. She had not supposed that Lady Fanny would be so formidable, but formidable she certainly was, in spite of her lack of inches; and her imperious way of speaking, coupled with her air of the great lady, quite threw Mrs. Challoner off her balance. She said somewhat lamely: "I have come to you, ma'am, to learn where I may find the Duke of Avon."

Lady Fanny's jaw dropped. She stared at Mrs. Challoner with a mixture of astonishment and indignation. "The Duke of Avon?" she repeated incredulously.

"Yes, ma'am, the Duke of Avon," reiterated Mrs. Challoner. "It is a matter concerning his honour, let me tell you, and I must see him at once."

"Good God!" said her ladyship faintly. A flash of anger came into her eyes. "How dare you come to me?" she said. "I vow it passes all bounds! I shall certainly not direct you where you may find him, and I marvel that you should expect it of me."

Mrs. Challoner took a firm hold on her reticule, and said with determination: "Either the Duke or her grace the Duchess I must see and will see."

Lady Fanny's bosom swelled. "You shall never carry your horrid tales to the Duchess, I promise you. I make no doubt at all it's a pack of lies, but if you think to make mischief with my sister, let me tell you that I'll not permit it."

"And let me assure you, ma'am, that if you try to prevent me seeing the Duke you will be monstrous sorry for it. Your ladyship need not suppose that I shall keep my mouth shut. If I do not obtain his grace's direction from you I'll make an open scandal of it, and so I warn you!"

Lady Fanny curled her lip disdainfully. "Pray do so, my good woman. Really, I find you absurd. Even were his grace ten years younger, I for one should never believe such a nonsensical story."

Mrs. Challoner felt more than ever that she had strayed into a madhouse. "What has his grace's age to do with it?" she said, greatly perplexed.

"Everything, I imagine," replied Lady Fanny dryly.

"It has nothing at all to do with it!" said Mrs. Challoner, growing more and more heated. "You may think to fob me off, ma'am, but I appeal to you as a mother. Yes, your la'ship may well start. It is as a mother, a mother of a daughter that I stand here to-day."

"Oh, I *don't* believe it!" cried Fanny. "Where are my lavender-drops? Mr poor, poor Léonie! Say what you have to: I shall not credit one word of it. And if you think to foist your odious daughter on to Avon, you make a great mistake! You should have thought of it before. I suppose the girl must be at least fifteen years of age."

Mrs. Challoner blinked at her. "Fifteen years, ma'am? She's twenty! And as for foisting her on to the Duke, if he has a shred of proper feeling he will make the best of it—though I am far from admitting her to be unworthy of the very highest honours—and accept her as a daughter (and, indeed, she is a sweet, dutiful girl, ma'am, and reared in a most select seminary) without any demur."

"My good woman," said Fanny pityingly, "if you imagine that Avon will do anything of the kind you must be a great fool. He has no proper feelings, as you choose to term them, at all, and if he paid for the girl's education (which I presume he must have done) I am amazed at it, and you may consider yourself fortunate."

"Paid for her education?" gasped Mrs. Challoner. "He's never set eyes on her! What in the name of Heaven is your la'ship's meaning?"

Fanny looked at her narrowly for a moment. Mrs. Challoner's bewilderment was writ large on her face. Fanny pointed to a chair. "Be seated, if you please," she said. Mrs. Challoner sat down thankfully. "And now perhaps you will tell me in plain words what it is you want," her ladyship continued. "Is this girl Avon's child, or is she not?"

Mrs. Challoner took nearly a full minute to grasp the meaning of this question. When she had realized its import she bounced out of her chair again, and cried: "No, ma'am, she is not! And I'll thank your la'ship to remember that I'm a respectable woman even if I wasn't thought good enough for Mr. Challoner. He married me for all he came of such high and mighty folk, and I'll see to it that his grace of Avon's precious son marries my poor girl!"

Lady Fanny's rigidity left her. "Vidal!" she said with a gasp of relief. "Good God, is *that* all?"

Mrs. Challoner was still fuming with indignation. She glared at Fanny, and said angrily: "All, ma'am? All? Do you call it nothing that your wicked nephew has abducted my daughter?"

Fanny waved her back to her chair. "You have all my sympathies, ma'am, I assure you. But your errand to my brother is quite useless. He will certainly not be moved to urge his son to marry your daughter."

"Will he not then?" cried Mrs. Challoner. "I fancy he will be glad to buy my silence so cheaply."

Fanny smiled. "I must point out to you, my good woman, that it is your daughter and not my nephew that would be hurt by this story becoming known. You used the word 'abduct'; I know a vast deal to Vidal's discredit, but I never yet heard that he was in the habit of carrying off unwilling females. I presume your daughter knew what she was about, and I can only advise you, for your own sake, to bear a still tongue in your head."

This unexpected attitude on the part of her ladyship compelled Mrs. Challoner to play her trump card earlier than she had intended. "Indeed, my lady? You are very much in the wrong, let me tell you, and if you imagine my daughter is without powerful relatives, I can speedily undeceive you. Mary's grandpapa is none other than a general in the army, and a baronet. He is Sir Giles Challoner, and he will know how to protect my poor girl's honour."

Fanny raised her brows superciliously, but this piece of information had startled her. "I hope Sir Giles is proud of his grandchild," she said languidly.

Mrs. Challoner, a spot of colour on either cheek-bone, hunted with trembling fingers in her reticule. She pulled out Mary's letter, and threw it down on the table before her ladyship. "Read that, ma'am!" she said in tragic accents.

Lady Fanny picked the letter up, and calmly perused it. She then laid it down again. "I have not a notion what it is about," she remarked. "Pray who may 'Sophia' be?"

"My younger daughter, ma'am. His lordship designed to run off with her, for he dotes madly on her. He sent her word to be ready to elope with him two nights ago, and Mary opened the letter. She is none of your frippery good-for-nothing misses, my lady, but an honest girl, and quite her grandpapa's favourite. She meant, as you have seen, to save her sister from ruin. Ma'am, she has been gone two days, and I say that the Marquis has abducted her, for I know Mary, and I'll be bound she never went with him willingly."

Lady Fanny heard her in dismayed silence. The affair seemed certainly very serious. Sir Giles Challoner was known to her, and she felt sure that if this girl were in truth her grandchild he would not permit her abduction to pass unnoticed. A quite appalling scandal (if it did not turn out to be worse than a mere scandal) seemed to be brewing, and however waspishly Lady Fanny might have predicted that her nephew would in the end create such a scandal, she was not the woman to sit by and do nothing to prevent it. She had a soft corner for Vidal, and a very real affection for his mother. She had also her fair share of family pride, and her first thought was to apprise Avon instantly of this disastrous occurrence. Then her heart failed her. This was no tale to pour into Avon's ears, at the very moment when his son had been obliged to leave the country for yet another offence. She had no clear idea of what the outcome of it all would be, or whether it would be possible to hush the matter up, but she determined to send word to Léonie.

She cast an appraising glance at Mrs. Challoner. She was a shrewd woman, and Mrs. Challoner would have been startled had she known how much that she had kept to herself Lady Fanny had guessed.

"I'll do what I can for you," Fanny said abruptly. "But you will do well to say nothing of this disagreeable matter to anyone. I shall repeat your very extraordinary story to my sister-in-law. Let me point out to you, ma'am, that if you raise a scandal you will lose the object you have in view. Once your daughter's name is being bandied from lip to lip I can assure you my nephew won't marry her. As to scandals, ma'am, I leave it to you to decide who will be most hurt by one."

Mrs. Challoner hardly knew what to reply. Lady Fanny's manner awed her; she was uncertain of her ground, for she had expected Lady Fanny to be horrified and alarmed. But Lady Fanny was so calm, so delicately scornful that she began to wonder whether she would be able to frighten the Alastairs with the threat of exposure after all. She wished she had her brother by, to advise her. She said rather pugnaciously: "And if I do keep silent? What then?"

Lady Fanny lifted her eyebrows. "I cannot take it upon myself to answer for my brother. I have informed you that I will tell my sister-in-law your story. If you will have the goodness to leave your address, no doubt the Duchess—or the Duke—will visit you." She stretched out her hand towards a little silver bell, and rang it. "I can only assure you, ma'am, that if wrong has been done his grace will certainly arrange matters honourably. Permit me to bid you good-day." She nodded dismissal, and Mrs. Challoner found herself rising instinctively from her seat.

The footman was holding the door for her to pass through. She said: "If I do not hear within a day, I shall act as I think best, my lady."

"There is not the smallest chance that you will hear within the day," said her ladyship coldly. "My sister is at the moment quite remote from London. You might perhaps hear in three or four days."

"Well . . ." Mrs. Challoner stood hesitating. The interview had not been conducted as she had planned. "I shall wait on you again the day after to-morrow, ma'am. And you need not think I'm to be fobbed off." She moved towards the door, but paused before she had reached it, and remembered to give Lady Fanny her direction. She then curtsied and withdrew, feeling a little discomfited and considerably annoyed.

Had she been able to transport herself back into the house five minutes later she would have been somewhat comforted. No sooner had the front door closed behind her than Lady Fanny flew up out of her chair, violently rang her hand-bell, and, upon the footman's return, sent him to find Mr. John Marling at once.

Mr. Marling entered the room presently to find his mamma in a distracted mood.

"Good heavens, John, what an age you have been!" she cried. "Pray shut the door! The most dreadful thing has happened, and you must go immediately to Bedford."

Mr. Marling replied reasonably: "I fear it will be most inconvenient for me to leave London to-day, mamma, as I am invited by Mr. Hope to accompany him to a meeting of the Royal Society. I understand there will be a discussion on the Phlogistic Theory, in which I am interested."

Lady Fanny stamped her foot. "Pray what is the use of a stupid theory when Vidal is about to shame us all with a dreadful scandal? You can't go to any society! You must go to Bedford."

"When you ask, mamma, what is the use of the Phlogistic Theory, and apparently compare it with Vidal's exploits, I can only reply that the comparison is ridiculous, and renders the behaviour of my cousin completely insignficant," said Mr. Marling with heavy sarcasm.

"I do not want to hear another word about your tiresome theory," declared her ladyship. "When our name is dragged in the mud we shall see whether Vidal's conduct is insignificant or no."

"I am thankful to say, ma'am, that my name is not Alastair. What has Vidal done now?"

"The most appalling thing! I must write at once to your aunt. I always said he would go too far one of these days. Poor, poor Léonie! I vow my heart quite aches for her."

Mr. Marling watched her seat herself at her writing-table, and once more inquired: "What has Vidal done now?"

"He has abducted an innocent girl—not that I believe a word of it, for the mother's a harpy, and I've little doubt the girl went with him willingly enough. If she didn't, I shudder to think what may happen."

"If you could contrive to be more coherent, mamma, I might understand better."

Lady Fanny's quill spluttered across the paper. "You will never understand anything except your odious theories, John," she said crossly, but she paused in her letter-writing, and gave him a vivid and animated account of her interview with Mrs. Challoner.

At the end of it, Mr. Marling said in a disgusted voice: "Vidal is shameless. He had better marry this young female and live abroad. I quite despair of him, and I feel sure that while he is allowed to run wild in England we shall none of us know a moment's peace."

"Marry her? And pray what do you suppose Avon would have to say to that? We can only hope and trust that something may yet be done."

"I had better journey to Newmarket, I suppose, and inform my uncle," said Mr. Marling gloomily.

"Oh John, don't be so provoking!" cried his mother. "Léonie would never forgive me if I let this come to Avon's ears. You must fetch her from the Vanes at once, and we will lay our heads together."

"It is impossible not to feel affection for my Aunt Léonie," announced Mr. Marling, "but have you considered, mamma, that she is capable of treating even this piece of infamy with levity?"

"It does not signify in the least. All you need do is to bear this letter to her, and bring her back to town," said Lady Fanny imperatively.

Mr. Marling, disapproving but obedient, arrived at Lady Vane's house near Bedford that evening. There were several people staying there, but he contrived to meet his aunt in a room apart. His countenance was so lugubrious that she asked him in quck alarm if anything were amiss?

"Aunt," said Mr. Marling gravely, "I am the bearer of bad tidings."

Léonie turned pale. "Monseigneur?" she faltered.

"No, ma'am, so far as I am aware my uncle enjoys his customary health."

"Ah, *mon Dieu*, it is Dominique! He has been shot in a duel? drowned in his yacht? dead of a fever? Speak, you!"

"My cousin is well, ma'am. Do not alarm yourself on that score. But the news is the worst imaginable."

"If he is well it cannot be the worst," said Léonie. "Please do not prepare me for a shock any more; I find it too alarming. What has happened to my son?"

"Madam, I regret to be obliged to soil your ears with the story, which I myself find excessively disagreeable. Vidal has abducted—I fear perhaps with violence—a young female of virtue and family."

"Oh, *mordieu*, it is the *bourgeoise!*" said Léonie. "And now Monseigneur will be more displeased than ever! Tell me it all!"

Mr. Marling regarded her with an expression of pained severity. "Possibly, my dear aunt, you would prefer to read it. I have a billet for you from my mother."

"Give it to me at once, then," said Léonie, and fairly snatched it from his hand.

Lady Fanny's agitated scrawl covered three pages. Léonie read them quickly, and exclaimed at the end that Fanny was an angel. She said that she would return to town at once, and upon her hostess coming into the room, greeted her with apologies, and the information that Lady Fanny was ill, and needed her. Lady Vane was all solicitude, and put a number of sympathetic questions to John which caused that conscientious young man to wriggle uncomfortably. She prevailed on Léonie to postpone her departure at least until next morning, and this Léonie consented to do out of consideration for her nephew, who had been travelling all day.

He and she set forth next day in her grace's huge travelling coach. Léonie did not seem to be greatly disturbed by her son's conduct. She said cheerfully that it was very odd of Dominique to abduct the wrong sister, and asked John what he supposed could have happened. John, who was feeling tired and annoyed, said that he could not venture a guess.

"Well, I think it was very stupid of him," said the Duchess.

Mr. Marling said austerely: "Vidal's conduct is nearly always stupid, ma'am. He has neither sense nor decency."

"Indeed?" said the Duchess dangerously.

"I have endeavoured again and again to interest him in serious things. I am his senior by six years, and I have not unnaturally supposed that my advice and frequent warnings would not go entirely unheeded. It seems I was wrong. The late scandalous happenings at Timothy's make it positively unpleasant for me to enter the clubs, where I am aware that I must be indicated to any stranger as the cousin of a notorious rake and—not to mince matters—murderer. Moreover——"

"I will tell you something, John," interrupted the Duchess. "You should be very grateful to Dominique, for of a certainty no one would point you out at all if you were not his cousin."

"Good God, aunt, do you imagine I wish to achieve notoriety in such a fashion? It is of all things the most repugnant to me. As for this latest exploit—well, I ascribe it very largely to my Uncle Rupert's influence. Vidal has always chosen to be intimate with him to a degree I and, I may say, my mother, have considered to be unwise in the extreme. I don't doubt he learned his utter disregard for morality from him."

"I find you insupportable!" stated the Duchess. "My poor child, it is quite plain to me that you are jealous of Dominique."

"Jealous?" repeated Mr. Marling, astounded.

"Of a certainty," nodded the Duchess. "To shoot a man dead: it is terrible, you say. For you could not do it. You could not shoot an elephant dead. To elope with a woman: it is scandalous! *Bien entendu,* but you, you could not persuade even a blind woman to elope with you, which I find not scandalous, but tragic."

Mr. Marling was unable to think of a suitable retort. His aunt, having disposed of him in this one withering speech, smiled affably, and patted his knee. "We will discuss now what I must do to rescue Dominique from this *impasse.*"

Mr. Marling could not resist the temptation of saying: "I apprehend that the unfortunate young female at present in his company is more in need of rescue."

"Ah, bah!" cried the Duchess, "it is is not possible to talk to you, for you are without sense!"

"I am sorry, ma'am, if I disappoint you, but you appear to regard this affair very lightly."

"I do not regard it lightly at all," said Léonie stiffly. "Only I do not believe that it is just as this Mrs. Challoner has told Fanny. If Vidal has taken her daughter to France I think she went very willingly, and the matter solves itself. Mrs. Challoner would have me believe that the one sister went with my son to save the other. *Voilà une histoire peu croyable.* I ask myself, if this were true where is the girl now? In England, *bien sûr,* for why should Vidal take to France someone he did not want?"

"I've thought of that too, Aunt Léonie, and I have the answer, though I am must afraid you will not credit it. If the story is true, Vidal will have taken her for revenge."

There was a long silence. The Duchess clasped and unclasped her hands. "That is what you think, John?"

"It is possible, ma'am, you'll agree."

"Yes. In a black mood Dominique might . . . I must go to Rupert at once! Why do we go so slowly? Tell them to hurry!"

"Go to my uncle?" John echoed. "I cannot conceive what good he will be to you!"

"No?" Léonie said fiercely. "I will tell you, then. He will go to France with me, and find Dominique and this girl."

"Lord, ma'am, do you tell me you'll go off to France with him?"

"Why not?" demanded Léonie.

"But, aunt, it will be thought prodigious strange if it becomes known. People will think you have run away with my uncle. Moreover, I consider him a most unsuitable escort for any lady, accustomed as you are, my dear ma'am, to every delicate attention to her comfort."

"I thank you, John, but I am quite in the way of running off to France with Rupert, and he will look after me very well," said her grace. "And now, *mon enfant,* if I am not to murder you we will talk no more of Vidal, or of Rupert, or of anything."

Some hours later aunt and nephew, each meticulously polite to the other, reached Lady Fanny's house in town. It was the dinner hour, and her ladyship was about to sit down to a solitary meal when the Duchess came quickly into the dining-room.

"Oh, my dearest love!" exclaimed Fanny, embracing her. "Thank heaven you have come! It is all too, too true!"

Léonie flung off her cloak. "Tell me at once, Fanny; he has abducted her? Truly he has abducted her?"

"Yes," Lady Fanny asseverated. "I fear so. That odious woman was here again to-day, and indeed she means mischief, and I don't doubt she'll make herself vastly unpleasant unless we can buy her off, which I thought of at once, only, my love, I do not know how in the world we are to do so unless you have a great deal of money by you, for I've not a penny. I declare I could kill Vidal! It is so unthinking of him to ravish honest girls—not that I believe she is honest for a moment, Léonie. The mother is a horrid, designing creature if ever I saw one, and oh, my dear, she brought the other sister here to-day, and 'twas that made me believe in her ridiculous story, for all I'm sure the most of it's a pack of lies. The child is quite provokingly lovely, Lèonie, and do you know, she makes me think of what I was at her age? As soon as I clapped eyes on her I saw that there was nothing could be more natural than for Vidal to be in love with her." She broke off as the serving-man came into the room to lay two more covers, and begged Léonie to be seated. Further discussion being impossible before the servant, she began to talk of the latest town gossip, and even, for want of something to say, asked her son kindly whether he would not like to go to the Royal Society to-night. John deigned no reply, but when dinner was over he informed the two ladies that although it was unhappily out of his power to repair to the Royal Society, he proposed to occupy himself with a book in the library.

Upstairs in the privacy of her boudoir, Fanny poured out
the rest of her tale. She said that Sophia Challoner had
scarce opened her little sulky mouth, but she could vow the
chit was furious at having Vidal stolen from her. "The veriest
minx, my dear! Oh, I know the signs, trust me! If the sister
is at all like her, and how can she not be? poor Vidal is most
horridly taken in. There's no doubt he took her off to France
with him, for if he did not, where is she? What shall we do?"

"I am going to Paris," Léonie said. "First I will see this Mrs.
Challoner. Then I shall tell Rupert he must take me to France.
If it is all true, and the girl is not a—what is the word, I want,
please?"

"I know what you mean, my love, never fear," Lady Fanny
said hastily.

"Well, if she is *not* that, then I must try to make Dominique
marry her, for it is not at all *convenable* that he should ruin
her. Besides, I am sorry for her," Léonie added seriously.
"To be alone like that, and in someone's power is very uncomfortable, I can assure you, and me, I know."

"The mother will never rest till she has caught Vidal, but
what of Justin, Léonie? I vow I'll have no hand in this. He
can be so excessively unpleasant, you know."

"I have thought of Justin, but though I do not like to deceive
him, I see that this time I must. If Dominique must marry
the girl I will make up a clever lie to tell him, and he must
not know that it was all due to Dominique's folly. That would
make him very enraged, *tu sais.*"

"He'll not believe you," Lady Fanny said.

"Yes, he will believe me, perhaps, because I do not lie to
him—ever," said Léonie tragically. "I have thought of it all,
and I am very miserable. I shall write to him one big lie, that
cousin Harriet is indisposed, and I have gone to stay with her,
and she is so old he will certainly not find that surprising.
Then, if it is necessary that Dominique marries this girl whom
already I detest, I will make him do it, only it will not appear
that I was ever in Paris, for I shall come home, and I shall
know nothing of Dominique at all. Then Dominique will
write to tell Monseigneur that he is married—and if it is true
the girl is Sir Giles' granddaughter it is not after all so very
dreadful—and I shall pretend how glad I am, and perhaps
Justin will not mind so much."

Fanny caught her hands. "My dearest love, you know he

will be furious, and when Justin is angry he is more dangerous than ever Dominique could be."

Léonie's lip trembled. "I know," she said. "But at least it will not be so bad as the truth."

❧ Chapter XI ☙

ON the following morning Mrs. Challoner, chancing to look out of the window, was edified to perceive a very elegant equipage drawn up at her door. She said instantly: "The Duchess!" and hurried over to the mirror to arrange her cap. She told Sophia that if she dared to speak a word outside her part she would lock her in her bedchamber for a week. Sophia was about to retort in kind when Betty opened the door and announced in a voice pregnant with awe: "The Duchess of Avon, mam!"

The Duchess came in, and Mrs. Challoner was so surprised she forgot to curtsy. She had expected a lady quite twenty years older than the youthful-looking creature who stood before her, and had prepared herself to meet something very formidable indeed. Great violet-blue eyes, a dimple, and copper curls under a chip-hat did not belong to the Duchess of her imagination, and she stood staring in a disconcerted way instead of greeting her grace with the proper mixture of pride and civility.

"You are Mrs. Challoner?" the Duchess said directly.

She spoke with a decided French accent, which further surprised her hostess. Sophia was also surprised, and exclaimed without ceremony: "Lord, are you Vidal's mamma, then?"

Léonie looked at her from her head to her heels till Sophia blushed and began to fidget. Then she once more surveyed Mrs. Challoner, who remembered her manners, told her daughter to hold her tongue, and pulled forward a chair. "Pray, will not your grace be seated?"

"Thank you," Léonie said, and sat down. "Madame, I am informed that your daughter has eloped with my son, which is a thing I find not very easy to understand. So I come to you that you may explain to me how this is at all possible."

Mrs. Challoner dabbed at her eyes with a handkerchief, and protested that she was nigh distracted with grief and shame. "For Mary is a good girl, your grace, and elope with his lordship she would never do. Ma'am, your son has abducted my poor innocent child by force!"

"*Tiens!*" said the Duchess with polite interest. "My son is then a house-breaker. He perhaps stole her from beneath your roof, madame?"

Mrs. Challoner let the handkerchief fall. "From under my roof? How could he do that? No, indeed!"

"It is what I ask myself," said the Duchess. "He laid a trap for her, perhaps, and seized her in the street, and carried her off with a gag and a rope."

Mrs. Challoner eyed her with hostility. The Duchess met her look limpidly, and waited. "You don't understand, ma'am," said Mrs. Challoner.

"Assuredly I do not understand. You say my son abducted your daughter with force. *Eh bien*, I demand of you how this could be done in the middle of London. I find M. le Marquis has been extremely clever if he could arrange so difficult a rape."

Mrs. Challoner flushed scarlet. "Ma'am! I must beg of you!"

"It is not then a rape?"

"Oh, I—yes, indeed and it is, and I will have justice done, ma'am, and so I tell you!"

"I too desire to have justice done," said the Duchess softly. "But I am not a fool, madame, and when you talk to me of rapes you talk of what I do not at all believe. If your daughter was not willing she could make a great outcry, and it seems to me that in London there is someone who will hear and come to her rescue."

"I see, ma'am, you have not heard the whole. Let me explain to you that it was not Mary his lordship wanted, but my little Sophia here. He has been for ever upon my door-step, and I fear, ma'am, he has quite turned the child's head. I blush to confess it to your grace, but he attempted to seduce Sophia, of course unbeknownst to me. I do not know what lies he told her, but he had it all arranged to

fly with her. I have reared her very strict, ma'am, and how
should she dream he did not mean marriage? She thought
he would take her to Gretna Green. Oh, I'll not deny it
was mighty foolish and wrong of her, but girls will have
these romantic fancies, your grace, and heaven knows what
persuasions his lordship may have used. No, Sophy, be quiet!"

Léonie looked at the indignant Sophia, and smiled. "You
present to me my son in a new rôle," she said. "I have
never known him to take so much trouble. It seems he was
in love with you quite *en désespéré.*"

"He did love me!" Sophia said chokingly. "He never looked
at Mary! Never!"

"Hold your tongue, Sophy! Not but what it is true, ma'am.
His lordship was mad for the child. But Mary took it into
her head 'twas not marriage he intended, and what she did
was to save her sister from ruin."

"It is of a nobility almost incredible, madame. What did
this Mary do?"

Mrs. Challoner threw out her hands dramatically. "She
took Sophia's place, ma'am. It was night, and she was masked,
for Sophia has found an old loo-mask gone from her drawer.
What she had in mind to do I know not, but she meant
to return, your grace. And all this was five days ago, and
there is no sign of my poor girl. His lordship has run off with
her to France."

"Indeed?" Léonie said. "You have good information, madame. Who told you that M. le Marquis has gone to France?
It is not known to many."

Mrs. Challoner cast a startled glance at Sophia. "I told
mamma," Sophia said sullenly.

"You interest me—oh, but very much, mademoiselle! You
thought, *en effet,* that he would go to Scotland, and he told
you that he would go to France."

"I see that your grace has guessed it!" Mrs. Challoner
said desperately. "Sophia, leave the room. I have something
of a private nature to say to her grace."

"I won't leave the room," Sophia answered rebelliously.
"You mean to make Vidal wed Mary, and it is not fair! He
loves me, me, me! Mary stole him, the mean cat, but she
shan't have him!"

"Ah, I perceive the truth!" said Léonie. "It is Miss Mary
Challoner who has abducted my son. I make her my compliments."

"It is no such thing!" broke in Mrs. Challoner. "Alas, it is true that Sophia here would have gone with my lord to France, and dreadful it is to me to have to own to it. But girls will be for ever reading romances, ma'am, as I make no doubt your grace knows. Yes, Sophia was swept off her feet by his lordship's wiles, but Mary stepped in with some scheme of her own to send my lord packing. She has saved her poor sister at the price of her own honour, ma'am!"

Léonie said thoughtfully: "It is strange, I find, that this so noble sister did not rather inform you, madame, of what mademoiselle here meant to do. You, who have reared your daughters with such strictness, could have arranged matters more easily, is it not so?"

"Indeed, and I do not know why Mary did not tell me, ma'am, but she is an odd secret girl, and will for ever be thinking she knows better than her mamma."

Léonie rose. She was smiling, but her dark eyes were bright with anger. "You do not know? Then me, I will tell you. It is plain to me that mademoiselle Mary has thought that she will become Madame la Marquise, and not her sister. As to that, we shall see. You have said to my sister that you will make one big scandal. *Vous pouvez vous éviter de la peine, madame;* it is I who will make the scandal. I do not desire that my son should have a *liaison* with your daughter, for she appears to me to be a young woman not at all *comme il faut.* I shall go to Paris at once, and I shall bring this clever Mary back to you in good time. And if you are so stupid that you cry aloud that the Marquis my son has carried off your daughter you will look even more foolish than you do now, for it will be seen that I am with M. le Marquis, and I think if I say I was with him all the time people will perhaps believe my word before that of Madame Challoner. *Que pensez-vous, madame?*"

Mrs. Challoner came to her feet in a hurry, and said loudly: "Ho, ma'am, and is that how it is to be? And do you think my poor deceived girl will have nothing to say to that fine tale? She shall declare her wrongs to the world, for I'll make her, and I'll see she is heard!"

Léonie gave a light, scornful laugh. *"Vraiment?* It is a story so silly, madame, that I think people will say *'quel tas de bêtises!'* and not at all believe you. And me I shall say only that this Mary forced herself upon my son, and I shall be believed, madame, do not doubt." She swept a curtsy,

ignored Sophia, who was gaping at her in astonishment, and
walked out of the room before Mrs. Challoner could collect
her scattered wits.

Sophia bounced out of her chair, crying: "There, mamma!
That's all your scheming has led to! Lord, I vow I could die
of laughing at you!"

Mrs. Challoner promptly boxed her ears. Sophia began at
once to cry, but her mother had gone to the window, and
was watching a liveried footman hand her grace into the
carriage. She said through her teeth: "I'm not finished yet,
Sophy, don't think it. We'll see who has the laugh, your
grace!" She turned quickly. "I'm going to make a journey,"
she said. "You'll be off to your Uncle Henry's house, Sophy,
till I come back, and see you behave yourself circumspectly!"

In the white house in Curzon Street Lady Fanny was
eagerly awaiting Léonie's return. When her grace came into
the boudoir she fairly pounced upon her, a dozen questions
tripping off her tongue. Léonie untied the strings of her
becoming hat, and threw it on the table. "Bah, *quelle vieille
guenon!*" she said. "I have frightened her a little, and I
tell you this, Fanny, I will not have Dominique ally himself
with the daughter of such a one. I go at once to France
to arrange the matter."

Lady Fanny regarded her shrewdly. "La, my dear, you're
in such a heat you'd best wait till you've cooled a little."

"I am not in a heat at all," Léonie said with great precision.
"I am of a coolness quite remarkable, and I would like to
kill that woman."

"You're in a rage, my love, don't tell me! You've forgotten
your English, which is a very sure sign, though I can't conceive why you should become so vastly French as soon as
you lose your temper."

Léonie stalked to the mantelpiece, picked up a vase from
it, and quite deliberately smashed it. Lady Fanny shrieked,
and cried out: "My precious Sèvres vase!"

Léonie looked down, conscience-stricken, at the pieces of
porcelain lying on the floor. "I do not behave like a lady,"
she said. "I did not know it was Sèvres. It was very ugly."

Fanny giggled. "Hideous, love! I've always hated it. But,
'pon rep, I thought you had learned to curb that dreadful
temper of yours! I vow you're as great a hoyden as ever you
were twenty years ago. What did that odious creature say
to make you so angry?"

Léonie said fiercely: "It is a trick, all of it, to make Dominique marry that girl. She thought she could make me afraid, but it is I who will make her afraid! Dominique shall not marry that—that—*salope!*"

"Léonie!" gasped Fanny, clapping her hands over her ears. "How dare you?"

"She is!" raged her grace. "And that mother, she is nothing but an *entremetteuse!* Me, I know very well her type! And she will be my Dominique's *belle-mère, hein?* No, and no, and no!"

Lady Fanny uncovered her ears. "Lord, my dear, don't put yourself about! Vidal won't want to marry the wench. But what of the scandal?"

"*Je m'en fiche!*" said Léonie crudely.

"And pray will Justin agree with you? My dearest love, there's been too much scandal attached to Vidal already, and you know it. I'll wager my diamond necklet that woman meant her vulgar threats. She'll create a stir, I know she will, and 'twill be monstrous disagreeable for all of us. I declare, it's too bad of Vidal! Why, if there's a word of truth in what that creature says—which, to be sure, I doubt, for I never heard such a rigmarole in my life—he did not even want the girl! And if you can think of anything in the world he did it for save to plague us I beg you will tell me!"

"John says, for revenge," Léonie answered, looking troubled. "I have a very big fear he may be right."

Lady Fanny's china-blue eyes widened. "Good God, my dear, surely even Vidal would not be such a fiend?"

Léonie had gone over to the window, but she turned quickly. "What do you mean—*even* Vidal?" she snapped.

"Oh, nothing, my dear!" said her ladyship hastily. "Not but what it would be the most dastardly thing, and I must say I am thankful my son is not of Dominic's disposition. I vow my heart positively bleeds for you, my love."

"And mine for you," said Léonie with awful politeness.

"Pray why?" demanded her ladyship, preparing for battle.

Léonie shrugged. "For a whole day I have been shut up in a coach with the so estimable John. It is enough, *mordieu!*"

Lady Fanny arose in her wrath. "I vow and declare I never met with such ingratitude!" she said. "I wish I had sent John to Avon, as I promise you I'd half a mind to."

Léonie softened instantly. "Well, I am sorry, Fanny, but

you said worse of my son than I said of yours, and you said it first."

For a moment it seemed as though her ladyship would stalk from the room, but in the end she relented, and said pacifically that she would not add to the disasters befalling the family by quarrelling with Léonie. She then demanded to be told how Léonie proposed to avert the gathering scandal.

Léonie said: "I do not know, but if it is necessary I will get that girl a husband."

"Get her a husband?" repeated Fanny, bewildered. "Who is he to be?"

"Oh, anyone!" Léonie said impatiently. "I shall think of something, because I must think of something. Perhaps Rupert will be able to help."

"Rupert!" almost snorted her ladyship. "As well ask help of my parrot! There's nothing for it, my dear; you will have to tell Avon the whole."

Léonie shook her head. "No. Monseigneur is to know nothing. I cannot bear it if there is to be more trouble between him and Dominique."

Fanny sat down limply. "I could shake you, Léonie; I vow I could! Avon will be in town again by the end of the week, and when he finds you and Rupert gone off together he'll come to me, and what, pray, am I to tell him?"

"Why, that I have indeed gone to Cousin Harriet."

"And Rupert? A likely tale!"

"I do not think that he will know whether Rupert is in London or not—or care."

"Take my word for it, child, he will know. And I'm to embroil myself in this affair, if you please! I won't do it!"

"Fanny, you will!—Dear Fanny?"

"I'm too old for these wild coils. If I do, I shall tell Avon I know nothing about you or Rupert or anyone. And you may inform Vidal from me that the next time he abducts a young female he need not come to me for aid." She got up, and began to look for the hartshorn. "If you dare to bring Rupert here I shall have an attack of the vapours." She went out, but a moment later put her head in at the door to say: "I've a mind to come with you. What do you think, my love?"

"No," said Léonie positively. "If Monseigneur finds us all gone he would think it very odd."

"Oh well!" said Fanny. "At least I should not have to face him with a mouthful of lies, which of course he will see through. However, if you are set on going with Rupert I'd as soon stay at home." She disappeared again, and Léonie picked up her hat, and once more tied it over her curls.

She took a chair to Half Moon Street, and was fortunate enough to find his lordship at home. Lord Rupert greeted her jovially. "I thought you were in Bedford, m'dear. Couldn't stand it, eh? I told you so. Devilish dull is old Vane."

"Rupert, the most dreadful thing has happened, and I want you to help me," Léonie interrupted. "It's Dominique."

Lord Rupert said testily: "Oh, plague take that boy! I thought we'd got him safe out of the country."

"We have," Léonie assured him. "But he has taken a girl with him!"

"What sort of a girl?" demanded his lordship.

"A—a hussy! A—I do not know any word bad enough!"

"Oh, that sort, eh? Well, what of it? You ain't turning pious, are you, Léonie?"

"Rupert, it is most serious. He meant to elope with the *bourgeoise*, and oh, Rupert, he has taken the wrong sister!"

Rupert stared at her blankly. "Taken the wrong sister? Well, I'll be damned!" He shook his head. "Y'know, Léonie, that boy drinks too much. If this don't beat all!"

"He wasn't drunk, *imbécile!* At least," added Léonie conscientiously, "I do not think he was."

"Must have been," said his lordship.

"I shall have to explain it all to you." Léonie sighed.

At the end of her explanation his lordship gave it as his opinion that his nephew had gone stark, staring mad. "Does Avon know?" he asked.

"No, no, not a word! He must not, you understand, and that is why we are going to France at once."

His lordship regarded her with profound suspicion. "Who's going to France?"

"But you and I, of course!" Léonie replied.

"No, I'm not," stated Rupert flatly. "Not to meddle in Vidal's affairs. I'll see him damned first, saving your presence."

"You must," Léonie said, shocked. "Monseigneur would not at all like me to go alone."

"I won't," said Rupert. "Now, don't start to argue, Léonie, for God's sake! The last time I went to France with you I got a bullet in my shoulder."

"I find you ridiculous," Léonie said severely. "Who is to shoot bullets at you now?"

"If it comes to that, I wouldn't put it above Vidal, if I go meddling in his concerns. I tell you I won't have a hand in it."

"Very well," Léonie said, and walked to the door.

Rupert watched her uneasily. "What are you going to do?" he asked.

"I am going to France," said Léonie.

His lordship requested her to have sense; she looked woodenly at him. He pointed out to her the extreme folly of her behaviour; she yawned, and opened the door. His lordship swore roundly and capitulated. He was rewarded by a beaming smile.

"You are *very* kind to me, Rupert," her grace said enthusiastically. "We will go at once, do you not think? For I am late already, five days."

"If you're five days behind that young devil you're too late altogether, m'dear," said his lordship sensibly. "Lord, Avon will murder me for this!"

"Of course he will not murder you!" said Léonie. "He will not know anything about it. When shall we start?"

"When I've seen my bankers. I'll do that in the morning, and I only hope the fellows don't take it into their heads I'm flying the country. We can catch the night packet from Dover, but don't bring a mountain of baggage, Léonie, if you want to travel fast."

The Duchess took him at his word, and when his coach arrived in Curzon Street next morning she had only one band-box to be put into it. "You can't travel like that!" he protested. "And ain't you taking your abigail along too?"

She rejected the suggestion with scorn, and pointed an accusing finger at the baggage already piled on the roof of the coach. After a lively dispute, in which Lady Fanny and her son joined, two of Lord Rupert's trunks were left behind in his sister's charge. An errand-boy, two loiterers, and a cook-girl were interested spectators of the start, and Mr. Marling delivered a lecture, which no one paid any attention to, on the amount of baggage he himself considered necessary for a gentleman to take to Paris.

When the coach at last moved forward Lady Fanny announced that she had the migraine, and went off upstairs, leaving Mr. Marling to order the disposal of the two trunks left on the pavement.

She expected to see his grace of Avon within three days. She saw him within two, greatly to her dismay. When his

name was announced she was reclining on a couch in her
withdrawing-room, her hands encased in chicken-skin gloves
(for an east wind had slightly chapped their soft whiteness),
yawning over the pages of *The Inflexible Captive*. She gave
a perceptible start, but recovered herself in an instant, and
greeted his grace with apparent delight.

"La, Justin, is it you indeed? I'm vastly glad to see you.
Only look at this book that John has given me! It is writ by
by that Bluestocking, Mrs. More. I find it amazingly dull, do
not you?"

His grace came over to the fire, and stood looking enigmatically down at her. "Amazingly, my dear Fanny. Do I
see you in your customary good health?"

Lady Fanny promptly launched into a recital of the many
ailments that afflicted her. It was a fruitful topic, and his
grace evinced enough polite interest to encourage her to
enlarge on it. She enlarged for twenty minutes and dis-
coursed on Dr. Cocchi's book, *The Pythagorean Diet, or
Vegetables only conducive to the Preservation of Health and
the Cure of Diseases*. His grace was urbanity itself. Lady
Fanny quaked inwardly, and began to falter in her account
of her indisposition. A short pause ensued. His grace took
snuff, and as he shut his elegant gold box said languidly: "I
understand, my dear Fanny, that there is to be a marriage
in our family."

Lady Fanny started upright on the couch. "A—a marriage?" she stammered. "Why—why—what do you mean,
Justin?"

His grace's brows rose a little; she thought there was a
gleam of malice in his eyes. "Doubtless I have been misinformed. I was under the impression that my niece is about
to espouse a gentleman of the name of Comyn."

"Oh!" gasped her ladyship, quite faint with relief. She
sank back upon her cushions. "Of course she'll do no such
thing, Justin. Why, have you forgot that I've sent her to
Paris to be out of the unfortunate young man's way?"

"On the contrary, I understood that you sent her there
to prevent a *mésalliance*."

"Well, but—but so it is!" said Fanny, taken aback.

His grace flicked a speck of snuff from his sleeve. "I should
inform you, my dear sister, that the marriage has my support."

Lady Fanny felt for her vinaigrette. "But I won't have it!

He's a nobody, Justin! I intend her to make a far better match. I made sure you would dislike it excessively. Pray, what in the world has come over you? You've never set eyes on young Comyn."

"I hesitate to contradict you, Fanny," said his grace politely, "but you will perhaps allow me to be not yet in my dotage. I have met and approved Mr. Comyn. He seemed to be a young gentleman of considerable presence of mind. I am only surprised that he should wish to ally himself with my niece."

Lady Fanny took a sniff at her salts, and regained strength enough to say: "I suppose you have gone mad, Justin. Let me tell you that I have every hope that Juliana will wed Bertrand de Saint-Vire."

His grace smiled. "I fear, my dear Fanny, that you are doomed to disappointment."

"I don't know what you mean, and I'm sure I don't desire to!" said her ladyship pettishly. "I might have guessed you would be monstrous disagreeable! And if you are come home early from Newmarket only to encourage Juliana in her waywardness I think it quite abominable of you."

"Pray calm yourself, Fanny; I am about to relieve you of my presence. You will no doubt be glad to learn that I am leaving London to-night."

Lady Fanny eyed him in considerable trepidation. "Oh indeed, Justin? May I ask where you propose going?"

"Certainly," replied his grace blandly. "But surely you have guessed?"

Lady Fanny stammered: "No—yes—pray, how should I guess? Where are you going?"

His grace moved towards the door. His eyes mocked her. "But to Cousin Harriet, my dear. Where else should I go?" He bowed, while she stared at him in mingled horror and suspicion, and before she had time to collect her wits, the door had closed behind him.

❧ Chapter XII ❧

WHEN Miss Marling heard that her dearest Mary was intending to become a governess she had the wit to keep her dismay to herself. It did not take the lively damsel long to discover the whole state of Mary's mind, and having discovered it she became instantly resolved on Miss Challoner's marriage to the Marquis. She lent a kind but disbelieving ear to Mary's steadfast disavowal of the tender passion, and when asked to aid her friend in the search for a genteel family, said frankly that she knew of none. Mary, with only a few borrowed guineas in her pocket, found that she was as much in Vidal's power as she had ever been, and since she feared that to take Tante Elisabeth into her confidence would lead only to her instant expulsion from the house, she threw herself on Juliana's mercy, and begged her to save her from Vidal. To be cast to the street in a foreign city was a fate from which even the redoubtable Miss Challoner shrank. She had a feeling that she was fighting in the last ditch, and when her appeal to Juliana was unavailing, there seemed to be no hope left of holding his lordship at arm's length.

Juliana, with a worldly wisdom learned no doubt from her mamma, pointed out the advantages of the match. She had no doubt, she said, that Vidal would make an odious husband, but Mary would be amazingly stupid not to take him, for more than half the dowagers in London wanted him for their own daughters.

Mary said unhappily: "I've begged you—I've prayed you to help me escape from this net. Do you care for me so little?"

"I love you so much I'm quite delighted to think you are to be my cousin," responded Miss Marling. She embraced Mary warmly. "Truly, my dear, I daren't smuggle you out of the way. I've promised Vidal I won't, and even if I did he would find you in a trice. What shall you wear at the ball to-night?"

"I don't go," Mary said in a flat voice.

"Good gracious, Mary, why not?"

"I am in your cousin's house under false pretences," Mary said bitterly, "she would not take me to these parties if she knew the truth."

"Well, she don't know it," replied Juliana. "Do come, my dear: Vidal will be there."

"I have no desire to meet his lordship," said Mary, and would say no more.

Mme. de Charbonne, the most easy-going of dames, made no more objection to Mary's remaining at home than she had made to her sudden arrival two days before. Mary had told her, in desperation, that she was under the necessity of earning a living for herself, and it was plain that madame—who upon hearing this news had regarded her young guest as a kind of *rara avis*—considered that balls must certainly be out of place for indigent young females. Upon being asked if she could recommend Miss Challoner to a suitable family she had said vaguely that she would bear it in mind, which did not sound particularly hopeful.

Having seen Juliana arrayed for her party in a rose-pink taffeta gown trimmed with chenille silver and spread over immense elbow-hoops; her hair dressed in her favourite *Gorgonne* style by no less a personage than M. le Gros himself; her person scented with cassia, Miss Challoner bade her farewell and prepared to spend a quiet evening in one of the smaller salons. She intended to apply herself seriously to the problem of escape, but in this she was frustrated by the appearance, not half an hour after Madame de Charbonne's and Juliana's departure, of Mr. Frederick Comyn.

She had already met Mr. Comyn once since their unfortunate encounter at Dieppe, and she supposed that he was apprised of her situation. His manner was extremely respectful, and she thought that she could detect a certain grave sympathy in his gaze.

When the lackey ushered him into the salon she rose, and curtsied to him, and perceived as she did so that his firm mouth was rather tightly compressed. He bowed to her, and said, more as a statement than a question: "You are alone, ma'am."

"Why yes," she answered. "Were you not informed at the door, sir, that Miss—that Madame is gone out to-night?"

Mr. Comyn said with a touch of gloom: "Your first premise was correct, ma'am. It is not Madame de Charbonne that I came hoping to see, but Miss Marling. I was indeed informed that she was gone out, but I ventured to inquire for yourself, ma'am, believing that you would be able to oblige me by divulging Miss Marling's present whereabouts."

Miss Challoner begged him to be seated. She had a shrewd notion that all was not entirely well between Miss Marling and her swain. Certain veiled remarks and flighty head-tossings on the part of Juliana had induced her to suppose that Mr. Comyn had somehow affronted his lady. She now perceived that Mr. Comyn wore the air of a man goaded beyond the limits of forbearance. She would have liked to give him some good advice on the proper way of treating Miss Marling, but feeling that their intimacy was not far enough advanced to permit of this, she merely replied: "Certainly, sir. Miss Marling is gone to a ball at the house of—I think—Madame de Saint-Vire."

She instantly realized from his expression that her frankness was ill-timed. A crease appeared between his brows; there was a distinct grimness in his face, which Miss Challoner privately thought became him rather well. "Indeed, ma'am?" he said levelly. "It is as I suspected, then. I'm obliged to you."

He seemed to be on the point of departure, but Miss Challoner ventured to stay him. "Your pardon, Mr. Comyn, but I think you are put out?"

He gave a short laugh. "Not at all, ma'am. I apprehend that I am merely unaccustomed to the manners obtaining in the Polite World."

"Will you not take me a little way into your confidence, sir?" Mary said gently. "Juliana is my friend, and I believe I may say I do in part understand her. If I could be of assistance to you—but I do not wish to appear vulgarly intrusive."

Mr. Comyn hesitated, but the kindness in Miss Challoner's face induced him to come back into the room, and sit down on a chair beside her. "You are very good, ma'am. I believe it is not unknown to you that there exists between Miss

Marling and myself a contract to wed, which, though un-happily a secret from the world, I at least have regarded as binding."

"Yes, sir, I know, and I wish you very happy," said Mary.

"Thank you, ma'am. Before I set foot in this town—a circumstance I am fast coming to regret—I should have received your extremely obliging good wishes with a gratitude unalloyed by misgiving. Now——" He stopped, and Miss Challoner watched the meticulous gentleman merge into an angry and scowling young man. "I can only suppose, ma'am, that Miss Marling has, upon reflection, perceived the force of her parent's arguments, and decided to bestow her hand elsewhere."

"No, sir, that I am sure she has not," Mary said.

He looked at her in a hurt way that touched her. "When I tell you, ma'am, that from the moment of my arrival in Paris Miss Marling has persistently encouraged the advances of a certain French gentleman not unconnected with her family, and has upon every occasion preferred his company to mine, you will hardly assure me that her affections are unchanged."

"But I do, sir," Mary said earnestly. "I do not know how she may have behaved to you, but you must bear in mind that she is as wilful as she is pretty, and delights, perhaps unwisely, in provoking people with her teasing ways. The gentleman you refer to is, I take it, the Vicomte de Valmé. I believe you have no need to feel alarm, Mr. Comyn. The Vicomte is no doubt entertaining, and his address is insinuating. But he is nothing but a rattle, when all is said, and I do not think for an instant that Juliana cares a fig for him."

"You know the Vicomte, ma'am?" said Mr. Comyn quick-ly.

"I have met him, sir."

Mr. Comyn said in a repressed voice: "You have been an inmate of this house for two days, ma'am, and I understand from Juliana that you do not go out. I infer therefore that you have met the Vicomte here—within the past forty-eight hours."

Miss Challoner said cautiously: "And if I have, sir, what is there in that to annoy you?"

"Only," replied Mr. Comyn sharply, "that Juliana denied that de Valmé had visited her here."

Miss Challoner, feeling very guilty, could think of nothing

to say. Mr. Comyn, rather pale about the mouth, said bitingly: "It is all of a piece. I begged Juliana, if she cared for me, not to be present to-night at a ball given by the Vicomte's parents. It was a test of her affection which I, foolishly, believed would not be too severe. I was wrong, ma'am. Juliana has been playing with me—I had almost said flirting with me."

Miss Challoner, feeling that it was time someone took the young couple in hand, proceeded to give Mr. Comyn her good advice on the management of a spoiled beauty. She tried to make him understand—but with indifferent success, since she did not understand it herself—that Juliana was so high-spirited that a breath of opposition induced her to behave outrageously. She told Mr. Comyn that to reproach Juliana, or to remonstrate with her was to drive her into her naughtiest mood. "She is romantic, Mr. Comyn, and if you desire to win her you should let her see that you are a man who will not brook her trifling. Juliana would love you to run off with her by force, but when you are gentle, sir, and respectful, she becomes impatient."

"You suggest, in fact, ma'am, that I should abduct Miss Marling? I fear I am quite unlearned in such ways. Her cousin, the Marquis of Vidal, would no doubt oblige her."

Miss Challoner coloured, and looked away. Mr. Comyn, realizing what he had said, coloured too, and begged her pardon. "I did not desire to elope with her, even were she willing," he continued hurriedly. "But she deemed it our best course, and when I was urged to it by a member of her family, I allowed my scruples to be overruled, and came to Paris with the express intention of arranging a secret marriage."

"Well, arrange it, sir," Miss Challoner advised him.

"I had almost done so, ma'am. I may say that I bear in my pocket at this moment the direction of an English divine at present travelling through France on his way to Italy. I came here to-night expecting to see Juliana, and to tell her that we have nothing more to wait for. And I find that she has gone, in defiance of my expressed wish, to a ball where the chief—the sole attraction is the Vicomte de Valmé. Madam, I can only designate such conduct as heartless in the extreme."

Miss Challoner paid very little heed to the last part of this speech, but said rather breathlessly: "You know of an English divine? Oh pray, sir, have you told my Lord Vidal?"

"No, ma'am, for——"

"Then do not!" Mary said, laying her hand on his. "Will you promise me that you will not tell him?"

"Madam, I regret infinitely, but you are under a misapprehension. It was Lord Vidal who told me."

Mary's hand fell again to her side. "When did he tell you?"

"This afternoon, ma'am. He was good enough, at the same time, to present me with a card for this ball at the Hôtel Saint-Vire. Apparently he knows his cousin better than I do. I never dreamed that she would go."

"This afternoon. . . . Oh, I hoped he would not be able to find a Protestant to marry us!" Mary exclaimed unguardedly. "What shall I do? What in the world shall I do?"

Mr. Comyn regarded her curiously. "Do I understand, ma'am, that a marriage with Lord Vidal is not your desire?"

She shook her head. "It is not, sir. I am aware that you must think my conduct—my compromising situation——" She got up, averting her face.

Mr. Comyn also got up. He possessed himself of both her hands, and held them in a comforting clasp. "Believe me, Miss Challoner, I understand your feelings exactly. I have nothing but the deepest sympathy for you, and if I can serve you in any way I shall count it an honour."

Miss Challoner's fingers returned the pressure of his. She tried to smile. "You are very kind, sir. I—I thank you."

The click of the door made her snatch her hands away. She turned, startled, and met the smouldering gaze of my Lord Vidal.

His lordship was standing on the threshold, and it was plain that he had seen Mary break loose from Mr. Comyn's hold. His hand was resting suggestively on the hilt of his light dress-sword, and his eyes held a distinct menace. He was in full ball dress, all purple and gold lacing, with a quantity of fine lace at his wrists and throat.

To her chagrin Miss Challoner felt a blush steal up into her cheeks. She said with less than her usual composure: "I thought you had gone to the Hôtel Saint-Vire, sir."

"So I infer, ma'am," said his lordship with something of a snap. "I trust I don't intrude?"

He was looking at Mr. Comyn in a way that invited challenge. Mary pulled herself together and said quietly: "Not

in the least, sir. Mr. Comyn is on the point of departure."
She held out her hand to this young man as she spoke, and
added: "You should use your card for the ball, sir. Pray do!"

He bowed, and kissed her fingers. "Thank you, ma'am.
But I should be very glad to remain if you feel yourself to
be at all in need of company."

The meaning of this was quite plain. My lord strolled
suggestively into the middle of the room, but before he could
speak Miss Challoner said quickly: "You are very kind, sir,
but I am shortly going to retire. Let me wish you good night—
and good fortune."

Mr. Comyn bowed again, favoured his lordship with a
slight inclination of the head, and went out.

The Marquis watched him frowningly till he was out of
the room. Then he turned to Miss Challoner. "You're on
terms of intimacy with Comyn, are you?"

"No," replied Mary. "Hardly that, my lord."

He came up to her, and gripped her by the shoulders. "If
you don't want to see a hole shot through that damned soft-
spoken fellow you'd best keep your hands out of his. Do
you understand, my girl?"

"Perfectly," said Miss Challoner. "You'll allow me to say
that I find you absurd, my lord. Only jealousy could inspire
you with this ill-placed wrath, and where there is no love
there cannot be jealousy."

He let her go. "I know how to guard my own."

"I am not yours, sir."

"You will very soon be. Sit down. Why are you not at the
ball?"

"I had no inclination for it, sir. I might ask, why are not
you?"

"Not finding you there, I came here," he replied.

"I am indeed flattered," said Miss Challoner.

He laughed. "It's all I went for, my dear, I assure you. Why
was that fellow holding your hands?"

"For comfort," said Miss Challoner desolately.

He held out his own. "Give them to me."

Miss Challoner shook her head. There was a curious lump
in her throat that made speech impossible.

"Oh, very well, ma'am, if you prefer the attentions of
Frederick Comyn!" said the Marquis in a hard voice. "Be
good enough to listen to what I have to say. I have discovered, through Carruthers, of the Ambassador's suite, that

there is a divine, lately passed through Paris, bear-leading some sprig of the nobility. They are bound for Italy by easy stages, and at this present are to be found in Dijon, where it appears they are making a stay of two weeks. He's the man to do our business for us. I am about to abduct you for the second and last time, Miss Challoner." She made no reply. His eyes reached her face. "Well, have you nothing to say?"

"I have said it all so many times, my lord."

He turned away impatiently. "Make the best of me, ma'am; you dislike me cordially, no doubt. I'll admit you have reason. But you may know, if it interests you, that I am offering what I have never offered to any woman before."

"You offer it because you feel you must," said Mary in a low voice. "And I thank you—but I refuse your offer."

"Nevertheless, ma'am, you'll start with me for Dijon to-morrow."

She raised her eyes to his face. "You cannot wrest me by force from this house, my lord."

"Can't I?" he said. His lip curled. "We shall see. Don't try to escape me. I should run you to earth within a day, and if you put me to that trouble you might find my temper unpleasant." He walked to the door. "I have the honour to bid you good night," he said curtly, and went out.

∞§ Chapter XIII §∞

MEANWHILE, to anyone who knew her, Miss Marling's reckless air of gaiety that night would have betokened an inward disquiet. She seemed to be in the highest spirits, but her eyes were restless, always searching the fashionable throng.

Paris had gone to Miss Marling's head, and the attentions of such a known connoisseur as the Vicomte de Valmé could not but flatter her. The Vicomte protested that his heart was under her feet. She did not entirely believe this, but a diet of admiration and compliments spoiled her for the criticisms of Mr. Comyn. When he first appeared at her cousin's house she had tumbled headlong into his arms, but this first unaffected rapture suffered a check. She proceeded to pour into her Frederick's ears a recital of all her pleasures and triumphs. He listened in silence, and at the end said gravely that although he could not but be glad that she had found amusement, he had not thought that she would be so extremely gay and happy away from him.

Partly because it was the fashion to be coquettish, partly from a feeling of guilt, Juliana had answered in an arch, provocative way that did not captivate Mr. Comyn in the least. Bertrand de Saint-Vire would have known just what to say. Mr. Comyn, unskilled in the art of flirtation, said that Paris had not improved his Juliana.

They quarrelled, but made it up at once. But it was an ill beginning.

Miss Marling made Mr. Comyn known to her new friends, amongst them the Vicomte de Valmé. Mr. Comyn, with a lamentable lack of tact, spoke disparagingly of the Vicomte,

154

whom he found insupportable. Truth to tell, the Vicomte, who was well aware of Mr. Comyn's pretensions, was impelled by an innate love of mischief to flirt outrageously with Juliana under the very nose of her stiff and disapproving lover. Juliana, anxious to awake a spark of jealousy in what at that moment seemed to her an unresponsive heart, encouraged him. All she wanted was to be treated to a display of ruthless and possessive manhood. If Mr. Comyn, later, had seized her in his arms in a decently romantic fashion there would have been an end to the Vicomte's flirtation. But Mr. Comyn was deeply hurt, and he did not recognize in these signs a perverted expression of his Juliana's love for him. He was young, and he handled the affair very ill. He was forbearing where he should have been violent, and found fault when he should have made love. Miss Marling determined to teach him a lesson.

It was this laudable resolve that took her to the Hôtel Saint-Vire. Mr. Comyn should learn that it was unwise to lecture and criticize Miss Marling. But because under her airs and graces she was really very much in love with him, she induced her cousin to provide him with a card for the ball.

The Vicomte de Valmé was her partner for the two first dances, and when they came to an end he took her off to a convenient alcove, and made intoxicating love to her. He was interrupted in this agreeable task by the sudden appearance of Vidal, who said unamiably: "Give me leave, Bertrand: I want a word with Juliana."

The Vicomte flung up his hands. "But I find you quite abominable, Dominique! Always you want words with Juliana! *J'y suis, j'y reste.* Have you yet slain me this Frederick?"

"Vidal, did you give Frederick a card for the ball?" Miss Marling asked anxiously.

"I gave it him, but I don't think he'll use it."

"*A la bonne heure!*" said the irrepressible Vicomte. He laughed impudently up at the Marquis. "For what do you wait, *mon cher?* You are infinitely *de trop.*"

"I await your departure—but not for long," said his lordship.

The Vicomte gave an exaggerated start. "A threat, Juliana! I scent it unerringly. He will presently shoot me: I am as good as dead, but if you give me the roses you wear at your breast I shall die happy."

Vidal's eye gleamed. "Will you go as happily through that window?" he inquired.

"By no means!" said the Vicomte promptly. He rose, and kissed Miss Marling's hand. "I surrender to *force majeure,* dearest Juliana. He has no *finesse,* our cousin. He will undoubtedly throw me out of the window if I linger."

"Well, I don't think it very brave of you to give way to him," said Miss Marling candidly.

"But, my adored one, observe his size!" implored the Vicomte. "He would be very rough with me, and spoil my so elegant coat. I go, Vidal, I go!"

Miss Marling waved an airy farewell, and turned to her cousin. "I find him excessively amusing, you know," she confided.

"I see you do," said Vidal. "Where is Mary Challoner?"

Miss Marling opened her eyes very wide. "Don't you like him, Vidal? I thought he was a friend of yours."

"He is," replied the Marquis.

"Well, it is very odd of you to threaten to throw your friends out of the window, I must say," remarked Juliana.

He smiled. "Not at all. It is only my friends that I would throw out of the window."

"Dear me!" said Juliana, finding the male sex incomprehensible.

His lordship picked up her fan, a delicate Cabriolet with ivory sticks and guards, pierced and gilt, and rapped her knuckles with it. "Attend to me, Ju. Do you mean to have Comyn, or not?"

"Good gracious, what in the world do you mean?" exclaimed Juliana.

"Answer, chit."

"You know I do. But I don't at all understand why——"

"Then you'd best stop flirting with Bertrand."

Miss Marling flushed. "Oh, I don't—flirt!"

"Don't you?" jibed his lordship. "I beg your pardon. But whatever it is that you do, stop. That's a kind cousinly warning."

She tilted her chin. "I shall do as I please, thank you, Vidal, and I'll not be lectured and scolded by either of you."

"Just as you like, Ju. Don't blame me when you lose your Frederick."

She looked startled. "I shan't lose him!"

"You're a fool, Ju. What's the game you're playing? Trying to make him jealous, eh? It won't work."

"How do you know it won't?" demanded Miss Marling, stung.

He looked down at her with lazy affection. "You've chosen the wrong man for these tricks of yours. What is it you want?"

She began to pleat the stiff silk of her gown. "I do love him," she said. "I do, Vidal!"

"Well?"

"If only he would—be a little more like you!" she said in a rush.

"Good God!" said the Marquis, amused. "Why the devil should he be?"

"I don't mean that I want him to be really like you," explained Miss Marling. "It's merely that—oh, I can't tell! But supposing you loved me, Dominic, and I—well, *flirted*, if you must use that horrid word—with another man: what would you do?"

"Kill him," said the Marquis flippantly.

She shook his arm. "You don't mean it, but I think perhaps you would. Vidal, you'd not let another man steal the lady you loved, would you? Do answer soberly!"

The smile still lingered on his lips, but she saw his teeth shut hard. "Soberly, Ju, I would not."

"What would you do?" inquired Miss Marling, momentarily diverted by curiosity.

His lordship was silent for a minute, and the smile faded, leaving his face strangely harsh. A tiny snap sounded under his fingers. He glanced down at them, and the grim look left his face. "I've spoiled your fan, Ju," he said, and gave it her back. Two of the sticks were broken at the shoulder. "I'll give you another."

Juliana was looking at him in considerable awe. "You haven't answered me," she said, with an uncertain laugh.

"What I might do is—happily for you—not in the least like what Comyn will do," he replied.

"No," she said sadly. "But can you understand that I wish it were?"

"My deluded child, one taste of my lamentable temper would send you flying into your Frederick's arms," said the Marquis, and rose. "Where's Mary Challoner?"

"She wouldn't come."

"Why not?"

"To say truth, Vidal, I believe she did not desire to meet you."

"Fiend seize her!" said his lordship unemotionally, and went off.

Miss Marling emerged from her alcove to find him gone. When he did not reappear she realized that he had left the ball, and had no difficulty in guessing his present whereabouts.

Nearly an hour later Mr. Comyn came up the wide stairway. His arrival was most inopportune, for he came in excellent time to see Miss Marling bestow one of her pink roses on the ecstatic Vicomte de Valmé.

She was standing just outside the ballroom, and she did not immediately perceive Mr. Comyn. The Vicomte took the rose reverently, and pressed it to his lips. He then bestowed it carefully inside his coat, and informed Miss Marling that it caused his heart to beat more strongly.

Miss Marling laughed at him, and at the same moment caught sight of Mr. Comyn. She had never seen so stern an expression on his face, and she was secretly rather frightened. She made the grave mistake of trying to brazen it out, and greeted him with a careless nod. "I vow I had quite given you up, sir!" she said.

"Yes?" said Mr. Comyn, icily civil. "Pray will you spare me five minutes alone, ma'am?"

Juliana gave a little shrug, but she dismissed the Vicomte. She showed Mr. Comyn a mutinous face, and said with a coldness that matched his: "Well, sir?"

"It does not seem to me to be well at all, Juliana. You could not bring yourself to forgo one ball to please me."

"Pray do not be absurd, Frederick!" she said sharply. "Why should I forgo it?"

"Merely because I begged you to, ma'am. Had you loved me——"

She was jerking her handkerchief between her fingers. "You expect a deal too much of me."

"Is it too much, then, to expect that you would prefer an evening spent in my company to one here?"

"Yes, it is!" Juliana answered. "Why should I prefer to be scolded by you? For that is all you do, Frederick; you know it is!"

"If my remonstrances seem to you to be in the nature of scolding——"

"Why must you remonstrate with me? I vow if that is how

you mean to treat me when we are married I would rather remain single."

Mr. Comyn grew paler. "Tell me in plain words, if you please, do you mean that?"

Juliana turned her face away. "Oh, well! I'm sure I don't want to quarrel with you, only every time you see me you behave in this disagreeable fashion as though I had no right to be at parties but must be for ever thinking of you. You think because you are used to live buried in the country I must be as dull as you are, but I have been bred very different, sir, I'll have you know."

"It is unnecessary to tell me that, ma'am, believe me. You have been bred to think of nothing but your pleasure."

"Indeed!" said Miss Marling, with rising colour. "Pray do not mince matters, sir! Inform me that I am selfish. I expect no less."

"If I think so, ma'am, you have no one but yourself to blame," said Mr. Comyn, deliberately.

Juliana's lip trembled. "Let me tell you that there are others who do not think so at all!"

"I am aware," bowed Mr. Comyn.

"I suppose you are jealous, and that is the whole truth!" cried Juliana.

"And if I am, have I no cause?"

"If you think I care for someone else I wonder that you don't try to win me back," said Miss Marling, stealing a look at him under her lashes.

"Then you have very little understanding of my character, ma'am. I do not desire a wife who could give me cause for jealousy."

"You need not have one, sir," said Miss Marling, her eyes very bright.

There was a short silence. Then Mr. Comyn said, holding himself very erect: "I take your meaning, ma'am. I hope you will not live to regret this night's work."

Juliana gave a defiant laugh. "Regret it? Lord, why should I? You need not think you are the only gentleman who has done me the honour to solicit my hand in marriage."

"You have played fast and loose with my affections, ma'am. I could laugh at myself for having been so taken in. To be sure, I should have known what to expect from a member of your family."

By this time each was in a royal rage. Juliana flashed back

at him: "How dare you sneer at my family? 'Pon rep, it is the greatest piece of impudence ever I heard! Perhaps you are not aware that my family consider you a Nobody?"

Mr. Comyn managed to keep his voice very level. "You are wrong, ma'am: I am well aware of it. But I was not aware until this moment that you would be guilty of the vulgarity of boasting of your noble connections. Allow me to point out to you that your manners would not be tolerated in my family."

"Your horrid family will not be called upon to tolerate me!" Juliana replied, quivering with anger. "I cannot conceive how I could have been fool enough to fancy myself in love with you. Faith, I believe I pitied you, and mistook that for love. When I think what a *mésalliance* I have escaped, I vow I find myself shuddering!"

"You should thank God, as I do, ma'am, that you have been saved from an alliance that could only end in the lasting misery of us both. I beg leave to bid you farewell, and I trust, ma'am, that you will be fortunate enough to be solicited in marriage next time by a man who will be blind to the folly and conceit of your nature." With which parting shot Mr. Comyn executed a low bow, and went downstairs without one backward look.

Rejecting the lackey's offer to summon a chair, he left the Hôtel Saint-Vire, and strode off down the street in the direction of his own lodging. He had not covered more than half the distance, when all at once he seemed to change his mind, and retraced his steps till he came to a side road. He turned down this, traversed a broad *place* and arrived presently, and for the second time that evening, at the Hôtel Charbonne.

The lackey who opened the door to him had ushered the Marquis of Vidal out not twenty minutes earlier, and his well-trained countenance betrayed surprise. Upon being asked if Miss Challoner were still up, he said cautiously that he would inquire, and left Mr. Comyn (whom he began to suspect of clandestine intentions) to kick his heels in the hall.

Miss Challoner, who had been sitting in a brown study, by the fire, started when the servant came in, and glanced at the clock. The hands pointed to a quarter past midnight.

"The Englishman who was here first to-night, mademoiselle, is here again," announced the lackey severely.

"Mr. Comyn?" she asked, surprised.

"Yes, mademoiselle."

Wondering very much what could have happened to bring

him back, Miss Challoner requested the man to admit him.
The lackey withdrew, and said later to his colleagues downstairs that the customs of English demoiselles were enough
to shock a decent Frenchman.

Meanwhile Mr. Frederick Comyn stood once more before
Miss Challoner, and said with less than his usual precision:
"I beg pardon, ma'am, to intrude upon you at this hour, but
I have a proposal to make to you."

"A proposal to make to me?" repeated Mary.

"Yes, ma'am. Earlier this evening I informed you that if it
lay within my power to serve you I should count myself
honoured."

"Oh, have you found a way of escape for me?" Mary said
eagerly. "Is that what you mean? I would welcome any way!"

"I am glad to hear you say as much, ma'am, for I fear that
what I have to propose to you will take you by surprise, and
even, perhaps, be repugnant to you." He paused, and she
noticed how hard his eyes were. "Miss Challoner, in touching
upon the extreme delicacy of your situation I do not desire,
believe me, to offend you. But your story is known to me; you
yourself have divulged as much to me as my Lord Vidal. Your
plight is desperate indeed, and while I can readily understand
your reluctance to wed his lordship, I am bound to hold with
him that nothing save marriage can extricate you from a
predicament that must necessarily blacken—though unjustly
—your fair name. Madam, I humbly beg to offer you my
hand in marriage."

Miss Challoner, who had listened to this amazing speech
with an expression of frank bewilderment on her face, recoiled. "Good gracious, sir, have you gone mad?" she cried.

"No, ma'am. Mad I have been for the past weeks, but I
am now in the fullest possession of my faculties."

Her suspicion that he had been drinking gave place to a
more exact comprehension of the true state of affairs. "But,
Mr. Comyn, you are plighted to Juliana Marling," she said.

He replied very bitterly: "I am happy to be able to inform
you, ma'am, that Miss Marling and I have cut the knot of
what each of us has been brought to regard as our en-
tanglement."

"Oh!" said Mary in distress. "Have you quarrelled with
Juliana, then? Dear sir, I do not know what has passed
between you, but if Juliana is to blame she will be sorry

soon enough. Go back to her, Mr. Comyn, and you will see that I am right."

"You mistake, ma'am," he replied curtly. "I have not the smallest desire to return to Miss Marling. Pray do not imagine that I am come to you in a fit of pique. I have for a week past realized the unwisdom of our betrothal. Miss Marling's conduct is not what I wish for in my wife, and her decision to release me from my obligations I can only regard as the greatest favour she has ever bestowed upon me."

Miss Challoner turned quite pale at this awful pronouncement, and sat weakly down on the couch. "But this is dreadful, sir!" she said. "You are speaking in anger, in a way that you will regret when you have had time to reflect."

"Madam, I speak not from anger but from infinite relief. Whether you choose to accept of my offer or not my betrothal to Miss Marling is at an end. I shall not conceal from you that I fancied myself to be much in love with her; nor shall I insult your intelligence by pretending an ardour for yourself which I can naturally have had no time to acquire. If you will be content with my respect and deep regard, ma'am, I shall count myself fortunate to have secured the hand of one whose character and conduct command my sincere admiration."

"But it is impossible!" Mary said, still feeling dazed. "Surely, surely all cannot be at an end between you and Juliana?"

"Irrevocably, ma'am!"

"Oh, I am sorry!" Mary said pitifully. "As for your offer, indeed I thank you, but how should we two wed without love, or even acquaintance?"

He said seriously: "At any other time, ma'am, such haste would be strange indeed. But your situation being what it is, you are bound to seek refuge in wedlock with all possible speed. Ma'am, allow me to speak with a plainness you may deem impertinent; I think you, as well as I, come to this marriage with a bruised heart. Forgive me, Miss Challoner, but having watched you I could not but suspect that you are not indifferent to my Lord Vidal. I do not inquire what are the reasons that induce you to refuse his suit; I say only, each of us is disappointed: let us endeavour, together, to heal our separate hurts."

She covered her face with her hands. She was so taken by surprise that her brain reeled. Here indeed was the answer

to her prayer, yet all she could say was: "Please leave me.
I must think, sir; I cannot answer you now. I know that I
ought to refuse your offer, but such is the hopelessness of my
position that I dare not even do that without a pause for calm
reflection. I must see Juliana; I can scarcely believe that all
is indeed as you say."

He picked up his hat at once. "I will withdraw, ma'am.
Pray think well over what I have said. I shall remain at my
present lodging until noon to-morrow, then, if I do not hear
from you, I shall depart from Paris. Permit me to wish you
good night." He bowed, and left the room, and after a few
moments Miss Challoner rose, and went slowly up to her
bedchamber.

She heard her hostess and Miss Marling come in an hour
later, and presently got up out of her bed, and slipped on a
dressing-gown, and went to scratch softly on Juliana's door.

Juliana called to her to come in. A sleepy tirewoman was
undressing her, and closely as she scrutinized the vivid little
face Mary could perceive nothing in it but a natural weariness.

"Oh, is it you, Mary?" Juliana said. "You should have
come; it was vastly entertaining, I do assure you." She began
to chatter of the people she had met, and the dresses she had
seen. Her eyes were bright and hard, her good spirits perhaps
rather feverish, but she deceived her friend. She sent the
abigail to bed when her dress was safely hung in the wardrobe, her jewels locked up, and her hair brushed free of
powder, and Mary ventured to ask whether Mr. Comyn had
been at the ball.

Juliana jumped into bed, saying: "Oh, don't speak to me
of that man! I cannot conceive how I was ever fool enough
to fancy myself in love with him. 'Tis all over between us; you
cannot imagine how glad I am!"

Mary looked at her worriedly. "But, Juliana, you did love
him—you do still!"

"I?" Miss Marling gave a scornful laugh. "Lord, how
solemn you are, my dear! I thought it would be famous good
fun to let him think I'd elope with him, but if you must know,
I never meant to marry him at all." She shot a quick look at
Miss Challoner's grave face. "I shall marry Bertrand de
Saint-Vire," she said, to clinch the matter.

This announcement startled Miss Challoner almost as much
as it would have startled the Vicomte, had he been privileged

to hear it. She said: "How can you talk so, Juliana? I don't believe you!"

Miss Marling laughed again. "Don't you, my dear? I make no doubt you think me monstrous heartless. Oh, yes, I can see you do! Well, we don't have hearts in our family, as you'll discover, I fear."

"You need not fear for me," said Mary calmly. "I am not going to marry Lord Vidal, I assure you."

"You don't know my cousin," replied Juliana. "He means to wed you, and he will—in Uncle Justin's teeth, too! Lord, I would give a guinea to see my uncle's face when he hears! Not that it would tell me much," she added pensively. She clasped her hands round her knees. "You've not yet met his grace, Mary. When you do——" she paused. "I can't advise you. I am for ever making up my mind just what I shall say to him, and then when the time comes I am not able to."

Miss Challoner ignored this. "Juliana, be frank with me: have you quarrelled with Mr. Comyn?"

"Lord, yes, a dozen times, and I thank heaven this is the last!"

"You will be sorry in the morning, my dear."

"It don't signify in the least. My mamma would never permit me to marry him, and though it is very good sport to plan an elopement it would be amazingly horrid to be really married to someone quite outside one's own world."

"I did not know you were as selfish as that, Juliana," said Miss Challoner. "I'll bid you good night."

Juliana nodded carelessly, and waited until the door was firmly shut behind her friend. Then she cast herself face downwards on her pillows and wept miserably.

Meanwhile Miss Challoner sought her own bed, and lay thinking of the strange proposal she had received.

Her disgust at Juliana's behaviour was untempered by surprise. By now she had reached the conclusion that the manners of the whole family of Alastair were incomprehensible to a less exalted person. My Lord Vidal was reckless, prodigal, and overbearing; his cousin Bertrand appeared to be a mere pleasure-seeker; Juliana, too, in whom Miss Challoner had suspected a warmer heart, was frivolous and calculating. From Juliana's and Vidal's conversation she had gleaned what she believed to be a fair estimate of the remaining members of the family. Lady Fanny was worldly and ambitious; Lord Rupert apparently wasted his time and substance on gambling and other amusements; his grace of Avon seemed to be a cold, unloving and sinister figure. The only one whom Miss Challoner felt any desire to know was the Duchess. She was inclined to think that Mr. Comyn was well rid of a bad bargain, and this conclusion brought her back once more to the consideration of her own difficulties.

It seemed ridiculous in an age of civilization, but Miss Challoner had no doubt that in some way or other Vidal would contrive to carry her off to Dijon. She believed that he was prompted more by his love of mastery than by his first chivalrous impulse. What he had said he would do he must do, reckless of consequence. He could not, she realized, drag an unwilling bride to the altar, but if he succeeded in transporting her all the way to Dijon she felt that she would be then in so much worse a predicament that marriage with him would be the only thing left to her. Against this marriage she was still firmly set. God knew she would ask nothing better than to be his wife, but she had sense enough to know that nothing but unhappiness could result from it. If he had loved her, if she had been of his world, approved by his family—but it was useless to speculate on the impossible.

She might steal away from this house very early in the morning, and lose herself in some back-street of Paris. She could not forbear a smile at her own simplicity. She would certainly lose herself, but it seemed probable that his lordship, who knew Paris, would have little trouble in finding her. She was without money and without friends; if she left the protection of Mme. de Charbonne's house she could see only one end to her career. Marriage with Mr. Comyn would be preferable to that. At least his degree was not immeasurably superior to hers; he did not seem to be a gentleman of very passionate affections, and she felt that she could succeed in making him tolerably happy. After all, she thought, neither of us is of a romantic disposition, and at least I shall be rid of this dread of sudden exposure.

Mr. Comyn was eating his breakfast some hours later when a surprised serving-maid ushered Miss Challoner into the room. The visit of a young and personable lady, quite unattended, and at such an unseasonable hour, roused all the abigail's curiosity. Having shut the door on Miss Challoner, she naturally put her ear to the keyhole. But as the conversation inside the room was conducted in English she soon withdrew it.

Mr. Comyn got up quickly from the table, and laid aside his napkin. "Miss Challoner!" he said, coming forward to greet her.

Mary, who was dressed in the grey gown and hooded cloak she had worn on the night of her abduction, gave her hand into his, and as he bent to kiss it, said in her quiet way: "Please inform me, sir, now that you have had time in which to reflect, do you not desire to return to Miss Marling?"

"Indeed, no!" said Mr. Comyn, releasing her hand. "Is it possible—do you in fact come in the guise of an envoy?"

She shook her head. "Alas, no, sir."

He was careful not to allow the disappointment he felt to creep into his voice. "I imagined, ma'am, that you had come to give me your answer to my offer. I need hardly assure you that if you will accept of my hand in marriage I shall count myself extremely fortunate."

She smiled, but rather wanly. "You are very kind, sir. I do not feel that I have any right to accept what I can only regard as a sacrifice, but my situation is desperate, and I do accept it."

He bowed. "I shall endeavour to make you comfortable, ma'am. We must now decide what were best to do. Will you not be seated?"

"You are breakfasting, sir, are you not?"

"Pray do not regard it, ma'am; I have had all I need."

Miss Challoner's eyes twinkled. "I, sir, on the other hand, am fasting."

He slightly pressed her hand. "Believe me, I perfectly understand that food at this moment is repugnant to you. Let us be seated by the fire."

Miss Challoner said meekly: "Food is by no means repugnant to me, Mr. Comyn. Pray allow me to share your breakfast. I am very hungry."

He looked rather surprised, but at once handed her to a chair by the table. "Why, certainly, ma'am! I will send to procure you a clean cup and plate." He went to the door and nearly fell over the serving-maid, who had not yet abandoned hope of catching a phrase spoken in her own tongue. His command of the French language being what it was, he was unable to deliver a rebuke, but he managed to ask for a cup and plate.

When these were brought Miss Challoner poured herself out some coffee, and spread butter on a roll. She proceeded to make a hearty meal. Mr. Comyn was assiduous in plying her with food, but he could not help feeling in a dim way that her attitude in face of a dramatic situation was a trifle mundane. Miss Challoner, biting a crust with her little white teeth, had also her private thoughts, and remembered other meals partaken in the company of a gentleman. This gave her a heartache, and since she had no notion of indulging in such a weakness, she said briskly: "Where are we to be married, sir? How soon can we leave Paris?"

Mr. Comyn poured her out another cup of coffee. "I have considered the matter, ma'am, and I have two plans to submit to you. It must, of course, be as you wish. We can, if you like, return to England, where I apprehend there will be no difficulty in arranging our immediate nuptials. I should point out to you, however, that in England our marriage must necessarily give occasion for comment. The alternative is to travel to Dijon, and there to find the English divine, whose direction was given to me by Lord Vidal. Should you choose this course, ma'am, I suggest that following upon the ceremony we should journey into Italy for a space. Against this scheme must be set my natural scruples, which urge me not to make use of the information provided by his lordship."

"I don't think that need trouble you," said Miss Challoner matter-of-factly. "Which of these plans do you prefer?"

"It is entirely for you to decide, ma'am."

"But really, sir——"

"Whatever you choose will be agreeable to me," said Mr. Comyn.

Miss Challoner, feeling that the argument might be interminable if embarked on, gave her vote for Dijon. She had no desire to return to England until comment had died down. Mr. Comyn then found several points in favour of her choice, and promised that they should set forward before noon. Miss Challoner informed him that she would need to buy herself some few necessities, as she had nothing but the clothes she stood in. Mr. Comyn was quite shocked, and asked her very delicately whether she had sufficient money for her needs. She assured him that she had, and while he went to order a post-chaise, she sallied forth to the nearest shops. Pride had forbidden her to bring any of the clothes of the Marquis's providing. She had, perforce, worn them at the Hôtel de Charbonne, but they were all carefully packed away now; gowns of tiffany with blonde scallops, gowns of taffetas, of dimity, of brocaded satin, cloaks richly trimmed with black lace, négligées so soft and fine they slid through the fingers; lawn shifts, point-lace tuckers, Turkey handkerchiefs—all the fineries of a lady of fashion, or—she thought, with a wry smile—of a light-of-love. She would not keep so much as one comb or haresfoot.

Shortly before noon they set forth on their journey. Both were rather silent, and until the chaise drew out of Paris they sat looking absently out of the windows, each one thinking sadly of the might-have-been.

Mr. Comyn roused himself at last from his abstraction to say: "I think it only right to tell you, ma'am, that I left a billet to be delivered to my Lord Vidal."

Miss Challoner sat bolt upright. "What, sir?"

"I could not but consider that I owed it to him to inform him of your safety and my intentions."

"Oh, you should never have done that!" Miss Challoner said, horrified. "Good God, what a fatal mistake!"

"I regret that you should disapprove, but I remembered that his lordship had made himself responsible for your well-being, and I could not reconcile it with my conscience to make this journey without apprising him of our contract."

Miss Challoner struck her hands together. "But don't you see, sir, that we shall have him hard on our heels? Oh, I would not have had you tell him for the world!"

"I beg you will not distress yourself, ma'am. Much as I dislike the least appearance of secretiveness I thought it advisable to write nothing of our destination to his lordship."

She was only partly reassured, and begged him to order the postillions to drive faster. He pointed out to her that greater speed would court disaster, but when she insisted he obediently let down the window, and shouted to the postillions. Not immediately understanding what he called to them these worthies drew up. Miss Challoner then assumed the direction of affairs, and whatever doubts the postillions had had concerning the nature of the journey were set at rest. Upon the chaise resuming its progress Mr. Comyn, pulling up the window, said gravely that he feared the men now suspected an elopement. Miss Challoner agreed that this was probably true, but maintained that it did not signify. Mr. Comyn said with a touch of severity that by informing the men, as well as he could, that he was her brother he had hoped to avert the least suspicion of impropriety.

Miss Challoner's ever lively sense of humour was aroused by this, and she slightly disconcerted Mr. Comyn by chuckling. She explained apologetically that after the events of the past week considerations of propriety seemed absurd. He pressed her hand, saying with feeling: "I believe you have suffered, ma'am. To a delicately nurtured female Lord Vidal's habits and manners must have caused infinite alarm and disgust."

Her steady grey eyes met his unwaveringly. "Neither, sir, I do assure you. I don't desire to pose as a wronged and misused creature. I brought it all on myself, and his lordship behaved to me with more consideration than perhaps I deserved."

He seemed to be at a loss. "Is that so, ma'am? I had supposed, I confess, that you had suffered incivility—even brutality—at his hands. Consideration for others would hardly appear to be one of his lordship's virtues."

She smiled reminiscently. "I think he could be very kind," she said, half to herself. "I am indebted to him for several marks of thoughtfulness." Her smile grew, though her eyes were misty. "You would scarcely credit it in one so ruthless, sir, but his lordship, though excessively angry with me at the time, was moved to provide me with a basin on board his yacht. I was never more glad of anything in my life."

Mr. Comyn was shocked. "It must have been vastly disagreeable to you, ma'am, to be—ah—unwell and without a female companion."

"It was quite the most disagreeable part of the whole adventure," agreed Miss Challoner. She added candidly: "I was vilely sick, and really I believe I should have died had his lordship not forced brandy down my throat in the nick of time."

"The situation," said Mr. Comyn austerely, "seems to have been sordid in the extreme."

Miss Challoner perceived that she had offended his sensibilities, and relapsed into a disheartened silence. She began to understand that Mr. Comyn, for all his prosaic bearing, cherished a love for the romantic, which Lord Vidal, a very figure of romance, quite lacked.

The journey occupied three days, and neither the gentleman nor the lady enjoyed it. Miss Challoner, of necessity the spokesman at every halt on the route, found herself comparing this flight with her previous journey to Paris, when the best rooms at all the inns were prepared for her, and she had nothing to do but obey my lord's commands. Mr. Comyn, in his turn, could not but feel that his companion behaved with a matter-of-factness quite out of keeping with the circumstances. She seemed more concerned with the ordering of meals at the inns, and the airing of sheets which she declared to be damp, than with the unconventional daring of the whole expedition. A natural female agitation would have given his chivalry more scope, but Miss Challoner remained maddeningly calm, and, far from betraying weakness or nervous fears, assumed the direction of the journey. The only betrayal of uneasiness which she permitted herself was her continual plea to travel faster. Mr. Comyn, who did not at all care to be bumped and jolted over bad roads, and who thought, moreover, that such a feverish pace made their progress appear like an undignified flight, several times remonstrated with her. But when he condemned the speed as dangerous, Miss Challoner laughed, and told him that if he had ever travelled with the Marquis he would not consider himself to be moving fast now.

This remark, and various others which had all to do with his lordship, at last induced Mr. Comyn to observe, not without a touch of asperity, that Miss Challoner did not seem to have disliked her late abduction so much as he had supposed. "I confess, ma'am," he said, "that I had imagined you desperate in the power of one whose merciless violence is, alas, too well know. Apparently I was mistaken, and from your present conversation I am led to assume that his lordship behaved with a respect and amiability astonishing in one of his reputation."

Her eyes twinkled a little. "Respect and amiability . . ." she repeated. "N-no, sir. His lordship was peremptory, overbearing, excessively quick-tempered, and imperious."

"And yet, ma'am, not repugnant to you."

"No. Not repugnant to me," she said quietly.

"Forgive me," said Mr. Comyn, "but I think you cherish a warmer feeling for Lord Vidal than I was aware of."

She looked gravely at him. "I thought, from something you said to me, that you had guessed I was not—indifferent to him."

"I did not know, ma'am, that it had gone so deep. If it is so indeed, I do not immediately perceive why you were so urgent to be quit of him."

"He does not care for me, sir," said Miss Challoner simply.

"Nor am I of his world. Conceive the very natural dismay that must visit his parents were he to ally himself with me. Fathers have been known to disinherit their sons for such offences."

Mr. Comyn was greatly moved. "Madam, the nobility of your nature is such that I can only say, I honour you."

"Nonsense!" said Miss Challoner sharply.

☙ Chapter XIV ❧

MISS MARLING partook of chocolate very late on the morning after the ball at the Hôtel Saint-Vire. It was after eleven when she awoke, and she did not look as though the long sleep had at all refreshed her. Her abigail noticed how woe-begone was the little face under the night-cap of point-lace, and drew her own conclusions. Miss Marling was pettish over the choice of a morning wrapper, and complained that her chocolate was too sweet. She demanded to know whether any note had been left for her, or if anyone had called to see her, and on being told that she had neither a note nor a visitor, she pushed her chocolate away, and said she could not drink the stuff, it was so vile.

She was still in bed trying to make up her mind whether or no to write to Mr. Comyn, when a message was brought to her that the Marquis of Vidal was below, and wanted to see her immediately.

She was so disappointed that the visitor was not Mr. Comyn, as she had at first been sure it must be, that tears rose to her eyes, and she said in a tight, hard voice: "I can't see him. I'm in bed, and I have the headache."

The lackey's footsteps retreated down the stairs, and in two minutes a far quicker step sounded, and a peremptory rap fell on the door. "Let me in, Ju; I must see you," said Vidal's voice.

"Oh, very well!" answered Juliana crossly.

The Marquis came in, much to the abigail's disapproval, and signed to that damsel to leave the room. She went, sniffing loudly, and Vidal strode over to the big bed, and stood

looking grimly down at Juliana. "The servants tell me Mary
Challoner left the house early this morning, and is not yet
returned," he said, without preamble. "Where is she?"

"Good gracious, how should I know?" said Juliana indignantly. She hitched one of her lace-edged pillows up higher.
"I dare say she has run away sooner than marry you, and
I vow I don't blame her, if you are in the habit of bursting
in on ladies abed in this horrid way."

"Oh, don't be missish, Ju!" said his lordship, with an impatient frown. "I left her in your care."

"Well, and what if you did? I can't be for ever with her.
She wouldn't have me, I'll be bound."

Vidal looked at her rather sharply. "Oh? Have you quarrelled?"

"Pray do not imagine everyone to be like yourself and for
ever being in a quarrel!" besought Miss Marling. "If people
are only kind to me I'm sure I am the last person to quarrel
with anyone."

His lordship sat down on the edge of the bed. "Now come
along, my girl: out with it!" he said. "What has happened
between you?"

"Nothing at all!" snapped Juliana. "Though I've little doubt
Mary thinks me as odious as she thinks you—not that I care
a fig for what she or anyone else thinks."

"I'll shake you in a minute," threatened the Marquis.
"What's between you two?"

Miss Marling raised herself on her elbow. "I won't be
bullied by you, Vidal, so pray don't think it! I think men
are the most hateful, cruel wretches imaginable, and I wish
you would go away and find your provoking Mary yourself."

There was a distinct break in her voice, and Vidal, who had
a soft corner for her, put his arms round her, and said with
unwonted cajolery: "Don't cry, child. What's to do?"

Miss Marling's rigidity left her. She buried her face in
Vidal's blue coat, and said in muffled accents: "I want to go
home! Everything is horrid in Paris, and I hope to heaven I
never come here again!"

Vidal carefully removed his lace ruffle from her clutching fingers. "Quarrelled with Comyn, have you? You're a
fool, Ju. Stop crying! Has he gone off? Shall I bring him back
to you?"

Miss Marling declined this offer with every evidence of

loathing, and releasing his lordship, hunted under her pillow for a handkerchief, and fiercely blew her small nose.

"I wonder . . ." Vidal stopped, and sat staring at the bedpost somewhat ominously.

Observing the darkling look in his eyes, Juliana said quickly: "What do you wonder? Please do not put on that murderous face, Dominic! It frightens me."

He glanced down at her. "I wonder whether Mr. Frederick Comyn has anything to do with Mary's disappearance?" he said.

"What a stupid notion!" commented Juliana. "Why in the world should he help Mary to escape?"

"From damned officiousness, belike," said Vidal, scowling. "I found the fellow here last night—mighty friendly with Mary."

"What!" Miss Marling stiffened. "Here? With Mary? What was he doing?"

"Holding her hands, curse his impudence."

"Oh!" Miss Marling turned quite pale with indignation. "The wicked, deceitful creature! She never breathed a word of it to me! And then to dare to scold me for quarrelling with Frederick! Oh, I could kill them both! Holding her hands at that hour of night! And then to turn jealous because I like to dance with Bertrand! Oh, it beats anything I have ever heard! I'll never forgive either of them."

Vidal got up. "I'm going round to Comyn's lodging," he said, and walked to the door.

"Don't kill him, Dominic, I implore you!" shrieked his cousin.

"For God's sake, don't be such a damned little fool, Juliana!" said the Marquis irritably, and departed.

The owner of Mr. Comyn's lodgings, a retired valet, opened the door to the Marquis, and admitted him into a narrow hall. On being asked for the English gentleman he said that M. Comyn had paid his shot, and left by coach a bare hour since.

"Left, has he? Alone?" demanded the Marquis.

The valet cast down his eyes. "The Englishwoman who came to see him—oh, but at a very strange hour, m'sieur!— was with him."

He stole a sly look upwards at the Marquis, and was startled by the expression on that dark face. "She was, eh?" said Vidal through his teeth. He smiled, and the valet retreated a pace, quite involuntarily. "Where have they gone? Do you know?"

"But no, m'sieur, how should I tell? The lady had no baggage, but M. Comyn took all of his. He said to me that he will not return, and he gave to me a letter to deliver in the Rue St. Honoré."

Light flashed in the Marquis's sombre eyes. "Where in the Rue St. Honoré, my man?"

"It was a letter to an English Marquis, m'sieur, at the Hôtel Avon."

"Was it, by God!" said Vidal, and promptly went off home.

The letter, addressed in Mr. Comyn's neat handwriting, was lying on the table in the wide hall. Vidal broke the seal, and ran his eye down the single sheet.

"My lord," wrote Mr. Comyn, *"I have to inform your lordship that my betrothal to Miss Juliana Marling being at an end, I have made bold to offer my hand in marriage to the lady lately travelling under your lordship's protection. I think it only proper to apprise your lordship of this step, since your lordship was good enough to take me into your confidence. Miss Challoner having been so obliging as to accept of my offer, we are leaving Paris immediately. Miss Challoner, while sensible of the honour your lordship does her in proposing for her hand, is highly averse from a marriage which she deems unsuitable, and from the outset doomed to unhappiness. Since I apprehend that this aversion is known to your lordship, it will be unnecessary (I am assured) to request your lordship to relinquish the pretensions which have become a menace to Miss Challoner's peace of mind.*

"I beg to remain, my lord, in all else,

"Your lordship's obedient servant to command,

"Frederick Comyn."

His lordship swore softly and long, to the admiration of a lackey, who stood reverently listening to his fluency. Then he proceeded to set his household by the ears, and the word flew round inside of ten minutes that the Devil's Cub was in a rare taking, and there would be bloodshed before nightfall. From the orders that followed one another like lightning off his lordship's tongue, it was apparent that he was going on a sudden swift journey, and when Fletcher was bidden send to the gates of Paris to find whether an Englishman accompanied by a lady had passed out of any one of them that morning, none of the household had any doubt at all of the nature of his lordship's journey.

"Damn my blood if I've ever seen the Cub so wild!" remarked his lordship's particular groom. "Ay, and I've known him a year or two."

"I've seen him wilder nor this," mused a footman, "but not for a female. And meself I'd say the Mantoni had more to her than this one, or that piece we had with us a couple of years back—what was her name, Horace? The beauty that threw a coffee-pot at the Cub in one of her tantrums."

"I'm not Horace to you, my lad," said Mr. Timms loftily. "And me knowing what I do, which is natural in his lordship's own gentleman, I'd advise you not to draw odious comparisons between Miss Challoner and those other trollops."

He went off to pack Vidal's cloak-bag, and was much scandalized to discover that he was not to accompany his master. When he ventured on an expostulation he was asked roundly whether he imagined my lord was unable to dress himself. Being a polite person he disclaimed, but this was precisely what he did think. He had a vision, horrible to a gentleman's gentleman, of my lord's cravat ill-tied, his hair uncurled, his dress carelessly arranged; and when Vidal flung the pounce-box, the haresfoot, and the rouge-pot out of the cloak-bag, he was moved to beg his lordship to consider his feelings.

Vidal gave a short bark of laughter. "What the devil have your feelings to do with it?" he demanded. "Put up a change of clothing, and my razors, and my night-gear."

Mr. Timms was ordinarily a timid creature, but where his profession was concerned he became possessed of great daring. He said firmly: "My lord, it's well known that it's me who has the dressing of your lordship. I have my pride, my lord, and to have you travelling amongst all these Frenchies, a disgrace to me, as you will, my lord, begging your pardon —oh, it's enough to make a man cut his throat, sir!"

Vidal, in his shirt sleeves, was pulling on his top-boots. He glanced up, not unamused, and said bluntly: "If you want a master you can dress like a painted puppet, you'd best leave my service, Timms. I'll never be a credit to you."

"My lord," said Mr. Timms, "if I may take leave to say so, there's not a gentleman in London, no, nor in Paris either, that can be a greater credit to his valet than what your lordship can be."

"You flatter me," said Vidal, picking up his waistcoat.

"No, my lord. I was three years with Sir Jasper Trelawney, who was thought to be a fine beau in his day. The clothes we had! Ah, that was a gentleman as was an artist. But the shoulders to his coats had to be padded so that it fair broke one's heart, and when it came to him wearing three patches on his face I had to leave him, because I'd my reputation to think of, like any other man."

"Good God!" said Vidal. "I trust my shoulders don't offend your sensibilities, Timms?"

"If I may take the liberty of saying so, my lord, I have seldom seen a finer pair. Whatever else may sometimes be amiss, our coats set so that it is a pleasure to see them done justice to." He assisted his lordship to struggle into one as he spoke, and smoothed the cloth with a loving hand. "When I was with Lord Devenish, sir," he said reminiscently, "we had to assist his lordship's legs a little with sawdust in the stocking. But even so they were never what one likes to see in a gentleman of fashion. Everything else about his lordship was as it should be; I believe I never saw a neater waist, and at that time, my lord, coats were worn very tight at the waist with whaleboned skirts. But below the knee his lordship fell off sadly. It took away from one's pride in dressing him, and sawdust, though helpful, is not like good muscle."

"I can imagine nothing more unlike," said Vidal, who was eyeing him in open astonishment. "You seem to have been hard put to it with your previous masters."

"That, my lord, was the trouble," replied Timms. "If your lordship will permit me, I will adjust this buckle. When I left Lord Devenish I was with young Mr. Harry Cheston for a space. Shoulders, legs, waist—all very passable. He wore his clothes very well, my lord; never a crease, nor a pin out of place, though he favoured vellum-hole waistcoats more than I could like. It was Mr. Cheston's hands that were his undoing. Do what one would, my lord, they were such as to render the perfection of his attire quite negligible. He slept every night in chicken-skin gloves, but it was of no use, they remained a vulgar red."

Vidal cast himself down in the chair by the dressing-table, and leaned back in it, surveying his valet with a half-smile curling his lips. "You alarm me, Timms, positively you alarm me."

Mr. Timms smiled indulgently. "Your lordship has no need

to feel alarm. I could wish that we wore a ring—not a profusion, sir, but one ring, possibly an emerald, which is a stone designed to set off the whiteness of a gentleman's hand—but since your lordship has a strong aversion from jewels we must forgo the adornment. The hands themselves, if your lordship will not think it impertinent, are all that I could wish."

His lordship, quite unnerved by this encomium, thrust them both into his breeches pockets. "Come, let me have it, Timms!" he said. "Where do I fall short of your devilish high standards? Let me know the worst."

Mr. Timms bent to dust one of his lordship's shining boots. "Your lordship can hardly fail to be aware of the elegance of your lordship's whole figure. In the twenty-five years during which I have been a gentleman's valet I have always had to fight against odds, as it were. Your lordship would be surprised to know how one inferior feature can ruin the most modish toilet. There was the Honourable Peter Hailing, sir, whose coats were so exactly cut to his figure that it needed myself and two lackeys to coax him into them. He had a leg such as is seldom seen, and his countenance was by no means contemptible. But it all went for nothing, my lord. Mr. Hailing's neck was so short that no neckcloth could be made to disguise it. I could tell your lordship of a dozen such cases. Sometimes it's the shoulders, at others the legs; once I served a gentleman with a fatal tendency to corpulence. We did what we could with tight-lacing, but it was not successful. Yet he was as handsome as your lordship, if I may say so."

"Spare my blushes, Timms," said the Marquis sardonically. "I don't aspire to be an Adonis. Out with it! What's my fault?"

Mr. Timms said simply: "Your lordship has none."

The Marquis was startled. "Eh?"

"None whatsoever, my lord. One could wish for greater care in the arrangement of the cravat, and a more frequent use of the curling-irons and pounce-box; but we have nothing to conceal. Your lordship will understand that a constant struggle against nature disheartens one. When your lordship found yourself in need of a valet, I applied for the post, being confident—with all respect, my lord—that though your lordship might affect a carelessness that one is bound to deplore, the figure, face, hands—your lordship's whole person, in short—were so exactly proportioned as to render the apparelling of your lordship a work of pleasure unmarred by any feeling of dissatisfaction."

"Good God!" said the Marquis.

Mr. Timms said insinuatingly: "If your lordship would permit me to place one patch—one only——"

The Marquis got up. "Content yourself with my perfect proportions, Timms," he said. "Where's that fellow Fletcher?" He strode out, calling to his major-domo, who came sedately up the stairs to meet him. "Well, man, are those damned lackeys to be all day about their business?" he demanded.

"John, my lord, is come in. At the Porte Saint-Denis, no one. At the Porte Saint-Martin, no one. I await the return of Robert and Mitchell, my lord, and will apprise your lordship instantly."

"No luck at the northern gates," the Marquis said, musing. "So he's not taking her back to England. Now what the devil's his game?"

Ten minutes later Fletcher came to find him again, and said impassively: "Robert reports, my lord, that shortly before noon a travelling chaise passed out of Paris by the Port Royal. It contained an Englishman who spoke French very indifferently, and one lady."

The Marquis's hand clutched on his riding-whip. "Dijon!" he said, with something of a snarl. "Damn his infernal impudence! Have the bay saddled, Fletcher, and send me a man to take a note to Miss Marling." He sat down at the writing-desk, and jabbed a quill in the standish. He scrawled one line only to his cousin. *"They're off to Dijon. I leave Paris in half an hour."* Having given this to a lackey, he picked up his hat and went off to Foley, his grace of Avon's banker.

When he returned, twenty minutes later, his light chaise was already awaiting him in the courtyard, and his groom was walking the bay up and down. A lackey was in the act of placing two band boxes in the chaise, but was checked by a thunderous demand to know what the devil he was about.

"They belong to the lady, my lord," explained the lackey nervously.

"Lady? What lady?" said Vidal, astonished.

He was answered by the appearance of his cousin in the big doorway. Miss Marling had on a highly becoming hat, tied under her chin with pink ribands, and carried a feather-muff. Her face wore a look of mulish determination. "Oh, so there you are at last, Vidal!" she said.

"What in the fiend's name brings you here?" asked the

Marquis, coming to her side. "There's nothing for you to do in this coil."

Miss Marling looked up at him defiantly. "I am coming with you."

"The devil you are!" ejaculated his lordship. "No, my fair cousin. I don't hamper myself with a petticoat on this journey."

"I am coming with you," repeated Miss Marling.

"You're not," said Vidal curtly, and beckoned to his groom.

Juliana caught at his wrist. "You shan't go without me!" she said in a fierce whisper. "You only care for your odious Mary, but she has run off with my Frederick, I'll have you know, and I'll come if I have to hire a post-chaise and travel alone! I mean it, Vidal!"

He looked down at her frowningly. "You do, do you? I doubt you won't relish this journey overmuch."

"You'll take me?" she said eagerly.

He shrugged. "I'll take you, but if I were your husband I'd soon school you, my girl." He handed her up somewhat urgently into the chaise, and said brusquely: "Does Tante know of this?"

"Well, she was gone out, but I felt a letter explaining as well as I could for the hurry I was in."

"Very well," Vidal said, and shut the door on her.

One of the lackeys put up the steps; the postillions were already in their saddles, and grooms stood to the horses' heads. Vidal pulled on his gloves, gathered the bay's bridle in his left hand, and mounted. "Port Royal!" he said to the postillions, and reigned the bay in hard to let the chaise pass out of the courtyard.

At the first post-stage Miss Marling insisted on descending from the chaise. While the horses were changed she favoured the Marquis with a pungent criticism of his manners, and the springs of the chaise. She said that never had she been so shaken and battered. She wondered that any man should be so brutal as to subject a lady to such discomfort, and declared that she vastly regretted having come on the journey.

"I thought you would," replied his lordship. "Perhaps it'll teach you not to meddle in my affairs."

"Your affairs?" gasped Miss Marling. "Do you imagine that I care a pin for your affairs? I've come on my own, Vidal!"

"Then don't grumble," he returned.

Miss Marling stalked back to the chaise in high dudgeon.

At the next halt she did not even look out of the window, but
at the end of another twelve miles, she alighted once more,
with her cloak held tightly round her against the sharp evening
wind.

It was dusk and the landscape was dim, with a grey mist
rising off the ground. The lamps on the chaise had been lit,
and a comfortable glow came from the windows of the small
inn.

"Vidal, can we not stay here for the night?" asked Miss
Marling in a fading voice.

His lordship was speaking to one of the ostlers. He finished
what he had to say, and then came leisurely towards his
cousin. He had put on his greatcoat, an affair of buff-coloured
cloth, with three capes at the shoulders. "Tired?" he said.

"Of course I am tired, stupid creature!" replied Miss Marling.

"Go into the inn," he commanded. "We dine here."

"I vow I could not eat a morsel!"

He did not pay any heed to this, but walked back to say
something to his groom. Miss Marling, hating him, flounced
into the inn, and was escorted by the landlord to a private
parlour. A fire had been kindled in the grate, and Juliana
drew up a chair and sat down, spreading her chilled fingers
to the warmth.

Presently the Marquis came in. He flung his greatcoat over
a chair, and kicked the smouldering logs to a small blaze.
"That's better," he said briskly.

"You have made it smoke," remarked Miss Marling in a
voice of long suffering.

He looked down at her with a hint of a smile. "You're
hungry, and devilish cross, Ju."

Her bosom swelled. "You have treated me abominably,"
she said.

"Fiddle!" replied the Marquis.

"You let me be jolted and bumped till the teeth rattled in
my head. You thrust me into your odious chaise as though I
were a mere piece of baggage, and you have not the civility
to stay with me."

"I never drive when I can ride," said his lordship indifferently.

"I make no doubt at all that had I been Mary Challoner
you would have been glad enough to have borne me company!"

The Marquis was snuffing one of the candles, but he looked up at that, and there was a glint in his eye. "That, my dear, is quite another matter,". he said.

Miss Marling told him roundly that he was the rudest creature she had ever met and when he only laughed, she launched into a speech of some length.

He interrupted her to say: "My good cousin, do you wish to catch up with our two runaways, or not?"

"Of course I do! But must we travel at this shocking speed? They cannot reach Dijon for two or three days, and we've time enough, I should have thought, to come up with them."

"I want to overtake them to-night," Vidal said grimly. "They are not three hours ahead of us now."

"What! Have we gained on them so fast? Then I take it all back, Vidal, every word. Let us go on at once!"

"We'll dine first," answered his lordship.

"How," demanded Juliana tragically, "can you suppose that I could *think* of food at such a time?"

"Do you know," said the Marquis gently, "I find you excessively tedious, Juliana. You complain of the speed at which I choose to travel; you talk a deal of damned nonsense about my incivility and your sensibilities; you spurn dinner as though it were poisoned; you behave in short like a heroine out of a melodrama."

Miss Marling was prevented from replying by the entrance of two serving-men. Covers were laid, and chairs placed at the table. The men withdrew, and Miss Marling said carefully: "You have a vast deal to say in my dispraise, Vidal. Pray, is it to be expected that I should feel no agitation? To be sure, I am sorry I complained of the speed, but to be left hour upon hour alone in a jolting chaise is enough to try the patience even of a Mary Challoner."

"No," said his lordship. A reminiscent smile softened his mouth for a brief moment. "Come and sit down."

She came, but told him that a glass of wine to revive her was all that was needed.

The Marquis shrugged. "Just as you please, cousin."

Miss Marling sipped her wine, and watched his lordship carve the capon. She shuddered, and said that she wondered at him. "For my part," she added, "I should have thought any gentleman of the least sensibility would have refrained from—from gorging when the lady in his company——"

"Ah, but I'm not a gentleman," said the Marquis. "I have it on the best of authority that I am only a nobleman."

"Good gracious, Vidal, who in the world dared to say such a thing?" cried his cousin, instantly diverted.

"Mary," replied his lordship, pouring himself out a glass of wine.

"Well, if you sat eating as though nothing mattered save your dinner I'm not surprised," said Juliana viciously. "If I were not so angry with her, the deceitful, sly wretch, I could pity her for all she must have undergone at your hands."

"Seeing me eat was the least of her sufferings," answered the Marquis. "She underwent much, but it may interest you to know, Juliana, that she never treated me to the vapours, as you seem like to do."

"Then I can only say, Vidal, that either she had no notion what a horrid brutal man you are, or that she is just a dull creature with no nerves at all."

For a moment Vidal did not answer. Then he said in a level voice: "She knew." His lip curled. He glanced scornfully at his cousin. "Had I carried you off as I carried her you would have died of fright or hysterics, Juliana. Make no mistake, my dear; Mary was so desperately afraid she tried to put a bullet through me."

"Tried to put a bullet through you, Dominic?" repeated Miss Marling incredulously. "I never heard a word of this before!"

"It is not a story that I should be likely to tell, since it don't redound to my credit," said Vidal drily. "But when you sit there full of airs and graces because you've been jolted over a bad road, and sneer at Mary——"

"I didn't sneer!" said Juliana hastily. "I'd no notion you behaved so dreadfully badly to her. You said you forced her aboard your yacht, but I never supposed that you really frightened her enough to make her fire at you. You need not be in a rage with me for saying so, Dominic, but when I saw Mary at your house she was so placid I made sure you'd not treated her so very brutally after all. Had you?"

"Yes," said Vidal bluntly. He looked at Juliana. "You think it was vastly romantic for Mary to be carried off by me, don't you? You think you would enjoy it, and you cannot conceive how she should be afraid, can you? Then think, my girl! Think a little! You are in my power at this moment, I may remind you. What if I make you feel it? What if I say to start with that you *shall* eat your dinner, and force it down your throat?"

Juliana shrank back from him involuntarily. "Don't, Vidal! Don't come near me!" she said, frightened by the expression in his face.

He laughed. "Not so romantic, is it, Ju? And to force you to eat your dinner would be a small thing compared with some other things I might force you to do. Sit down, I'm not going to touch you."

She obeyed, eyeing him nervously. "I—I wish I hadn't come with you!" she said.

"So did Mary, with more reason. But Mary would have died sooner than let me see that she was afraid. And Mary, my love, is not my cousin."

Juliana drew a long breath. "Of course, I didn't think that you would really force me to eat," she said. "You—you merely startled me."

"Well, I shall force you if you don't take care," said his lordship. He carved a slice of breast, and handed it to her. "Don't be tiresome, Juliana. Eat it, and forget your sensibilities. You've not much time."

Juliana took the plate meekly. "Oh, very well," she said. "I must say, Dominic, if you looked at Mary in that dreadful threatening way I can almost forgive her for running off with Frederick." She stole a sidelong look at him. "You were not very kind to Mary, apparently."

"Kind!" ejaculated Vidal. "No, I was not—kind."

Juliana ate another morsel of capon. "You seem to me to have behaved as though you hated her," she remarked.

He said nothing. Juliana peeped at him again. "You're very anxious to get her in your power again, Vidal. But I don't quite know why you should be, for you meant to marry her only because you had ruined her, and so were obliged to, didn't you?"

She thought that he was not going to answer, but suddenly he raised his eyes from the contemplation of the dregs of his wine. "Because I am obliged to?" he said. "I mean to marry Mary Challoner because I'm devilish sure I can't live without her."

Juliana clapped her hands with a crow of delight. "Oh, it is famous!" she exclaimed. "I never dreamed you had fallen in love with my staid Mary! I thought you were chasing her through France just because you so hate to be crossed! But

when you flew into a rage with me for saying she was too
dull to be afraid of you, of course, I guessed at once! My
dearest Dominic, I was never more glad of anything in my
life, and it is of all things the most romantic possible! Do, do
let us overtake them at once! Only conceive of their astonishment when they see us!"

"Mary knows I am hard on her heels," Vidal answered,
with a little laugh. "At every stage I meet with the same tale:
the English lady was anxious to lose no time. She's used to my
way of travel, Juliana; she'll whisk your Frederick to Dijon
in a manner highly discomposing to his dignity."

"It is possible," said Miss Marling stiffly, "that Frederick
and not Mary will have the ordering of the journey."

Vidal chuckled. "Not if I know my Mary," he replied.

Twenty minutes later they took the road again. Dinner had
revived Miss Marling's spirits, and she made no demur at
entering the chaise again. Knowing that she was within reach
of her Frederick she could not now drive fast enough, and her
only fear was that they might overshoot their mark. Somewhere on the route Frederick and Mary must have halted for
the night, and Miss Marling was inclined to stop at every
village they passed, in case the fugitives might be there.

She occupied herself in planning the scene that lay before
her, and had decided on the speech she would make when
there was a sudden crash, and she was hurled against the side
of the chaise. There was a dreadful bump, the smash of
breaking glass, and Miss Marling, considerably shaken and
dazed, tried to right herself only to find that the seat of the
coach was now at a very odd angle, and the off-door almost
where the roof should have been. She heard the trampling of
the horses plunging in alarm, and the voices of the postillions.
Then the off-door was wrenched open, and Vidal said sharply:
"Are you hurt, Ju?"

"No, but what has happened?—Oh, I have cut myself!
Oh, this dreadful glass! It is too bad of you, Dominic! I said
we were driving at a wicked pace, and now see what has
happened!"

"We've lost a wheel," explained his lordship. "Reach up
your hands to me, and I'll pull you out."

This feat was performed in an expeditious if somewhat
rough-and-ready fashion. Juliana was swung down on to the
road, and left to examine her hurts while his lordship went
to see that the frightened horses were unhurt. When he

came back he found his cousin in a state of seething indignation. She demanded to know where they were, how he proposed to come up with the runaways, where they were to sleep, and whether anyone cared enough to bind up her bleeding hand or not.

The Marquis performed this office for her by the light of one of the chaise lamps, and told her not to be in a taking over a mere scratch. He said that they were, providentially, only a quarter of a mile from the next village, where they could obtain a lodging for the night in one of the cottages.

"What?" shrieked the afflicted Miss Marling. "Sleep in a horrid peasant's cottage? I won't! You must find another chaise at once! At once, Vidal, do you hear?"

"I hear," said his lordship coolly. "Now, don't be nonsensical, Juliana. You'll do well enough. For all I know there may be an inn you can stay at, though I won't vouch for the sheets. There's no hope of repairing the chaise till the morning, for Richards will have to ride to the nearest town to find a smith. I'm sending him off now, and for the present you must make the best of it. We shall catch our runaways in time, don't doubt it."

Miss Marling, overcome by the ignominy of her position, sank down on the bank by the roadside and gave way to her emotions. The postillions regarded her with interested sympathy; Richards coughed in embarrassment; and my lord, raising his clenched fists to heaven, prayed to be delivered from every female but one.

◄§ *Chapter XV* §►

AT about the same time that the Marquis of Vidal's chaise lost a wheel, the Duchess of Avon and Lord Rupert Alastair arrived in Paris, and drove straight to the Hôtel Avon.

"What had we best do first, Rupert?" her grace asked anxiously, as the chaise drew into the courtyard.

"Have some dinner," replied his lordship, with a prodigious yawn. "If there's anyone in the house, which I doubt."

"But why should you doubt? We know that Dominique is in Paris!"

"Lord, Léonie, don't be so simple! Dominic's lax, but damme, he wouldn't bring his mistress to your house." Lord Rupert heaved his body out of the corner of the chaise, and looked out of the window. "Place looks as deserted as a tomb," he remarked, opening the door.

A solitary lackey came out of the house, attracted by the noise of the arrival, and began to say that his lordship was out of town. Then Lord Rupert sprang from the chaise, and the lackey, recognizing him, looked very much taken aback, and as though he did not know what to say.

Lord Rupert eyed him appraisingly. "One of Lord Vidal's servants, aren't you?" he said. "Where's his lordship?"

"I couldn't say, my lord," answered the lackey cautiously.

"Won't say, more like," said Rupert. He turned, and gave his hand to Léonie who was descending from the chaise. "There's one of Vidal's fellows here, so it looks as though the boy had been here. Odd, damned odd."

The Duchess shook out her crushed skirts with a purposeful air, and looked at the lackey, who was staring at her aghast. "It is you who are my son's servant? *Bon!* Where is milor'?"

"I don't know, your grace. He's not in town."

"Is there anyone in the house?" demanded the Duchess.

"No, your grace. Only the servants, that is."

Léonie pounced on this. "Why is it then that the house is full of my son's servants and yet he is not here?"

The lackey shifted uneasily from one foot to the other. "His lordship left Paris this afternoon, your grace."

Léonie turned to Lord Rupert, throwing out her hands. "But it is *imbécile!* Why should he leave Paris? I don't believe a word of it. Where is Fletcher?"

"Mr. Fletcher and Mr. Timms have both gone out, your grace."

"What, has his lordship gone off without his valet?" demanded Rupert.

"Yes, my lord."

"I am going into the house," announced Léonie.

Rupert watched her go, and looked at the lackey again. "Come on, out with it, my man: Where's his lordship?"

"My lord, indeed I could not say. If your lordship would wait till Mr. Fletcher comes in, maybe he would know."

"It looks to me like a damned fishy business," said Rupert severely, and followed Léonie into the hall.

He found her grace trying to pump the housekeeper. When she saw him Léonie said: "Rupert, it is what I do not at all understand! She says the girl was never here. And I do not think she is lying to me, for she is my servant, and not Dominique's."

Lord Rupert divested himself of his heavy Rockelaure. "Well, if Vidal's got rid of the wench already, I'd say it's quick work," he remarked admiringly. "Stap me, if I know how he manages it! I always found 'em cling so there was no shaking the dear creatures off at all."

Léonie cast him a glance of scorn and swept upstairs. The housekeeper would have followed her, but his lordship detained her, and broached the matter nearest his heart. The housekeeper was shocked to learn that the travellers had not yet dined, and hurried away to order a meal to be prepared at once.

When Léonie saw Rupert again dinner was on the table, and his lordship had just come in from a visit to the stables. He took his seat opposite Léonie, and said with a puzzled

air: "Blister me if I can make head or tail of this coil.
Vidal's damned lackeys are as close as a lot of oysters.
Y'know, Léonie, the boy's a marvel, so he is. *I* never could
keep a servant who didn't blab all my affairs to the world."

"He is coming back," Léonie said positively. "I have looked
in his room, and all his clothes are there."

Lord Rupert coughed. "Anything else, my dear?" he asked,
with delicacy.

"Nothing," said Léonie. "It is very curious, do you not
think? For where can the girl be?"

"That's what beats me," confessed Rupert. "Not but what
I never thought to find her here. But if she's not, why is
Vidal? That's what I don't understand. Now, I've been talking to the grooms. All I can find is that Vidal left Paris by
the Port Royal to-day. Naturally, I don't like to ask 'em
point-blank if he'd a wench with him, and none of 'em——"

"Why not?" interrupted the Duchess.

"Burn it, you can't ask lackeys questions like that, Léonie!"

"I do not see why not. I want to know, and if I do not
ask who will tell me?"

"They'll never tell you, anyway, my dear," his lordship
informed her.

Dinner was over when Fletcher at last put in an appearance, and Rupert and Léonie had repaired to the library.
Fletcher came in, sedate as ever, and begged her grace's
pardon for having been out when she arrived. Léonie brushed
that aside, and once more demanded to know her son's
whereabouts.

"I think, your grace," he answered guardedly, "that his
lordship has gone to Dijon."

Lord Rupert stared at him. "What in the fiend's name
does he want in Dijon?" he asked.

"His lordship did not tell me, my lord."

Léonie smote her hands together. "*Voyons*, I find it insupportable that no one can tell me anything about my
son! Speak, you! Was that girl with M. le Marquis?—No,
I will not be quiet, Rupert! Was she with him, Fletcher?"

"I beg your grace's pardon?" Mr. Fletcher was all polite
bewilderment.

"Do not beg my pardon again, or I shall become enraged!" Léonie said dangerously. "It is no use to tell me you
do not know of any girl, for me I am well aware that
M. le Marquis had one with him when he left England.

That is not a thing extraordinary. It is true, is it not?"

Mr. Fletcher cast an appealing glance at Lord Rupert, who said testily: "Don't stare at me, man! We know the girl was with his lordship."

Mr. Fletcher bowed. "As your lordship says."

"Well, has she gone to Dijon?"

"I could not say, my lord."

Léonie eyed him with hostility. "Did she leave this house with M. le Marquis?"

"No, your grace. She was not with his lordship when he set forward on his journey."

"There you are, my dear!" said Rupert. "Vidal's got rid of her, and we may as well go home again before Avon gets wind of the affair."

Léonie told Mr. Fletcher he might go, and when the door had closed behind him, she turned to Rupert with an expression of great anxiety on her face. "Rupert, it becomes more and more serious!"

"Devil a bit!" said his lordship cheerfully. "You can't get away from it, the girl's not with Vidal now, so I don't see we've aught to worry over!"

"But Rupert, you do not understand at all! I have a very big fear that Dominique may have cast her off—in a rage, *tu sais.*"

Lord Rupert disposed his limbs more comfortably in his chair. "I shouldn't wonder if he had," he agreed. "It don't concern us, thank the Lord!"

Léonie got up, and began to move about the room. "If he has done that it is a crime one does not forgive. I must find her."

Lord Rupert blinked. "If she ain't with that precious son of yours what do you want with her now?" he inquired.

"Do you think I will permit my son to abandon a girl in Paris?" Léonie said fiercely. "That is noble, yes! I tell you, I have been alone in a great city and there is nothing I do not know of what may happen to a girl who has no protector."

"But you said this wench was a——"

"I may have said it, but that was because I was angry. I do not know what she is, and I will find her immediately. If Dominique has done her a wrong he shall marry her."

Lord Rupert clasped his head in his hands. "Hang me, if I know what you're about, Léonie!" he said. "Here's me dragged out of England to help you save the Cub from an adventuress, as I thought, and now you say the boy's to marry her!"

Léonie paid not the slightest heed to this. She went on pacing the room until suddenly an idea came to her, and she stopped short. "Rupert, Juliana is in Paris!"

"What of it?" said his lordship.

"But do you not see, that if Vidal has been staying here of course Juliana has met him?"

"Do you think she might know why the plaguey boy has gone off to Dijon?" inquired Rupert hopefully. "That's what bothers me. Why Dijon?"

Léonie wrinkled her brow in a puzzled manner. "But why, Rupert, is it Dijon that bothers you? I find the whole of this affair so very strange and without reason that for Dominique to have gone to Dijon is a bagatelle."

"Well, I don't know," Rupert said. "It's such a devilish queer place to go to. Dijon! What in the fiend's name would anybody want there? I'll tell you what it is, Léonie, the boy's behaving mighty oddly." He shook his head. "The ninth earl was given to these turns, so they say. It's a bad business."

Léonie stared at him. Lord Rupert tapped his forehead significantly. Léonie said in great indignation: "Are you telling me that my son is mad?"

"We'll hope he ain't," Rupert said pessimistically, "but you can't deny he's behaving in a manner no one would call sane. Dijon! Why, it's absurd!"

"If you were not Monseigneur's brother, Rupert, I should have one big quarrel with you. Mad! *Voyons*, he is not so mad as you, for you have not any sense at all. Let us go to find Juliana."

They found, not Juliana, but her hostess, laboriously writing what seemed to be a very long letter. When they were ushered into her boudoir she displayed as much startled surprise as could be expected of anyone so habitually placid. She got up to embrace Léonie, almost falling upon her neck. "*Mon Dieu,* is it you, Léonie?" she said, with a fat gasp. Then she held out a checking hand. "Not my cousin Justin? Do not say my cousin Justin is here!" she implored.

"Lord, you wouldn't see me here if he was in Paris!" said Rupert reassuringly.

"If Fanny is here, I cannot face her!" stated madame in

palpitating tones. She pointed to her desk, and the scattered sheets of gilt paper. "I am writing to her now. Why have you come? I am glad, yes, but I do not know why you have come."

"Glad, are you? Well, it don't sound like it," commented his lordship. "We've come chasing after that plaguey nephew of mine, and a devilish silly errand it is."

Madame sank down on to a spindle-legged chair, and stared at him with her mouth open. "You know, then?" she faltered.

"Yes, yes, we know everything!" Léonie said. "Now tell me where is Dominique, Elisabeth? Please tell me quickly."

"But I do not know!" cried madame, spreading out her two plump hands.

"Oh, *peste!*" said Léonie impatiently.

"Come now, that's the only thing we *do* know," said his lordship. "Vidal's gone to Dijon."

Madame looked from him to Léonie in blank bewilderment. "To Dijon? But why? Gracious God, why to Dijon?"

"Just what I said myself, cousin," replied Rupert triumphantly. "I don't say the boy hasn't his reasons, but what the devil he can want in Dijon beats me."

"Let me see Juliana," interrupted the Duchess. "I think perhaps she will know where is my son, for he is fond of her, and I feel very certain that she has seen him."

Madame gave a start. "Juliana?" she echoed hollowly. "Alas, then, you do not know!"

Lord Rupert looked at her with misgiving in his face. "Burn it, I believe you're going to start a mystery now. What's to do? Not that I want to know, for I've enough on my hands as it is, but you'd best tell us and so be done with it."

Thus encouraged, madame delivered her terrific pronouncement: "Juliana has eloped with Vidal!"

The effect of this on her hearers was to bereave them, momentarily, of all power of speech. Léonie stood staring in astonished incredulity, and Lord Rupert's jaw dropped perceptibly. Léonie found her tongue first.

"Bah, what a piece of nonsense!" she said. "I do not at all believe it!"

"Read that!" commanded madame dramatically, and handed her a crumpled sheet of paper.

It contained a brief message in Juliana's sprawling char-

acters: *"My dear Tante, pray do not be in a taking, but
I have gone with Vidal. I have No Time to write more, for
I am in Desperate Haste. Juliana."*

"But—but it is not possible!" stammered Léonie, growing
quite pale.

Lord Rupert snatched the letter unceremoniously out of
her hand. "Here, let me read it!" he said. His eyes ran over
the sheet. "Damme, if this doesn't beat all!" he ejaculated.
"Oh, there's not a doubt about it: the boy's gone stark,
staring crazy." He struck the paper with his hand. "It ain't decent, Léonie! I've naught to say against him abducting this
other wench: there's no harm in that. But when he takes
to running off with his cousin, blister it, it's time he was
clapped up!"

Mme. de Charbonne followed this rather imperfectly. "I
do not understand. Vidal has eloped with Juliana, that is
seen. But why, I ask you? Is it not permitted that they wed?
Now they make a scandal, and Fanny will come here, and I
am afraid of Fanny."

Léonie, who had possessed herself of Juliana's letter again,
said stubbornly: "I do not believe it. Dominique does not
love Juliana. There is a mistake. I remember, too, that Juliana is going to marry the Nobody."

Madame de Charbonne said that she still did not understand. Upon the matter being made plain to her, she remarked thoughtfully: "Ah, that is the young Englishman,
without doubt. He comes very often to see Juliana."

"What, is Frederick Comyn in Paris, too, then?" demanded
Rupert.

"That is the name," nodded madame. "A young man *tres
comme il faut*. But Juliana is going to marry Dominique."

"No!" said Léonie firmly. "He does not want to, and he
shall not."

"But, my dear, he has eloped with her, and he must
certainly marry her."

"Lord, that's nothing, Elisabeth!" said Rupert. "Juliana
ain't the only girl Vidal's eloped with. I'll tell you what it
is, the boy's a Bluebeard."

"Stop saying that he has eloped with Juliana!" ordered
Léonie, her eyes flashing. "I do not know why he has taken her
away, but of a certainty he has a reason."

"Taken her to Dijon, too," said my lord thoughtfully.
"Y'know, the more I think on it the less I believe in this Dijon

rubbish. It don't make sense. I can swallow the rest, but I'll admit that worries me."

"It is of all things the most incomprehensible," agreed madame.

"But you are *imbécile*, Rupert! To go to Dijon, that is not a great affair! Many people go to Dijon: it is nothing!"

"Do they?" said his lordship sceptically. "Well, I never met anyone that did. Why should they? What's to do at Dijon? Tell me that!"

"It is a town, Rupert, is it not? Then, of course, people go there. I do not find that part incomprehensible. But that Vidal should run away with Juliana—*voyons*, that is so incomprehensible that I do not believe it." She turned to Madame de Charbonne. "Do not write to Fanny! Me, I will arrange everything."

Madame sighed. "Very well, my dear. I do not want to write to Fanny, I am sure. It has been a very perplexing day, very *énervant*, I assure you. I ask myself, where, too, is the other girl? But that is not my affair, only that I think it very strange to depart without a word to me."

"What other girl?" asked Rupert, puzzled.

"The girl that was the friend of Juliana. Juliana asked her to visit us. She was in Paris with her aunt, and Juliana invited her to stay in my house."

Léonie brushed this aside. "I am not interested in Juliana's friend. She is not at all *à propos*."

"No, my dear, but I think it odd that she should go away like that."

"Belike she's gone with Vidal too," Lord Rupert said sarcastically.

Léonie refused to be diverted by this artless suggestion. She had been thinking hard, and now said: "If the Nobody—what is his name, Rupert?—Comyn. I will remember. If M. Comyn is in Paris, I think Juliana has eloped with him. Naturally, she would not tell you that, Elisabeth. If Vidal is with them, it is, *sans doute*, to make it to appear quite respectable. They had fled, perhaps to Dijon, and Vidal went to—to—*en chaperon*, in effect."

Lord Rupert listened to this in considerable astonishment. "Do you tell me Vidal's gone to play propriety?" he asked blankly. "*Vidal?* No, rabbit it, that's too much! You're the boy's mother, and of course you're bound to make the best of him, but to say he's gone to a silly place like Dijon to be a duenna to Juliana—Lord, you must be besotted, my dear!"

An irrepressible dimple peeped in Léonie's cheek. "It is not perhaps very probable," she admitted. "But he has not eloped with Juliana. I know he has not! It is all so strange that it makes my head ache, and I see that there is only one thing to do."

Lord Rupert breathed a sigh of relief. "You're a sensible woman, Léonie, 'pon my soul you are. If the luck favours us we'll reach home before Avon gets back from Newmarket."

Léonie tied the strings of her cloak under her chin, and shot a mischievous look at his lordship. *"Mon pauvre*, we are not going home."

Lord Rupert said disgustedly: "I might have known it. If ever there was a female with silly, wild notions in her head——"

"I am very sensible. You said so," Léonie pointed out, twinkling. "We will start very early in the morning, Rupert, and go to Dijon." She paused, and added buoyantly: *"Du vrai*, I find it *fort amusant*, you know. For it seems to me that my poor Dominique has now two ladies he must marry *à l'instant*, which is a thing not permitted. It does not amuse you, Rupert?"

"Amuse me?" gasped his lordship. "Amuse me to go junketing through France after that young devil and his pack of females? No, it don't! Bedlam's the place for Vidal, and damme, when I think of trying to explain all this to Avon I've a strong notion I'll end there myself." With which his lordship seized his hat and cane, and bidding his open-mouthed cousin a curt farewell, flung open the door for Léonie to pass out.

❧ Chapter XVI ❧

BY the time Miss Challoner and Mr. Comyn reached Dijon, neither regarded the coming nuptials with anything but feelings of profound depression, although each was determined to be married as soon as was possible. Mr. Comyn was prompted by his sense of propriety, and Miss Challoner by her dread of the Marquis's arrival.

They reached Dijon late in the day, and put up at the best inn. Miss Challoner desired Mr. Comyn to wait upon the English divine at once, but he was firm in refusing to go until the morning. He contended that it would be thought a very odd thing were he to demand to see the divine at the dinner-hour, and he informed Miss Challoner that if she supposed him to be afraid of my Lord Vidal, she quite mistook the matter. It was Miss Challoner's wish to leave Dijon for Italy immediately the wedding was over. Mr. Comyn was quite agreeable, but if there were the least chance of the Marquis's arrival, it would be more consonant with his dignity (he said) to await him in Dijon. He had no desire to escape a meeting with his lordship, and he pointed out to Miss Challoner that since Vidal was known to be deadly with his pistols, a hurried flight to Italy would savour very much of fright.

Miss Challoner, always reasonable, could appreciate the feelings which prompted Mr. Comyn to linger in Dijon, but dreaded the issue. She condemned the whole practice of duelling, and Mr. Comyn agreed that it was a stupid custom, and one that should be abolished.

On the morning following, he went to wait upon Mr.

Leonard Hammond, who was staying with his young charge at a château about three miles distant from the town. Miss Challoner, left to her own devices, found herself nervously listening for the sound of wheels, and continually getting up to look out of the window. This would not do, she decided; and since she hardly expected Mr. Comyn to return before noon she tied on her hat, and went out for a walk. It may have been the state of mind she was in, but she could find little to interest her, and having looked at three milliners' shops, and four mantua-makers, she went back to the inn to await Mr. Comyn's return.

He came in shortly before noon. He was unaccompanied, and looked grave. Miss Challoner said anxiously: "Did you not find this Mr. Hammond, sir?"

Mr. Comyn carefully laid his hat and riding-whip on a chair. "I was fortunate enough to find the gentleman at the château," he replied, "but I fear I have little dependence on him performing the rite of marriage for us."

"Good God!" cried Miss Challoner. "Do you mean that he refuses?"

"Mr. Hammond felt, ma'am, certain qualms which, when I consider the extreme delicacy of the circumstances, I cannot deem altogether unreasonable. My request he could not but think a strange one, and in short, ma'am, I found him very loth to take a part in so equivocal an affair."

Miss Challoner was conscious of a stab of impatience. "But you explained to him—you persuaded him, surely?"

"I endeavoured to do so, ma'am, but with indifferent success. Happily—or so I trust it may be found—I had my card about me, which in part reassured him as to my standing and credentials. I venture to think that had I been able to be private with him a little longer I might have prevailed with him. But, as we apprehended, he is a guest in the château, and his host—a gentleman of a choleric disposition—broke in on us with some demand which I, insufficiently conversant with the French tongue, was unable to understand. Mr. Hammond, not being desirous (as one might readily comprehend) of presenting to the Comte such a dubious visitor as I must have seemed, was at pains to be rid of me. I had nothing to do but to take my leave. I did so, with what grace I could assume under conditions which I found vastly disconcerting, and begged Mr. Hammond to be so good as to wait upon us here this afternoon."

Miss Challoner had listened to this speech with great patience. At the end of it she said, trying not to sound waspish: "But will he, sir?"

"I am inclined to believe so, ma'am." A smile disturbed the primness of Mr. Comyn's face. "When he showed reluctance, I promised to return to the château to seek another interview with him. A needy divine, ma'am, who has the good fortune to be in charge of a young gentleman making the Grand Tour, has of necessity to be careful of the company he keeps. I, Miss Challoner, appeared to be of so disreputable a character that Mr. Hammond, at the mere hint of a second visit, acceded to my request. I venture to think that when he has made your acquaintance he will see the matter in a more favourable light."

She had to laugh. "Of the pair of us, sir, it is you who are the most respectable, I fear. If this provoking Mr. Hammond knows my—my lamentable story he will scarcely look on me with approval."

"He does not, ma'am. Though not apt in the fabrication of lies, I was able to deceive the reverend gentlemen. With your leave, I will now bespeak luncheon."

"I suppose there is nothing else to be done," agreed Miss Challoner, accepting the situation.

Luncheon was served in the private parlour, but Miss Challoner's appetite had forsaken her. She was so sure that the Marquis would pursue her that even an hour's delay fretted her unbearably. Mr. Comyn said gently that he wished he could convince her of the impossibility of his lordship's preventing the marriage. But Miss Challoner, having by now acquired a very fair knowledge of the Marquis's temper, could not be convinced. Feeling, however, that her prospective bridegroom had already a good deal to put up with, she tried not to appear anxious. Had she but known it her consideration was wasted, for Mr. Comyn had a profound belief in the frailty of female nerves, and would have felt himself to be more master of the situation had he been obliged to allay her alarms. Her calm appeared to him to be the expression of an unimaginative nature, and instead of admiring her control, he wondered whether she was stupid, or merely phlegmatic.

Towards three o'clock Miss Challoner's inward fears were justified. A clatter of hooves and carriage wheels announced the arrival of a chaise. Miss Challoner grew rather pale,

and put out her hand towards Mr. Comyn. "It's my lord,"
she said unsteadily. "Please do not allow him to force you
into a duel! I cannot bear to bring so much trouble on
you!" She got up, twining her fingers together. "If only we
were safe married!" she said despairingly.

"Madam, if this is indeed his lordship, I propose, to save
you from his importunities, to inform him that we are married," said Mr. Comyn. He too rose, and glanced towards the
door. A voice there was no mistaking was heard outside,
raised in a peremptory demand. Mr. Comyn's lips tightened.
He looked at Miss Challoner for a moment. "It seems that
you were right, ma'am," he said drily. "Do you desire me to
say that we are already wed?"

"Yes," she answered. "No—I don't know. Yes, I think."

A quick step was coming down the passage; the handle
of the door was twisted violently round, and the Marquis
of Vidal stood on the threshold, booted and spurred, and
with raindrops glistening on his greatcoat.

His gaze swept the room, and came to rest on Miss
Challoner, standing motionless beside her chair. "Ah, Miss
Challoner!" he said. "So I find you, do I?" He strode forward, casting aside the riding-whip he carried, and gripped
her by the shoulders. "If you thought to escape me so easily,
you were wrong, my dear."

Mr. Comyn said in a voice of polite coldness: "Will your
lordship have the goodness to unhand my wife?"

The grip on Miss Challoner's shoulders tightened so suddenly that she winced. The Marquis glared at Mr. Comyn, his
breath coming short and fast. "What?" he thundered. "Your
wife?"

Mr. Comyn bowed. "The lady has done me the honour to
wed me this day, my lord."

The Marquis's fierce eyes reached Miss Challoner. "Is that
true? Mary, answer me! Is it true?"

She stared up at him; she was as white as her tucker.
"Perfectly, sir. I am married to Mr. Comyn."

"Married?" he repeated. "Married?" he almost flung her
from him. "By God, then, you shall be widowed soon
enough!" he swore.

There was murder in his face; one stride brought him to
Mr. Comyn, who felt instinctively for his sword-hilt. He had
no time to draw steel; my lord's lean fingers had him by

the throat, choking the life out of him. "You dog! You little damned cur!" my lord said through his shut teeth.

Miss Challoner, seeing the two men swaying together in the throes of a desperate struggle, started forward, but before she could reach the combatants a piercing scream came from the doorway, and Miss Marling, just arrived on the scene, flew across the room, and cast herself into the fray.

"You shall not! you shall not!" shrieked Miss Marling. "Let him go, you wicked, wicked brute!"

Miss Challoner, who saw that Mr. Comyn was hopelessly over-weighted, looked round for a suitable weapon. She caught sight of the water-jug still standing on the table, and with her usual presence of mind picked it up. "Stand aside, Juliana!" she said coolly, and dashed the water impartially over both men. Miss Marling, having paid no heed to the warning, also received her share, and fell back, gasping.

The sudden shock must have sobered his lordship, for he released his grip on Mr. Comyn's throat, and put up his hands to wipe the wet out of his eyes. Mr. Comyn went staggering backwards, feeling his neck, and coughing. Miss Marling ran to him, sobbing: "Frederick! oh, my poor Frederick, are you hurt?"

It was to be seen that Mr. Comyn had lost his prim punctiliousness. He thrust her off unceremoniously, and said angrily: "Hurt? No!" He tried to straighten his damaged neckcloth. He was in as great a rage as the Marquis by this time, and stuttered a little in his haste to utter his challenge. "Swords or pistols?" he demanded. "Choose your weapon, and choose it quickly."

"No!" cried Juliana, trying to fling her arms round him. "Vidal, you shall not! Frederick, please, please, be calm!"

He disengaged himself from her clinging hands. "Madam, I have nothing whatsoever to say to you," he snapped. "Be good enough to stand away from me! Well, my lord? Which is it to be?"

The Marquis was looking at Miss Challoner with an odd smile lifting the corners of his mouth. "Mary, you little wretch!" he said softly. He turned his head, and his eyes hardened again as they rested on Mr. Comyn's pale countenance. "Either will do your business for you, you treacherous cur!" he said. "Choose which you will."

Juliana wrung her hands. "Oh, you'll kill him! I know you will!" she wailed.

"I shall," said his lordship silkily.

Miss Challoner grasped the edge of the mantelpiece. "This has gone far enough," she said. "Please listen to me for a moment."

Mr. Comyn, who was struggling with his top-boots, said quickly: "Nothing you can say will deter me from fighting his lordship! Pray hold your peace! We will have this out with swords, my lord, and I trust that I may be able to rid the world of one whose instincts are more those of a beast than of a gentleman of breeding."

"Oh, but you will never succeed in killing him!" almost wept Miss Marling. "Oh, Frederick, I am sorry for everything! Don't fight Vidal! I implore you not to!"

Mr. Comyn turned a flint-like face towards her. "Madam, I have already informed you that I have nothing to say to you. I do not know why you are here, but you come in excellent time to felicitate me. Miss Challoner has done me the honour to marry me."

Miss Marling clutched at a chair-back for support. "Married?" she faltered. "Oh, oh, oh!"

Only Miss Challoner paid any heed to this fit of mild hysterics. The Marquis took off his greatcoat, coat, and boots, and stood in his shirt and breeches, testing the flexibility of his slim blade. The Dresden ruffles of his shirt fell over his hands, but Mr. Comyn rolled up his own sleeves with business-like haste. He cast his lordship a look of angry dislike, and as he pulled his rapier from the scabbard, he said in a low, unsteady voice: "You have called me by some names I will presently force down your throat, sir. I take leave to tell you that your persecution of the lady who is my wife——"

But that fatal word fanned the flame of his lordship's passion. He said, white-lipped: "Damn you to hell, you shall not long call her so!" He thrust the table back against the wall, and turned. "On guard!"

"I am at your service," said Mr. Comyn.

There was the briefest of salutes; then the blades hissed together with a venom that brought Miss Challoner from Juliana's side in a flash. She cried out: "Shame! shame on you both! Put up! put up! I am not married, no, and shall not be to either of you!"

Her words fell on deaf ears. The duel was too desperate an affair to permit of either man's listening to her. Each was in a white heat of fury; each meant to make an end of the other.

The rapier was not Vidal's weapon, but his wrist had great strength and cunning, and he fought with a dashing brilliance disconcerting to the more careful fencer. His sword play was dangerous, he took risks, but drove his opponent hard. Mr. Comyn's fencing was neat, and it was plain he had been well-taught, but my lord had a pace which he lacked, and broke through his guard time after time. He recovered always, and by some dexterous parry escaped the death that threatened, but he was hard-pressed, and the sweat rolled down his forehead in great drops.

Juliana, realizing what was going on, abandoned her hysterics, and cowered in the chair hiding her face in her hands, and sobbing. Miss Challoner stood beside her, intently watching the swift thrust and parry of the swords.

"Make them stop! Oh, good God, can no one make them stop?" wept Juliana, shuddering as steel rang against steel in a scuffle of blades.

"I hope very much that they will make an end of each other!" said Miss Challoner, stiff with anger.

"How can you say such a thing?" gasped Juliana. "It is all your fault! Oh, but *married!* married!"

The stockinged feet padded on the bare floor; Mr. Comyn, disengaging above the wrist, was forced back hard against the table. Miss Challoner saw his guard waver, and knew all at once that he was spent. The Marquis followed up his advantage ruthlessly, and Miss Challoner, forgetting her pious wish, seized one of the discarded coats, and ran in on the swords, catching at them through the heavy cloth. She threw herself in the way as the Marquis lunged; Mr. Comyn's blade was entangled in the coat, but his lordship's point flashed under it, driven by the whole force of his arm. It seemed as though to check were an impossibility; Juliana, peeping through her fingers, gave a scream of warning and horror. The Marquis's point glanced up Miss Challoner's arm, ripping her gown at the shoulder, and was wrenched back.

The sword went spinning, my lord caught Miss Challoner's swaying form in his arms, his face as white as hers. "Mary! Mary!" he said hoarsely. My God, what have I done?"

"Murderer! You have killed her!" panted Mr. Comyn, and came up close as though to snatch Miss Challoner away from him.

He was thrust aside. "Stand off from her!" the Marquis shot at him. "Mary, look at me! Mary, my little love, my precious girl, I've not killed you!"

Miss Challoner, who had half fainted, more from shock than actual hurt, opened her eyes and achieved a wan smile. "It's nothing," she whispered. "The—the—veriest pin-prick. Oh, what did you call me?"

The Marquis lifted her quite off her feet, and carried her to the armchair just vacated by Juliana. He put her gently down in it, and saw the red stain at the neck of her gown. Over his shoulder he threw an order at Mr. Comyn. "Get the flask from my greatcoat!"

Juliana cried: "Oh, there is blood on her dress! Mary, are you dreadfully hurt?"

Without the smallest hesitation the Marquis ripped open the front of Mary's grey gown, and laid bare the injured shoulder. It was a very slight wound, the sword point having caused no more than a long scratch, but it was bleeding a little. Mary tried to pull her gown up over it, repeating that it was nothing, but was told not to be a fool. This was very much in his lordship's usual manner, and she could not forbear a smile.

"No, it's only a scratch," Vidal said, with a sigh of relief. He pulled his handkerchief from his breeches pocket and bound the wound up deftly. "Little fool!" he scolded. "Do you know no better than to run in on a fight? You might have been killed!"

"I thought I was going to be," said Miss Challoner in rather an uncertain voice. She lifted her hand to her head. "I feel a little dizzy. I shall be well in a moment."

Mr. Comyn, whose face now wore a very thoughtful expression, came to my lord's elbow with the flask of brandy. Vidal snapped it open, and put it to Mary's lips, his other arm encircling her. "Come, drink this!" he said.

Mary tried to push it away. "Oh, no, I so very much dislike it! I am better now—truly, I am better now!"

"Do as I bid you!" commanded his lordship curtly. "You know me well enough to be sure I'll make you."

Mr. Comyn said protestingly: "Really, sir, if she does not want it——"

"Go to the devil!" said his lordship.

Miss Challoner meekly sipped a small quantity of the brandy, and raised her eyes to see the Marquis smiling down at her with so much tenderness in his face that she hardly recognized him. "Good girl!" he said, and dropped a light kiss on her hair.

His eye fell on Mr. Comyn again, and hardened. He removed his arm from about Miss Challoner, and stood up. "You may have married her," he said fiercely, "but she is mine, do you hear me? She was always mine! You——! do you think I shall let you take her? She may be ten times your wife, but, by God, you shall never have her!"

Mr. Comyn, having regained control over his temper, showed no sign of losing it again. "As to that, sir, I believe a word with you alone would be timely." He looked fleetingly at Juliana, who was standing by the window, her face quite rigid. "Juliana—Miss Marling——" he said.

She gave a shudder. "Do not speak to me!" she said. "Oh, Frederick, Frederick, how could you do it? I did not mean a word that I said! You should have known I did not! I hope I never set eyes on you again!"

Mr. Comyn turned away from her to Mary, who was trying to collect her scattered wits. "Madam, I believe nothing will serve now but frankness. But I await your pleasure."

She got up, steadying herself with a hand on the arm of the chair. "Do what seems best to you," she said faintly. "I must be alone a little while. I am not quite myself yet. I'll go up to my chamber. For God's sake, gentlemen, let there be no more fighting. I am not worth it."

"Juliana, go with her!" said Vidal sharply.

Miss Challoner shook her head. "Please let me be alone. I don't need Juliana, or anyone."

"I'll not go!" Juliana said. "If she is hurt I vow it serves her right! She stole Frederick from me by a hateful trick, and I wish her joy of him, and she shan't have him!"

Miss Challoner gave a little laugh that broke in the middle, and went to the door. Mr. Comyn opened it for her to pass out, and what seemed to be the entire staff of the inn was disclosed in the passage. The landlord and his wife, two serving-maids, a cook, and three ostlers, were all gathered round the door, and had evidently been listening to everything that had been going on inside the parlour. They looked very sheepish upon the door being so suddenly opened, and dispersed in a hurry. Mr. Comyn said sarcastically that he was happy to be a source of so much interest, but since he spoke in English no one understood him. The landlord,

who had stood his ground, began to say that so scandalous
a fracas in a respectable house could not be permitted. Lord
Vidal turned his head, and spoke one soft, short phrase. The
landlord looked very much taken aback, excused himself,
and withdrew.

Meanwhile, Miss Challoner had walked straight past the
group of servants, down the passage to the coffee-room, out
of which the stairs rose to the upper floor. She entered it,
holding her torn dress together, in time to hear a jovial voice
say in English: "Burn it, the place is deserted! Hey, there!
House!"

Miss Challoner looked quickly towards the door. A tall,
rakish man of middle age was standing there, his Rockelaure
thrown open to display a rich suit of purple cloth with gold
lacing, and a fine flowered waistcoat. He did not perceive
Miss Challoner, and conscious of her dishevelled appearance,
she drew back into the ill-lit passage. The landlord, hearing
the shout, came hurrying past her, and was greeted by a
fluent demand to know what the devil ailed the place that
there wasn't so much as a groom to be seen.

The landlord's apologies and explanations were cut short
by the somewhat tempestuous entrance of a copper-headed
lady in a gown of green taffeta, and a cloak clutched round
her by one small hand. "It is not at all deserted, because my
son is here," asserted this lady positively. "I told you we
should find him, Rupert. *Voyons,* I am very glad we came
to Dijon."

"Well, he ain't here so far as I can see," replied his
lordship. "Damme, if I can make out what this fellow's talking about!"

"Of course, he is here! I have seen his chaise! Tell me
at once, you, where is the English monsieur?"

Miss Challoner's hand stole to her cheek. This imperious
and fascinating little lady must be my lord's mother. She
cast a glance about her for a way of escape, and seeing a
door behind her, pushed it open, and stepped into what
seemed to be some sort of a pantry.

The landlord was trying to explain that there were a great
many English people in his house, all fighting duels or having
hysterics. Miss Challoner heard Lord Rupert say: "What's
that? Fighting? Then I'll lay my life Vidal is here! Well,
I'm glad we've not come to this devilish out-of-the-way place

for nothing, but if Vidal's in that sort of a humour, Léonie, you'd best keep out of it."

The Duchess's response to this piece of advice was to demand to be taken immediately to her son, and the landlord, by now quite bewildered by the extremely odd people who had all chosen to visit his hostelry at the same time, threw up his hands in an eloquent gesture, and led the way to the private parlour.

Miss Challoner, straining her ears to catch what was said, heard Lord Vidal exclaim: "Thunder an' Turf, it's my mother! What, Rupert too? What the devil brings you here?"

Lord Rupert answered: "That's rich, 'pon my soul it is!"

Then the Duchess's voice broke in, disastrously clear and audible. "Dominique, where is that girl? Why did you run off with Juliana? What have you done with that other one whom I detest infinitely already? *Mon fils,* you must marry her, and I do not know what Monseigneur will say, but I am very sure that at last you have broken my heart. Oh, Dominique, I did not want you to wed such an one as that!"

Miss Challoner waited for no more. She slipped out of the pantry, and went through the coffee-room to the stairs. In her sunny bedchamber, looking out on to the street, she sank down on a chair by the window, trying to think how she could escape. She found that she was crying, and angrily brushed away the tears.

Outside, the Duchess's chaise was being driven round to the stables, and a huge, lumbering coach, piled high with baggage, was standing under her window. The driver had mounted the box, but was leaning over to speak to a fat gentleman carrying a cloak-bag and a heavy coat. Miss Challoner started up, looked more closely at the coach, and ran to the door.

One of the abigails who had lately had her ear glued to the parlour door, was crossing the upper landing. Miss Challoner called to her to know what was the coach at the door. The abigail stared, and said she supposed it would be the *diligence* from Nice.

"Where does it go?" Miss Challoner asked, trembling with suppressed anxiety.

"Why, to Paris, *bien sûr, madame,*" replied the girl, and was surprised to see Miss Challoner dart back into her room. She emerged again in a few moments, her cloak caught hastily round her, her reticule, stuffed with her few belongings, on her arm, and hastened downstairs.

No one was in the coffee-room, and she went across it to the front door. The guard of the *diligence* had just swung himself up into his place, but when he saw Miss Challoner hailing him, he came down again, and asked her very civilly what she desired.

She desired a place in the coach. He ran an appraising eye over her as he said that this could be arranged, and asked whither she was bound.

"How much money is needed for me to travel as far as Paris?" Miss Challoner inquired, colouring faintly.

He named a sum which she knew to be beyond her slender means. Swallowing her pride, she told him what money she had at her disposal, and asked how far she could travel with it. The guard named, rather brutally, Pont-de-Moine, a town some twenty-five miles distant from Dijon. He added that she would have enough left in her purse to pay for a night's lodging. She thanked him, and since at the moment she did not care where she went as long as she could escape from Dijon, she said that she would journey as far as Pont-de-Moine.

"We shall arrive before ten," said the guard, apparently thinking this a matter for congratulation.

"Good heavens, not till ten o'clock?" exclaimed Miss Challoner, aghast at such slow progress.

"The *diligence* is a fast *diligence*," said the guard offendedly. "It will be very good time. Where is your baggage, mademoiselle?"

When Miss Challoner confessed that she had none, he obviously thought her a very queer passenger, but he let down the steps for her to mount into the coach, and accepted the money she handed him.

In another minute the driver's whip cracked, and the coach began to move ponderously forward over the cobbles. Miss Challoner heaved a sigh of relief, and squeezed herself into a place between a farmer smelling of garlic and a very fat woman with a child on her knee.

❧ Chapter XVII ❧

UPON the Duchess of Avon's entry into the parlour, Vidal had come quickly towards her, and caught her in his arms. But her opening speech made him let her go, and the welcoming light in his eyes fled. His heavy frown, so rarely seen by her, descended on his brow. He stepped back from Léonie, and shot a scowling look at Lord Rupert. "Why did you bring my mother here?" he said. "Can you not keep from meddling, curse you?"

"Easily, never fear it!" retorted Rupert. "Fiend seize you, d'ye think I want to go chasing all over France for the pleasure of seeing you? Bring your mother? Lord, I've been begging and imploring her to come home ever since we started out! God bless my soul, is that young Comyn?" He put up his glass, and stared through it. "Now what the plague are you doing here?" he inquired.

Léonie put her hand on Vidal's arm. "It is of no use to be enraged, *mon enfant*. You have done a great wickedness. Where is that girl?"

"If you are speaking of the lady who was Miss Challoner," replied Vidal icily, "she is upstairs."

Léonie said quickly: "*Was* Miss Challoner? You have married her? Oh, Dominique, no!"

"You are entirely in the right, madame. I have not married her. She is married to Comyn," said his lordship bitterly.

The effect of this pronouncement on the Duchess was unexpected. She at once turned to Mr. Comyn, who was trying to put on his coat again as unobtrusively as possible, and caught his hand in both her own. "*Voyons*, I am so very

glad! It is you who are Mr. Comyn? I hope you will be
very happy, m'sieur. Oh, but *very* happy!"

Juliana gave a strangled cry at this. "How can you be so
cruel, Aunt Léonie? He is betrothed to me!"

"Damme, if he's betrothed to you how came you to go
off with Vidal?" demanded Lord Rupert reasonably.

"I didn't!" Juliana declared.

"I said it was not so!" said her grace triumphantly. "You
see, Rupert!"

"No, I'll be pinked if I do," replied his lordship. "If it
was Comyn you ran off with, why did you say you'd gone
with Vidal, in that devilish silly note of yours?"

"I didn't run off with Frederick! You don't understand,
Uncle Rupert."

"Then whom in the fiend's name did you run off with?"
said his lordship.

"With Vidal—at least, I went with him, but of course I
did not elope, if that is what you mean! I hate Vidal! I
wouldn't marry him for the world."

"No, my girl, you'd not have the chance," struck in the
Marquis.

Léonie at last released Mr. Comyn's hand, which all this
time she had been warmly clasping. "Do not quarrel, *mes
enfants*. I find all this very hard to understand. Please explain to me, one of you!"

"They're all mad, every one of 'em," said Rupert with
conviction. He had put up his glass again, and was observing
his nephew's attire through it. "Blister it, the boy can't spend
one week without being in a fresh broil! Swords, eh? Well,
I'm not saying that ain't better than those barbarous pistols
of yours, but why in thunder you must be for ever fighting.—
Where's the corpse?"

"Never mind about that!" interrupted Léonie impatiently.
"I will have all of this explained to me at once!" She turned
once more to Mr. Comyn, who had by now pulled on his
boots and was feeling more able to face her. She smiled
engagingly at him. "My son is in a very bad temper and
Juliana is not at all sensible, so I shall ask you to tell me
what has happened."

Mr. Comyn bowed. "I shall be happy to oblige you, ma'am.
In fact, when your grace entered this room, I was about
to make a communication of a private nature to his lordship."

Vidal, who had gone over to the fireplace, and was staring

down into the red embers, lifted his head. "What is it you have to say to me?"

"My lord, it is a communication I should have desired to impart to you alone, but if you wish I will speak now."

"Tell me and be done with it," said my lord curtly, and resumed his study of the fire.

Mr. Comyn bowed again. "Very well, sir. I must first inform your lordship that when I had the honour of making Miss Challoner's acquaintance at the house of Mme. de Charbonne in Paris——"

Léonie had sat down in the armchair, but started up again. *"Mon Dieu,* the friend of Juliana! Why did I not perceive that that must be so?"

"Because if anyone spoke a word about aught save Dijon you would not listen," said Rupert severely. "And that reminds me, Vidal: what in thunder brought you here? I've been puzzling over it all the way, and stap me if I can make it out."

"I had a reason." Vidal answered briefly.

"It does not matter in the least," said her grace. "But it was very stupid of me not to see that of course the friend of Juliana must be this Mary Challoner. It was stupid of you too, Rupert. More stupid."

"Stupid of me? Lord, how the devil should I guess Vidal would take his——" He encountered a sudden fiery glance from his nephew, and stopped short. "Oh, very well!" he said. "I'm mum."

"So you went to Tante Elisabeth?" cried Juliana. "I see!"

Mr. Comyn, who had waited in vain for the interruptions to cease, saw that he must be firm if he wished to make himself heard in this vociferous family. He cleared his throat, and continued loudly: "As I was saying, my lord, when I first had the honour of making Miss Challoner's better acquaintance I was under the impression that not only was your lordship's suit disagreeable to her, but that you yourself were constrained to wed the lady out of consideration—which I confess surprised me—for her reputation, and were not prompted by any of the tenderer feelings. Being convinced of this, I had little compunction, upon Miss Marling's sundering our secret betrothal, in offering for Miss Challoner's hand; an arrangement which I believed would be preferable to her than a marriage with your lordship."

My Lord Rupert, who had been listening in rapt admiration to this speech, said in what he imagined to be a whisper:

"Wonderful, ain't it, Léonie? Never heard aught to equal it. The boy always talks like that, y'know."

Juliana said throbbingly: "Indeed, Frederick? And the marriage was, I need hardly ask, more to your taste than our contract?"

"Madam," replied Mr. Comyn, looking steadily across at her, "when you informed me that you had no desire to wed one so far removed from your world as myself, it mattered very little to me whom I married. I had for Miss Challoner a profound respect; and on this I believed it would be possible to lay the foundations of a tolerably happy marriage. Miss Challoner was so obliging as to accept of my offer, and we set forth immediately for this town with what speed we could muster."

"Hold a minute!" besought Rupert, suddenly alert. "Why Dijon? Tell me that!"

"You take the devil of a time arriving at the point of your story," struck in the Marquis impatiently. "Be a little more brief, and to hell with your periods."

"I will endeavour, my lord. Upon the journey——"

"Damn it, am I never to know why you came to Dijon?" said Rupert despairingly.

"Hush, Rupert! Let Mr. Comyn speak!" reproved Léonie.

"Speak? The dratted fellow's never ceased speaking for the past ten minutes," complained his lordship. "Well, go on, man, go on!"

"Upon the journey," repeated Mr. Comyn with unwearied patience, "I was gradually brought to realize that Miss Challoner's affections were more deeply involved than I had supposed. Yet I could not but agree with her that a marriage with your lordship would be unsuitable in the extreme. My determination to marry her remained unshaken, for I believed your lordship to be indifferent to her. But when the late accident occurred it was apparent to anyone of the meanest intelligence that you felt for the lady all the most tender passions which any female could wish for in her future husband."

The Marquis was watching him intently. "Well, man? Well?"

The question was destined to remain unanswered. A fresh interruption occurred. The landlord scratched on the door, and opened it to say: "There is another English monsieur desires to see M. Comyn. He calls himself M. Hammond."

"Tell him to go to the devil!" said Lord Rupert irritably.

"Never heard of the fellow in my life! He can't come in now."

"Hammond?" said the Marquis sharply. He strode up to Mr. Comyn, his eyes suddenly eager. "Then you've not done it? Quick, man, it was a lie?"

"It was a lie, my lord," answered Mr. Comyn quietly.

Lord Rupert listened open-mouthed to this interchange, and glanced hopelessly at the Duchess. Her eyes had begun to twinkle, and she said frankly: "It is quite incomprehensible, *mon vieux*. Me, I know nothing, and no one tells me."

"Plague take it, I won't have it!" roared his lordship, goaded beyond endurance. "What's a lie? Who's this fellow Hammond? Oh, I'll end in Bedlam, devil a doubt!"

"Shall I tell the English monsieur that M. Comyn is engaged?" asked the landlord doubtfully.

"Bring him in here at once!" commanded Rupert. "Don't stand there goggling, fatwit! Go and fetch him!"

"Yes, go and fetch him," said the Marquis. He was still looking at Mr. Comyn, but he was frowning no longer. "Good God, Comyn, do you know how near to death you have been?" he asked softly.

Mr. Comyn smiled. "I am aware, my lord. The heat of the moment—excusable, you will agree—being happily past, I can make allowances for the very natural fury of a man deeply in love."

"Mighty good of you," said his lordship with a rather rueful grin. "I'll admit I'm a thought too ready with my hands." He turned as the door was once more opened to admit a gentleman dressed in a black habit and bands, and a Ramillies wig. "Mr. Hammond?" he said. "In a very good hour, sir!"

The cleric looked him over with patent disapproval. "I have not the pleasure, I think, of your acquaintance, sir," he said frigidly. "I am come here, much against my will, at the request of Mr.—ah—Comyn."

"But it is I who need your services, sir," said his lordship briskly. "My name's Alastair. You are, I believe, making the Grand Tour in charge of Lord Edward Crewe?"

"I am, sir, but I fail to understand what interest this can be to you."

Light broke upon Lord Rupert with dazzling radiance. Suddenly he smote his knee and called out: "By the holy Peter, I have it! The man's a parson, and that is why you came to Dijon! Lord, it's as plain as the nose on your face!"

Mr. Hammond looked at him with acute dislike. "You have the advantage of me, sir."

"Eh?" said Rupert. "Oh, my name's Alastair."

Mr. Hammond flushed angrily. "Sir, if this is a pleasantry it is one that in no way amuses me. If you summoned me here, Mr. Comyn, for some boorish jest——"

Léonie got up, and came towards him. "But do not be enraged, m'sieur," she said kindly. "No one jests, I assure you. Will you not be seated?"

Mr. Hammond thawed a little. "I thank you, ma'am. If I might know whom I have the honour of addressing——?"

"Oh, her name's Alastair, too," said Rupert, who was fast lapsing into a rollicking mood.

Mr. Comyn intervened hastily as the divine showed signs of deep offence. "Permit me, my lord! Let me make you known to her grace the Duchess of Avon, sir. Also her grace's son, my Lord Vidal, and her grace's brother-in-law, Lord Rupert Alastair."

Mr. Hammond recoiled perceptibly, and stared in horror at the Marquis. "Do I understand that this is none other than that Marquis of Vidal who—sir, if I had known, no persuasion would have sufficed to draw me into this house!"

The Marquis's brows lifted. "My good sir," he said, "you are not sent for to condemn my morals, but to marry me to a certain lady at present staying in this inn."

Léonie cried out, aghast: "But you cannot, Dominique! You said that she is married to M. Comyn!"

"So I thought, madame, but she is not."

"Sir," said Mr. Hammond very furiously, "I shall perform no marriage service!"

Lord Rupert looked at him through his quizzing glass. "Who *is* this fellow?" he inquired haughtily. "I don't like him, stap me if I do!"

"Dominique," Léonie said urgently, "I cannot talk to you here, with all these people. You say you will marry this girl, but it seems to me that it is not all necessary, for first she runs away with you, and then with M. Comyn, so that I see very well she is like that mother and sister whom I have met."

He took her hands. "Maman, when you have seen her you will know that she is not like them. I am going to marry her." He drew her over to the window, and said gently: "*Ma chère*, you told me to fall in love, did you not?"

"Not with a girl like this one," she replied, with a small sob.

"You will like her," he persisted. "Egad, she's after your own heart, maman! She shot me in the arm."

"*Voyons*, do you think that is what I like?" Léonie said indignantly.

"You'd have done it yourself, my dear." He paused, staring out of the window. She watched him anxiously, and after a moment he turned his head and looked down at her. "Madame, I love her," he said curtly. "If I can induce her to take me——"

"What's this? Induce her! I find you absurd, *mon enfant*."

He smiled faintly. "She ran off with Comyn sooner than wed me, nevertheless."

"Where is she?" Léonie asked abruptly.

"In her bed-chamber. There was an accident. When Comyn and I had our little affair, she threw herself between us, and my sword scratched her."

"Oh, *mon Dieu!*" Léonie exclaimed, throwing up her hands. "It is not enough to abduct her! No, you must wound her also! You are incorrigible!"

"Will you see her, maman?"

"I will see her, yes, but I promise nothing. Dominique, have you thought of Monseigneur? He will never, never permit it! You know he will not."

"He cannot stop it, madame. If it leads to an estrangement between us I am sorry for it, but my mind is made up." He pressed her hand. "Come to her now, *ma chère*." He led her back into the room. "Comyn, since you know Miss Challoner's room and I do not, will you have the goodness to escort my mother to her?"

Mr. Comyn, who was talking earnestly to Mr. Hammond, turned at once, and bowed. "I shall be happy to do so, sir."

Rupert called out: "Hey, where are you off to, Léonie? Tell me, do we spend the night in this place?"

"I don't know," Léonie answered. "I am going to make the acquaintance of this Mademoiselle Challoner."

She went out, followed by Mr. Comyn, and his lordship shook his head gloomily. "It won't do, Vidal. You can talk your mother over, but if you think your father will stand this you don't know him. Lord, I wish I were well out of it!" He became aware of his nephew's coatless and bootless state. "For God's sake, boy, put your clothes on!" he begged.

Vidal laughed, and sat down to pull on his boots. His uncle observed them through his glass with considerable interest. "Did Haspener make those for you, Vidal?"

"Lord, no!" said the Marquis scornfully. "What, does he make yours still? These are a pair of Martin's."

"Martin, eh? I've a mind to let him make me a pair. I don't like your coats, I don't like your stock-buckle, your hats have too rakish a cock for a man of my years, your waistcoats are damned unimaginative, but one thing I'll allow: your boots are the best made in the town, ay, and the highest polished. What does your fellow use on 'em? I've tried a blacking made with champagne, but it ain't as good as you'd expect."

Mr. Hammond broke in on this with unconcealed impatience. "Sir, is this a moment in which to discuss the rival merits of your bootmakers? Lord Vidal! Finding me adamant, Mr. Comyn has favoured me with an explanation of this extraordinary situation."

"He has, has he?" said the Marquis, looking round for his coat.

"Devilish fluent, he was," nodded Lord Rupert. "Y'know, Vidal, it's a bad business, but you can't marry the girl. There's the name to be thought on, and what's more, Justin."

Mr. Hammond cast him a fulminating glance, but addressed himself to the Marquis. "My lord, his explanation leaves me horrified, I may say aghast, at the impropriety of your lordship's behaviour. My instinct, sir, is to wash my hands of the whole affair. If I relent, it is out of no desire to oblige one whose mode of life is abhorrent to me, but out of compassion for the unfortunate young female whose fair name you have sullied, and in the interests of morality."

Lord Rupert stopped swinging his eyeglass, and said indignantly: "Damme, I'd not be married by this fellow if I were you, Vidal. Not that I'm saying you should be married at all, for the thing's preposterous."

Vidal shrugged. "What do you suppose I care for his opinion of me so long as he does what I want?"

"Well, I don't know," said his lordship. "Things are come to a pretty pass, so they are, when any plaguey parson takes it on himself to preach a damned sermon to your face. Why, in my father's time—you never knew him: devilish bad-tempered man he was—in his time, I say, if the chaplain said aught he didn't like—and from the pulpit, mind you!—he'd throw his snuff-box at him, or anything else he had to hand . . . Now what's to do?"

The Duchess had come back into the room in a hurry. "She is not there, *mon fils*," she announced, not entirely without relief.

"What?" Vidal said quickly. "Not there?"

"She is not in the inn. I do not know where she is. No one knows."

The Marquis almost brushed past her, and went out. Léonie sighed, and looked at Rupert. "I cannot help being a little glad that she has gone," she confessed. "But why does she run away so much? I find it not at all easy to understand."

Juliana, who had been sitting for a long time by the fire, staring into it, now raised her voice. "You don't want Vidal to marry her, Aunt Léonie, but indeed she is the very one for him. She loves him, too."

"*Eh bien*, if she loves him I understand less than ever why she runs away."

"She thinks she is not good enough for him," said Juliana.

Mr. Hammond picked up his hat. "Since I apprehend that the unfortunate female I came here to serve has departed, I shall beg to take my leave. To perform this marriage service would have been vastly repugnant to me, and I can only be thankful that the need for it no longer exists."

The Duchess's large eyes surveyed him critically. "If you are going, m'sieur, it is a very good thing, for I find you infinitely *de trop*, and in a little while I shall be out of all patience with you."

Mr. Hammond's jaw dropped perceptibly at this unexpected severity, and he became extremely red about the gills. Lord Rupert pressed his hat and cane upon him with great promptitude, and lounged over to open the door. "Outside, Sir Parson!" he said cheerfully.

"I shall relieve your grace of my unwelcome presence at once," announced Mr. Hammond awfully, and bowed.

"Never mind your civilities," recommended his lordship. "They come a trifle late. But one word in your ear, my buck! If you bandy my nephew's name about in connection with this affair, my friend Lord Manton will look for another bear-leader for his cub. Do you take me?"

"Your threats, sir, leave me unmoved," replied Mr. Hammond. "But I can assure your lordship that my one desire is to forget the prodigiously disagreeable events of this day." He grasped his cane tighter in his hand, tucked his hat under his arm, and went out, very erect and stiff.

Lord Rupert kicked the door to. "Let's hope that's the last we'll see of that fellow," he said. "Now what's all this about Vidal's wench? Gone off, has she? Well, that's one problem off our hands."

"That is just what I thought," sighed the Duchess. "But Dominique is in love with her, and I fear very much he will try to find her, and if he does he says he will marry her, which is a thing I find very worrying."

"Marry her? What does the boy want to marry her for?" asked his lordship, puzzled. "It don't seem sense to me. First the girl's off with him, then she has a fancy for young Comyn —oh, are you there, my boy? Well, it makes no odds—and now I'll be pinked if she hasn't gone off again, though whom she's gone with this time is beyond me."

Mr. Comyn said gravely: "Your lordship is mistaken in Miss Challoner. I can explain——"

"No, no, don't do that, my boy!" said Rupert hastily. "We've had enough explanations. What we want is dinner. Where's that rascally landlord?" He went to the door, but as he opened it he bethought himself of something, and looked back. "Burn it, if we do get rid of Vidal's wench there's still that silly chit Juliana. What's to be done with her?"

Juliana said in a small, dignified voice: "I am here, Uncle Rupert."

"Of course you're there. I've eyes in my head, haven't I?" said his lordship testily. "Though why you're here the Lord only knows. Well, there's naught for it: you'll have to marry young Comyn here, unless Vidal will have you, which I don't think he will. Lord, was there ever such a family?"

Mr. Comyn was regarding Juliana fixedly. She did not look at him, but blushed, and stammered: "I do not want to— to marry Mr. Comyn, and he does not want to marry m-me."

"Now don't start to make a lot more difficulties!" begged his lordship. "You can't go chasing all over France with a man, and leaving silly letters for a born fool like Elisabeth, and stay single. Why, it's unheard of!"

"I did not go with a—a man!" said Juliana, blushing more deeply still. "I went with my cousin."

"I know you did," said Rupert frankly. "That's what's bothering me."

The Duchess was pondering over her own worries, but this caught her attention, and she fired up. "It is perfectly respectable for Juliana to go with my son, Rupert!"

"It ain't," said Rupert. "She couldn't have chosen a worse companion. Now don't be in a heat, Léonie, for God's sake! I don't say the chit wasn't as safe with Vidal as with that devilish dull brother of hers, but there ain't a soul will believe that. No, we'll have to set it about that she went off with Comyn, and you can tell Fanny, for I'll be damned if I do."

Léonie glanced from her niece's hot face to Mr. Comyn's intent one, and drew her own conclusions. "Juliana shall not marry anyone at all if she doesn't want to, and no one will make a scandal because I am here, and so it is quite *convenable*," she said. "Go and order dinner, Rupert. Me, I must at once find Dominique before he does anything dreadful."

She pushed his lordship, protesting, out of the room, and looked back to say with her roguish smile: "M. Comyn, I think it would be a very good thing if you gave this foolish Juliana a big shake, and then perhaps she will not be foolish any more. *Au revoir, mes enfants*." She whisked herself out of the room, but before she had time to shut the door she heard Mr. Comyn say in a low voice: "Miss Marling—Juliana—I implore you, listen to me!"

Léonie took Rupert's arm confidingly. "That goes very well, I think. We are doing a great deal, you and I, *n'est-ce pas?*" She gave a gurgle of laughter. "We have made Juliana a *mésalliance*, which will enrage poor Fanny, and perhaps Monseigneur too, and now perhaps we shall keep Dominique away from that girl, and that will please Monseigneur, and he will forgive us. Let us find Dominique."

Lord Rupert professed himself to be utterly without desire to find his nephew, and went off to the kitchens to order and inspect his dinner. Léonie heard her son's voice raised in the courtyard at the back of the house, and looked through a window to see him giving instructions to his groom. She promptly hurried out to him, and demanded to know what he was doing.

He looked at her with a trace of impatience in his face. He was rather pale, she thought, and there was a frown in his eyes. "Madame, Mary has run from me to hide herself

in France with naught but an odd guniea or two in her pocket. I must find her. It touches my honour, not my heart
alone."

"Do you know where she has gone?" Léonie asked. "I
do not want any girl to be ruined by you, but——" She
stopped, and sighed.

"I don't know. She was not seen to leave the inn, unless
by one of the abigails, who, curse the wench, is gone off
to visit her mother. She can't be far."

"It seems to me," Léonie said slowly, "that this Mary
Challoner does not at all wish to marry you, *mon enfant.*
What I do not know is why she does not wish it. If it is because she loves you, then I understand very well, and I
am infinitely sorry for her, and I think I will help you—
unless I do not like her. But perhaps she does not love
you, Dominique, which is not incomprehensible if you have
been unkind. And if that is so, then I say you shall not
marry her, but I will arrange something. You see?"

"Good God, madame, what arrangement is possible now?
In the eyes of the world I've ruined her, though I swear to
you I did not seduce her. What can I do but give her my
name?"

"It is very difficult," admitted the Duchess. "But you cannot force her to marry you, Dominique."

"I can, and I will," he replied grimly. "After—it shall be
as she wishes. I am a fiend and a brute, no doubt, but not
such a fiend that I would force more than my name on
her, be sure." His groom came out of the stables, leading
a riding-horse. He caught his mother's hands in a tight clasp.
"Forgive me, maman!" he said. "I must marry her."

Her fingers clung to his. "Oh, my dearest dear, you shall
do anything you like, but when you have found her bring her
to me, and I will arrange it, and then perhaps Monseigneur
will not be so very angry with you."

He hesitated. "I'd do it, but I don't desire his wrath should
fall on you, maman."

She smiled, and shook her head. "He will be angry with
me a little, perhaps, but he will forgive me because he
knows that I am not at all respectable, *au cœur,* and I
cannot help doing outrageous things sometimes."

"I wish you had not come," he said. He released her
hands, and turned away from her to order the groom to
lead his horse round to the front of the inn. He glanced back

at Léonie to say briefly: "I must get my riding-whip," and disappeared into the house.

She followed him down the passage to the private parlour. He went in quickly—too quickly for Juliana and her Frederick, who were seated hand in hand on the settle by the fire.

The Marquis cast them a cursory glance, and picked up his whip and greatcoat. Juliana said radiantly: "It was all a mistake, Vidal! We do love each other, and we have been monstrous unhappy, both of us, but we shall never, never quarrel again."

"You affect me deeply," said Vidal. He nodded to Comyn, and there was a glint of humour in his eyes. "Do you expect me to felicitate you? My God, I had her on my hands for three days. I should beat her if I were you."

He turned to go out again, but the way was blocked by his uncle, who came in with a dusty bottle in one hand, and a glass in the other.

"Is that you, Vidal?" he said jovially. "'Pon my soul, I'm devilish glad we came to this place, though I'll admit I was against it. That fat rogue there has six dozen bottles of this in his cellar. I've bought the lot, and as good a port as ever I tasted, too. Here, wait till you roll this round your tongue, my boy." He poured out a glass of the burgundy, and gave it to his nephew.

The Marquis tossed it off, and set down the glass. "Quite tolerable," he said.

"God bless the boy, that's no way to treat a wine like this!" said Rupert, shocked. "We'll broach the port after dinner, and if you throw that down your throat as though it was nothing in particular, I'll wash my hands of you, and so I warn you."

"I'm not dining," the Marquis replied. "Out of the way, Rupert, I'm in a hurry."

"Not dining?" echoed his lordship. "But Vidal, there's a capon and a trifle of veal, and as sweet game-pie in the oven as you could wish for." His nephew put him firmly aside, and strode out, leaving him to shake his head in great disapproval. "Mad!" he said. "Stark staring crazy!"

"It is you who are mad," said Léonie with conviction. "You have bought all those bottles of wine, which is a great madness, for how in the world can you take them to England?

I will not sit in a chaise with six dozen bottles of burgundy. It is not at all *comme il faut*."

"I can hire a coach for 'em, can't I?" retorted Rupert. "Now don't start arguing, Léonie: I've been dragged all over France on as silly an errand as ever I heard of, and never a word of complaint out of me. I'll admit you were in the right about Dijon. If you hadn't insisted on coming here I'd not have found this burgundy. And now I've found it, damme, I'm going to carry it back to London with me!"

"But Rupert, it is not so important——"

"It's a deal more important than Vidal's silly affairs," said his lordship severely. "There's some sense in coming to Dijon to pick up wine like this."

Mr. Comyn, who had been gazing at him in wonderment, ventured to say: "Hire a coach to carry wine?"

"Why not?" said his lordship.

"But——" Mr. Comyn could not go on.

"*Eh bien*, if you hire a coach for it I do not mind at all," Léonie said, satisfied. "It seems to me a very good notion."

Mr. Comyn suddenly bowed his head in his hands and gave way to mirth.

ᴥ Chapter XVIII ᴥ

MISS CHALLONER had much time for reflection during the stage-coach's slow progress to Pont-de-Moine, and not many miles had been covered when, her first impetuous impulse to fly having abated, she became extremely fearful of the consequences of her action. Her purse was now woefully slim, and she supposed that the cost of a night's lodging would make an end of the few remaining coins lent her by Miss Marling.

She did not know what to do, a state of affairs repugnant to one of her orderly habit of mind. To be stranded in the middle of a strange country seemed to her the worst fate that could befall any young female, and no amount of sensible argument could convince her that it was no worse than to be stranded, penniless, in England.

She first bent her mind to the problem of reaching Paris, but after some consideration she decided that her determination to return there was without reason. Having no acquaintance in Paris, and no intention of claiming assistance from the English Embassy, there could be little point in striving to get to the capital. It might even be better for her to seek employment in some smaller town. She reflected that if my Lord Vidal still sought her he would suppose Paris to be her objective, in which case anywhere in the world would be preferable to her.

The Duchess of Avon's words continued to ring in her ears. Well, the Duchess need not suppose that Miss Mary Challoner was going to thrust herself into the noble family of Alastair. She would rather die—no, that was absurd. She did not wish to die in the least. Lord, she was becoming like Juliana, and falling into a habit of foolish exaggeration! She gave herself an inward shake. Her situation, though disagreeable, was not desperate. Though it seemed unlikely that she could obtain genteel employment without proper credentials, there must be some work to be found, and to be sure she had no right to be over-nice after the adventures she had passed through. The realization of her sudden and undeserved loss of character provoked a dismal frame of mind which was hard to shake off. She began to consider the several occupations open to her, and by the time she had run through such depressing trades as milliner, seamstress, serving-maid, and washerwoman, she was feeling very doleful indeed. On the whole, the life of a serving-maid seemed to be the most agreeable of those debased professions. She thought that she would endeavour to find a suitable post, and as soon as she had saved enough money to pay for the journey she would go back to England, where more congenial employment might, with a little ingenuity, be found. Even if she had the means at her disposal she would not return to England yet, for no doubt the packet would be watched for some time to come, if not by the Marquis, certainly by her own family. Later, when all hue and cry had died down, and she was in a fair way to being forgotten, it would be safe to venture back, though never, she determined, to within reach of her own people.

Having made up her mind to become a serving-maid, she found herself without anything much to think of except the events of the past few days, and she was soon confronted by a fresh alarm: that the Marquis, upon discovering her flight, would pursue her immediately. She at once perceived that to board the Paris stage had been an act of supreme folly, for my lord would naturally suppose her to be escaping to Paris, and would have not the slightest difficulty in catching up with the slow-moving coach. At the same time, no one had actually seen her set forth, although one abigail must have a very good notion whither she had gone. It was possible that his lordship might first scour Dijon and the surrounding countryside, which would give her time to hide herself. There was also the Duchess to be reckoned with, and Miss Challoner, during the days of her journey in his lordship's company, had been led to believe that her wishes were very nearly paramount with him. From what she had said upon seeing him, it seemed certain that she would exert all her influence to induce him to abandon his unfortunate *liaison*. There was the tall man, too, who, Miss Challoner guessed, was probably his lordship's uncle. Between them they should be able to hold the Marquis in check.

Her hand crept up surreptitiously under her cloak to feel the wound on her shoulder. The Marquis's fine handkerchief was still knotted round it. She thought she would keep that handkerchief always, in memory of one brief moment when she had been sure that he loved her.

Tears stung her eyelids; she forced them back, casting a timid look round the coach to see whether anyone was looking at her. The stout woman was asleep, with her jaw sagging; two farmers were earnestly conversing opposite to her, and judging from his stentorous breathing she thought the man on her left was also asleep.

Well, that one moment's conviction would comfort her in the lonely future. He had called her—but, after all, it was dangerous to recall his words, or the look on his face, or the gentle note in his voice.

She had thought—it seemed a long time ago now—that if only he had loved her she could marry him, but she had not considered then what it would mean to him to marry one so far beneath him. Perhaps his father would cast him off; it might even be in his power to disinherit him, and from all she had heard of his grace he was quite capable of doing that. She did not think that his love would survive exclusion from his own order, nor could she for an instant contemplate dragging him down to the society of lesser men. She thought, a little sadly, that she had seen too clearly how a man could sink to be able to cheat herself into supposing that the Marquis would maintain his position. Her own father had been disowned by his father, and he had ceased to associate with his old friends, because he had been looked at askance, as one who had committed the unforgivable sin. If the Duke of Avon had it in his power to disinherit his son, the Marquis would soon find himself condemned to the society of Miss Challoner, and Uncle Henry Simpkins, and their like. The very notion was so incredible that had her heart been less heavy she would have smiled at it.

It had grown dark inside the coach, and very chilly. Miss Challoner drew her cloak more tightly round her, and tried to ease her cramped limbs. It did not seem as though they would ever arrive at Pont-de-Moine. At every halt, of which there were many, she waited hopefully to be set down, but though one of the farmers had alighted, and two other persons entered the coach, no summons had yet come for her. She had no means of ascertaining the time, but she felt sure she had been travelling for many hours, and had begun to wonder whether the guard had forgotten her, and long passed Pont-de-Moine, when the coach stopped again before a well-lighted inn, and the door was pulled open.

The guard announced Pont-de-Moine in a stentorian voice which woke the fat woman with a jerk. The child, drowsing in her arms, set up a whimper, and Miss Challoner descended thankfully on to the road.

The guard, who apparently took a friendly interest in her, jerked his thumb towards the open door of the inn, and said that she had best bespeak a bed for the night there. She looked at the inn doubtfully, fearing from its well-kept appearance that it might be beyond her means to stay there, and inquired whether there was not some smaller hostelry to which she could repair.

The guard scratched his chin, and ran his eyes over her thoughtfully. "Not for you, there is not," he said bluntly. "There's only a tavern, at the end of the village, but it's not fit for a decent woman to enter."

Miss Challoner thanked him, and rather recklessly pressed a silver coin into his hand, thereby depleting her slender hoard still further.

She watched the guard climb on to the box again, and feeling somewhat as though she had lost her only friend in all France, she turned, and walked resolutely into the inn.

She found herself in a small well-hall, with the stairs running up to a couple of galleries on the first and second storeys. The place was lit by swinging lamps, and had several doors leading out of it, on one side. On the other an archway afforded a glimpse of a comfortable coffee-room.

Out of this apartment the landlord came bustling, a lean man with a sharp face, and a habit of sniffing. He came bowing, and rubbing his dry hands together, but when he saw that his visitor was quite unattended, his manner changed, and he asked her in a curt way what she wanted.

She was unaccustomed to meet with incivility, and instinctively she stiffened. She replied in her quiet, well-bred voice, that she had alighted from the stage, and required a bed-chamber.

Like the guard, the landlord eyed her up and down, but in his glance was no friendliness, but a distinct look of contempt. Solitary females travelling by stage were not wont to put up at his inn, which was a house catering for the nobility and gentry. He asked warily whether her abigail was outside, with her baggage, and perceived at once, from her sudden flush and downcast eyes, that she had no abigail, and probably no baggage either.

Until this humiliating moment Miss Challoner had not considered her extremely barren state. She knew quite well in what a light she must appear, and it took all her resolution not to turn and run ignominiously away.

Her fingers clasped her reticule tightly. She lifted her head, and said calmly: "There has been an accident, and my baggage is unhappily left behind me at Dijon. I expect it to-morrow. Meanwhile I require a bed-chamber, and some supper. A bowl of broth in my room will suffice."

It was quite evident that the landlord did not place any belief in the existence of Miss Challoner's baggage. "You have come to the wrong inn," he said. "There is a place down the street for the likes of you."

He encountered a look from Miss Challoner's fine grey eyes that made him suddenly nervous lest her story might after all be true. But at this moment he was reinforced by the arrival of his wife, a dame as stout as he was lean, who demanded to know what the young person wanted.

He repeated Miss Challoner's story to her. The dame set her arms akimbo, and gave vent to a short bark of laughter. "A very likely tale," she said. "You'd best be off to the *Chat Griz*, my girl. The *Rayon d'Or* does not honour persons of your quality. Baggage in Dijon indeed!"

It did not seem as though an appeal to this scornful lady would be of avail. Miss Challoner said steadily: "I find you impertinent, my good woman. I am English, travelling to rejoin my friends in the neighbourhood, and although I am aware that the loss of my baggage must appear strange to you——"

"Vastly strange, mademoiselle, I assure you. The English are all mad, *sans doute,* but we have had many of them at the *Rayon d'Or,* and they are not so mad that they permit their ladies to journey alone on the *diligence.* Come, now, be off with you! There is no lodging for you here, I can tell you. Such a tale! If you are English, you will be some serving-maid, very likely dismissed for some fault. The *Chat Griz* will give you a bed."

"The guard on the stage warned me what kind of a hostelry that is," replied Miss Challoner. "If you doubt my story, let me tell you that my name is Challoner, and I have sufficient money at my disposal to pay for your bed-chamber."

"Take your money elsewhere!" said the woman brusquely. "A nice thing it would be if we were to house young persons of your kind! Don't stand there staring down your nose at me, my girl! Be off at once!"

A soft voice spoke from the stairway. "One moment, my good creature," it said.

Miss Challoner looked up quickly. Down the stairs, very leisurely, was coming a tall gentleman dressed in a rich suit of black cloth with much silver lacing. He wore a powdered wig, and a patch at the corner of his rather thin mouth, and there was the hint of a diamond in the lace at his throat. He carried a long ebony cane in one hand, and a great square emerald glinted on one of his fingers. As he descended into the full light of the lamps Miss Challoner saw that he was old, although his eyes, directly surveying her from under their heavy lids, were remarkably keen. They were of a hard grey, and held a cynical gleam.

That he was a personage of considerable importance she at once guessed, for not only was the landlord bowing till his nose almost touched his knee, but the gentleman had in every languid movement the air of one born to command.

He reached the foot of the stairs, and came slowly towards the group by the door. He did not seem to be aware of the landlord's existence; he was looking at Miss Challoner, and it was to her and in English that he addressed himself. "You appear to be in some difficulty, madam. Pray let me know how I can serve you."

She curtsied with pretty dignity. "Thank you, sir. All I require is a lodging for the night, but I believe I must not trouble you."

"It does not seem to be an out-of-the-way demand," said the gentleman, raising his brows. "You will no doubt inform me where the hitch lies."

His air of calm authority brought a smile quivering to Miss Challoner's lips. "I repeat, sir, you are very kind, but

I beg you will not concern yourself with my stupid affairs."

His cold glance rested on her with a kind of bored indifference that she found disconcerting, and oddly familiar. "My good child," he said, with a touch of disdain in his voice, "your scruples, though most affecting, are quite needless. I imagine I might well be your grandfather."

She coloured a little, and replied, with a frank look: "I beg your pardon, sir. Indeed, my scruples are only lest I should be thought to importune a stranger."

"You edify me extremely," he said. "Will you now have the goodness to inform me why this woman finds herself unable to supply you with a bed-chamber?"

"I can scarcely blame her, sir," said Miss Challoner honestly. "I have no maid, and no baggage, and I arrived by the stage coach. My situation is excessively awkward, and I was very foolish not to have realized sooner what an odd appearance I must present."

"The loss of your baggage is, I fear, beyond my power to remedy, but a bed-chamber I can procure for you at once."

"I should be very grateful to you, sir, if you would."

The Englishman turned to the landlord, who was humbly awaiting his pleasure. "Your stupidity, my good Boisson, is lamentable," he remarked. "You will escort this lady to a suitable chamber."

"Yes, monseigneur, yes indeed. It shall be as monseigneur wishes. But——"

"I do not think," said the Englishman sweetly, "that I evinced any desire to converse with you."

"No, monseigneur," said the landlord. "If—if mademoiselle would follow my wife upstairs? The large front room, Célestine!"

Madame said resentfully: "What, the large room?"

The landlord gave her a push towards the stairs. "Certainly the large one. Go quickly!"

The Englishman turned to Miss Challoner. "You bespoke supper, I believe. I shall be honoured by your presence at my own table. Boisson will show you the way to my private *salle*."

Miss Challoner hesitated. "A bowl of soup in my chamber sir——"

"You will find it more entertaining to sup with me," he said. "Let me allay your qualms by informing you that I have the pleasure of your grandfather's acquaintance."

Miss Challoner grew rather pale. "My grandfather?" she said quickly.

"Certainly. You said, I think, that your name is Challoner. I have known Sir Giles any time these forty years. Permit me to tell you that you have a great look of him."

In face of this piece of information Miss Challoner abandoned her first impulse to disclaim all relationship with Sir Giles. She stood feeling remarkably foolish, and looking rather worried.

The gentleman smiled faintly. "Very wise," he commented, with uncanny perspicacity. "I should never believe that you were not his granddaughter. May I suggest that you follow this worthy female upstairs? You will join me at your convenience."

Miss Challoner had to laugh. "Very well, sir," she said, and curtsied, and went off in the wake of the landlady.

She was allotted what she guessed to be one of the best chambers, and a serving-maid brought her water in a brass can. She emptied her reticule on to the dressing-table, and somewhat ruefully inspected the collection thus displayed. Luckily she had slipped a clean tucker into it, and when carefully arranged round her shoulders this concealed the tear in her gown. She combed out her hair, and dressed it again, washed her face and hands, and went downstairs to the hall.

The presence of a countryman had been providential, but that he should be acquainted with her grandfather, and knew her identity, was a calamity. Miss Challoner had no idea what she was going to say to him, but some explanation was clearly called for.

The landlord was awaiting her at the foot of the staircase, and he met her with a respect as marked as his late contempt. He led the way to one of the doors leading from the hall, and ushered her into a large parlour.

Covers were laid on the table in the centre of the room, and the apartment was lit by clusters of wax candles in solid chandeliers. Miss Challoner's new friend was standing by the fireplace. He came forward to meet her, and taking her hand at once remarked on its coldness. She confessed that she was still feeling chilly, and told him that the stage had been full of draughts. She went to the fire, and spread out her hands to the blaze. "I find this very welcome, sir," she said, smiling up at him. "You are indeed kind to invite me to sup with you."

He surveyed her somewhat enigmatically. "You shall let me know later how I may serve you further," he said. "Will you not be seated?"

She walked to the table, and sat down at his right hand. A liveried servant came in noiselessly, and set soup before them. He would have stayed behind his master's chair, but a slight sign dismissed him.

Miss Challoner drank her soup, realizing suddenly that it was many hours since she had partaken of food. She was relieved to find that her host did not seem to require an immediate explanation of her peculiar circumstances, but talked gently instead on a number of impersonal subjects. He had a caustic way with him, which Miss Challoner found entertaining. There was often a twinkle in her eye, and since her knowledge was sufficiently wide (for, unlike her friend Juliana, she had not wasted her time at school), she was able not only to listen, but to contribute her own share to the conversation. By the time the sweetmeats were set on the table she and her host were getting on famously, and she had quite lost any shyness that she might at first have felt. He encouraged her to talk, sitting back in his chair, sipping his wine, and watching her. To begin with, she had found his scrutiny a little trying, for his face told her nothing of what he might be thinking, but she was not the woman to be easily unnerved, and she looked back at him, whenever occasion demanded, with her usual friendly calm.

She could not be rid of the conviction that she had met him before, and the effort to remember where brought a crease between her brows. Observing it, her host said: "Something troubles you, Miss Challoner?"

She smiled. "No, sir, hardly that. Perhaps it is ridiculous of me to suppose it, but I have an odd feeling that I have met you before. I have not?"

He set his glass down, and stretched out his hand for the decanter. "No, Miss Challoner, you have not."

She was tempted to ask his name, but since he was so very much older than herself she did not care to appear in the least familiar. If he wished her to know it no doubt he would tell her.

She laid down her napkin, and rose. "I have been talking a great deal, I fear," she said. "May I thank you, sir, for a pleasant evening, and for your exceeding kindness, and so bid you good-night?"

"Don't go," he said. "Your reputation is quite safe, and the night is still young. Without wishing to seem idly curious, I should like to hear why you are journeying unprotected, through France. Do you think I am entitled to an explanation?"

She remained standing beside her chair. "Yes, sir, I do think it," she answered quietly. "For my situation must seem indeed strange. But unhappily I am not able to give you the true explanation, and since I do not wish to repay your kindness with lies it is better that I should offer none. May I wish you good-night, sir?"

"Not yet," he said. "Sit down, my child."

She looked at him for a moment, and after some slight hesitation, obeyed, lightly clasping her hands in the lap of her grey gown.

The stranger regarded her over the brim of his wineglass. "May I ask why you find yourself unable to proffer the true explanation?"

She seemed to ponder her reply for a while. "There are several reasons, sir. The truth is so very nearly as strange as Mr. Walpole's famous romance that perhaps I fear to be disbelieved."

He tilted his glass, observing the reflection of the candlelight in the deep red wine. "But did you not say, Miss Challoner, that you would not lie to me?" he inquired softly.

Her eyes narrowed. "You are very acute, sir."

"I have that reputation," he agreed.

His words touched a chord of memory in her brain, but she was unable to catch the fleeting remembrance. She said: "You are quite right, sir: that is not my reason. The truth is there is someone else involved in my story."

"I had supposed that there might be," he replied. "Am I to understand that your lips are sealed out of consideration for this other person?"

"Not entirely, sir, but in part, yes."

"Your sentiments are most elevating, Miss Challoner. But this punctiliousness is quite needless, believe me. Lord Vidal's exploits have never been attended by any secrecy."

She jumped, and her eyes flew to his face in a look of startled interrogation. He smiled. "I had the felicity of meeting your esteemed grandparent at Newmarket not many days

since," he said. "Upon hearing that I was bound for France
he requested me to inquire for you on my way through Paris."

"He knew?" she said blankly.

"Without doubt he knew."

She covered her face with her hands. "My mother must
have told him," she said almost inaudibly. "It is worse, then,
than I thought."

He put his wineglass down, and pushed his chair a little
way back from the table. "I beg you will not distress yourself, Miss Challoner. The rôle of confidant is certainly new to
me, but I trust I know the rules."

She got up and went over to the fire, trying to collect her
thoughts, and to compose her natural agitation. The gentleman at the table took snuff, and waited for her to return.
She did so in a minute or two, with a certain brisk determination that characterized her. She was rather pale, but completely mistress of herself. "If you know that I—left England
with Lord Vidal, sir, I am more than ever grateful for your
hospitality to-night, and an explanation is beyond doubt due
to you," she said. "I do not know how much you have learned
of me, but since no one in England knows the whole truth, I
fear you may have been quite misinformed on several points."

"It is more than likely," agreed her host. "May I suggest
that you tell me the whole story? I have every intention of
helping you out of your somewhat difficult situation, but I
desire to know exactly why you left England with Lord Vidal,
and why I find you to-day, apparently alone and friendless."

She leaned towards him, her face eager. "Will you help
me, sir? Will you help me to obtain a post as governess in
some French family, so that I need not go back to England,
but can maintain myself abroad?"

"Is that what you want?" he inquired incredulously.

"Yes, sir, indeed it is."

"Dear me!" he remarked. "You seem to be a female of
great resource. Pray begin your story."

"In doing so, sir, I am forced to betray the—folly—of my
sister. I dare say I need not ask you to—to forget that part
of the tale."

"My memory is most adaptable, Miss Challoner."

"Thank you, sir. You must know then that I have a sister
who is very young, foolish as girls are sometimes, and very,
very lovely. Her path was crossed, not so long ago, by the
Marquis of Vidal."

"Naturally," murmured her host.

"Naturally, sir?"

"Oh, I think so," he said, with a faintly satirical smile. "If she is—very, very lovely—I feel sure that the Marquis of Vidal would cross her path. But continue, I beg of you!"

She inclined her head. "Very well, sir. This part of the story is very hard to tell, for I do not wish to give you to understand that the Marquis—forced his attentions upon an unwilling female. My sister encouraged him, and led him to suppose that she was—that she——"

"I comprehend perfectly, Miss Challoner."

She threw him a grateful look. "Yes, sir. Well, the end of it was that the Marquis induced my sister to consent to fly with him. I discovered their assignation, which was for eleven o'clock one evening. I should explain that the billet his lord-ship sent my sister, appointing the hour, fell into my hands, and not hers. There were reasons, sir, into which I shall not drag you, which prevented me from informing my mother of this dreadful elopement. I need not tell you, sir, that his lordship did not contemplate marriage. It seemed to me that I must contrive not only to stop the actual flight, but to put an end to an affair that would only mean Sophia's ruin. When I look back I marvel at my own simplicity. I con-ceived the notion of taking Sophia's place in the coach, and when he discovered the imposture it was my intention to make him believe that Sophia and I had planned it between us, for a jest. I thought that nothing would more surely disgust him." She paused, and added drily: "I was quite right."

The gentleman twisted the emerald ring on his finger. "Do I understand that you carried out this remarkable plan?" he inquired.

"Oh, yes, sir. But it went sadly awry."

"That was to have been expected," he said gently.

"I suppose so," she sighed. "It was a silly plan. Lord Vidal did not discover the cheat until next morning, when we reached Newhaven. To find myself by the sea was a shock to me. I had not guessed that his lordship intended to leave England. I entered the inn on the quay in his company, and in the private room he had engaged I discovered myself to him." She stopped.

"I can well imagine that Lord Vidal's emotions baffle de-scription," said the gentleman.

She was looking straight in front of her. She nodded, and

said slowly: "In what followed, sir, I do not wish to lay any blame on Lord Vidal. I played my part too well, not dreaming of the revenge he would take. I must have appeared to him—I *did* appear to him—a vulgar, loose female." She turned her head towards him. "Are you acquainted with Lord Vidal, sir?"

"I am, Miss Challoner."

"Then you will know, sir, that his lordship's temper is extremely fiery and uncontrolled. I had provoked it, and it—it was disastrous. Lord Vidal forced me to go on board his yacht, and carried me to Dieppe."

The gentleman felt for his quizzing-glass, and raised it. Through it he surveyed Miss Challoner. "May I ask what were his lordship's tactics?" he inquired. "I feel an almost overwhelming interest in the methods of daylight abduction employed by the modern youth."

"Well, it was not very romantic," confessed Miss Challoner. "He threatened to pour the contents of his flask down my throat, thereby rendering me too drunk to resist." She saw a frown in his eyes, and said: "I fear I shock you, sir, but remember that his lordship was enraged."

"I am not shocked, Miss Challoner, but I infinitely deplore such a lack of finesse. Did his lordship carry out this ingenious plan?"

"No, for I submitted. To be made drunk seemed to me a horrid fate. I said I would go with him. It was very early, and there was no one on the quay, so that I could not call for help, even had I dared. And since his lordship threatened to strangle me if I made the least outcry, I am sure I should not have dared. I went on board the yacht, and as our passage was rough, I was most vilely unwell."

A smile flickered across her hearer's countenance. "My sympathies are with Lord Vidal. He no doubt found you most disconcerting."

She gave a little laugh. "I think you don't know him very well, sir, for it is one of the nice things about him that he was not disconcerted, but on the contrary, extremely prompt in dealing with the situation."

He was looking at her rather curiously. "I thought that I knew him very well indeed," he said. "Apparently I was wrong. Pray continue: you begin to interest me vastly."

"He has a dreadful reputation," she said earnestly, "but he

is not wicked at heart. He is nothing but a wild, passionate, spoiled boy."

"I am all admiration for your shrewdness, Miss Challoner," said the gentleman politely.

"It is true, sir," she insisted, suspecting him of irony. "When I was sick on that yacht——"

He raised one thin hand. "I accept your reading of his lordship's true nature, Miss Challoner. Spare me a recital of your sufferings at sea, I beg of you."

She smiled. "They were excessively painful, sir, I assure you. But we arrived at length at Dieppe, where his lordship had planned to spend the night. We dined. His lordship had, I think, been drinking aboard the yacht. He was in an ugly mood, and I was compelled, in the end, to protect my virtue in a somewhat drastic manner."

The gentleman opened his snuff-box, and took a pinch delicately. "If you succeeded in protecting your virtue, my dear Miss Challoner, I can readily believe—knowing his lordship—that your methods must have been exceedingly drastic. You perceive me positively agog with curiosity."

"I shot him," she said bluntly.

The hand that was raising the pinch of snuff to one nostril was checked for a brief moment. "Accept my compliments," said the gentleman calmly, and inhaled the snuff.

"It was not a very bad wound," she told him. "But it sobered him, you see."

"I imagine that it might do so," he conceded.

"Yes, sir. He began to realize that I was not—not vulgarly coy, but in deadly earnest."

"Did he indeed? A gentleman of intuition, I perceive."

Miss Challoner said with dignity: "You laugh, sir, but it was not very amusing at the time."

The gentleman bowed. "I beg your pardon," he said solemnly. "What happened next?"

"His lordship insisted that I should tell him all that I have told you. When he had heard me out he said that there was only one thing to be done. I must marry him at once."

The keen eyes lifted from the contemplation of the enamelled snuff-box, and were suddenly intent. "We have reached the point where you interest me extraordinarily," said that smooth voice. "Proceed, Miss Challoner."

She looked down at her clasped hands. "I could not consent to so wild a scheme, sir, of course. I was forced to decline his lordship's offer."

"I do not think I am a fool," said the gentleman pensively. "But although I can sympathize with your reluctance to marry so dissolute a gentleman as Lord Vidal, your predicament was such that I do not immediately perceive what forced you to decline."

"The knowledge, sir, that Lord Vidal did not care for me," answered Miss Challoner in a low voice. "The knowledge also that in marrying me he would be making a—a deplorable *mésalliance*. I do not desire to discuss that, if you please. I requested his lordship—since I could hardly return to England—to escort me to Paris, where I hoped to find some genteel employment, such as I described to you."

The quizzing-glass was raised again. "You appear to have confronted your somewhat unnerving situation with remarkable equanimity, Miss Challoner."

She shrugged. "What else could I do, sir? Vapours would not have helped me. Besides, I had his lordship sick on my hands with some slight inflammation of the wound I had given him, and as he was bent on doing a number of imprudent things I had too much to do in preventing him to think very much of my own troubles."

"From my brief acquaintance with you, Miss Challoner, I feel moderately convinced that you did prevent Lord Vidal's imprudence."

"Oh yes," she answered. "He is quite easy to manage, if—if one only knows the way."

The quizzing-glass fell. "His lordship's parents should be anxious to meet you," said the gentleman.

Her smile was twisted. "I am afraid not, sir. I do not know whether you are acquainted with his grace of Avon?"

"Intimately," he said, with the ghost of a laugh.

"Oh, then——" She broke off. "In short, sir, I refused Lord Vidal's offer, and we——"

"But were you not about to make some observation concerning his grace of Avon?" he interposed urbanely.

"I was, sir, but if you are intimate with him I will refrain."

"Pray do not. In what monstrous light has this gentleman appeared to you?"

"I have never set eyes on him, sir. I only judge him by what I have heard, and by things that Lord Vidal has from time to time let fall. I suppose him to be a man of few morals and no heart. He seems to me a sinister person, and is, I believe, quite unscrupulous in attaining his ends."

The gentleman appeared to be amused. "I am far from contradicting you, Miss Challoner, but may I inquire whether you culled this masterly description from Lord Vidal's lips?"

"If you mean, did Lord Vidal tell me so, no, sir, he did not. Lord Vidal is, I think, attached to his grace. I go by common report, a little, and by the very lively fear of her uncle evinced by my friend Miss Marling. His lordship merely gave me to understand that his father was uncannily omniscient, and had a habit of succeeding in all his objects."

"I am relieved to hear that Lord Vidal has so much respect for his grace," remarked the gentleman.

"Are you, sir? Well, having formed this opinion, I could not but feel that so far from desiring to meet me, his grace would very likely disinherit Lord Vidal if his lordship married me."

"You draw an amiable portrait, Miss Challoner, but I can assure you that whatever his grace's feelings might be he would never follow so distressingly crude a course."

"Would he not, sir? I did not know, but I am very sure he would not countenance his son's marriage to a nobody. To continue: Lord Vidal, discovering that I was once at school with his cousin, Miss Marling, brought me to Paris, and consigned me to her care until such time as he could find an English divine to marry me. Miss Marling was secretly betrothed to a certain Mr. Comyn, but their betrothal was broken off—irrevocably, as I thought—and Mr. Comyn, being a gentleman of great chivalry, offered his hand to me, to enable me to escape from Lord Vidal. Though I blush to confess it, sir, such was my desperate need, that I consented to elope with Mr. Comyn to Dijon where Lord Vidal had found an English divine. Unfortunately, Mr. Comyn thought it incumbent on him to leave a note for his lordship, apprising him of our intention to wed. The result was, sir, that Lord Vidal, accompanied by Miss Marling, overtook us at Dijon before the knot was tied. There was a painful scene. Mr. Comyn, desiring to protect me from his lordship's—coercion —announced that we were man and wife. Lord Vidal, with the object of making me a widow, tried to choke the life out of Mr. Comyn. In which I think he would probably have succeeded," she added, "had there not been a jug of water at hand. I threw it over them both, and my lord let Mr. Comyn go."

"A jug of water!" he repeated. His shoulders shook slightly. "But continue, Miss Challoner!"

"After that," she said matter-of-factly, "they fought with their swords."

"How very enlivening! Where did they fight with—er—their swords?"

"In the private parlour. Juliana had hysterics."

"It is quite unnecessary to tell me that," he assured her. "What I should like to know is what was done with Mr. Comyn's body?"

"He wasn't killed, sir. No one was hurt at all."

"You amaze me," said the gentleman.

"Mr. Comyn would have been killed," Miss Challoner admitted, "but I stopped it. I thought it was time."

The gentleman surveyed her with distinct admiration, not untouched by amusement. "Of course I should have known that you stopped it," he said. "What means did you employ this time?"

"Rather rough-and-ready ones, sir. I tried to catch the blades in a coat."

"I am disappointed," he said. "I had imagined a far neater scheme. Were you hurt?"

"A little, sir. His lordship's sword scratched me, no more. That ended the duel. Mr. Comyn said that he must tell Lord Vidal the truth about us, and feeling myself somewhat shaken, I retired to my chamber." She paused, and drew a long breath. "Before I had reached the stairway, his lordship's mother arrived, accompanied, I think, by Lord Rupert Alastair. They did not see me, but I—I heard her grace—say to Lord Vidal—that he must not marry me, and I—I got into the *diligence* for Paris, which was at the door, and—and came here. That is all my story, sir."

A silence fell. Conscious of her host's scrutiny, Miss Challoner averted her face. After a moment she said: "Having heard me, sir, do you still feel inclined to assist me out of my difficulty?"

"I am doubly anxious to assist you, Miss Challoner. But since you have been so frank, I must request you to be yet franker. Am I right in assuming that you love Lord Vidal?"

"Too well to marry him, sir," said Miss Challoner in a subdued voice.

"May I aesk why 'too well'?"

She raised her head. "How could I, sir, knowing that his parents would do anything in their power to prevent such a marriage? How could I let him stoop to my level? I am not of his world, though Sir Giles Challoner is my grandfather. Please do not let us speak any more of this! My mind is made up; my one dread now is that his lordship may pursue me to this place."

"I can safely promise you, my dear, that while you remain under my protection you are in no danger from Lord Vidal."

The words were hardly out of his mouth when the sound of voices outside came to Miss Challoner's ears. She grew very white, and half rose from her chair. "Sir, he has come!" she said, trying to be calm.

"So I apprehend," he said imperturbably.

Miss Challoner cast a frightened look round. "You promised I should be safe, sir. Will you hide me somewhere? We must be quick!"

"I still promise that you shall be safe," he replied. "But I shall certainly not hide you. Let me recommend you to be seated once more . . . Come in!"

One of the inn servants came in looking rather scared, and firmly shut the door. "Milor', there is a gentleman outside demands to see the English lady. I told him she was supping with an English milor', and he spoke through his teeth, thus: 'I will see this English milor',' he said. Milor', he has the look of one about to do a murder. Shall I summon milor's own servants?"

"Certainly not," said milor'. "Admit this gentleman."

Miss Challoner put out her hand impulsively. "Sir, I beg you will not! If my lord is in one of his rages I cannot answer for what he may do. I have a great alarm lest your years should not protect you from his violence. Is there no way I can escape from this room unseen?"

"Miss Challoner, I must once more request you to be seated," said milor', bored. "Lord Vidal will lay violent hands on neither of us." He looked across at the serving-man. "I do not in the least understand why you are standing there goggling at me," he said. "Admit his lordship."

The servant withdrew; Miss Challoner, standing still beside her chair, looked down rather helplessly at her host. She wondered what would happen when my lord came in. A clock had chimed midnight somewhere in the distance not long since; it was a very odd hour at which to be found supping with a strange gentleman, however venerable he might be, and she feared that the Marquis's jealous temper might flare up with disastrous results. There seemed to be no hope of making her host understand that the Marquis in a black rage was scarcely responsible for his actions. The gentleman was maddeningly imperturbable: he was even smiling a little.

She heard a quick step in the hall; Vidal's voice said sharply: "Stable my horse, one of you. Where is this Englishman?"

Miss Challoner laid her hand on the back of her chair, and grasped it as though for support. The servant said: "I will announce m'sieur."

He was cut short. "I'll announce myself," said his lordship savagely.

A moment later the door was flung open, and the Marquis strode in, his fingers hard clenched on his riding-whip. He cast one swift smouldering glance across the room, and stopped dead, a look of thunderstruck amazement on his face. "Sir!" he gasped.

The gentleman at the head of the table looked him over from his head to his heels. "You may come in, Vidal," he said suavely.

The Marquis stayed where he was, one hand still on the doorknob. "You here!" he stammered. "I thought . . ."

"Your reflections are quite without interest, Vidal. No doubt you will shut that door in your own good time."

To Miss Challoner's utter astonishment the Marquis shut it at once, and said stiffly: "Your pardon, sir." He tugged at his cravat. "Had I known that you were here——"

"Had you known that I was here," said the elder man in a voice that froze Miss Challoner to the marrow, "you would possibly have made your entrance in a more seemly fashion. You will permit me to tell you that I find your manners execrable."

The Marquis flushed, and set his teeth. An incredible and dreadful premonition seized Miss Challoner. She looked from the Marquis to her host, and her hand went instinctively to her cheek. "Oh, good God!" she said, aghast. "Are you——can you be——?" She could get no further.

The look of amusement crept back into the gentleman's eyes. "As usual, you are quite right, Miss Challoner. I am that unscrupulous and sinister person so aptly described by you a while back."

Miss Challoner's tongue seemed to tie itself into knots. "I can't—I would not—there is nothing I can say, sir, except that I ask your pardon."

"There is not the smallest need, Miss Challoner, I assure you. Your reading of my character was most masterly. The only thing I find hard to forgive is your conviction that you had met me before. I don't pretend to be flattered by the likeness you evidently perceived."

"Thank you, sir," said the Marquis politely.

Miss Challoner walked away to the fireplace. "I am ashamed," she said. Real perturbation sounded in her voice. "I had no business to say what I did. I see now that I was quite at fault. For the rest—had I known who you were I would never have told you all that I did."

"That would have been a pity," said his grace. "I found your story extremely illuminating."

She made a hopeless little gesture. "Please permit me to retire, sir."

"You are no doubt fatigued after the many discomforts you have suffered to-day," agreed his grace, "but I apprehend that my son—whose apologies I beg to offer—is come here expressly to see you. I really think that you would be well advised to listen to anything he may have to say."

"I can't!" she said, in a suffocated way. "Please let me go!"

The Marquis came quickly across the room to her side. He took her hands in his strong clasp, and said in a low voice: "You should not have fled from me. My God, do you hate me so much? Mary, listen to me! I'll force nothing on you, but I beg of you, accept my name! There's no other way I can right you in the eyes of the world. You must wed me! I swear to you on my honour I'll not hurt you. I won't come near you unless you bid me. Father, tell her she must marry me! Tell her how needful it is!"

His grace said placidly: "I find myself quite unable to tell Miss Challoner anything of the kind."

"What, have you been one hour in her company and not seen how infinitely above me she is?" the Marquis cried hotly.

"By no means," said the Duke. "If Miss Challoner feels herself able to become your wife I shall consider myself to be vastly in her debt, but out of justice to her I am bound to advise her to consider well before she throws herself away so lamentably." He regarded Miss Challoner blandly. "My dear, are you sure you cannot do better for yourself than to marry Vidal?"

A laugh escaped the Marquis. He drew Miss Challoner closer. "Mary, look at me! Mary, little love!"

"I am of course loth to interrupt you, Vidal, but I desire to inform Miss Challoner that there is no reason why she should accept your hand unless she chooses." The Duke rose, and came towards them. The Marquis let Miss Challoner go. "You appear to be a woman of so much sense," said his grace, "that I find it hard to believe you can really desire to marry my son. I beg you will not allow the exigencies of your situation to weigh with you. If marriage with Vidal is distasteful to you I will arrange matters for you in some other way."

Miss Challoner gazed down into the fire. "I cannot . . . I—the Duchess—my sister—oh, I do not know what to say!"

"The Duchess need not trouble you," said his grace. He walked to the door, and opened it. He glanced back, and said languidly: "By the way, Vidal's morals are rather better than mine." He went out, and the door closed softly behind him.

The Marquis and Miss Challoner were left confronting one another. She did not look at him, but she knew that his eyes never wavered from her face. He made no movement to recapture her hands; he said slowly: "Until you ran away with Comyn, I never knew how much I loved you, Mary. If you won't marry me, I shall spend the rest of my life striving to win you. I'll never rest till I've got you. Never, do you understand?"

A smile trembled on her lips. "And if I do marry you, my lord? You'll let me go my own road? You'll not come near me unless I wish it? You'll not fly into rages with me, nor tyrannize over me?"

"I swear it," he said.

She came to him, her eyes full of tender laughter. "Oh, my love, I know you better than you know yourself!" she said huskily. "At the first hint of opposition, you'll coerce me shamefully. Oh, Vidal! *Vidal!*"

He had caught her in his arms so fiercely that the breath was almost crushed out of her. His dark face swam before her eyes for an instant, then his mouth was locked to hers, in a kiss so hard that her lips felt bruised. She yielded, carried away half-swooning on the tide of his passion. But in a moment she struggled to get her hands free, and at once his hold on her slackened. She flung up her arms round his neck, and with a queer little sound between a sob and a laugh, buried her face in his coat.

⊷ Chapter XIX ⊷

MISS CHALLONER appeared at the breakfast hour next morning rather shy, her face delicately tinged with colour. She found both the Marquis and his father in the parlour, and an elderly dapper little Frenchman whom she discovered to be his grace's valet.

The Marquis carried her hand to his lips, and held it there for a moment. His grace said in his bored voice: "I trust you slept well, child. Pray be seated. Gaston, you will take my chaise immediately to Dijon, where you will find her grace."

"*Bien, monseigneur.*"

"You will bring her to this place. Also my Lord Rupert, Miss Marling, and Mr. Comyn. That is all, Gaston."

There had been a day when Gaston would have been appalled by such an order, but twenty-five years in Avon's service had left their mark.

"*Bien, monseigneur,*" he replied without the smallest sign of surprise and bowed himself out.

The Marquis said impetuously: "I'll make that fellow Hammond marry us, Mary, at once."

"Very well," said Miss Challoner equably.

"You will be married," said his grace, "in Paris, at the Embassy."

"But, sir——"

"A little coffee, my lord?" said Miss Challoner.

"I never touch it. Sir——"

"If his grace wishes you to married at the Embassy, my lord, I won't be married anywhere else," stated Miss Challoner calmly.

The Marquis said: "You won't, eh? Sir, it's very well, but it will cause a deal of talk."

"I rather think that it will," agreed Avon. "I had no time on my way through Paris to arrange the details. But I have no doubt that my friend Sir Giles will have done so by this time."

Miss Challoner regarded him in frank wonderment. "Is my grandfather in Paris then, sir?"

"Certainly," said his grace. "I should tell you, my child, that officially you are in his company."

"Am I, sir?" Miss Challoner blinked at him. "Then you did meet him at Newmarket?"

"Let us say, rather, that he came to find me at Newmarket," he amended. "He is staying in an hôtel which he has hired for some few weeks. You, my dear Mary, are at present keeping to your room, on account of some slight disorder of the system. The betrothal between yourself and my son is of long, though secret standing. Hitherto"—his grace touched his lips with his napkin, and laid it down. "Hitherto, both Sir Giles and myself have refused our consent to your marriage."

"Have you?" said Mary, quite fascinated.

"Obviously. But Vidal's banishment to France so attacked your sensibilities, my dear child, that you seemed to be in danger of going into a decline. This induced Sir Giles and myself to relent."

"Oh, no!" begged Miss Challoner. "Not a decline, sir! I am not such a poor creature!"

"I am desolated to be obliged to contradict you, Mary, but you were certainly on the brink of a decline," said Avon firmly.

Miss Challoner sighed. "Well, if you insist, sir . . . What next?"

"Next," said Avon, "the Duchess and myself came to Paris to grace the ceremony with our presence. We have not yet arrived, but we shall do so in a day or two. I imagine we are somewhere in the neighbourhood of Calais at the moment. When we do arrive we shall hold a rout-party in your honour. You will be formally presented to society as my son's future wife. Which reminds me, that I cannot sufficiently praise your admirable discretion in refusing to go about when you sojourned with my cousin Elisabeth."

Miss Challoner felt herself bound to say: "There is one

person who met me at the Hôtel Charbonne, sir. The Vicomte
de Valmé."

"You can leave Bertrand to me," interposed the Marquis.
"This is all very well thought of, sir, but when does our
marriage take place?"

"Your marriage, my son, takes place when Miss Challoner
has had time to buy her bride-clothes. I shall leave you to
decide the rest. My ingenuity falls short of planning your
wedding trip."

"You surprise me, sir. I shall take you into Italy, Mary.
Will you come with me?"

"Yes, sir, with all my heart," said Mary, smiling at him.
His hand went out to her across the table. The Duke said
drily: "Delay your affecting demonstrations a moment longer,
Vidal. I have to inform you that your late adversary was,
when I left England, on the road to recovery."

"My late adversary?" frowned his lordship. "Oh, Quarles!
Was he, sir?"

"You do not appear to feel any undue interest in his fate,"
remarked Avon.

The Marquis was looking at Mary. He said casually: "It
makes no odds to me now, sir. He can live for all I care."

"How very magnanimous!" said his grace with gentle satire.
"Perhaps it may interest you to learn that the gentleman has
been—er—induced to make a statement which obviates the
need for your exile."

Vidal turned his head, surveying his father with candid
admiration. "I should like to know how you induced him to
make such a statement, sir, I admit. But I did not leave
England for fear of the runners."

Avon smiled. "Did you not, my son?"

"No, sir, and you know it. I left at your command."

"Very proper," said his grace, rising. "I have no doubt I
shall be weak enough to command your return—when you
get back from Italy." His eyes rested for an instant on Miss
Challoner. "I comfort myself with the reflection that your
wife will possibly be able to curb your desire—I admit, a
natural one for the most part—to exterminate your fellows."

"I shall try not to disappoint you, sir," said Miss Challoner
demurely.

It was past noon when Gaston returned with his charges.
Miss Challoner felt extremely nervous of meeting the Duchess
of Avon, but that lady's entrance put all her fears to flight.

Her grace came into the parlour like a small whirlwind, and
cast herself into her husband's arms. "Monseigneur!" she
cried joyfully. "I am so very glad you have come! I thought
I should not have to tell you anything about it, but it is all so
difficult I cannot manage it in the least, and Rupert will
not try because he only thinks of getting all that wine home.
Monseigneur, he has bought dozens and dozens of bottles of
wine. I could not stop him. He says first he will hire a coach,
and now he says no, it must go by canal."

"It must undoubtedly go by canal," said his grace, betraying a faint interest. He removed his ruffle from his wife's
clutch. "May I ask, Léonie, why you must needs elope with
Rupert in this distressing fashion?"

"But do you not know, then?" she demanded. "If you don't
know, why are you here, Monseigneur? You are teasing me!
Where is Dominique? Gaston said that he was with you."

"He is," said his grace.

"Then of course you know. Oh, Monseigneur, he says he
will marry that girl, and I have a great fear she is like the
sister whom I found detestable!"

The Duke took her hand and led her to Miss Challoner.
"You shall judge for yourself," he said. "This is Miss Challoner."

The Duchess looked sharply up at him, and then at Mary,
who stood still and looked gravely back at her. Léonie drew
a long breath. "*Voyons,* are you the sister of that other one?"
she demanded, not very lucidly.

"Yes, ma'am," said Mary.

"*Vraiment?* But it is not at all credible, I find. I do not
want to be rude, but——"

"In that case, my love, you had better refrain from making
the comparisons that are on the lips of your very unguarded
tongue," interposed his grace.

"I was not going to say anything indiscreet," the Duchess
assured him. "But I say one thing. If you do not like it,
Monseigneur, I am sorry, but I am not going to permit that
my son abducts this Mary Challoner and then does not marry
her. I say he shall marry her at once, and Rupert shall
fetch that Hammond person, who has the manners of a pig."

"These continued references to Mr. Hammond—a gentleman quite unknown to me—I find most tedious," complained
his grace. "If his manners are those of a pig, I beg that Rupert
will refrain from fetching him."

"But you do not understand, Justin. He is a priest."

"So I have been led to infer. I believe it will not be necessary for us to disturb him."

The Duchess took Miss Challoner's hand, and held it. She faced her husband resolutely. "Monseigneur, you must listen to me. When I thought that this child was—was——"

"Pray do not continue, my dear. I understand perfectly. If you will permit me to——"

"No, Monseigneur," she said firmly. "This time it is I who must speak. When I thought this child was not a respectable person, I said Dominique should not marry her. I made Rupert bring me to Dijon because I thought I would be very clever and arrange everything so that you would never know——"

"This touching but misplaced confidence in your powers of concealment, *ma mie*——"

"Justin, you shall listen to me!" said the Duchess. "Of course I might have known you would find out—how did you, Monseigneur? It was very clever of you, I think. No, no, let me speak!—I meant that Dominique should not marry Mademoiselle Challoner. But now I have seen her, and I am not a fool, me, and she is a person entirely respectable, and this time I do not care what you may say, Dominique is to marry her."

His grace looked down at her impassively. "Quite right, my dear. He is," he said.

The Duchess opened her eyes very wide indeed. "You do not *mind*, Monseigneur?"

"I cannot conceive why I should be supposed to mind," said his grace. "The marriage seems to be eminently desirable."

The Duchess let go of Miss Challoner to fling out her hands. "But, Monseigneur, if you do not mind why did you not say so at once?" she demanded.

"You may perhaps recall, my love, that you forbade me to speak."

The Duchess paid no attention to this, but said with her usual buoyancy: "*Voyons*, now I am quite happy!" She looked at Mary again. "And you—I think you will be very good to my son, *n'est-ce pas?*"

Miss Challoner said: "I love him, ma'am. I can only say that. And—and thank you—for your——"

"Ah, bah!" Léonie said. "I do not want to be thanked.

Where is Rupert? I must tell him at once that everything is arranged."

Lord Rupert, who had evidently been detained outside, came into the room at this moment. He seemed preoccupied, and addressed himself at once to his brother. "Damme, Avon, I'm devilish glad you've come!" he said. "The Lord knows I never thought I should want to see you, but we're in a plaguey difficulty."

"No, we are not, Rupert!" Léonie told him. "It is all arranged."

"Eh?" His lordship seemed surprised. "Who arranged it?"

"Oh, but Monseigneur, of course! They are to be married."

Rupert said disgustedly: "Lord, can't you think of aught beside that young fire-eater of yours?" He took hold of one of the silver buttons on his grace's coat, and said confidentially: "It's a mighty fortunate thing you've arrived, Avon, 'pon my soul it is. I've got six dozen of burgundy, and about three of as soft a port as ever I tasted, lying back in Dijon. I bought 'em off the landlord of some inn or another we stayed at, and the devil's in it I can't pay for 'em."

"Monseigneur, I am quite *ennuyée* with this wine," said Léonie. "Do not buy it! I do not wish to travel with bottles and bottles of wine."

"May I request you to unhand me, Rupert?" said his grace. "If you have purchased port it must of course go by water. Did you bring a bottle with you?"

"Bring a bottle? Lord, I've brought six!" said Rupert. "We'll crack one at once, and if you don't find I'm right— well, you've changed, Justin, and that's all there is to it."

Léonie said indignantly: "Rupert, I do not care what you do, but I wish to present you to Mademoiselle Challoner, who is to marry Dominique."

His lordship was roused to look round. "What, is she here?" He perceived Mary at last. "So you're the girl that confounded nevvy of mine ran off with!" he said. "I wish you joy of him, my dear. A pretty dance you've led us. You'll forgive me if I leave you at this present. There's a little matter demanding my attention. Now, Avon, I'm with you."

Léonie called after him: "But Rupert, Rupert! Where are Juliana and M. Comyn?"

Rupert looked back from the doorway to say: "They'll be here soon enough. Too soon for my liking. Stap me if ever

I saw such a pair for ogling and holding hands. It's enough to turn a man's stomach. Their chaise fell behind."

He went out as he spoke, and Léonie turned to Miss Challoner with a gesture of resignation. "He is mad, you understand. You must not be offended with him, for presently he will recover, I assure you."

"I could not be offended, ma'am," said Miss Challoner. "He makes me want to laugh." She moved a little away from the Duchess. "Madame, are you—are you sure that you wish me to marry your son?"

Léonie nodded. "But yes, I am quite sure, *petite*." She sat down by the fire, and held out her hand. "Come, *ma chère*, you shall tell me all about it, please, and—I think, *not* cry, *hein?*"

Miss Challoner dabbed at her eyes. "No, ma'am, certainly not cry," she said rather tremulously.

Ten minutes later Miss Marling came in to find her friend seated at the Duchess's feet, with both her hands clasped in Léonie's. She said brightly: "Oh, Aunt Léonie, is it all decided, then? Has my Uncle Justin given his consent? I vow it is famous!"

Léonie released Miss Challoner and stood up. "Yes, it is quite famous, as you say, Juliana, for now I am to have a daughter, which will amuse me very much, and Dominique is to make no more scandals. Where is M. Comyn? Do not tell me you have quarrelled again?"

"Good gracious, no!" replied Juliana, shocked. "Uncle Rupert met us in the hall, and he took Frederick off with him to that room over the way. I think they are all there. I am certain I saw Vidal."

"*Voyons*, it is insupportable!" said her grace. "Do they all go off to drink Rupert's wine? I won't have it!" She went quickly out into the hall with Miss Challoner, who followed in the direction of her accusingly levelled finger, and frankly laughed. Through the archway that gave on to the coffee-room the outraged Duchess could see her son, seated on the edge of a table with one foot swinging, and a glass in his hand. Lord Rupert was in the background, holding a bottle, and speaking to somebody outside Léonie's range of vision. A burst of laughter set the seal to her grace's wrath. She promptly walked into the coffee-room, saw that not only Mr. Comyn, but her husband also, was there, and said reproachfully: "But I find you extremely rude, all of you!

One would say this wine of Rupert's, of which I have already heard enough, was of more importance than the betrothal of Dominique. *Ma fille,* come here!"

Miss Challoner came and shook her head. "Dreadful, madam!" she said.

"Devil a bit!" said Lord Rupert. "We're drinking your health, my dear." He saw Vidal smile across at Miss Challoner, and raise his glass in a silent toast, and said hastily: "That'll do, Vidal, that'll do! Don't start fondling, for the love of God, for I can't bear it. Well, what d'ye say, Justin? Will you buy it or not?"

His grace sipped the wine, while Lord Rupert watched him anxiously. The Duke said: "Almost the only evidence of intelligence I find in you, Rupert, lies in your ability to pick a wine. Decidedly I will buy it."

"Now that's devilish good of you, 'pon my word it is!" said his lordship. "Damme, if I don't let you have a dozen bottles of it!"

"Your generosity, my dear Rupert, quite overwhelms me," said his grace with polite gratitude.

Léonie stared at his lordship. "Let Monseigneur—oh, but that is too much, *enfin!*"

"No, no," replied his lordship recklessly. "He shall have a dozen: that's fair enough. Give your mother a glass, Vidal —oh, and what's the girl's name? Sophia! Give her a glass too, for I've——"

"Mary!" snapped the Marquis, with a sudden frown.

His uncle was quite unabashed. "Mary! so it is. Sophia was t'other one. Well, give her a glass, my boy. I've a toast for you to drink."

Léonie accepted the glass her son handed her. "Yes, it is true that I wish very much to drink to my son and daughter," she said. "Go on, Rupert."

His lordship raised his glass. "Dijon!" he said quite unheeding, and drank deeply.
